A Plot to Die For

ALSO BY ARDAL O'HANLON

Brouhaha
The Talk of the Town

ARDAL O'HANLON
A Plot to Die For

**SIMON &
SCHUSTER**

London · New York · Amsterdam/Antwerp · Sydney/Melbourne · Toronto · New Delhi

First published in Great Britain by Simon & Schuster UK Ltd, 2026

Copyright © Ardal O'Hanlon, 2026

The right of Ardal O'Hanlon to be identified as author of this work
has been asserted in accordance with the Copyright, Designs and Patents Act, 1988.

1 3 5 7 9 10 8 6 4 2

Simon & Schuster UK Ltd, 1st Floor
222 Gray's Inn Road, London WC1X 8HB

For more than 100 years, Simon & Schuster has championed authors and the
stories they create. By respecting the copyright of an author's intellectual property,
you enable Simon & Schuster and the author to continue publishing exceptional
books for years to come. We thank you for supporting the author's copyright
by purchasing an authorised edition of this book.

No amount of this book may be reproduced or stored in any format, nor may it
be uploaded to any website, database, language-learning model, or other repository,
retrieval, or artificial intelligence system without express permission. All rights
reserved. Enquiries may be directed to Simon & Schuster, 222 Gray's Inn Road,
London WC1X 8HB or RightsMailbox@simonandschuster.co.uk

Simon & Schuster Australia, Sydney
Simon & Schuster India, New Delhi

www.simonandschuster.co.uk
www.simonandschuster.com.au
www.simonandschuster.co.in

The authorised representative in the EEA is Simon & Schuster Netherlands BV,
Herculesplein 96, 3584 AA Utrecht, Netherlands. info@simonandschuster.nl

Simon & Schuster strongly believes in freedom of expression and stands against
censorship in all its forms. For more information, visit BooksBelong.com

A CIP catalogue record for this book is available from the British Library

Hardback ISBN: 978-1-3985-3957-0
Trade Paperback ISBN: 978-1-3985-3958-7
eBook ISBN: 978-1-3985-3959-4
Audio ISBN: 978-1-3985-3960-0

This book is a work of fiction. Names, characters, places and incidents are either
a product of the author's imagination or are used fictitiously. Any resemblance
to actual people living or dead, events or locales is entirely coincidental.

Typeset in Sabon by M Rules

Printed and Bound in the UK using 100% Renewable Electricity at CPI Group (UK) Ltd

To my mother, Teresa

Chapter 1

Finn O'Leary handed his access control card to Paulette the receptionist.

'How does it feel?'

'Weird.'

He had expected to feel somewhat deflated or possibly elated. He'd expected to feel something. It was quite weird to him that he felt nothing at all. Leaving the BBC after eight years and, what was it, four-hundred-odd shows felt strangely anticlimactic. But he didn't tell Paulette that. He suspected that she was the 'inside source' who routinely sold stories to the tabloids. To humour her, and to satisfy his own curiosity once and for all, Finn, dressed in his customary plaid shirt flapping over an old T-shirt, leaned an elbow on the counter and looked around conspiratorially, before lowering his bearded face towards her. Paulette pushed her biscuits to one side and looked up into the inviting lakes that were his eyes.

'To tell you the truth, Paulette, this place has gone to the dogs. I was pushed out.'

'Oh my God!'

'Shh! Between myself and yourself, they're replacing me with Ant and Dec.'

'What?'

'Yes.'

'But Ant and Dec, they're not gardeners, Finn.'

'That's right. They wouldn't know a rose from a dandelion. It's the new policy, you see, Paulette, do you mind if I . . . ?'

Finn helped himself to one of her ginger snaps. There was a man, about sixty-five, fidgeting on a lurid yellow sofa in a corner of the reception area of the otherwise nondescript BBC building in Bloomsbury. A quick glance at his hands told Finn that he was a guitarist, long fingernails on the right hand for plucking, calluses on the left from many years of fretwork. If there was any doubt about it, a guitar rested on the sofa beside him. They briefly made eye contact. An '80s pop-star, Finn reckoned, the sleeveless denim jacket and sun-bleached hair the giveaway. And, he surmised, he was still big in Malta, given the pheasant's-eye he sported illegally in a buttonhole of the jacket. It was a tiny scarlet wildflower, according to his learned eye, the *adonis microcarpa*, a rare and protected species found in Malta. But Finn let it go. He wasn't the judgemental type.

'Yeah, you see, they want less gardening advice, more banter. All part of the drive to reach a younger audience.'

'I am so sorry. That's just terrible.'

'Ah well! Keep it under your hat, Paulette. See ya.'

If his hunch about the receptionist was correct, he'd be reading about Ant and Dec's new gardening show in the papers next week. Needless to say, Ant and Dec weren't replacing him. The truth was that his show was more popular than ever. The BBC had begged him to stay. But he'd asked for an extended leave of absence on account of his mother. She'd had an accident some months earlier, a fall. He'd been over and back to Ireland on numerous occasions since then to sit by her bedside in the rehab hospital. But now, finally, to his immense relief, she was home. And it was his 'turn' to mind her. 'Turn' was not the right word, as if spending time with his mother was a chore. And neither was 'obligation', although that was the word his sister used to admonish him ad nauseam during their regular Zoom calls. It was a choice, freely made, and he was looking forward to it, a proper six-month-long sabbatical from his horticultural and media obligations, and an overdue opportunity to reconnect with his family and his hometown of Abbeyford. He'd just slipped away from the farewell champagne on the third floor, without even saying a proper goodbye to Isabella, his ex-wife and long-time producer, to make it in time for his flight.

'You're that guy? The Irish guy? The celebrity gardener?'

The toothy, perma-tanned musician pointed at Finn. Finn smiled back at him, not without warmth, but not with a lot of warmth either. He was a purist, despite his laid-back, jocular demeanour and populist appeal, and passionate to the point of self-destruction about his gardening principles. He didn't like, as a rule, people who picked precious wildflowers. And more than anything, he hated being labelled a celebrity. Or as he often said himself, 'libelled' a celebrity.

'*Garden Nightmares*! Eh? What a show! Brilliant.'

'Truly groundbreaking,' quipped Finn drily, realizing that his pun was probably lost on the slightly distracted muso.

If he was honest, his TV show, although great fun to do and a hit by all the relevant metrics, was anything but original. By way of format, it was a fairly standard makeover show. Mind you, his solutions weren't always the most obvious ones.

'You're better on the radio,' the man carried on hoarsely, still gigging by the sound of it, or at the very least singing loudly in the shower.

Finn towered over the former pop star. The latter was presumably about to appear on one of the Sunday morning chat shows and, judging by the book under his arm, promote a memoir.

'I actually took up gardening because of you.'

'Oh?'

Finn wasn't expecting that.

'Yeah, mate, I was at the lowest point of my life. Turned on the radio one Sunday morning, looking for a religious service I suppose, I was really desperate. There you were banging on about bedroom plants.'

'Well, I can only apologize.'

'No. It was the way you talked about them, mate, the passion, the humour, the ... irreverence. It was like, you were a preacher. It's like you knew I was listening.'

Finn, allergic to compliments as a rule, was getting uncomfortable. He spotted his taxi driver waving discreetly from the other side of the revolving door.

'That day instead of jumping in a lake, mate, I went to the garden centre, and I tell you, I bought every plant you mentioned on that show, even the Rose of Jericho.'

'You were in a bad way.'

Paulette the receptionist was listening intently to the musician's confession. Her ears were practically quivering.

'Never looked back thanks to you, Finn. Married again, yeah, have a little boy now, Kneil with a K, lovely boy, bit sensitive, and if I say so myself, mate, I have the finest garden in Surbiton. Ask anyone!'

'I'll take your word for it. I'm sorry ...'

It was not uncommon for strangers to come up to Finn – in the street, in the pub, on the train – and tell him their life stories. But it was never comfortable.

'Here!'

The singer thrust a hardback into his hand. It was called *One Hit Wonder*.

'It's about my addiction. One hit, do you get it? That's all it took. There's a whole chapter in there about my love of gardening. And ... my debt to you. Such a coincidence, this.'

'Wow. Yes.'

'Serendipity, mate.'

Finn never knew what that word meant. He wasn't sure if it was a good thing or a bad thing, but nodded along anyway, a profound expression on his handsome, weather-beaten face. Rarely stuck for a consoling word – on air at any rate – he was momentarily speechless. He tried to think of something appropriate to say. Although he couldn't think of the man's name, or recall any details about his career, he thought it best to pretend that he did. It must be a pop star's worst nightmare, he imagined, to be forgotten by the public.

'You're still going strong.' Finn slapped him on the back. 'Amazing voice.'

'Thanks mate. Just back from Malta, actually. Did a couple of nights at the Lynx.'

Finn smiled. As his mother used to say, he should have been a detective.

'Wettest April on record over there but a decent crowd all the same. They knew all the words.'

'I'm not surprised. By the way. You know it's against the law.'

He pointed at the red flower in the man's buttonhole.

Perhaps, after all, he was a bit judgemental, at least, when it came to conservation.

'*What?* No, mate, no.'

The singer looked genuinely upset.

'Do you think I …? No! That was a gift. From the Mayor of Valletta herself. She's a fan.'

'Oh. Sorry, eh … mate. Can't wait to read it.' He held up the book, as the indignant man was ushered away to his interview.

More and more of late, Finn had been making a habit of putting his foot in it. Having a pulpit could be a dangerous thing, giving one a false sense of security, or perhaps even a sense of entitlement. He glanced over at Paulette, visualizing next week's headline, 'Maverick Gardener and Suicidal Pop Legend in BBC Bust-up'.

On the way back to his flat in Highgate through the sleepy slick-wet Sunday morning streets of London to pack his bags, his mind turned to his mother, Maura, as it had every day for the past few months. It was chaos, by all accounts, in Abbeyford. His sister, Eimear, not remotely impressed by Finn's high-profile career in the UK, had organized and, as she reminded him repeatedly, *paid* for a full-time carer for his mother, now that she was home.

Meanwhile, in a somewhat unusual arrangement, their father, Redmond, was currently living apart from their mother. Theirs was a deeply loving but complicated relationship and had been for as long as he could remember. And Finn was now forty-ish. But anybody who knew his father – possibly the most contrary man alive – would vigorously agree that his mother's recovery was best served by Redmond continuing to live at least a good ten miles away from her. Thinking of his father, Finn's dodgy right shoulder automatically tensed, sending a spasm of pain shooting into his neck.

What on earth, he asked himself not for the first time, was he letting himself in for?

Chapter 2

'Now Aoife, as you know, I don't want to make a big deal about this,' said the headmaster, sitting smugly on the edge of his desk, looking like an ad for knitwear.

'And yet something tells me you are going to make a big deal about this, Giles?' Aoife smiled, still standing, having refused the offer of a seat, not planning on staying long to indulge her boss's latest lunchtime power trip.

Her composure slightly unnerving him, Giles shifted his pert buttocks on the desk to regain his position of strength as per the body language training course she knew for a fact he'd taken and, what's more, claimed as an expense from the school budget. In doing so, he accidentally knocked over a turmeric and ginger shot he'd just opened, the foaming yellow liquid spreading over the tabletop.

'I'll get that, Giles.'

'You're fine. It's nothing,' he pooh-poohed as if he'd meant to spill it as part of his advanced mind games.

Ignoring his protests, she whipped off her scarf, a cheap pinky-green satin number, and wiped up the spillage, even going so far as to dab at the smudge on his blue chinos, which didn't help his growing discomfort.

'Thank you, Aoife. That's ... There's been a complaint.'

'Another one?'

'And it is my duty as headmaster of St Joseph's to bring it to your attention.'

Aoife glanced at her watch. She had 3rd year French at two, but had arranged to meet a friend and ally to deal with an urgent Tidy Towns matter before that. There'd been another act of sabotage from, she suspected, a nearby town.

'You were seen, last Thursday I believe, hugging one of the boys!'

Aoife's face darkened. That caught her on the hop. Her regular summonses to McCabe's office were usually to do with being late for school or leading the boys astray with allusions to revolutionary Marxism. This was a new one.

'Now, I'm sure there's a perfectly innocent explanation for you embracing a ... a ... a ruttish teenager raging with hormones.'

'Ruttish! Giles! *Really?*'

'As safeguarding officer in this establishment, as well as headmaster, it is my primary obligation to protect the welfare of each and every student. What would the parents think if they knew one of the more, if I may say so, attractive teachers was seen in a ... a ... clinch with their little darlings?'

It was true that she'd hugged one of the boys. Or rather he, Justin, a particularly vulnerable pupil, had hugged her last Thursday as he did most days. She was a hugger by nature, she had to admit, or more to the point available for hugs to those who really, really needed them. That didn't make her some sort of predator, as McCabe seemed to be implying.

'Who brought the complaint?'

'It doesn't matter who brought the complaint. What do you have to say for yourself?'

'Was it you who complained, Giles? To yourself?'

'You know full well GDPR forbids me from revealing the source.' He pursed his lips triumphantly as he retreated around his desk to the safety of his swivel chair.

GDPR was by far the best thing ever to happen to upholders of the status quo like Giles McCabe.

'Let me get this straight. You the headmaster witnessed me comforting a boy, a boy with all sorts of issues, a victim of bullying, no less, and then you reported it to the safeguarding officer who also happens to be you.'

'Look, Aoife, I'm prepared to let it go on this occasion,' he said, toying with the zip of his thick-knit, quarter-zip jumper. 'But let this be a warning to you.'

'Thank you, Giles. I will learn from this. From this moment onwards, I will try and restrain my baser impulses.'

If her antagonist was aware of the sarcasm, he pretended not to show it.

'Great.'

'Was there anything else?'

'You're fine. No hard feelings.'

She smiled at him pitifully as she exited the room, slamming the door behind her, the waft of chewing gum and damp coats in the corridor filling her nostrils. *If anything, she thought, McCabe looked like he was in need of a good hug himself.*

It being a Monday, Abbeyford was fairly quiet as Aoife strode briskly from the school in her platform runners, a witty retort here, a reprimand there, an encouraging word to a shivering boy in the playground shelter here, an accurate kick of the football that elicited a cheer there. She bowed, indifferent to the scuff mark on her white Scholls, the unnecessary altercation with her headmaster already but a hazy memory.

Aoife Prendergast had an enviable ability to banish negative thoughts from her mind, even towards blowhards like Giles, being able to quickly refocus on the important things in life. You'd know her from a distance by her carefree gait. She had a charisma she wasn't aware of, an approachability. No airs and graces about her, was the common consensus, the ultimate compliment in a faded glory like Abbeyford. People were drawn to her even when she was in a hurry as she was now on her shortened lunch break.

She took a shortcut through Davin's Lane, gratified to see the murals depicting vignettes from Abbeyford's history had been freshly painted. Most of the shops in the winding alleyway, apart from the old cobbler's and the new artisan bakery, were boarded up or closed for the day. Nothing much happened in town until Tuesday, when the delivery vans finally arrived to restock the shops after the weekend. Aoife emerged in Market Square, where she was hit by a blast of wind and the sense of the powerful presence of the River Barrow flowing fifty yards to her left.

She waved at the chemist, Fionnuala Boyle, who was entering the Medical Hall with a slice of quiche from Deevy's, and kept walking up John Street, climbing steadily away from the river, before taking a left onto the Grange, the buildings becoming steadily more residential until finally she turned right into the Dyke Road and stopped beside a copper beech hedge. There she waited for Michael Dunlop at the pedestrian gate of the Abbeyford tennis club. She didn't have a fob. She wasn't a member. There were goosebumps on her arm. In her haste, she'd left her coat in the staff room at school. And her phone was in her coat pocket. So she couldn't call Michael.

'You're late,' she said, when he eventually came out.

'I'm late? I thought you'd stood me up,' he countered in a cultivated Australian accent, lighting a cigarette. 'I was hoping you'd stood me up,' he added archly, all too aware that when Aoife called on a weekday, there was bound to be some sort of an assignment involved. And with the Tidy Towns campaign cranking up for the year, there was always lots to be done.

'No such luck, Michael. Everybody else was busy.'

'I was the last on your list? I should be offended.'

'The others all have proper jobs,' she teased.

'Ouch! Just because I'm an Aussie doesn't mean I don't have feelings. I'll have you know I'm flat out today, like a lizard drinking.'

Michael was his usual unhurried self. Although it was a dull, chilly day, he was wearing sunglasses and bedecked entirely in whites, a pristine tennis shirt tucked into his neat shorts, not a crease to be seen, or a drop of sweat on his chiselled, olive-skinned face. He clearly hadn't been playing tennis that morning. An incongruous pair of shiny brown Oxfords on his feet underlined the fact. The only member of the club that ever wore whites in what was in fairness an unstuffy small-town set-up, Michael Dunlop didn't care what anybody inside or outside the organization thought about him.

'I'm sorry, Michael, what has you so busy today?'

'Admin,' he sighed, dramatically, as if he was running a multinational conglomerate instead of a tiny sports facility. After three of four drags of his cigarette, he showily discarded it on the footpath just to wind Aoife up.

Aoife, not rising to the bait, automatically picked up the butt and put it in her pocket. She looked warmly at one her closest friends, raising her eyebrows at his ridiculous costume.

'Leading by example, Aoife. You know me. Trying to civilize the natives.'

He did play tennis, and to a high standard by all accounts. And although he'd never actually produced a much-promised certificate or evidence of Garda vetting, was even known to coach on occasions. But today he'd been engaged in his administration duties. This was a role he voluntarily performed three days a week. Over the heads of the committee, and most of the ageing membership, distrustful of change, he'd been of late busily upgrading the club website. Using his programming skills – without, it should be said, ever presenting proof of his technical qualifications there either – he had already created a platform for making payments online. He was now currently in the process of developing a simple court-booking system.

'Honestly, Eefs, they'd prefer to scowl at the court-hoggers and not play at all, than book a court online,' he said, waspily, as he lit another Marlboro Gold.

'You're going to die, if you're not careful.'

'Oh no. Deep down. They love me; they know I'm indispensable. Oh you mean the cigarettes?'

Aoife smiled indulgently. He could be a very annoying man, but she loved him all the same.

Nobody knew what Michael did to make ends meet. Nobody knew much about Michael at all, not even one of his better friends, Aoife. Something in tech, or crypto, or possibly espionage. That, as far as she was concerned, was part of his appeal. His unreadability behind his shades.

He, a bit of an attention-seeker, did nothing to disabuse the speculation. As far as she was concerned, he was a breath of fresh air: provocative, flamboyant and unconventional and in a town where grievances tended to fester for generations, not afraid of open confrontation.

She'd met him at the rallies against the waste incinerator just over a year ago and took an instant liking to him. He'd only recently materialized in Abbeyford at the time. Unlike her, he had no obvious connection to the town but threw himself into a controversy, that she, in her typically righteous way, led from the front. Michael, a man in his early thirties, had cheerfully admitted that he had no real interest in environmental concerns per se but the quickly escalating protest was 'exciting' and 'something to do' and 'a way to get to know people'. She welcomed his youthful energy, his disruptive instincts and his all-in mentality once he'd committed to the cause. Like herself, he'd paid a high price for his involvement in the campaign, an outrage that bonded them for life.

Aoife by contrast, had deep roots in the town. The Prendergasts, she'd often been told, had arrived with the Normans in the 12th century. On the 2nd of May 1169, to be precise, Maurice de Prendergast sailed into Bannow Bay with ten knights and sixty bowmen. And while their fortunes had ebbed and flowed in the meantime – her father being the last of the level-crossing railwaymen – their attachment to the south-east had never wavered. That was why she, in her capacity as secretary of the Abbeyford Tidy Towns committee, was so affronted that a further act of vandalism had taken place on her watch, and why she on her lunch break had recruited Michael to help undo the damage.

Aoife led him to the edge of town, just before the WELCOME TO ABBEYFORD sign on the Ennismore Road.

'There.'

She pointed at a picnic table.

'What am I looking at here, Eefs?'

'Arson!'

Upon closer inspection, Michael agreed that the table had indeed been set on fire. No real damage was done to the structure but the wood was badly scorched. Michael couldn't help laughing. Not at the mindless arson attempt. But at the idea of a picnic table anywhere in Abbeyford never mind at the side of a busy road. As somebody who'd once lived in Byron Bay, he knew all about dining al fresco.

'It's not funny.'

'I'll wager nobody, not one person, has ever dined at that table.'

'That's not the point, Michael.'

'In fact, I doubt if anybody has ever even sat at that table.'

'True but it looks nice. That's the point. It's a feature. Creates a good impression on visitors. Particularly visiting judges.'

He didn't know the first thing about removing scorch marks, but Michael wasn't going to refuse Aoife. And Aoife knew that. Despite her best efforts and those of the Tidy Towns volunteers, they didn't have the resources or, in his opinion, the know-how to compete at the very highest levels of the contest. They were also, apparently, dealing with a not-so-subtle campaign by somebody or other to undermine all their good work. Michael had a flash of inspiration.

'Did you hear Finn O'Leary is back in town?'

Aoife's eyes lit up. Michael, amused, watched her as she, an open book, processed that information, her mind sifting through the possibilities that revelation presented to her.

'You'd be a terrible poker player, Aoife.'

Not only was she a person who spoke her mind, she wasn't very good at concealing her feelings. Or her plans, one of which, Michael could see clearly, was to prevail upon a world-famous gardener to help – no, *transform* – this year's Tidy Towns campaign. Aoife always thought big.

Aoife's brother, who now lived in the United States, had been one of Finn's best friends at school. Although a couple of years younger than them, she remembered Finn fondly as a gentle, easy-going, observant sort who didn't mind her joining in their games. More pertinently, she was a genuine fan of Finn's evangelical gardening, and unlike some of the local people who tended to be suspicious of success, was proud of his association with the town.

'How long has he been home?'

'About a week now as far as I know. He called Harry.'

Harry was Michael's partner and another of Finn's oldest friends.

'Said he'd see him at choir tomorrow night. Finn's bringing his mother.'

'Is he now? Interesting. Very, very interesting.'

'I mean, it would be too cringe just to ask him straight out, even for you.'

There was nothing Michael loved more than winding people up, a habit, Harry had warned him, that would get him into a lot of trouble one of these days.

'Don't worry, Michael.' Aoife winked. 'I'll be very diplomatic.'

Michael suppressed a laugh at what he considered to be one of Aoife's delusions. She nodded towards the table.

'Do your best, I've got to get back to school.'

PART 1

Chapter 3

Finn and his mother's new carer, Happiness, eyed each other warily through the rear-view mirror. It was probably fair to say she hadn't warmed to him since he'd arrived home. She was, he decided, feeling territorial. She also, he gathered, had strong views about children's obligations to their parents. Although a modest man by nature, in his own estimation, he had confidence in his ability to charm the stoniest of souls. He'd win her around. Eventually.

Happiness, lips pursed and leaning forward over the steering wheel, drove the short distance from the house to the community centre. More used to an automatic, Finn deduced, she drove the whole way in first gear. The groaning Yaris pleaded with Finn to do something. Finn, at six foot two, was a little cramped in the back seat and too afraid of distracting Happiness to say anything. His mother, Maura, sitting contentedly in the passenger seat, asked for the tenth time, 'Where are we going again?'

'We are going to sing, Maura.'

'Of course!' Maura laughed. 'I'll forget my own head next. We're going to choir practice, Finn,' she explained, turning around to her son, as if he was the one who'd fallen while walking in the Comeragh Mountains.

Despite her accident and the resulting brain bleed that

had left her bed-bound and delirious for the best part of five months, she looked younger than her seventy-two years. Having been a teetotaller all her life probably helped. Mind you, that description no longer applied, as he'd discovered the night he'd landed, a week ago, when Happiness had brought her a vermouth spritz. It was garnished with a twist of orange peel and a sprig of rosemary from the next-door neighbour's garden. He could tell the rosemary was from Burke's because of the noodle of golden retriever hair caught in the needles. The pair of them settled down to watch an episode of *Death in Paradise*. Somebody had fallen off a balcony. Were they pushed? Or did they jump? Finn had to smile when his mother insisted, as she always used to do when they watched detective shows when he was a boy, that they all write down who they thought the murderer was. Finn, much to Happiness' disgust, guessed correctly.

'We got the recipe on Alan thingy. Titmouse.'

It took a few moments for Finn to realize his mother was referring to the vermouth.

'Titchmarsh,' Finn said, the name of a bitter rival setting his teeth on edge.

'He's very good. Not quite as good as you, love. But he's very funny.'

There was a lot to unpack in that speech. Enough to keep a therapist in work for years. Finn wasn't quite sure if it was supposed to be a compliment or not.

'I prefer Titchmarsh,' Happiness declared firmly. He was absolutely sure that was not a compliment.

Not only had Maura been clean-living, she'd also been a keen hiker. That surely helped her rehab too. He'd never forget the call from his sister the previous autumn telling him to come home immediately. He'd been on location near

Hebden in North Yorkshire trying to extricate a house from its cage of invasive bamboo when Eimear called. Maura wasn't expected to live more than a few days after she'd slipped near the Mahon Falls while out walking with a retirement group. The thing that probably saved her in the end, more than the abstemiousness and the penchant for outdoor activity, was the complete absence of stress in her life. Her refusal to even countenance stress. Bearing in mind she'd been a district health nurse who'd seen it all, every stress and strain known to man, every pain and privation. Every type of death, natural and unnatural. And to top it all, she'd married possibly the most stubborn, wilful man that had ever walked the earth.

His father, Redmond, was what was known as a force of nature, whimsical and unpredictable and oblivious to the havoc he tended to leave in his wake. Apart from that, he was great. His intentions were good. It was only later in life, on reflection, long after he'd escaped to England, that Finn could in any way appreciate his father's idiosyncratic point of view. At the same time, he took great satisfaction in his own refusal, even as a child, to bend to Redmond's will. If he achieved nothing else in life that would be something.

Despite having to put up with this selfish man and his infuriating ways, Maura was determinedly stress-free and relatively free of cynicism too. She'd never, as far as Finn could remember, lost her temper and never raised her voice. Commuting from London, he visited her in the hospital as often as he could, particularly in the first few weeks after the accident. Then he held her hand and told her what a wonderful mother she was. What a wonderful woman she was. And he meant it. He wasn't sure if Maura even recognized him. She spoke mostly gibberish in two languages,

English and Irish. In her delirium, she often referred to the children she'd lost to pirates and the terrible things that had happened in the mother-and-baby home, but those events didn't seem to correspond in any way to her own biography. And then, much to Eimear's disgust, he had to go back to London to finish the latest series of *Garden Nightmares*. Did he absolutely have to go back? That was the question that tore away at his conscience. Well, he was contractually obliged to return to work for one. There was a team waiting for him. A production company. A demanding network. Not to mention millions of viewers and the forlorn householders whose runaway gardens were derailing their lives. But what about his obligation to his parents? To his father? Was he being entirely honest about his altruistic motives in returning home to help care for his ailing mother? Or was he just running away from Isabella? From responsibility?

It was Happiness who suggested Maura join the choir. His mother resisted at first, still a bit disorientated after her fall, and her confidence somewhat dented. But it proved to be one of the many ideas Happiness had that seemed to be changing Maura's life for the better.

Although only partially sighted now, Maura pointed to where she imagined local landmarks to be as if Finn were a tourist visiting the town for the first time.

'That's the river. The River Barrow! Did you know it's the second longest river in Ireland?' she claimed, proudly.

Protective of her charge and overly fond of the horn, Happiness beeped anybody and anything that came within ten yards of the vehicle.

'Imbecile!'

Imbecile, it was becoming clear, was one of her favourite words and, as far as she was concerned, half the town was deserving of that tag. Another of her favourite words was, mystifyingly at first to Finn's ears, Dundee.

Following the arcane one-way system, a mazy route devoid of logic, devised by a deranged town planner, by the looks of it, to prevent people from ever leaving the town, they had crossed over the New Bridge, built in the 1970s, and turned right onto Quay Street followed by a quick left into Parnell Street where the shopfronts were painted gaily – orange and fuchsia and bottle green, the windowsills and surrounds in wilfully contrasting colours – till they found themselves in the heart of the so-called medieval quarter outside a vape shop.

'You complete Dundee!' Happiness shouted at a guard who had stopped the traffic for a moment to allow an elderly man with a little pooch curled under his arm to cross the road. Out of curiosity, Finn did a quick Google search on his phone. He discovered that 'Dundee' was not only the name of a Scottish city, but was also a term of abuse synonymous with stupidity in Nigeria. Who knew? Apparently, according to a report on BBC Sport anyway, it was used widely in Nigeria ever since a hapless tour of that country back in 1972 by the Scottish football team Dundee United. Happiness had his mother at it too. Only this morning, he recalled, Maura referred to her husband as a 'big Dundee'. They were discussing Redmond's latest idiocy, his decision to refuse on principle the state pension to which he was entitled.

'Him and his principles. The big Dundee,' Maura had scoffed.

They carried on uphill through the town, the car audibly panting by now, around the early-18th-century church, St Mary's, erected by the Board of the First Fruits and then downhill again past the remains of the early-13th-century Norman church. That was also confusingly called St Mary's. By way of compensation for any dereliction or lack of amenities in Abbeyford, somebody – most likely the deranged town planner himself – had commissioned a series of giant murals on spare walls and in laneways, celebrating the history of the town with an emphasis on the glory days before the Anglo-Norman invasion. In fact, by the looks of it, he'd probably painted the murals himself.

'There's Aoife now. Isn't she lovely?' His mother pointed at the gable end of Morrissey's Bar and Undertakers on the corner of Little Richard Street and Main Street, the painting so big even Maura couldn't miss it.

'And what's-his-name … ? Oh, it's gone.'

Finn gave her every chance before prompting her.

'Strongbow.'

'Strongbow, the very man, he was the leader of the Normans, did you know that, Happiness?'

'No, Maura, I did not.'

'Not the worst of them. Aoife was the daughter of a local Gaelic chieftain. They got married.'

Opposite the big mural was a smaller one, on the crumbling wall of a makeshift car park. Although Finn was no art expert, it looked like a pastiche of a Rembrandt composition featuring local luminaries. He recognized the footballer who'd enjoyed a decent career in England by the blue hoops of his Queen's Park Rangers jersey. The telescope in the hands of another suggested a famous astronomer whose name escaped him.

'Beethoven,' his mother proclaimed.

'No, Maura, Beethoven was a dog,' Happiness corrected her gently.

'Bateman,' Finn remembered. 'William Bateman. Wasn't he supposed to have discovered Uranus?'

'He's very clever,' his mother whispered to Happiness. 'You wouldn't know it to look at him.'

'I can hear you, mammy.'

'Not as clever as Eimear, now. She's a genius.'

They were momentarily stuck in traffic. The driver of a car in front had stopped for a chat with a pedestrian. It was a good long chat. Happiness rolled down the window.

'Dundee. Move!'

Finn, still studying the mural, did a double-take. One of the figures was holding a shovel.

'Hey! Is that? Is that supposed to be me?'

Finn was a bit put out. The proportions were all wrong. The head was too big, surely. His own teeth were straighter and cleaner than that. And he wasn't that scruffy, was he? This was a travesty.

'I forgot to ask. How is Isabella?'

Pulled away from his thoughts on who the artist might be and what he might do to *his* face, Finn paused at his mother's question. It was only a matter of time before his mother would have remembered Isabella's name and asked him about her. He had decided not to tell her that his marriage was over. Not yet. He didn't want to disappoint her. Or indeed to try and articulate the various reasons for what was after all an inevitable and amicable break-up. Or to acknowledge the certainty that it was in fact over.

'She's grand, mammy.'

Eventually, after doing multiple laps of the town, they re-crossed the river this time by the Old Bridge, a nine-arched bridge in continuous use since 1340, took a right turn and after driving past the timber yard, the crematorium and the drab Celtic Tiger-era apartment block, streaks of algae running down the walls, they arrived intact at the community centre. Only a direct descendent of the Anglo-Norman settlers with the psycho-geography of the town hardwired into their DNA could have navigated their way around the town. Or somebody as indefatigable as Happiness.

Once safely in the car park, Finn uncurled himself and helped his mother from the car. It was an unseasonably sunny April evening, with only a slight chill in the air. Happiness retrieved Maura's stick from the boot. Somehow she'd managed to park what was after all a very small vehicle across three parking spaces just outside the entrance to the community centre, placing a crudely drawn disabled badge in the window by way of justification.

'I have applied for permission. Your mother is entitled.'

Finn wasn't going to argue. He took Maura by the arm and together they walked towards the door. An imposing cut-stone building, the community centre, as his mother reminded him, was a former workhouse. It only dawned on him that her habit of naming local landmarks and geographical features was for her own benefit and not for his. Her worst fear, he realized, was that she would lose her memory. And at her peak she'd had a phenomenal memory containing zettabytes of detail about everybody and everything that moved in Abbeyford.

The institution was now home to council offices, meeting rooms, a small museum of rural life and a crèche. It had been derelict when he was a child, and haunted to this day, they say, by the Victorian poor.

His mother was very light and unsteady on her feet. Happiness edged Finn out of the way and took Maura's arm.

'She is my responsibility.'

'Of course.'

Maura looked over her shoulder at Finn with a loving smile, but it seemed to him that his mother felt safer being chaperoned into choir practice by her fiercely loyal carer rather than her own son. Although still sharp and spirited, she had become worryingly frail and clearly quite anxious when she was out and about. And he, the guilt rising in his gut like reflux, hadn't been around as much as he would have liked. Being home now, he was determined to make amends.

Chapter 4

Beside the door was a small and neatly maintained triangular planting area dominated by an acer. Unusually for Ireland, an evergreen. Finn, although he might not like to admit it, had inherited a streak of his father's contrariness. While he was hailed for his wild, imaginative, some would say 'unhinged' gardens, he was often chastised for his lack of colour. A sore point with him. There were a thousand shades of green, ten thousand, for God's sake, and all of them beautiful. He'd tell people curious about his aversion to colour that he was slowly working his way through the whole spectrum but was still on green for the time being. That philosophy, it seemed, didn't impress the judges at Chelsea who had yet again passed him over for a gold medal. Another sore point with Finn. He bent down to inspect the plant, instantly happier on his hunkers. An *acer sempervirens* if he wasn't mistaken.

'You know your stuff.'

'Did I say that out loud?'

'Don't worry, Finn. We all talk to ourselves around here. Maybe you'd like to help?'

A woman who looked vaguely familiar pointed at a sign in the vegetation.

'The Tidy Towns? We're in with a good shout this year.'

'I bet you say that every year.'

She smiled at him. He wasn't wrong. The Tidy Towns Competition was a big deal throughout Ireland. He knew that. And this woman knew that he knew that. His mother in her heyday was a leading light in the local branch. And he understood the almost demented pride that people have in their home place, no matter how big a kip it was. Practically every settlement in the country, city, town and village competed ferociously for the prize of a Tidy Towns accolade. It did wonders for local self-esteem, not to mention tourism. Planting, typically, was a big part of the effort, but a busman's holiday was the last thing he needed right now. And while he did admire the unusual acer and the native fern, it pained him to see the likes of dogwood and comfrey in the same small space. That was just asking for trouble.

'Are you okay, Finn? You're frowning.'

'No, it's just ... Dogwood and comfrey are so rampant, they'll swamp the other plants. Whoever did that should be shot.'

'A bit harsh but I'll take my punishment.'

Arms up, she surrendered.

'I'm so sorry,' he laughed. 'I didn't mean ... It's actually not that bad.'

'You can show us all how it's done.'

Her face lighting up again, she let that hang for a beat waiting for a reaction. Waiting for a yes. *A bit forward*, Finn thought. *A bit of an edge to her, despite the breezy manner. Someone to be avoided.*

He still couldn't place her, local definitely, her accent not entirely disguised by her excellent elocution. He reddened slightly – the colour of the more conventional *acer palmatum atropurpureum* – embarrassed by his ability to recognize plants but not people, not to mention his ability to put his foot in it.

'We actually have a committee meeting coming up. You should join us.' She was persistent, that was for sure.

Finn got the distinct impression that she wasn't going to take no for an answer. It was almost like she'd known he was going to be there and had been waiting to accost him.

Casually dressed in jeans and runners and a light mohair jumper of cobalt blue, she was self-possessed, in her late thirties. Her face was open and amused, her chestnut hair, an afterthought. She looked to him like someone who slept well as a rule. The sleep of the just. He was envious.

'This is a bit awkward, isn't it?' she said, enjoying watching Finn squirm as he tried to retrieve her name. She was more than vaguely familiar.

'It's on the tip of my tongue. You a teacher by any chance?' he guessed.

'I'm genuinely impressed.'

Finn glanced down at her hands.

'The paper cuts on your fingers. Bit of a giveaway.'

'Very observant. You should be a detective.'

'That's what my mother used to say.'

'You comparing me to your mother?'

She laughed, a single earring in the shape of an ancient cowbell making a tinkling sound as she did so. It was the sole accoutrement adorning her make-up-free face.

'Aoife! Aoife Prendergast!' It suddenly came to him.

It was the way she covered her mouth with her hand when she laughed.

'Of course. How could I forget? Conor's annoying little sister!'

'That's me! As annoying as ever.'

Conor Prendergast was one of Finn's best friends in Joey's. St Joseph's boys' secondary school. He stuck out his hand.

'Oh, very formal,' she said, taking his hand. 'Good evening, Mr O'Leary, how do you do? Welcome back to Abbeyford.'

Aoife pulled Finn in for a hug. Very forward indeed. Nobody had hugged him like that for quite a while, not even Isabella, now that he thought of it. Although he was still in regular contact with Conor, who lived in San Francisco and worked in tech, he hadn't laid eyes on Aoife since Conor's wedding some ten years earlier.

'You sang "Tears of a Clown",' he recalled. 'The night of the wedding, in the bar.' He pointed at the little triangular garden.

'Better singer than a gardener.'

They were just about to go inside to begin the vocal warm-up when a loud revving noise drew their attention to the entrance of the car park. A snarling silver G-Wagen lurched aggressively towards an athletically lean man who was holding an ice-cream cone. The quarry, for want of a better word, didn't blink. Subtly tanned with a decent head of floppy black hair, he calmly turned towards the powerful machine and took a lick of his ice cream. At which point, the butch 4x4 lurched forward again, braking perilously close to the man's shoes. Cool as you like, sock-less, a crisp white shirt tucked into his ankle-length black jeans, the man stood his ground. He reminded Finn of a matador staring down a bull.

'That's Michael. Michael Dunlop,' Aoife explained, before adding under her breath, 'He's not going to take this lying down. Michael!'

She called after him, in full school-teacher mode now,

as she, followed by Finn, moved swiftly towards the altercation.

Michael nonchalantly walked around to the driver's door. With a grin on his face, he smeared his ice cream over the front windscreen. The driver, squat, middle-aged, with a shoulder-length shock of grey curly hair, rolled down the window, spluttering obscenities at this affront to the symbol of his manliness. It was then that Michael threw the remains of his 99 onto the driver's lap. Some of the bystanders, Aoife included, marvelled at his audacity. Michael, loving the drama, bowed gracefully to his audience.

In a right rage now, the man unbuckled his seatbelt and leapt out of the tank with an agility that belied his years. He crouched, adopting a convincing boxer's stance but, Finn thought, fully expecting to be held back. This he duly was by a glamorous woman, four or five bangles on each arm, as well as by some of the choristers. She did a double-take as Finn himself stepped in between the two men. Between his powerful frame and his calming horse-whisperer presence, not to mention his minor fame, he commanded instant respect.

Finn immediately recognized the aggressor as Barry Duggan, a tight ball of energy who ran a fleet of waste disposal lorries in the town. He also owned or at least was the face of the controversial new waste incinerator outside the town. The ice-cream and raspberry-ripple stain on the crotch of his grey Prada track pants slightly undermined his cred as a pugilist.

'I'll fucking kill ya, Dunlop! So I will. You're a dead man! Do you hear me?' Duggan roared as he got back into his monstrous car. He sounded like he had laryngitis, all throat no diaphragm, in such a tizzy he'd forgotten to breathe, but the elongated vowels were pure Abbeyford.

Michael, unruffled, turned to Aoife and said in a laconic accent that sounded vaguely Australian to Finn.

'I wouldn't mind, but I was enjoying that ice cream.'

'Leave it, Michael. He's not worth it,' she said.

'Oh don't you worry, Eefs. We have something planned for him. Something big. Who's your boyfriend?'

She turned to Finn.

'Ignore him! Michael can be – how should I put it? – very provocative. There've been times I've wanted to run him over myself. This is Finn, Finn O'Leary. An old friend of Conor's.'

'Ah, a celebrity in our midst. I heard you were home, mate. We're honoured.'

Michael took out his phone and without asking put his arm around Finn and took a selfie.

'They'll never believe it back home. Do you have any idea how big you are in Oz?'

'Well, I've been out there a few times.'

There was something a bit contrived about Michael's accent, a bit exaggerated.

'Your accent? It's hard to place. It's not Melbourne. Definitely not Perth?'

Michael reddened a little, his boldness briefly deserting him, but he held eye contact with Finn nonetheless.

'Oh, you know, little Michael moved around a lot as a child. My parents came with me, ha-ha. Dad was a ... geologist. Mum, she was religious. She once composed a hymn, you know. Just the words. She wasn't a very musical mummy.'

It might have been the dissociative way he referred to himself in the third person, or the nervous laughter, or the tiny hesitation before settling on an occupation for his father, or maybe it was the excessive detail, but whatever it was Finn was sure that Michael was lying. Not that it mattered to him what Michael did. Strangely, though, he believed the bit about Michael's mother composing a hymn.

'Right. And by the way just for the record, I'm not a celebrity,' Finn couldn't let it lie. He tried to be blasé about this bugbear of his but could hear the strain in his voice. 'I'm just a common gardener. I mean, an ex-gardener actually, not one of the ... ' – he searched his brains trying to come up with a sure-fire, incontrovertible celebrity – '... one of the Rolling Stones.'

Finn winced, embarrassed that that was the best he could come up with in the moment.

'Who?' Michael asked witheringly.

'Finn's come home to help with the Tidy Towns campaign.' Aoife broke the tension.

'Oh, that is so thoughtful of you,' Michael said. 'Harry told me you were a good sport. I thought, not gonna lie, the fame might have gone to your head.'

The penny dropped.

'Oh, you're Harry's Michael.' Finn softened. 'He mentioned you were a bit of a smart-arse, on the phone.'

Michael seemed pleased.

'How sweet!'

Harry Boyle, a boyhood friend, had always been excitable, overwrought, a geyser waiting to erupt. During his conversation with him the other day, he also tearfully confided in Finn that Michael was not only a smart-arse, but that he kept him on his toes.

'And – ' Finn had no reason not to come clean – 'he told me that you completely changed his life. For the better.'

'Did Harry really say that?' Michael beamed, his eyes

becoming moist, the studied coolness visibly evaporating into the ether.

'I can well believe it,' Finn said, vigorously shaking his hand.

Aoife eased the men apart. Meanwhile, Barry Duggan, climbing down from his car, was still bulling. As he entered the building he roared across at Michael.

'Just you wait, Dunlop, just you wait.'

'Ooh, I'm scared.'

'You go on ahead, Finn. Just need to have quick word with Michael,' said Aoife.

'Oh right.'

Thus dismissed, Finn sauntered towards the building while Aoife and Michael huddled in conference. He looked back. So that was Harry's enigmatic partner. And that was Conor's vivacious sister. So much time had passed. He had never really noticed her when they were younger. Well, that was not strictly true. But a three- or four-year age gap had seemed chasmic back then, unbridgeable. Besides, there was an unwritten rule that sisters were off-limits. He remembered her then as being warm and playful and assured. Not to mention headstrong. In that regard, it seemed that she hadn't changed much.

The choir was already in full swing. Straining an ear, he discerned to his surprise a rather upbeat version of the Nirvana song 'Smells like Teen Spirit', accompanied by a somewhat unexpectedly jaunty piano. Whether it was the tension in the car park, or the encounter with Aoife, or the jarring music, he had a strange feeling in his bones that this was going to be no ordinary night.

Chapter 5

Finn, in his youth, like most of the boys in town had messed around inside the workhouse before it was restored. It was there he'd had his first drink. And his first kiss – no, not with Aoife. It had actually been, now that he thought of it, with Aoife and Conor's older sister, Neasa, during a game of spin-the-bottle. Conor didn't speak to him for weeks afterwards.

   A listed building, it had been erected in 1841, according to the date stone above the Tudor-arched double doors. Although the workhouse was by a stretch the most substantial and handsome structure in Abbeyford, it was tucked away on a side street, the old Graiguenamanagh Road, unseen by the coach-loads of tourists who, after visiting the Cistercian abbey outside the town, stopped for sandwiches in Deevy's on John Street. On a five-acre plain on the less populated west side of the river, it was a bit unorthodox architecturally and thus pleasing to Finn's ever-questioning eye. Built in dressed limestone blocks of different shapes and sizes and varying hues of grey and brown, it was, by Finn's count, thirteen-bayed and two storeys tall except for a protruding double-fronted gabled end set at right angles to the main block, which was three stories high. The shape of a chaise-longue. The windows were diamond-paned, timber-framed and in his opinion tweely painted red. On many of the sills there were window boxes teeming with geraniums, lobelia and petunia, the profusion of colour giving him a headache.

For a once-foreboding place that used to house up to two thousand destitute people at any one time, it sure had some quirky decorative features including, would you believe, a belvedere. *A belvedere in a workhouse! That was a bit incongruous*, he thought, *if not downright cruel.* Like some sort of a sick joke. Even if the former residents, starving peasants for the most part recently evicted from the land, were actually allowed to avail of the vista – big if! – they wouldn't have had the strength to climb the stairs! What would you see from that eyrie now, he wondered, ever the adventurer.

There was nothing wrong with Finn's sense of direction. Turning right at the end of the corridor to the left of the reception desk, he soon found a likely staircase that led to the viewing point. Facing east, beyond the willows and limes and oaks that lined the Barrow, he saw the grand old grain stores and flour mills on the far quayside of what was once a great river port; downriver to the south, its sails billowing in the gentle breeze, he could see the *Lady Jane*, a restored famine ship from the 1840s that once transported thousands of stricken townsfolk to America and was now a remarkably popular tourist attraction; and there was the town, handsome from his current perspective, rising steeply towards St Mary's Church on Butler's Hill; behind that, beyond the remnants of the old Anglo-Norman walls, he couldn't fail to notice the futuristic waste incinerator that dominated the skyline. Aesthetically, it was beautiful in its way, a gleaming windowless rhombus, like a giant, upturned foil container. The smoke from its twin pencil-thin chimneys rose into the early evening sky.

Rehearsals were held weekly in meeting room 2 which, he din't need to be told – such was the gusto with which the choir were now singing 'Sweet Child o' Mine' – was at the end of the corridor to the right of the reception area. The old refectory apparently. There were about thirty-five people in attendance, the numbers swollen by rumours of Finn's appearance. People who'd never met him wanted to have a good look at him in the flesh. Tip-toeing into the room, it delighted his heart to see his mother in such raptures among the altos. As a district health nurse covering a wide area, and not bound by such petty conventions as a working day, she'd never had much time to pursue such pleasures before her retirement.

Happiness held her sheet music before her although he doubted Maura could see it. Since the fall, Maura's peripheral vision was seriously impaired and, despite her protests to the contrary, she wasn't able to read.

The otherwise irascible Happiness seemed to have infinite patience when it came to his mother. Last night, Maura hung on her every word as she read aloud a few chapters of a Golden Age detective novel. Finn himself, the guts of a bottle of mediocre Spanish red to the good, was equally riveted. He was not just drawn in by the ingenious puzzle at the heart of the plot but by Happiness' utter conviction in the telling. To say her narration was animated was an understatement. Of course, it should be noted, almost everything Happiness said sounded dramatic.

'You do not put eggs in the fridge.'

She'd scolded him after breakfast that morning. Coming

from her, that pearl of wisdom sounded like the third secret of Fatima. With her precise articulation and hypnotic West African phonetics, she emphasized every key moment of the story, every word. Whether Happiness read the book out of duty or pleasure, whether it was for Maura or herself, he couldn't say. Either way it had a remarkable effect on his mother.

Over her glasses, his mother's keeper lasered Finn with a look of disdain, as if to say she was disappointed but not at all surprised by his late arrival.

Apart from Aoife, a wavering alto, and her friend Michael, a countertenor by the sounds of it, and supremely confident too like all countertenors, he didn't know many of those present. The bestubbled entrepreneur Barry Duggan, a rasping tenor, was there of course, furiously rubbing the ice-cream stain on his expensive, voluminous pants with a babywipe as he sang. Alongside Aoife, he saw the sultry Cher lookalike with the bangles, a watchful woman, presumably Barry's wife, in a figure-hugging tracksuit more wisteria than lilac, and possibly more suited to dance class or kick-boxing than choir practice, a lady whose voice fell somewhere intriguingly between an alto and a soprano.

Finn caught the eye of a bespectacled teddybear of a man in a cord jacket. It was the unmistakable figure of Harry Boyle, a bass. Harry was now a doctor, a beloved GP in town, and a bass since he was about eight years old. He gave Finn a big wave. Always quite a theatrical chap, the irrepressible Harry and he had been inseparable in primary school.

From his position just inside the door, Finn further scanned the room looking for more familiar faces. Somewhat aloof behind a host of sopranos stood Harry's ex-wife, Fionnuala. Under a severe bob, she was as ever elegantly dressed in a navy-blue blazer and matching skirt, the collar of the jacket rounded in a vintage style and the buttons round and plump softening an otherwise business-like image. She looked like somebody who worked in mergers and acquisitions rather than as a local chemist in a provincial town. Fionnuala didn't catch his eye.

Rather than stand apart from the crowd, Finn quietly tried to insinuate himself among the tenors but was stopped short by the choirmaster closing his fist and pulling it downwards in a stagey motion. Everybody stopped singing apart from Michael, who continued falsetto for the craic.

'Ay ay ay ay ay ay, where do we go now, where do we go ... oo ... oo ... ?'

'Prick!' muttered Barry Duggan. 'Always looking for attention.'

'Duggan!' Harry Boyle growled in a basso profondo that near shattered the windows. 'Leave Michael alone!'

'Gentlemen, please, settle!' commanded the choir leader, a diminutive bald man called Noel 'Wolfgang' Whelan, but more commonly known as Wolfie.

Harry Boyle, a highly strung sort by nature, was a bit agitated. Nervously, he swallowed whole a mini Crunchie bar, wiping his hands on his trousers. Although the situation was tense, Finn smiled. This was pure Harry. Quick to advance and quick to retreat. A cauldron of cortisol, he had a habit of eating when he was nervous, had done ever since he was a child. And he was nearly always nervous.

'We have a new member, it seems,' said Wolfie, with only a tiny note of sarcasm in his voice.

'Oh, please God, no!' said Maura. 'Finn can't sing. He's a crow.'

Some people seemed to think this was quite amusing.

'Thank you, mother. I had no intention …'

'He can play the accordion though. Can't you, love?'

'Mammy … please …'

'He has medals.'

'Have you any choir experience, Finn?' asked the choirmaster.

Finn although a lover of music and even, as the exacting quizzers at the Boogaloo in Highgate would surely attest, an authority on music, was definitely not a singer. No. He didn't even sing in the car. He didn't even hum.

'Right, not to worry, what are you? We're very short of baritones. Let's start at the lower range,' said Wolfie, fingering a low G with his left hand. Finn had no idea what he was supposed to do. His leg started to tremble.

'Relax the shoulders there. Good man. Make an O, a nice big O with your mouth.'

'Honestly I don't think it's—'

'What do you think, boys and girls?' Wolfie asked the chorus.

'Go on, Finn. You can do it.' Aoife winked at him.

'Come on for flip's sake,' an old woman chimed in. 'We don't have all night.'

'Finn! No!' cautioned Maura.

'Thinks he's too good for us, so he does,' muttered a buttoned-up tenor.

'Yeah, too big for his boots.' Somebody else nodded in agreement.

Wolfie played a selection of notes from the lower end of the scales. Finn, now in a sweat, tried to vocalize the notes appropriately but they all sounded the same and none of them sounded pretty. Singing in public was literally his worst nightmare. He was suddenly back in the school hall, eleven years old, playing Arvide Abernathy in *Guys and Dolls*. Harry, as Miss Adelaide, brought the house down, as did Aoife's brother Conor as Sky Masterson. But when it came to Finn's turn to sing 'More I Cannot Wish You', he couldn't help noticing the parents, teachers and the whole shoal of pre-pubescent boys before him begin to shift and fidget in their seats. Then the shoulders started to shake and the giggling began, a contagion that quickly spread around the room and even onto the stage. Soon the entire audience and most of the cast were in heaps, doubled-up in helpless convulsions. At that point Finn's tongue stuck to the roof of his mouth. Harry Boyle, to his credit, tried to save his friend's blushes and finished the song on his behalf. But it was too late. His humiliation was complete. And now, decades later, the kinder members of the choir were looking at the ceiling, trying to rein in the developing merriment. Maura did her best but couldn't control herself, while Happiness remained her usual impassive self. Mind you she did fold her arms in quiet satisfaction.

'Better gardener than a singer.' Aoife said, relieving the tension.

'Touché.'

Finn could only laugh himself. Small-town Ireland would quickly find a way to pull you back down to earth, not that Finn was unmoored in any way. At least he didn't think he was. He didn't have any 'notions' about himself, did he? If he did have notions, about his celebrity status, say, or his expertise, he knew well, they'd soon be identified by the notion police, a sizeable force that included most of the population, and that he would soon be unceremoniously disabused of them.

Wolfie rubbed his hand through his non-existent hair.

'Finn, that's grand, very good. We'll let you know when we have a vacancy. Would you mind ... eh ... putting on the kettle there? Now. Back to the start.'

'Dum dum dum dum dum dum dum ...'

As the choir launched into the Guns 'n' Roses classic again, Finn retired to the kitchenette and made himself a cup of tea. There was liquorice root tea and squeezable honey for the more serious singers. One jar had a skull and crossbones label. Ominous, Finn thought, I might give that a miss. He almost slipped on a tiny tube on the floor. It was a stick of lip balm. Orange flavour. Finn threw it in the bin and helped himself to a cup of Barry's tea. Finn had huge respect for England and the English – he was an Anglophile – but, in his opinion, etiquette and ceremony aside, they didn't know how to make a decent cup of tea. After centuries in India and East Africa with access to the world's finest tea fields, you'd think they'd know better.

If anything, Wolfie and the choir had notions about themselves, with their penchant for 90s rock bangers. It was probably a mistake to come home. What was he expecting? What he needed more than anything else was peace and quiet. To be on his own for a while. He had forgotten how claustrophobic the town could make him feel. How small! He loved his mother but felt like a little boy in her presence, slightly naughty and a bit useless. He tried to ring Isabella, more out of habit than necessity. But he knew in his heart she'd already left London.

After about half an hour, the choir took a break. Finn was shooed out of the kitchen by one of the older ladies, Kitty somebody or other, a friend of his mother's and the attractive woman he took to be Barry Duggan's wife. The latter smiled at him seductively.

'I've always wanted to meet you! I'm your biggest fan.'
'Thank you.'
'You must visit our garden. We have super big plans. I think you are just the man.' She winked, salaciously, handing him a business card that read MONIKA KOVAČIĆ-DUGGAN, CHARTERED PHYSIOTHERAPIST.

Once the coffee break was over, the singers reassembled. Without any obvious cue from Wolfie they spontaneously embarked on an extraordinarily moving a capella version of 'What The World Needs Now'. All differences between the various members were set aside. All the troubles and cares of the world were briefly forgotten. Nothing else mattered as the community came together in uplifting song. Their faces were ecstatic. Finn, he had to admit, was envious. How he wished he could sing. How he wished he belonged somewhere. No matter where he was in the world he had always felt between places. Now, on an open-ended career break, not to mention a six-month 'trial separation' from Isabella – a fudgy way of saying a permanent split – he'd felt like an interloper in London. And although he'd only been home in Abbeyford for a week or so he still felt like a stranger, a bit of an exotic specimen, like a ghost orchid. He was outgoing and affable by nature. Too outgoing and too affable probably for Isabella's liking. But his celebrity, a word he had come to loathe, was a kind of force field around him that tended to nip intimacy in the bud. On the one hand it acted as a magnet. People had no problem coming up to him and confiding in him, asking him gardening questions and telling him their whole life story. But it also repelled people from getting too close. He felt sometimes that he was not so much a person as a personality. Maybe it was all in his own head. He was possibly guilty of projecting onto others the idea that they were somehow projecting onto him. Finn wished he had something in his life as transcendent as this. He found himself clicking his fingers in time to the gentle swing of the music until a reproving look from Happiness made him see the error of his ways. Even though he wasn't directly involved, the song carried him away to what he could only describe as a holy place. It was a perfect moment in time. A group of disparate people sustaining a B4 for what seemed like an eternity. He could only imagine how the choristers themselves must be feeling.

Suddenly, a strange gurgling sound broke the magic spell. Michael Dunlop doubled over in what appeared to be great pain. He was tearing at his throat, as if it was on fire, struggling to breathe. The singing abruptly ceased. Those around him, unsure as to what they should do, moved back to give him space.

'Typical!' said Barry Duggan. 'There he goes again. Always acting the maggot.'

'For God's sake. He's having a heart attack.'

'It's just indigestion. Get up, Dunlop, ya clown!'

Within seconds though, Michael had collapsed to the floor, not before convulsing violently, vomiting and evacuating his bowels. Finn noticed a small tattoo on the back of his hand. It was, if he was not mistaken, a bell of some sort. A cowbell.

Murmurs of shock and concern quickly gave way to panic as those around him realized that this was no joke. Michael did seem like the type to perform outrageous pranks but this was definitely not a ruse. Nor was it a health scare, major or minor. Finn could see that his pupils were dilated and he'd been foaming at the mouth. He was, very obviously, now dead. Harry Boyle, surprisingly light on his feet for a big man, bounded over to the now lifeless body.

'Oh, Michael, Michael! My beautiful boy!' Harry showered the dead man's face with kisses. Although a doctor he was evidently too shocked and distraught to even think of giving CPR. That responsibility fell on Aoife, but it was too late. She dutifully went through the motions. After giving it everything she had for ten minutes, Finn took over. To his surprise, Michael's body already felt quite cool. Curious. And his skin felt clammy. Harry's ex-wife, Fionnuala, tried her best to console Harry, as did Finn and the others, but he flung himself over Michael's body and refused to move.

'What am I going to do now?' he wailed, a heartbreaking plea matching anything previously heard in the old workhouse, a bird-scattering cry that reverberated high over Abbeyford and the surrounding countryside.

Chapter 6

The guards were called. It was not that anybody necessarily suspected foul play. But Michael was a young man in good health, so they needed to observe the formalities. Kitty Doyle, a retired postmistress and an oracle on medical matters as well as everything else, insisted he'd died of 'sudden death syndrome'. It was going around apparently.

'Sure didn't a young hurler in Wexford town drop dead only three weeks ago out on the pitch on the stroke of half-time?'

Although not a qualified practitioner, Kitty was adamant that her diagnosis was correct. A notorious hypochondriac, there were few ailments she hadn't suffered from at one time or another. She, according to one wag present, had more than likely died suddenly herself on many occasions before miraculously springing back to life and therefore knew of what she spoke. Maura, who was an actual qualified nurse, had her doubts. As did Finn. But it was Happiness who was the first to say it out loud.

'It was murder!'

It was she who called the guards, on Maura's behalf, much to the consternation of almost everybody else present, even the most law-abiding citizens among them.

An outraged Barry Duggan and his equally incensed

wife, Monika, left the scene at high speed after Harry in a fog of grief accused Barry of having something to do with Michael's death. Some of the others, despite the mind-numbing shock, left the premises too before the guards arrived.

Finn knew why. The guards were personae non gratae in Abbeyford and had been for almost a year now.

It had all started when Barry Duggan had got planning permission to build the new state-of-the-art waste incinerator just off the motorway to the north-east of the town. Where he got the money and how he got permission to erect such a facility in a rural area, on wooded land no less, managed by a state-owned forestry body, was long a source of speculation and anger. A protest group was quickly formed to stop the project. They were concerned not just about the potential damage to the environment and to community health but to tourism as well. Aoife and the Tidy Towns committee were particularly exercised after all their efforts over the previous decades.

The protestors were led by Aoife, by Finn's own father, the legendary Redmond 'Rio' O'Leary, and by the now deceased, Michael Dunlop. They had had modest success at first. Thanks to their objections, the courts and the planning authorities had ruled that the incinerator be scaled down in size. Instead of being the biggest such unit in Europe, it was only going to be allowed to burn a max of a mere 500,000 tonnes of rubbish per annum. Guarantees were given about the great benefits that would accrue to the area in terms of employment and, somewhat mind-bogglingly, the clean electricity that would be generated by the incinerator and donated to the national grid.

Once construction commenced on the site, the campaign

escalated. Aoife was the reasonable and articulate voice of the movement. Redmond, a mischievous environmentalist and radical in his own offbeat way was chief strategist, while Michael was either a loose cannon or a secret weapon depending on which side of the fence you were sitting on. Although his father was heavily involved, Finn had paid little attention to the protests. His father was always heavily involved in something or other. Finn had only the sketchiest idea of what was going on but his frequent visits to Ireland only took him as far as his mother's hospital bed in Dublin, so his information was second-hand at best. He hadn't fully realized how heated the issue had become on the ground.

Eventually, after lengthy delays and after a number of earth-moving vehicles were sabotaged, Aoife, Redmond and Michael were arrested on a charge of vandalism. Better known as the Abbeyford Three, they became a cause celebre nationwide, which only encouraged them more. After Duggan's company was granted a temporary injunction preventing the protestors from blocking access to the site, the Three were summarily jailed for breaching court orders.

Nobody came out of the experience well, apart from Michael, ironically. He, a blow-in to the town, was embraced as a folk hero by some of the locals and as a bonus found love with Harry. Aoife was grudgingly allowed to teach again at St Joseph's after an appeal to the board of management, but was overlooked for promotion to the position of principal. The grasping incumbent, Giles McCabe, had been looking for an excuse to get rid of her ever since.

Redmond, by all accounts, had become even more reclusive and more eccentric if that was possible and was now living in his weird, self-built eco-lodge in the woods.

According to Maura, Finn wasn't to worry. They were still very much a couple. They just didn't see each other very often. And as a result, they were getting on better than ever.

Barry Duggan Senior wasn't satisfied by the outcome either. His incinerator, an award-winning design, a tourist landmark in its own right if only people could see sense, and a bona-fide boon to the town, was smaller and less profitable that it ought to have been. Not only that. But he, despite all he had done for the town – sponsoring the soccer team, paying for people's medical treatments in Dublin, flying people to Hungary for crowns and hair transplants – had been ostracized by half of Abbeyford.

However, it was the guards that came off worst. They were regarded as having been heavy-handed, and accused of taking Duggan's side in the dispute.

'They were only doing their jobs,' Maura reasoned, her record of service to the town, the long-running rumour that she had the gift of second sight, giving her extra chevrons on her sleeve, and her voice added weight. But after seeing beloved local figures like Aoife and her own husband in handcuffs and the innocent-looking Australian lad banged-up in Mountjoy prison, people swore they would never speak to the guards again.

Dusk settled. While waiting for the police to arrive, Finn and Aoife were milling around just outside the front door.

'You okay?'

'Poor Michael.'

Aoife wasn't in a talkative mood. Finn, an experienced radio broadcaster as well as a television gardener, instinctively filled the silence.

'I worry about Harry.'

Aoife looked right through him.

'Sorry,' he backtracked. 'Not the time.'

She really didn't want to talk. He wished there was something he could say or do to make things better. On the radio, he invariably found the right words: some jovial advice for the callers, a gardening tip here, an expert answer to a query there. Of late, though, it was noted that he was straying more and more from the garden path, so to speak. The thing is, he was far more interested in the questioners' life stories than their gardening woes. His show was becoming a bit of a free-for-all, the studio a confession box. Eyebrows were raised at Broadcasting House, not least by Isabella who was not just Finn's wife but also his producer.

'*Zapatero, a tus zapateros*!' she had chided him in her laconic, measured way with just a touch of frost, but her point was well made. She was probably right. A shoemaker should stick to his shoes. Incidentally Isabella, whose mother was from Salamanca, tended to only speak Spanish when she was upset. But it had dawned on Finn early on in his career that many of his callers weren't just looking for advice on pruning and splicing and red spider mite. (That reminded him, in answer to a caller who was at her wits' end thanks to a particularly indestructible mite, he suggested she shoot them! Preferably with a machine gun. The BBC switchboard lit up that morning. It even made the *Daily Mail*. ROGUE IRISH GARDENER GUN SHAME.) No. They were often lonely. Or bereaved. Or burdened with a secret. They wanted to be heard. But for somebody who prided himself on being such a good listener, with the ratings to prove it, he realized just a little too late that he hadn't really been listening to his wife. If he had, he'd have noticed she'd been speaking a lot more Spanish of late.

'That acer. Does it look alright to you?' Finn asked.

Aoife turned on the flashlight on her phone and shone it towards the plant.

'Well, it's not exactly full of life anymore if that's what you mean,' she said drily.

Finn rubbed one of the now inexplicably wilted leaves between his fingers.

'Curious. It's wilted.'

Aoife's spirit, which had been wandering, rejoined her body with a jolt.

Chapter 7

At about 9 pm an ambulance arrived, hot on the heels of the on-call doctor. A couple of minutes later the guards arrived in two cars, one unmarked and unremarkable, and the other a brand-new electric vehicle in the usual Garda yellow with blue trimmings. *They were taking a chance with an EV,* Finn thought, recalling the story of the criminal mastermind in Dublin who kept canisters of petrol in the boot of his car so as he could outwit the cops who'd been following him. He famously led them on a wild goose chase high in the Wicklow mountains. When they all eventually ran out of fuel, casual as you like, the crime magnate cheerily refilled his tank with his own supply. Waving goodbye, he went on his nefarious way while his hapless pursuers were left scratching their heads as the mist descended in the Sally Gap.

'Ah, it's yourself.'

It was a fella Finn remembered from the high school, ambling pigeon-toed towards him from the unmarked car.

'Special!'

'Nobody calls me that anymore, Finn. It's just Xavier. Xavier Keane.'

'Sorry.'

'No, you're grand. It's just. It has connotations. Howarya Aoife.'

Aoife walked away in disgust. Xavier looked pained.

Francis Xavier Keane, known as Special Effects on account of his initials, was now of all things a detective Garda. He hadn't changed a bit. Same fresh eager face, high cheekbones you'd need crampons to climb. Same gormless expression. The hair still resembled a palm tree, fronds falling away from a central parting. The suit was sharp though, and not cheap, slim-fitting, olive green in something of a mod revival style. Finn nodded in admiration. Special beamed.

'Cheers! C'mere to me! Now that I have you. Treehouses.'

'What about them?'

'No, it's just Niamh is at me to put one up for the children. A house in a tree.'

'I understand.'

'A one bedroom would suffice, I'd say. Do you think it's a runner?'

'Well, it would depend. Like what sort of a tree is it?'

'I haven't a fecking clue, Finn, to be honest with you. I don't know one tree from the next. I mean I'd pay you.'

The things people asked him to do! It was hard to believe Xavier was a cop. A sensitive soul, he'd always been a snazzy dresser, a great man for the polo shirts and tailored trousers while the rest of them were slumming around in jeans and Oasis T-shirts. The band, not the brand. A woman a head smaller than Xavier and a good ten years younger joined them and coughed loudly to announce her presence.

'Oh, sorry, yes. This is Detective Inspector Valerie Kilcoyne.'

Xavier stressed the 'inspector' part with just a hint of bitterness.

'What's the story?' said Valerie brusquely.

She was a Mayo woman, pony-tailed, in a no-nonsense trouser suit she reluctantly wore because you weren't allowed to wear Mayo football tops while on duty. Her eyes moved warily as if she was surrounded by a pack of dingoes. You immediately felt guilty in her presence. Felt like confessing to something or other. That or running away. But you knew if you ran, she'd catch you and with a few choice karate moves bring you down, leaving you with at the very least a limp for the rest of your life.

Finn filled the detectives in on what happened in great detail. Unnerved by Valerie, he even told her why he himself was at the choir practice and why he was back home in Abbeyford. He even touched on his recent relationship woes.

'I'm more interested in this evening, Mr O'Leary, if you don't mind.'

She typed everything he said with her right hand into an iPad that was balancing precariously in her left hand.

'I could lend you a pen, if that's handier,' offered Finn.

'We're trialling these fecking iPads at the minute. Another brainwave from HQ.' Xavier shrugged, what-can-you-do, at Finn.

'This fella is stuck in the past.' Valerie nodded towards her colleague. 'We won't know till we've tried it, will we, Xavier?' Turning to Finn, she continued, 'It's got all sorts of apps. A camera. Built-in theodolite. The works. Could save us a lot of time in the long run.'

'Interesting,' said Finn.

'It's a joke, so it is,' Xavier sneered. 'Over in Wexford town. Main problem. They're robbing the iPads out of the squad cars. You couldn't make it up.'

When Finn got to the bit about Barry Duggan threatening Michael in the car park, Valerie nodded knowingly.

'Typical Duggan. All hat, no cattle.'

'I don't know, Valerie,' her colleague argued. 'He has a lot of cattle. As well as a fairly big hat. Very big hat in fact. I mean he doesn't actually wear one.'

'I understand.'

'And by cattle, I mean . . .'

He shadow-boxed to illustrate his point.

'Duggan's one mad, bad hombre.'

Valerie scoffed.

'All gate, no house.'

'She hates it here. Thinks it's too quiet.'

She didn't disagree with her colleague.

'Valerie gets very bored in the station. Very moochy. Nice way to go all the same,' said Xavier.

'What?'

'No, I mean. "What a Wonderful World". Great song.'

'Xavier, I'm not sure you should be saying things like that out loud. Michael was in his thirties. There's no good way to go.'

'Yeah, no, of course, it's just . . . Doing something like that. Something you love. Singing. Surrounded by people who love you. I was in the choir myself until . . . well, you know the score. It doesn't matter.'

'Here we go.' Valerie threw her eyes up to heaven.

Xavier looked close to tears.

'It's alright for you, Valerie. You're not from around here. They deleted me from the WhatsApp.'

Finn broke the awkward silence that followed.

'Look, I know it's probably a stupid question. But is there a chance, do you think, is it possible that Michael was murdered?'

'Ah now. Are ya mad?' Xavier exclaimed. 'Murder in

Abbeyford? We haven't had a murder here in forty-two years.'

'That doesn't mean anything,' said Valerie.

'You'd love a murder. She'd love a murder.'

'I wouldn't love a murder. Just because we haven't had one in forty-two years it doesn't mean we'll never have one, Xavier. Unlike you I'm a realist. Only a matter of time if you ask me.'

'Believe me, Finn. There's nothing she'd like more. It's all she talks about. Sure you tried to reopen that one from back in the '80s?'

'Well, no one else ever seemed too bothered.'

'You should have joined the fecking Rio de Janeiro police instead of the Gardai.'

'The De Burgh case?' Finn inquired.

Xavier nodded.

'What do you know about the De Burgh case?' Valerie was in like a bullet.

'Nothing. I was two at the time!'

Which was not strictly true. Well, it was true that he was only two years old when Eamonn 'Rameses' De Burgh vanished without trace. But seeing as how Rameses – so called because of his extravagant goatee – had been a close friend of Finn's parents and that they often discussed his sinister disappearance and presumed murder in Finn's presence, it wouldn't be true to say he knew absolutely nothing about the case. Xavier was droning on.

'The only excitement we had 'round here in the last six months was this big smuggling operation. And that was pure luck. I was going for a wee in this lay-by on the M9. Middle of the night. We were just coming off a job. Anyway, there was a lorry parked there. Driver fast asleep.

Next thing I hear voices from inside the container. People talking. In a strange language. So naturally I wake up the driver. Big Bulgarian lad. Who panics. Makes a run for it. But, you know, he's about forty stone, doesn't get far, does he? Valerie here rugby-tackles him around the legs. The long and the short of it. We open the trailer to find a million euros worth of cigarettes.'

'Wow.'

'Two million,' Valerie chipped in.

'Two million.'

'And a pair of refugees.'

'Right,' Finn whistled.

'From Somalia, I believe they were. Somalian.'

'Eritrean, actually. From Eritrea.'

'Whatever. We're not playing Trivial Pursuit, Val. They got on at Le Havre apparently. The Bulgarian fella swore he knew nothing about it. The refugees. We never knew whether he did or he didn't, did we? But either way we smashed the ring as they say. He talked. The Bulgarian. Dragan somebody. Cool name, Dragan.'

'Dragan Petrov.'

'Thank you. She's like Wikipedia. Special crimes got involved. Dublin of course were beyond delighted. They got all the main players this end. The Drumms. Of course her nibs here gets promoted to DI.'

Valerie showed him her badge by way of confirmation. Or more to the point by way of rubbing it in. Xavier paused and swallowed the memory while waiting for Finn to ask the obvious question. He'd clearly told this story before. Many, many times before. Finn obliged, inviting him to continue with a raised eyebrow.

'Me? Funny you should ask. I was invited in for a "chat"

by the brass. Breslin, he's the super, tore strips off me, so he did.'

'No?'

'Yes. I was severely reprimanded.'

Valerie sniggered. Xavier ignored her.

'For, wait for it now, urinating in a public place.'

Finn bit down hard on his lower lip.

'Can you believe that? Story of my life, Finn. I should have got a medal.'

'Right. That's ... Sorry to hear that, Xavier.'

'That piss, forgive my language, was worth two million quid. Liquid gold. Anyway. It's all in the past. What do you say?'

'About what?'

'The treehouse!'

'Oh, right, yes, I'll call around in a couple of days and have a look. Sorry, detective, what happens now?'

'Call me Valerie. The doctor will examine the body. Confirm the cause of death. I'm sure there won't be an issue.'

'More's the pity, says you,' Xavier interjected, still licking his wounds.

'He never stops. We'll have to give the coroner a shout as a matter of course.'

'If we can find him.'

'There'll be an autopsy.'

'He races pigeons, all over the world. The coroner.'

'It's the pigeons who go away,' Valerie said, her patience at breaking point. 'The coroner stays at home and waits for the pigeons to fly back to the coop.'

'Oh right. I didn't know that. Sorry.'

'C'mon.'

As the bickering detectives made their way into the community centre, Aoife rejoined Finn. She was pale and subdued. Not knowing what else to do, he patted her on the shoulder. Suddenly she kneeled down at the base of the acer tree. Finn thought she was going to be sick.

'Not on the plants, Aoife.'

Immediately she stood up again holding two cigarette butts one in each hand. They studied them. Two cigarettes, each one only half-smoked.

'Strange,' mused Finn. 'Can't imagine they'd harm the tree.'

'Marlboro Gold!'

'What? Are they particularly strong?'

'Michael smoked Marlboro Gold,' Aoife said. 'Two of them. He always smoked two half cigarettes instead of one full one.'

'I see.'

Finn didn't see at all.

'He was very health conscious like that, Michael,' she clarified. 'The closer you get to the butt, the more toxic it is apparently.'

'Makes sense, I suppose. In a deluded way.'

'Michael was complicated. He must have been here.'

Finn thought about that for a moment. Due to the earlier altercation, the choir had schismed into smaller and quieter groups than usual during the break. Aoife had been drinking coffee with some teacher colleagues in the corridor. Finn himself was being fussed over by his mother's friends, as if he was a new baby and oblivious to anything else that might have been going on.

'*Something* happened during that break,' said Aoife, looking down at the wilted tree.

Chapter 8

Morrissey's was almost too good to be true, a sort of fantasy of a traditional Irish pub. But here's the thing: it was all authentic, defiantly quaint, its original fixtures and fittings varnished with the breath and tears of Abbeyford's residents since early Victorian times. The shop, just inside the front door to the right, was still a going concern, although its limited stock – cornflakes, soap, cans of motor-oil – was eclectic to say the least. Likewise, the undertaking business was no gimmick. More of an obligation at this stage in the game than a lucrative sideline, they still did three or four funerals a week in a bespoke and old-fashioned way. There's nothing they wouldn't do for the community, the Morrisseys. They'd wine them, dine them, ferry them home and eventually bury them. After the burial, the send-offs back in the bar often bordered on legendary.

Finn loved Morrissey's. In a town of some thirty pubs, it was usually his first port of call. Although in fairness he eventually got around to them all. Its fabled snugs were shrines to bygone times when deals were sealed with spit and a handshake, where love matches were made for better or for worse, and rebellions plotted inevitably for worse. As far back as 1848, the story goes, a group of Young

Irelanders huddled in one such smoky corner before their ill-fated march on Kilkenny. To this day they say there's a tunnel that leads directly from the pub to the outside world. Michael Collins himself, no less of a man, with the pub surrounded by the Black and Tans, availed himself of it during the War of Independence. The shot glass from which the rebel leader drank a 'ball-of-malt' was displayed reverently in a glass case on the wall alongside a trove of photographs, original metal advertising signs and quirky bric-a-brac that told the story of Abbeyford and its hinterland. In pride of place over the hearth there hung one of the original pikes used in the battle of Vinegar Hill in 1798. Incidentally, if there really was such an escape route beneath the pub, Hector, the current proprietor and fifth-generation Morrissey, wasn't saying.

Hector didn't say much about anything though. However, despite being a taciturn character, as well as a qualified embalmer, he was well liked in the town. A gangling, inoffensive sort, he always had an air of distraction about him. You couldn't not like him even though he'd been spoilt as a child and enjoyed inherited wealth. And that was one of the worst things you could be accused of in a place where most people didn't have much. But strangely people felt sorry for him.

The whole town knew that Hector's heart wasn't in hospitality (or for that matter handling dead bodies) although in his own passive way he oversaw what was by any standards a fairly smooth operation. Although he had trained to be a pilot, he was forced into taking over the family business after his father's death. He largely succeeded by staying out of the way, a philosophy Finn was coming to respect more and more every day. Always a bit of a dreamer, Hector spent most of his time pursuing his expensive hobbies. When he wasn't flying small planes from the aerodrome in New Ross, he was flying drones. When he wasn't flying drones, he was going to toy fairs in England and adding to his vast collection of toy cars, leaving the bar in the capable hands of Eve Duggan. A gadget man and something of a drone pioneer locally, Hector famously used to deliver pints to his customers during the pandemic lockdowns via drone. For that if for nothing else he was considered a hero. More recently he had started to fly prescriptions from the nearby Medical Hall to sick people in isolated areas.

Now, there he was, leaning over the bar, his ear close to the mouth of an estate agent wrapped in a gilet by the name of Declan Doyle, a son of Kitty, and the chairman of the Tidy Towns Association, who was relaying the big news of Michael's death. Hector had that familiar faraway look in his eyes. If anyone else apart from Finn had been watching, they would have noticed a tiny tear rolling down his cheek. Hector, of course, was sorry to hear that Michel had died, but he was, truth be told feeling, even sorrier for himself. Now, he calculated, he'd probably have to stay at home and sort out Michael's funeral instead of going to the Ashington Vintage Toy Fair in West Sussex, where he had his eye on a rare 1966 Matchbox Citroen DS.

It was Eve Duggan who served Finn and Aoife. Eve was the wife of Barry Duggan's eldest son, Barry Duggan Junior. By all accounts, it was Eve who really ran the show at Morrissey's – and in her marriage.

'Would tea have harmed that acer? Or coffee?' Aoife asked.

'No. Definitely not. But what if . . . No, it's ridiculous.'

'No, go on.'

'Maybe, this may sound far-fetched, Aoife, what if there was something in his tea?'

'Poison?'

'I know, it's too ridiculous for words. I'm sorry I mentioned it.'

'No, no, go on! You might be on to something. Just say it. I won't judge.' Aoife sat up.

Finn shook his head.

'It's just that acer was perfectly healthy before the rehearsal.' Finn frowned.

'You look like your father when you frown.'

'Don't say that!'

'I like your father.'

He painted a scenario for her.

'Michael had a cup of tea at the break.'

'He always did,' Aoife confirmed.

'He went outside for a smoke, as usual. He smoked two Marlboro Golds. Then he threw away the dregs of the tea, as you do. And ... no. It doesn't make sense.'

'What you're saying is,' Aoife continued his thought, 'whatever was in the tea was toxic enough to harm the acer tree. And strong enough to kill Michael when he came back inside.'

Finn was sorry he'd embarked on this type of idle speculation. There was a danger you could come across as a fool. Aoife had seemed so sensible earlier on, so together. So carefree, before Michael's demise. And now here she was, like himself, indulging in outlandish conspiracy theories. Obviously she'd had a shock. Shock could be disorientating. That goes without saying. But he had to confess, there was a nagging doubt in his own mind. Healthy trees don't just die for no reason. And neither do healthy men. He didn't want to say it out loud because that would mean acknowledging that he'd witnessed a murder, but from the moment he saw Michael fall he knew intuitively that Michael had ingested poison. His first thought, given the dilated pupils, was some sort of nightshade. The dilation could of course have been caused by anything, a variety of plant-based poisons, anti-depressants, cocaine. And besides it would have taken hours for the effects to kick in. But then there was the cramping, the diarrhoea and vomiting, the burning throat. Barbados nuts sprang to mind. Not that he ever tried them himself. Although once while working in Mexico, his local fixer had used some oil extracted from the extremely toxic seeds of the Barbados nut to treat a fungal infection between Finn's toes. Mind you, priding himself on being a patient man, he wasn't inclined to rush to conclusions.

'If you think there was something in Michael's tea, why don't you say it to the police?'

Aoife looked at him with disbelief.

'I don't talk to the guards. Besides they wouldn't take me seriously. They have me down as a troublemaker as it is. You should tell them.'

'Me?'

'You seem very pally with Xavier Keane. Anyway, people listen to you.'

'Do they? That's news to me. They'll think *I'm* a loon.'

'What are you saying? Do you think I'm a loon?'

Finn hesitated.

'I think you're grieving. You've lost a close friend. And yes, if you don't mind me saying so, you're beginning to sound like a bit of a loon.'

She regarded him fondly, appreciating his attempt to lighten the mood.

'You're a national treasure, Finn. Everybody is so proud of you around here. I have followed your career with great interest.'

In his experience, for every one who approached him shyly or without compunction, for an autograph or a brush with 'celebrity', to celebrate or sneer at his fame, there were two or three more who went out of their way to act as if they didn't know him from Adam and fastidiously avoided the subjects of gardening or television. They, it turned out, were often his biggest fans.

Aoife encouraged him to look around the bar. There were a number of patrons literally staring at him, watching his every move, his every sip. Many of them raised their glasses in toast to him. He raised his back.

'Just tell them to test a soil sample. And check the cups or whatever.'

Finn rubbed his beard. There'd be no harm, he supposed, in asking Xavier to order some sort of toxicology test on the soil. For all he knew they were doing exactly that. Despite his natural inclination to stay out of it, he found himself slowly unrolling a sock and dipping a toe in the water. Michael's skin, he remembered, was strangely clammy and cold though he'd been singing powerfully only moments before he fell. That, his mind racing again, suggested monkshood or maybe lily of the valley. As most of his knowledge of poisons and their symptoms was derived from old detective novels rather than botanical textbooks he decided it was wise to keep his ignorance to himself.

'I'm pretty sure somebody washed the cups,' Finn said.

'*What?*' Aoife shouted, before quickly powering her voice down to a whisper. 'Who washed the cups, for God's sake?'

'It was one of the older ladies. I never saw her before in my life.'

'Kitty?'

'No. Not Kitty. I know Kitty. There was a little mousey one. Did you see her there? She was in pink, remember.'

'Monika Duggan?'

He could tell that Aoife was dying for it to be Monika. She didn't like the Duggans, for good reason.

'No. Older. Much older. Mid-sixties. Well-dressed. Expensive perfume. Hints of Bergamot and May Rose.'

'Bergamot and May Rose? Really? You can tell? What are you, some sort of perfume sommelier?'

'No. It's just ... I did a documentary once in Grasse. I have a highly developed nose.'

Aoife studied his nose. It was actually a little bent out of shape, the result of an accident when he'd hit himself in the face with a spade about twenty years ago.

'It's hard to believe such a deformed hooter is so ... finely tuned,' she mused, insensitively, before declaring: 'Tara Wallace!'

'Who?'

'Oh my God, of course. Lady Tara Wallace. The novelist.'

'Oh right. Yes. My mother reads her books. I didn't know she was royalty?'

'We just call her "lady" because of her haughty ways. Bit of a recluse really. Very unusual to see her at choir. Very unusual indeed.'

'What are you suggesting? Tara killed Michael?'

'Think about it. She hasn't been to choir in months. Turns up the night Michael dies.'

'Pure coincidence. So did I. I was there tonight. First time ever.'

Aoife carried on as if she hadn't heard him.

'And ... And, Finn, she washes the cups. Including the cup that contained the evidence of the poison.'

'Aoife! You're in shock. You're letting your imagination run away with itself. Somebody washed the cups. Big deal. It's what people do.'

'You didn't.'

'People apart from me.'

'Look at what sort of books Tara writes, Finn: historical fiction, with quite a lot of grisly deaths. Mostly deaths by poison! She's an expert.'

Finn was getting a bit worried about Aoife by now. Her eyes blazing, she was on a roll, accusing an elderly reclusive writer of being a potential murderer on the extremely tenuous basis that a handful of her fictional characters, at various junctures in Irish history, if he remembered correctly, were poisoned.

Aoife asked Eve for a pen and paper. Eve removed her glasses which had steamed up on her return to the crowded bar.

'It's cold down in the cellar.'

She'd just changed a keg and was now effortlessly taking three different orders while the lugubrious Hector, his lips parched, helped himself to a pint of Beamish. Eve handed Aoife a notebook and pen.

'Thanks, Eve.'

'No bother at all. Sorry about Michael. Lovely chap.'

Nothing was any bother to Eve. A mere five foot four, she was a human dynamo in jeans and a Doors T-shirt, personable and even-tempered. She'd left school at the age of fifteen, but most people agreed she'd be well able to run a small country never mind a bar. If only she wasn't married to Barry Duggan Junior.

Aoife and Finn moved to a quiet-ish corner beside the grand piano. She started writing furiously in the notepad Eve had provided.

'What are you doing?'

'What does it look like? I'm compiling a list of suspects.'

Finn looked over her shoulder.

'Excuse me. What am I doing there?'

'Everybody who was at choir practice is a suspect. Including you.'

'Right, I see.' Finn grabbed the notebook. 'And my *mother*! Seriously?'

Aoife grabbed the notebook back.

'Everybody. Until we can eliminate them. Obviously there's a hierarchy. A hierarchy of suspects.'

As Aoife continued to write, Finn's gaze wandered to the grand piano. It was a Steinway, finished, he was impressed to see, in a Macassar ebony from Sulawesi.

'Wow.'

He ran his hand along the smooth brown and black grains. He looked up at the wall. There was a photograph of Sir Nicholas Nguyen-Bow sitting at the piano. The renowned composer of West End musicals was a frequent visitor to Abbeyford near where he had a stud farm. He was often to be found, in a low-key way, playing on this, his own custom-made instrument, to a small but knowing audience.

'Obviously, Barry Duggan is top of the list, right?' Aoife said in a more reasonable manner.

'Of course. No argument there.'

'He has any amount of motives. He hated Michael. He threatened to kill him. You heard it yourself.'

'Yes,' Finn agreed, allowing himself against all his instincts to be drawn into Aoife's grief-stricken knee-jerk pseudo-detecting. She was a very persuasive person. Racking his brains, trying to be helpful, he recalled: 'And it was Monika who made the tea.'

'Did she now? Why didn't you tell me that before?'

'I'm telling you now. It's only just come to me.'

'*You see!* They might be in it together.'

He had to confess it was intoxicating – if that was not too crass a term in the circumstances – speculating as to who might have murdered Michael. If, he qualified, Michael had in fact been murdered. It didn't take away from the seriousness of the situation, or the genuine shock they were all experiencing, but it was … intoxicating. That was the word, rightly or wrongly, he kept coming back to. He just had to make sure in his own mind his interest was sparked by genuine curiosity and not the magnetism of the person beside him.

'Who else had a motive?'

Aoife pointed at a name on the list in block capitals.

'*Fionnuala Boyle!*'

Finn was startled. Harry's ex-wife was a paragon of virtue. A parody of the virtues, all seven of them – chastity, temperance, charity, diligence, kindness, patience and humility. She was the last person he'd have put on the list.

'You're not honestly … Have you met Fionnuala? She's practically a nun.'

'And all the nuns in this country are innocent? Are they?'

Good point, Finn thought.

'Think about it. Harry left Fionnuala for Michael. She must have been humiliated. Beneath that froideur, she could be a raging torrent for all we know.'

'Nice word.'

'Torrent?'

'Froideur. I bet you don't get to use that very often.'
'I teach French. And don't forget, Fionnuala's a chemist.'
'Oh come on.'
'She has the means. She'd know how to make a lethal concoction, wouldn't she?'

He objected to people getting all interrogative, asking a question after expressing an opinion, forcing you to agree or disagree with them. As if there were only yes or no answers. It was an infuriating habit of his father's. Even if he agreed with his father, which wasn't often, he invariably found himself adopting an opposing point of view. So insistent was Redmond on the rightness of his own views, and so dismissive was he of anybody else's opinions, Finn just couldn't give him the satisfaction of agreeing with him on anything.

'So we start with Barry and Monika. And then Fionnuala,' Aoife declared.

It looked suspiciously like he'd just been roped into a murder investigation. Or willingly jumped into one. There was no stopping Aoife. Conor, her brother, was the same, once he got an idea into his head. Finn hardly saw him the last year at school, so fixed was he on his studies and his determination to get into MIT. The Prendergasts were an extraordinary family, materially poor by any standards but driven, with a huge emphasis on education, and yet at the same time humble and selfless. They'd do anything for anyone. He made one last feeble attempt, thinking of the happy, relaxed if slightly melancholy sojourn he'd planned, to resist.

'Aoife! You're not yourself. Shouldn't we just leave this to the guards?'

'And what will they do? They still don't know what happened to Eamonn De Burgh, and that was over forty years ago. It's up to us, Finn. Michael was my friend and I will find out who did this to him, I have to – and think of Harry! He needs to know the truth as well.'

Finn sighed. What was he getting himself into at all?

'Right. Okay. What about Lady Tara then?'

'Her too. We need to speak to them all. For all we know she and Michael might have had some connection.'

'Maybe he was the long-lost son she'd rejected?' he mumbled sarcastically. 'Bent on revenge. Tara killed him before he killed her.'

'Very good.'

'Or maybe he was a reincarnation of one of the people she bumped off in her novels.'

'Now you have it. At the very least she's an authority on poisons. We know that. She might be able to give us a steer on what exactly was used.'

'*If* Michael was murdered. Big if. And my mother? What should we do with her? Should we bundle her into a car and take her to a disused shed? Blindfold her and waterboard her until she talks?'

'There's very little your mother doesn't know. Now, are you having another?'

He nodded at his empty glass. This could be a long night.

PART 2

Chapter 9

Finn woke up in his mother's bedroom with a start. He'd been having the dream again about being late for an exam; a maths exam that he was unprepared for in the first place, having lost all his school books. It was an annoying dream that was not in any way related to him sleeping in his parents' bed, its distinct scent – a commingling of Imperial Leather soap, Lenor fabric conditioner, his father's piney sweat, the 1980s generally and a touch of damp from the en suite shower – irritating his nose. His father, a forester by profession, hadn't washed his hair with shampoo for about ten years. Nor had he used soap products. It was no wonder his parents had agreed to live apart. No, the dream predated Finn's return home. Isabella had put it down to stress. Couldn't every dream be attributed to stress? For a second he couldn't remember why he'd set the alarm so early. Then it came to him and he suddenly wanted to be four years old again curled up between his parents after a nightmare.

It must have been over their fifth – or was it their sixth? – whiskey that himself and Aoife had arranged to meet first thing in the morning at Barry Duggan's premises to interview Barry about Michael's death. He sat up in bed. Who did they think they were? The whole situation was ludicrous. His wife had just left him. He had possibly witnessed a murder. A murder he was now by the looks of it actively investigating. And as if that wasn't enough, he was currently sleeping in his mother's bed. No wonder he was stressed.

The reason he was sleeping in his mother's bed was that Happiness had been allocated his old room. He could hear her greeting the new day by way of song, a hymn, a warbly 'What a Friend We Have in Jesus', through the wall. Since her accident, Maura herself was not able to use the stairs and was currently occupying the 'good' room which had been converted into a boudoir. Finn was determined, once he'd handed in his notice to Aoife and stood down from this foolish escapade, notwithstanding his obligation to his mother, to find himself a flat.

Finn knocked on the door of the old sitting room, a room he rarely entered as a child, except to illicitly explore the bookcase for his father's botanical and horticultural treasures and his mother's detective novels, and later as a teen to raid the drinks cabinet for his father's whiskey collection. The rather grand bookcase and drinks cabinet, a two-door early twentieth century affair in solid mahogany, was still there, along one wall. At the other end of the room in the bay window stood an interloping IKEA wardrobe in solid MDF, blocking the view of Redmond's rose garden. And in place of the couch was a surgical bed in which lay Maura, raring to go.

'Where's Happiness?'

Charming.

'It's her day off, Mammy.'

In his youth, the sitting room had been off-limits as a rule so as it would always be in perfect condition for receiving visitors. As far as Finn could recall, although there were always plenty of visitors in the house, none were important enough to merit entry to that particular sanctum. Short of a US president calling, or The Beatles, he couldn't imagine who would fit the bill. He escorted his mother to the bathroom across the hall (formerly Redmond's office) where she performed her ablutions while keeping up an entertaining stream of commentary.

'Your father is impossible. You know about the rhododendrons?'

'No.'

'He has this thing.'

She laughed gummily as she cleaned her dentures with a toothbrush.

'A crusade, he calls it. He won't rest until he's killed them all.'

'Yep, sounds like Dad alright.'

'He wants to rid the whole country of rhododendrons, can you believe it?'

He could well believe it.

'Like St Patrick and the snakes. You should go and see him.'

Finn helped Maura get dressed.

'Poor Rameses. You know he was here the night he disappeared.'

Where had that come from?

'In the house?'

'In this room. Himself and your father were in here drinking whiskey.'

She lowered her voice.

'They were arguing.'

'What were they arguing about, Mammy?'

'Oh that was a long time ago. Where's Happiness?'

'It's her day off. She's going to Dublin I think.'

'Oh yes, you told me that. I'm such a featherhead.'

He prepared his mother a simple breakfast, as instructed, of tea with toast and honey. Happiness appeared in the living room wearing a white Trinity College Dublin sweatshirt and flouncy skirt. Although her face didn't show it, it was obvious that she was in a buoyant mood. It occurred to Finn that thus far he had never seen her smile. And so he resolved there and then that he would make it his business, his mission in life, before the summer was out, to make the ironically named Happiness laugh.

'I didn't know you went to Trinity?'

'I didn't,' she scowled.

'Sorry.'

'Her daughter,' Maura chipped in. 'Grace.'

'Grace is studying Bess at Trinity College,' Happiness announced proudly.

'Bess?'

Finn was confused.

'You mean Queen Elizabeth the First? History?'

'No, Mr Dundee, I mean Business, Economics and Social Studies.' She enunciated each syllable and even added a few extra syllables for emphasis. 'Lord preserve us. She got a scholarship for your information.'

'Finn never went to college,' said Maura matter-of-factly.

Happiness picked up a knife. Finn recoiled.

'Your mother doesn't like the crusts.'

Shaking her head at Finn's utter incompetence, she started cutting the crusts off Maura's toast.

'I know,' laughed Maura. 'I'm such a baby.'

'You have worked hard all your life, Maura. You are entitled to a treat.'

After breakfast they dropped Happiness at the bus stop in Market Square, damp vegetable traders setting up their stalls in the morning drizzle. Lifting his left buttock off the driver's seat, Finn removed a piece of paper from his back pocket and followed Aoife's directions to her house. The drawing she'd added for the craic was a surprisingly accurate representation of her tiny cottage, a restored gate house on a level crossing about two miles from the town. He hadn't needed the directions at all, having spent much of his youth in and out of what was once the Prendergast family home. A cycle path now ran along what was once a branch line off the old Dublin–Wexford railway.

Ignoring Finn's belated attempt to call off the venture, Aoife and Maura were alarmingly gung-ho, planning on having the case wrapped up before Aoife's first class at 10 am. A herd of Friesian cows in a nearby field raised their impassive heads and lowed pitifully at their folly. Finn didn't disagree with them.

'He has only the one kidney.'

'Who's that now, Mammy?'

'Barry Duggan.'

'He only found out in his forties. When he got the gout.'

What ever happened to patient confidentiality, Finn muttered under his breath. And how was that relevant? As far as he knew, the seat of empathy was in the amygdala and not the kidneys.

'I was very friendly with his wife. His first wife, Imelda. He definitely changed after the gout.'

'He changed long before the gout, Maura,' Aoife corrected her gently.

'You love prawns, don't you Finn?'

'Well, yes.'

'Imagine if you weren't allowed to eat prawns?'

She let that appalling prospect settle for a moment.

'Or chocolate or red meat or wine? All the good things in life.'

'That would be disappointing alright, Mammy, but I don't think I'd necessarily become a murderer if I was deprived of them.'

'You'd be angry.'

'Maybe.'

'He changed after he expanded the business, Maura,' Aoife insisted. 'After he took over AAAAA Waste in Waterford City.'

Between the two of them, they told Finn what they knew of Barry Duggan. He was a townie. His father had a little garage on Emmett Street but was more often than not to be found in the less salubrious pubs of the town, the few pubs he hadn't been barred from. His mother was a seamstress.

'She made your communion outfit. Do you remember?'

How could he forget? A blue suit made out of felt modelled surely on the classic Trumpton fireman's outfit complete with belt and buckle and shiny buttons. The boys called him Barney McGrew for months afterwards. Pugh, Pugh, Barney McGrew, Cuthbert, Dibble and Grub. The trousers were too tight and too short, details his friends didn't overlook as they taunted him mercilessly in the playground. He could forgive his mother a lot but that – what he now suddenly realized was a sympathy commission to Duggan's mother – still rankled.

'He looked adorable, Aoife.'

'He still does,' said Aoife.

Finn caught Aoife winking at him in the rear-view

mirror, the bell in her left ear faintly tinkling as she chuckled away at her own quip.

'You'll have to show me the photos some time, Maura. Give me one for my wallet.'

Finn was amused not so much by the quality of her flirty banter but by her playfulness generally.

The Duggans lived in a flat above the garage. Officially, Barry left school at the age of fifteen, but the truth was that he rarely attended school at all, ever – primary or secondary. By all accounts he worked in the garage morning, noon and night, from about the age of five. He was already buying and selling cars in his teens. Everybody loved him. They gave him the benefit of the doubt even after the time he was charged with a spree of burglaries.

'He was never convicted,' Maura pointed out.

The judge liked him. Felt sorry for him. Believed in second chances. Cheeky, good-humoured, clever Barry could spin yarns with the best of them, a talent that went a long way in a place like Abbeyford. He bought his first waste disposal lorry when he was nineteen, and shortly afterwards married his childhood sweetheart, Imelda.

'Terrible eczema, poor Imelda.'

Again with the uncharacteristic breach of ethics. Finn turned to his mother, not the same woman he knew and loved before the fall, but possibly more fun and certainly less circumspect.

'All her kidneys intact, Mammy?'

His mother carried on, oblivious to his jibe. Together the happy couple set up AA Waste Management and before long they had Barry Junior.

'I taught him at Joey's just after I started,' Aoife reminisced. 'Nice kid. But troubled.'

'They were a great team. Barry drove the lorry. Imelda did everything else. Whatever you do in a new company, books and so on. Orders.'

'When she wasn't busy scratching herself.'

'What?'

'The eczema. Oh, never mind.'

Finn couldn't help it. Again his mother wasn't distracted by his impertinence. In fact, prompted by Aoife, she was only warming to her theme.

'They bought out an existing waste company.'

'AAAAA in Waterford City?' Finn said to show he'd been listening.

'No, ya big Dundee,' Maura said. 'AAA here in Abbeyford. And then they moved to the old sales yard.'

'The cattle mart. They're still there. That's where we're going now.'

'Imelda died about … what was it, Aoife … five years ago?'

'Fifteen, Maura.'

'I'm such a goose. I've lost all track of time. Poor Imelda.'

Maura blessed herself.

'Crohn's in the end. Barry was beside himself.'

This was where the story became vague. It was around that time that he either fell in or fell out with a 'bad shower', Aoife wasn't sure. Apparently Barry's father had crossed the wrong people. She didn't know if it was some sort of a gambling debt or if somebody's honour had been offended in some way. Either way, Barry changed and not for the better.

'It was the gout. It can do awful things to a man,' Maura insisted.

'Gout is a remedy, and not a disease, Maura,' Aoife argued. 'Swift.'

'Nonsense.'

Aoife effortlessly recited a ditty from the back seat.

> *'As if the gout should seize the head.*
> *Doctors pronounce the patient dead,*
> *But, if they can by all their arts,*
> *Eject it to th'extremest parts,*
> *They give the sick man joy, and praise*
> *The gout that will prolong his days.'*

'She's a teacher,' Maura whispered to Finn. 'Likes to show off.'

'I can hear you, Maura.'

Turning stiffly towards Aoife, Maura asked her: 'What would Swift know anyway? Wasn't he the one who suggested people should eat their own children?'

'I think that was supposed to be a joke, Mammy. Swift was a satirist.'

'Pretty sick joke if you ask me.'

Eventually Duggan bought AAAAA Waste in Waterford. That was a big operation and them having all the local government contracts in the region. Of course there were questions about where Duggan got the money for the expansion. In a small town there were always questions when anybody did well for themselves. Aoife, without saying as much, seemed to be implying that Barry had some sort of a silent partner, whether he wanted one or not.

'That's unfair,' objected Maura, who usually had a soft spot for the underdog. 'He was always a hard worker.'

The pair of them agreed that without Imelda, Barry threw himself into his work with a new and ruthless zeal, rebranding his company as AAAAAAAAAA Waste Solutions. 10 As in total.

'Like a cry for help,' Finn mused without getting any sort of a reaction.

Within months, Barry Duggan, alone or in tandem with his shadowy backers, had driven most of his rivals out of business and was soon overseeing the leading waste management company in the whole of the south-east.

'Hundreds of trucks.'

'Twenty-eight, Maura.'

'We're here.' Finn took a deep breath. 'Are you sure you want to go through with this?'

Chapter 10

Between the excessive amount of whiskey the night before and the nervous knots in his stomach, Finn didn't feel well. Aoife, who'd consumed a similar amount of whiskey without any obvious ill effects, nodded enthusiastically, as did his mother.

At Aoife's behest Finn drove into the yard, the Yaris dwarfed by the lorries coming and going in their distinctive pink livery. A large hoarding on one of the hangars featured Barry himself dressed in a tux like a Vegas crooner with his arms outspread above the caption, MY WASTE!

They parked outside the office. 'Office' was possibly too grand a term for what was essentially a pair of rectangular prefabs, one on top of the other, fixed together with steel beams. A set of aircraft passenger stairs led to the upper storey, which was currently padlocked.

'Mammy, do you mind waiting in the car? It won't take a sec.'

'You must be joking. I wouldn't miss this for the world.'

The secretary, a middle-aged woman with short, dyed-black hair, a pair of round glasses and a two-piece tweed suit, was dipping a croissant into a flat white.

'How are ya, Birdy!' said Aoife casually. 'We're looking for Barry.'

'He's not here,' the secretary snapped, not looking up from her breakfast.

Aoife, clearly unwelcome, was unfazed but at the same time acknowledged the inefficacy of her rookie approach by smiling self-deprecatingly at Finn. Winsomely, she put her hand over her mouth.

'Fidelma! Is it yourself?' said Maura. 'Haven't seen ya in ages.'

Birdy/Fidelma's face loosened.

'Ah Maura. What brings you here?'

She stood up, brushed the crumbs off her jacket, walked around to the other side of the desk and gave Maura a hug, a tear forming in her eye. Finn could see the bird resemblance alright. Like a thrush or something.

'Just hoping to have a quick chat with Barry about a little job. Nothing urgent.'

'Sure you know Barry would do anything for you, Maura. Try outside at the wash station.'

Finn was aware of two men, bodies tense in green AAAAAAAAAA overalls with the little pink logo on the breast pocket, sitting on a couch at the far end of the Portakabin. The taller one was sallow and bald with an extremely lush and well-groomed beard, tattoos creeping above his collar. The other fella was wiry with sandy hair and a pasty complexion. They were playing Grand Theft Auto on one of many TV screens in front of them. The other screens showed CCTV images of the interior and exterior of a luxury home. Their uniforms were remarkably clean for waste-disposal operatives.

Despite her obvious affection for Maura, Fidelma, a sister of Barry's first wife, Imelda, as it turned out, had pulled a fast one. It was Barry Duggan Junior who was washing a truck, and not the chief suspect himself.

'Mrs O'Leary. Miss Prendergast.'

'Aoife.'

'And I know you off the telly.'

Barry Junior's face reddened in Finn's presence. He thrust out a hand sheathed in a thick rubber glove. He was a shy man, head bowed. Wouldn't look the trio in the eye.

'You keep them lorries fierce clean,' Finn said, his boyhood accent and local inflections coming to the fore, attracting a wry sideways glance from Aoife. 'Sure what's the point,' he continued. 'Says you, if they're only going to get dirty again, what?'

Finn tried to sound jocular but now that he thought of probably sounded a bit patronizing.

'Daddy likes everything to be right. Eve was saying you were in the pub last night.'

'We were actually hoping to speak to your father,' said Aoife.

Finn noticed that Aoife had a lovely warm, compassionate way with people when she wanted to. He could imagine her in the classroom. Barry relaxed a little, safe in her presence.

'You think he killed Michael?'

There was a moment's silence.

'That's what Eve said anyways. She heard you talking about it.'

'Ha. Did she now?' said Aoife. 'Nothing gets past your Eve.'

'She's a good listener right enough. The best. Daddy's not here at the minute. He's in Croatia.'

Aoife caught Finn's eye. *Convenient*, her eye said.

'Himself and herself, Monika, went first thing this morning. Dragged me out of bed, so he did, at half three to give the pair of them a lift to the airport.'

Barry Junior slowly removed his cumbersome gloves and lit a cigarette with a trembling hand. They were Marlboro Gold.

'What brings them to Croatia, do you mind me asking?'

'Wedding. One of Monika's cousins. I know what you're thinking. But it was booked months ago.'

'Were you not invited?'

'I was.'

Again there was a moment's silence, as the man, misty-eyed, took a long drag on his fag.

'But Eve wasn't.' He crushed the cigarette under the heel of his welly. It was only half-smoked.

'Eve wasn't invited to the wedding.'

It was said more in sorrow than anger. But that slight clearly affected him deeply.

'Anyway, somebody has to mind the shop.'

Washing lorries didn't look like the work of a high-powered executive.

'He hasn't ... what do you call it? ... absconded, if that's what you're thinking. They'll be back next weekend. I'm sure he'll be delighted to talk to yiz.'

'If it's not too impertinent, Barry, where were you last night?'

'Me?'

Barry looked from his right foot to his left foot. He put on his gloves again and picked up the power hose.

'I was actually at the community centre.'

If Aoife and Finn were slightly stunned by this revelation, they didn't show it. Maura did audibly.

'Oh.'

'Yeah. For an AA meeting.'

He let that land, smiling humourlessly at their discomfort.

'About six o'clock, I think. I was gone before the choir started.'

'Right.'

'And where were you after that?'

'You're not usually this blunt. On the radio.'

'They say you should never meet your heroes, Barry,' said Aoife at Finn's expense.

Barry accidentally pressed the button on the hose, spraying Finn's jeans.

'Sorry, Finn. I was ... don't say this to Eve if you're talking to her ... I was in Finnegan's.'

Finnegan's was another pub in town.

'Hey Barry!'

A piercing voice in an eastern European accent called from the office door. It was the tall, muscle-bound one. Barry winced, his hangdog face reddening again.

'We need coffee, Barry? Americano for me with oat milk. Flat white for Karl.'

Barry Junior tried to put his hands in the pockets of his overalls in what he imagined was a nonchalant way. But with the bulky gloves they didn't fit. The poor man was mortified, especially in front of Finn.

'No, it's not ... It's just ... I lost a bet.'

'Right.'

'To Dominik there. Bit of craic, you know.'

'Café Madremonte,' the man referred to as Dominik shouted in no uncertain terms. 'Not from Spar like last time. Okay? And don't forget, oat milk!'

Finn got the distinct impression that Barry Junior was the sort of man that lost a lot of bets.

Back in the car, Aoife whipped out her notepad and added Barry Junior's name to the list of suspects.

'What, because of the cigarette? It's going to be a very long list at this rate.'

'He was shifty.'

'So was the secretary. Not to mention yer man, Game of Thrones, and his scrawny friend. Everybody looks shifty depending on how you look at them.'

'He was at the community centre, wasn't he? He had the opportunity. We'll get our hands on the CCTV. See if he entered the rehearsal room.'

'CCTV! We're not the FBI, Aoife. This is not a game.'

In the face of her determination, he let it rest. Finn and Maura said goodbye to Aoife at St Joseph's Boys school and carried on home. They'd arranged to meet again at the Medical Hall at lunchtime, ostensibly to pick up Maura's prescription but really, for a probing chat with Fionnuala Boyle.

Chapter 11

In the meantime, Finn and his mother enjoyed a pleasant morning together in the stillness of his boyhood home. After diligently doing her physical exercises, driven by the hope of regaining her full strength, they tackled the *Irish Times* crossword to test her mental faculties. Finn took great pleasure in watching his mother's delighted reaction when she solved a clue correctly. It was also nice to have the one-to-one time with her. Much as he appreciated Happiness, he wasn't himself when she was around. And it occurred to him, not for the first time, that in all his visits home in the past twenty years, his father had been invariably there, dominating the conversation, trying to initiate some debate or argument about one of his many bugbears. His mother, patience personified, didn't always get a look-in. Finn knew intimately his father's family history, his passions and interests, his hopes and dreams, his 'solutions' to all the world's problems. Although he was a loving man in his own way, and caring, he had a tendency to talk over everybody else. Much as Finn tried, it had proved next to impossible to have private conversations with his mother when his father had so much to say. Redmond's moving out was, counter-intuitively, something of a rare, selfless act on his part. Deep down, he knew the best way to contribute to Maura's recovery was by not being there! Between Redmond's absence and the effects of her accident, Maura had won a new-found freedom to express herself. She laughed in a way she never had before. She was indiscreet. Memories and thoughts drifted up from her subconscious and were articulated unfiltered. Finn treasured these moments with her, getting to know her properly as a human being and not merely as a mammy.

'Your father and Rameses were best friends.'

Finn casually poured a cup of tea, not saying anything in case he might discourage her from going further.

'They fell out.'

'Sure you know Daddy,' Finn said, noncommittally.

'They fell out over eggs!'

'Eggs?'

'I shouldn't be telling you this,' she whispered. 'Eagle eggs.'

Among his many achievements, Redmond had been peripherally involved in re-introducing the golden eagle to Ireland in the late 1970s. To his immense satisfaction, a breeding pair settled in the Comeraghs, above Coomshimgaun Lough. Maura in a trance-like state recalled the night in March of 1982 during the Big Snow when Rameses called around to the house. It had come to Redmond's attention that three eggs had been stolen from the eagle's nest. Naturally, he suspected Rameses.

'Rameses was a tree surgeon. He could shinny up a tree like a squirrel.'

Rameses was also an egg collector. Obviously the rarer the egg, the more he wanted it. Of course since 1954 it was illegal to steal any bird's egg, never mind the eggs of an endangered species.

'It drove your father mad. But he was very fond of

Rameses. We both were. He might have turned a blind eye to some eggs. Crows, I suppose. No shortage of them. Even curlews and lapwings and skylarks and what have you. But not his precious eagles.'

That night, according to Maura, Redmond gave Rameses an ultimatum. If he didn't return the eggs to the nest, he would have no choice but to report him.

'This was forty-odd years ago. Your father had no problem with the guards back then.'

Rameses denied he had anything to do with it, the theft. Words were exchanged. They nearly came to blows apparently. Then Rameses stormed out into the blizzard and was never seen again. Finn was captivated by his mother's story. For some reason he was more interested in what happened to Rameses than what happened to Michael.

'Did he return the eggs?'

'We don't even know if he stole them in the first place. Your father isn't always right, you know, despite what he might think.'

When Redmond went to check the nest a couple of days later, two of the three eggs had been replaced. Finn quizzed his mother on what she thought might have happened, but Maura was getting tired. Somebody definitely stole the eggs. It could have been Rameses, she conceded, or somebody known to Rameses. Or, she told him, waving her hand, it could have been anybody. When they searched his house, the guards found hundreds of illegally collected eggs but not the missing golden eagle's.

'It could have been sold.'

And then she added: 'The lake was frozen that night. If Rameses was up there, he might have fallen through the ice.'

'So you don't think it was foul play?'

'I don't know. It's a very deep lake. They say the deepest in Ireland. Did I tell you about my new carer? She's a Nigerian lady. Happiness.'

Chapter 12

Aoife made it to Joey's just in time for her first class of the day. She knew that Giles McCabe would note her time of arrival from his office overlooking the playground. She didn't give a whit what he, a shameless careerist, thought. Not just a careerist but a stickler too. And a populist. She particularly didn't like the way he pandered to some of the more nativist parents in trying to keep the number of foreign nationals in the school to a minimum.

She loved teaching, the engagement, the banter, the everyday challenge of helping fourteen-year-old boys reach their potential. What she didn't care for was school politics, dealing with a fifty-year-old man who had fully realized his potential as a petty despot, and for whom Aoife was a challenge, a threat, as he saw it, a mocking, dissenting voice to be crushed. Easier said than done though, for he hadn't anticipated the force of nature that was Aoife Prendergast.

Aoife's father had died when she was in her early teens, his pneumonia-prone lungs finally packing in after one rain-soaking too many. He in turn had been raised in a mother-and-baby home, and despite the hardship and neglect he'd obviously endured there, he didn't dwell on it. Nor did he mope. She remembered him as a quiet, obliging, uncomplaining man. He worked hard, smoked his pipe and read his books. He never seemed to sleep. If she ever got up during the night for a drink of water, she'd find him in his threadbare armchair, smoking and reading, happier awake than asleep. His eyes would light up when he saw her. He'd gather her in his arms and lull her to sleep with a poem or an off-the-cuff story. It wasn't by accident she developed a fierce thirst deep in the night.

It was from her mother, who died of a heart attack not long after her father, that Aoife had inherited her stubborn streak and her endless passion for social justice. Although they didn't have much themselves, her mother was often to be found delivering meals on wheels to the elderly. When she wasn't doing that, she'd be outside SuperO, collecting for one charity or another, or visiting the truly poor. And although they lived a few miles out of town, in the cottage at the railway crossing – which she finally managed to buy back from the state transport company – vagrants and travellers knew they would not be denied a meal or a few coppers to send them on their way. Channelling the memory of her parents, Aoife, in her role as a schoolteacher at St Joseph's, vowed never to leave any child behind. She was also determined to do everything in her power to make Abbeyford the best possible place to live and breathe. Hence her role in the Tidy Towns organization. And her resolve to root out any murderers who might be lurking in the long grass. *Vincit veritas*. That as her father constantly reminded her was the motto of the Prendergasts. *Truth Prevails*.

After class, during first break, she hurried the couple of hundred yards to the community centre, McCabe's eyes, no doubt, trained on her back. There she asked the manager, a friend of hers named Donal Kirby, if she could have a look at the CCTV footage from the previous night. Donal smiled.

'Ha. Don't know what you're up to. But you're not the first one to ask for it. The guards were here earlier.'

So the guards were taking Michael's death seriously. Donal didn't seem remotely interested in why Aoife might be looking for the footage. But he had a son in Aoife's class, a shy boy with alopecia who idolized Aoife, and Donal credited her with helping the lad come out of his shell. So whatever she wanted to do was okay by him.

'Did you give it to them?'

'No.'

'Good.'

'For the simple reason, Aoife, it doesn't exist.'

'What?'

'Last night. In fact every Tuesday night the CCTV here is switched off.'

'Why?'

The manager of the community centre hummed and hawed.

'Look. I don't want to get anybody into trouble. Let's just say, a mutual friend of ours asked me to turn it off. I don't know if it's an affair or if he's not supposed to be here of a Tuesday, or maybe he's just camera-shy. No idea. I thought what's the harm. To be honest with you, we don't really need CCTV here at all. But there was a grant going, you know yourself ...'

Once the hard-pressed Donal started, grateful to have sounding board as empathetic as Aoife, he wasn't going to be shushed.

'And we need all the help we can get. Sure the place is falling down. What we do need, and I've been saying this since day one is a proper coffee machine ...'

'Donal. Who was it? Who asked for the CCTV to be switched off?'

Donal looked around. Aoife leaned in. He gave her a name.

'Don't say it was me told you. I have enough on my plate.'

Aoife whistled.

'Interesting. Thanks Donal. Did you tell the guards?'

'God no.'

'I owe you one.'

Chapter 13

At five past one, Finn and Maura entered the pharmacy. Fionnuala had retained the original shopfront, with the old Medical Hall sign in gold lettering on a racing-green background. And while she also kept the three arched windows either side of the doorway, the interior was now spacious and fluorescent. Gone were the apothecary cabinets and glass jars he remembered as a boy when her father, Mr Flynn, a deeply religious man with something of an un-Christian temper, dispensed medications and unwanted advice from behind the walnut counter. Harry Boyle had dared him once to ask Mr Flynn if he sold condoms. As expected, Flynn lost the head completely and chased Finn out of the shop, calling him, among other things, a fornicator who would rot in hell. In such a tizzy was he, he even took the trouble to ring Redmond and Maura that evening to warn them of the eternal peril that faced their reprobate son if he didn't mend his ways. Redmond had a good laugh at that and shook Finn's hand.

'Put it there, boy!'

Although he could see that his mother found it quite amusing too, ever the peace-maker, she kept a straight face and made him write a letter of apology to Mr Flynn.

Poor Fionnuala. She had never quite managed to escape

from under the wimple of the Catholicism in which she was reared. Nowadays, she dressed beautifully in expensive clothes but always demurely. Unlike her parents, she drank good wine but only in moderation. As a debater at university, she was intelligent with a dry wit, but kept her more progressive opinions to herself. She ran a state-of-the-art contemporary pharmacy with a full range of medical and beauty supplies (including condoms), but maintained the traditional exterior. She had always been an intense woman, poised in a way that suggested she was forced to draw on extraordinary reserves of energy just to maintain an equilibrium, torn between a desire to get down on her knees and a desire to let herself go.

While Finn was waiting for Maura's prescription – painkillers, a diuretic and some sleeping pills – Aoife rushed in. She paid for some lozenges and made a big show of accidentally bumping into them.

'Oh hi, fancy meeting you here.'

At which point Maura, who was looking forward to her afternoon nap, asked the bemused assistant to tell Fionnuala she was here. They really weren't very good at this undercover caper. The assistant looked them up and down, popped away for a moment and popped back again.

'She's out the back. You're to go on through.'

At the back of the premises was a small courtyard. There was some garden furniture, a table and chairs in grey rattan, pushed into one corner. In the opposite corner stood a life-sized statue of the Virgin Mary coiled in ivy. After much agonizing, Fionnuala had decided to leave her there, paint flaking, a residual concern regarding the consequences for her soul of dumping a holy statue in a skip being the overriding factor in her decision. Along the back wall separating the yard from the hairdressers' beyond were a number of potted plants, including an *olea europaea* and a whopping *chamaerops humilis* that both looked to Finn starved of light. A bit like Fionnuala herself.

She was kneeling on a cushion on the paving stones in the centre of the courtyard, as if in worship. Alongside her was Hector Morrissey, the proprietor of Morrissey's Bar, of all people, in a fleece that had seen better days. The object of their reverence was a drone. Neither looked up. Maura sat down on one of the garden chairs while Aoife and Finn stood watching as Fionnuala, deep in concentration, tucked her thick black hair behind her ears. She then placed two paper prescription bags into a larger receptacle. It looked at a glance like a sort of stiff plastic tote bag, sturdy with a pair of handles. Hector then hooked the handles onto an attachment on the underside of the drone. Fionnuala, pale and anxious, stood up and smoothed out the pleats of her sleek poplin skirt as Hector, a far cry from the morose figure he cut in the pub last night, switched on the drone and stared intently at his controller. The machine, buzzing menacingly like a nest of hornets, rose suddenly about twenty feet in the air. There was a scrap of paper sellotaped to the undercarriage with what appeared to be Hector's name and number on it.

'In case she comes down. I've lost them before.'

Animated like a boy on Christmas Day, Hector, his tongue protruding from his mouth, entered the co-ordinates for the destination of the drone.

'Wait,' Fionnuala instructed. Hector guided the drone back to earth, while Fionnuala, tall and bony, hurried inside.

'What's in the bag?'

'Oh, it's just a prescription for an old boy out by Pipestown. A few beta-blockers, eye drops, that sort of thing.'

'McQuaid!' Maura shouted triumphantly as if she'd just answered a clue in the *Irish Times* crossword, instantly recognizing the symptoms of the patient out in Pipestown.

'Mammy!'

'Andy McQuaid. Hard to believe he's still going.'

'What's the range?'

'This yoke? She could do about fifty kilometres no problem, as far as Thomastown and back,' Hector explained enthusiastically, delighted to be asked. 'Fifty kilometres an hour. Depends on the weather of course. Although we're only allowed thirty kilometres an hour, can you believe that? And this a medical emergency. Mind you, McQuaid is only three kilometres out the road.'

Fionnuala materialized again.

'Hector! That information is not for public consumption.'

'She guessed,' he defended himself, pointing at Maura.

Hector went down a tad in Finn's estimation. Nobody likes a squealer.

Fionnuala seemed to feel a bit better about herself and the current undertaking after adding a family pack of fruit pastilles to the carrier bag as well as a paperback book. After reassuring Fionnuala about the infallibility of the technology, Hector directed the drone skywards high over the town and on to the little hamlet of Pipestown. Meanwhile, she rang the patient's wife to let her know the delivery was due and stayed on the line until it arrived six minutes later. The woman on the other end of the phone seemed terrified, as if the gadget would go rogue and destroy her house, frightening her hens to death in the process. It was hardly surprising given the list of do's and don'ts, mostly don'ts, that Fionnuala issued to her in her typically hushed and ominous tone. Stay inside. Don't go within twenty feet of the drone. Lock up the hens. Wait for a full minute after the drone departs before picking up the bag. For fear of decapitation, Finn supposed.

Aoife and Finn crowded around the monitor. When the drone landed outside the McQuaid house, Finn could hear the lady scream.

'It's here. May the Lord save us.'

Hector pressed a button which released the bag from the device, and expertly manoeuvred the drone out of the farmyard and over a copse of willow. He zig-zagged over hill farms dotted with sheep, across the motorway, around the incinerator and back to the Medical Hall in Abbeyford.

'I had one shot down last year,' he said by way of explanation for the erratic trajectory of the drone. 'An English hippie woman, would you believe, lives in that cottage out in Broomfield, you know with the sculptures outside, totem poles or whatever. Said I was annoying her dog.'

'A hippie with a shotgun.' Aoife shook her head sadly. 'That's a good one. Whatever happened to peace, love and understanding?'

'You tell me.'

Fionnuala accompanied them all to the street. As Hector placed his equipment in the boot of a sea-green fifteen-year-old Mercedes estate, she asked him.

'What do I owe you, Hector?'

Hector refused to take any money. He did, however, try to give Fionnuala a parting hug, which she resisted firmly but politely with a handshake. The publican applied some lip balm to his sorely desiccated lips and attempting to put the chapstick in his pocket, dropped it on the footpath. It was no surprise, given the shallow pockets of the shabby fleece.

Finn picked it up. It was orange-flavoured. He handed it back to Hector. Where had he seen a similar little cylinder recently?

'Thanks, Finn.'

Hector drove away disappointed – his default disposition, in fairness – smoke belching from the exhaust.

'You wanted to see me, Maura,' Fionnuala said curtly, interrupting Finn's train of thought.

Maura, no flies on her, expressed her fears about the events of the previous evening and framed her interest in speaking to Fionnuala as a request for advice. Finn admired her deviousness.

'Mammy gets very anxious you see, Fionnuala,' Finn joined in. 'I'm sure it's nothing. But she got it into her head that you would be the best person to talk to. You being so ... sensible.'

Fionnuala bristled, although how she could be surprised at that characterization, Finn couldn't say.

'So level-headed,' he doubled down before he could stop himself. Being described as sensible and level-headed could be regarded as an insult in towns like Abbeyford where the craic was paramount. He regretted his words as soon as he said them. To her suspicious ears it might have sounded like Finn was calling her a dry-shite. A dreaded and uniquely Irish term of abuse, etymology unknown, dry-shite sounds mild and innocent enough on the surface but it is actually one of the worst things you can be called. You will usually hear it from a good friend who only has your best interests at heart. On being called a dry-shite, in other words outed as dry and boring, a bit of a party pooper, you are instantly challenged to reassess your whole life, or at the very least to change your plans for the evening. It implies that you are not only letting yourself and your friends down, but that you are, it was not a stretch to say it, guilty of in some way, given the emphasis on having a relentlessly good time, letting the whole country down as well.

Fionnuala looked from Finn to Aoife.

'Eh, I was just on my lunch break,' Aoife extemporized. 'Ran into these guys. As you do.'

Aoife coughed pathetically. And held up her lozenges.

'There's a bug going round the school.'

Fionnuala nodded, and after retrieving a beaker of sorts from the shop, ushered the trio towards Café Madremonte a few doors down.

Fionnuala and Harry Boyle had been a couple for as long as Finn could remember. While they had been acquainted as children, it was after a school debate between Joey's and the Mercy when they were both fifteen that Harry asked her to be his girlfriend. The motion, Finn recalled, was 'It's a Man's World'. Harry brought the house down against the motion in his flamboyant, facetious way while Fionnuala sensibly and level-headedly demolished his arguments, citing biology and law and of course the bible, leading the convent team to victory and possession of the Mary O'Connor perpetual trophy.

Contrary to popular wisdom, they complemented each other beautifully. She was a calming influence on Harry, loyal to a ludicrous degree, and a legendary listener, always there to console him when he was feeling low. Which was often. And Harry made Fionnuala laugh, and taught her to dance. He even made her father laugh, no mean feat, and defended her fiercely when she was teased. Which was often, at least until she'd gone to college in Dublin, when she semi-reinvented herself. With her rigorous and analytic mind and infinite patience, she helped Harry to focus on his studies and ultimately to secure a place in medical school. Although she somewhat tempered his excesses and indeed cleaned up his vomit, literally and metaphorically, she was no killjoy. If anything, she facilitated him. They were as close as two people could be. Well, until Harry ran off with Michael.

Finn noted a TO LET sign in a window above the café. And a NO CUP, NO COFFEE sign on the door. Although it was lunch-time, there weren't too many diners inside. Arepas and empanadas were not yet in huge demand in these parts, the locals tending to favour foot-long rolls sweating in cellophane, or better still the full steaming carvery lunch to get them through the afternoon. And although the coffee in Café Madremonte was reputed to be the best in the county, the thought of having to carry your own cup around with you was an imposition too far for most citizens, if not an actual affront to their civil liberties. Ana, the diminutive proprietor, her hair covered in a red bandana, plonked a carafe of water on the table and took their orders. Fionnuala carefully poured water into her receptacle offering both Maura and Finn a sip, but not Aoife.

'You have a bug,' she said pointedly, holding eye contact for a second too long.

'I am so sorry about Harry,' said Maura. 'He was so young.'

'Harry?' Fionnuala put her hand to her breast. 'What happened to Harry?'

'We don't know for sure. It might have been a heart attack or a seizure of some sort or it might have been ...'

'She means Michael,' said Finn.

'Michael Dunlop? What happened to Michael?' asked Maura, alarmed.

'He died last night, Mammy. You were there.'

Finn had noticed that his mother tended to be more confused in the early afternoon when she was tired. Although on this occasion he wasn't sure what she was up to. She might have been just acting that way to throw Fionnuala off her guard.

'Of course. Michael. Sorry. What a goose I am. We think he might have been killed.'

Fionnuala blanched. She nodded to herself, licked her top lip, and looked at each of them in turn. Finally, gravely, she said.

'The thought had crossed my mind.'

She took a sip of her water.

'No. Let me put that another way.'

She composed herself, doing that fussy thing with her hair again, pushing it back behind her ears.

'I think there's a chance that he might have taken his own life. Accidentally, I should add. And it's partly my fault. Phenelzine!'

Fionnuala, once she had decided to confide in her friends, didn't hold back. It seems Michael had always suffered from depression, but after his incarceration his symptoms had gotten worse. Harry had prescribed various antidepressants but nothing seemed to work. He eventually settled on phenelzine.

'One of the MAOs.'

'The what?'

'The monoamine oxidase inhibitors. Don't get me wrong. It's a wonderful medicine. And I'm not blaming Harry. It blocks the monoamine oxidase in the blood. Increases the serotonin levels in the brain. Just wonderful. It was the right medicine. But Michael was the wrong patient.'

Fionnuala outlined the reasons why in her opinion Michael shouldn't have been prescribed phenelzine.

'I said all this to Harry.'

First of all, he suffered from hay fever that would have necessitated antihistamines, which would have reacted badly with the antidepressant. Secondly, Michael was partial to alcohol and, she hesitated, before continuing with a heavy heart, 'Opiates. Fentanyl. I saw it with my own eyes in Crete.'

Fionnuala, along with the two children she had with Harry, Nora and Nina, had gone on holiday with Harry and Michael some six months earlier.

'It was glorious. Chania in October is just perfect. Have you been? The girls adored Michael. Then one evening I found him in a stupor by the pool – there was a small pool on the roof of the hotel. I was worried about him so I looked in his bag. The little man bag. There was a number of fentanyl patches in there. Ten, twelve, maybe. Naturally, I was furious. On account of the girls. So I confronted him next morning. He swore he'd never touch the stuff again. I stupidly believed him.'

When asked by Aoife if she had dispensed the fentanyl patches, Fionnuala was horrified at the insinuation.

'I don't know how he got his hands on them. He certainly didn't get them from me.'

Ana, with perfect timing, placed a halloumi salad decorated with cherry tomatoes and pomegranate seeds in front of Fionnuala and a selection of empanadas, beef and potato, and cheese and spinach on the table for the others to share.

She hovered at the table, clearly waiting for an introduction. Aoife obliged.

'Ana, this is Maura's son, Finn. He's home from England.'

Ana wiped her hand on her apron and shook Finn's hand. She winced at how rough his skin was.

'*Espera!*'

Before they could resume their discussion, Ana returned with a plastic tube and, without asking, rubbed some hand cream matter-of-factly into Finn's gnarly, spade-worn skin. This considerate gesture almost brought a tear to his eye.

'You work too hard, amigo. You want coffee?'

'Sure.'

Aoife raised an eyebrow. Even Fionnuala, paler than usual, and that was saying something, a part of her absently reliving the scene in that rooftop spa in Crete, was surprised. Only in rare cases, usually involving homelessness or some sort of chronic hardship, did Ana make exceptions to her no-cup rule.

Fionnuala, cutting a piece of lettuce into a tiny perfectly square fragment, resumed her story.

'I thought he had changed. I see a lot of him, Michael ... *saw*, I should say, as I'm sure you'll appreciate. Myself and Harry are still friends. Best friends. It seems so strange to say that as if I were still a schoolgirl. But I don't know how else to put it. But then yesterday ...'

She chased an uncooperative pomegranate seed around the plate with her fork.

'Yesterday at the launch I couldn't help noticing he ate quite a lot of cheese!'

'Cheese? What difference would that make?'

Before choir practice the day before, at 6 pm, she explained, there'd been a reception in Deevy's to celebrate the latest pottery collection of a local ceramicist.

'I wasn't invited,' said Aoife, peeved.

'Neither was I,' said Maura. 'Mind you I never liked her pottery. Vaginas mostly.'

Finn was quite shocked to hear his mother say that word out loud.

'Aged gouda. Femke had it especially imported from the Netherlands.'

'That's the artist,' Aoife explained to a bewildered Finn.

'She's Dutch,' Fionnuala continued. 'Michael must have eaten half a block. Drank a lot of wine too. He knew the risks.'

'I don't understand. Was he allergic to cheese?'

'Tyramine. The cheese contains tyramine, which of course exacerbates the potency of the phenelzine. Between the phenelzine, the wine and the cheese, the antihistamines and possibly the fentanyl, he was taking a huge chance.'

Ana, her hair newly released from the bandana almost doubling her height, presented Finn with a mug of her legendary coffee.

'*Mi taza es tu taza.*' Ana beamed at her own play on words.

'Very good, Ana,' Aoife said while the others were still figuring out what she was saying.

'It's my cup. Don't break it. Next time, bring your own.'

Finn took a sip. It was good. He offered everybody else a drink which they all, except Fionnuala, accepted. Her face had changed, not just in colour but in shape too.

'I didn't come down in the last shower, you know.'

'What do you mean, Fionnuala?'

'I know what you're all thinking. I loved Michael. I didn't wish him harm despite ...'

Fionnuala's mouth tightened.

'This ... intervention,' she, her poise deserting her, spat bitterly, 'or whatever this is, doesn't fool me for an instant. You know me better than that, Finn. As long as Harry was happy, I was happy. Hard as that is to believe for some people.'

She didn't want people feeling sorry for her. She knew how they talked. How they joked. How they laughed behind her back. Her father took great satisfaction in telling her that it gave him no satisfaction whatsoever to tell her it was God's retribution for her liberal ways. Her main priority, her only priority, was her daughters. Since Harry left, she maintained levelly, he had become a better father, a better, more complete person.

'Harry blossomed.'

Of course, she suspected from an early age, while they were still at school, that Harry was gay. She knew before Harry himself did. But she loved him.

'I didn't know Harry was gay,' Maura exclaimed, a crumb of cold cheese-and-spinach empanada falling from her mouth.

He had convinced himself that he was straight. They had twenty-two wonderful years together and two beautiful children. Deep down she knew there was something missing, a sadness at the core of his being, and had braced herself for the day the emergence of his true self would rupture their lives. When he finally met Michael, she wasn't going to stand in his way. Harry, she insisted, would never have done anything to upset her, not deliberately, and would not have moved in with Michael without her explicit blessing.

'It was I who left him.'

If anything, she was grateful to Michael for making Harry happy in a way that she never could. He was more present than ever. More fun.

'Despite appearances, nothing really changed for us. We're still in the house, the house Harry's parents left him. Harry drops in almost every day. The only difference is I don't have to deal with his emotional baggage. As you know, Finn, Harry can be volatile. Irrepressible I believe is the word. So Michael was in a way the best thing that ever happened to us. As a family. Things might have changed for other people around town but not for us. Now I need to get back to work.'

With that, she paid the bill and, dignity personified, she exited the café, not before saying.

'If I wanted to poison somebody, I'd make sure it was undetectable.'

For a few moments nobody spoke. Then Finn cleared his throat. There was a bit of a crust of an empanada stuck in it.

'Well, look I don't know about you but I think Fionnuala was telling the truth,' he declared.

'*What?*' asked Aoife, incredulously.

'If you ask me, she is fundamentally incapable of lying.'

'Oh don't be so naive, Finn.'

'It's clear as day, Aoife. Michael died a natural death. Well, not natural as such. But due to his own poor decisions.'

'I'm surprised at you. I really am. You know perfectly well he was poisoned. And you don't understand women at all.'

That thistled a little. Although, he rued, she was probably right. A squirt of sweat tickled his temples. He really didn't like confrontation.

'She played you. All that guff about the opiates. Blackening Michael's good name.'

'I believed her.'

'Maura, did you know your son was so gullible? Everything she said was considered, deliberate, I would go as far as to say, rehearsed. To misdirect us from what she put in that cup.'

'I thought Barry Duggan killed him.'

'We don't know for sure who killed Michael. But I know this: Fionnuala is furious. You can tell. Beneath that façade, that calm, measured façade, she's hopping mad. And ... and trying to implicate Harry ...'

'What are you talking about? She'd do anything for Harry.'

'That was just despicable. Were you even listening, Finn?'

'Just like his father,' said Maura.

'Thanks, Mammy.'

A runnel of sweat now trickled down his back, his spinal ravine. He was feeling the pressure. He looked to his mother for support. She was nodding away at Aoife.

'Telling us what Harry prescribed, Maura, you heard her, subtly shifting the blame on to him.'

'Aoife, you're reading too much into it. Yes, she's hurt, and yes, perhaps she's putting a brave face on it, her situation, who wouldn't, but why would she kill him?'

'Are you messing? Playing devil's advocate? It would be a surprise if she didn't kill him. I'd kill him if I was Fionnuala. Fionnuala had the perfect life until Michael came along. Now with Michael out of the way she can have Harry to herself again.'

A pond of sweat had by now formed in the small of Finn's back. It felt like fish, little minnows, were already swimming in it.

'Mammy, she might listen to you. Tell Aoife she's being preposterous. What do you think? Do you think Fionnuala is capable of murder?'

His mother looked towards the ceiling for a second before smiling beatifically.

'I think the lady doth protest too much.'

Et tu, mother. Aoife, her face quite flushed, said that she had to get back to class.

'Oh, by the way, it was Wolfie who asked for the CCTV to be turned off.'

'Who?' asked Finn.

'Noel Whelan,' his mother said, 'the choirmaster.'

'What?'

'I'll go and see him later,' Aoife announced, pushing her chair back. 'Alone.'

Finn was a little shook by her attitude, as well as being sweaty and frankly damp. He was surprised by how this relative stranger was able to affect him physically as well as mentally, but didn't want to analyse what that might mean. All he knew was that he definitely didn't want to fall out with Aoife, but at the same time he wasn't going to be railroaded into accusing Fionnuala of wrongdoing. Nor was he going to be ousted from the case. He could be as headstrong as the next person. If they were going to solve this murder, they would have to do it systematically and with clear heads. First things first, he needed to dry himself off.

'Those ham pandas were very nice,' said Maura, rising unsteadily to her feet.

'Empanadas.'

'Will I see you at the Tidy Towns meeting later, Maura?' Aoife asked Maura from the door, studiously ignoring Finn.

'Of course you will, dear. Finn will bring me, won't you?'

He nodded. Before he brought his mother home, he went up to the counter, thanked Ana for the coffee and enquired about the flat to let above the café.

'No, no. It is too small for a big strong handsome man like you. And it smells.'

What sort of a person was Ana? What sort of a businesswoman? She didn't stock sandwiches. Refused to sell coffee to anybody who didn't have their own vessel. And now here she was doing her damnedest to dissuade him from renting her flat. How did she make a living at all? Finn wasn't fussy at the best of times, and right now he really, really needed his own space so, in desperation, he dug his heels in. After a few minutes, Ana relented and agreed to show him the flat the following day.

Chapter 14

Later that day, Finn and Maura collected Happiness, a bustle of bags and satisfaction, from the bus. After the weary traveller had soaked her feet in hot water, he left the ladies to their tea and went off to pay an overdue visit to his father.

On the way, passing a dried-up waterfall, an image of Hector Morrissey's blistered lips sprang to mind. For someone who spent a good part of every day wetting his whistle with porter it was surprising just how chapped his lips were. Why was there a tube of lip balm on the floor of the kitchenette off the community centre rehearsal room? He'd thought nothing of it at the time. But it was orange-flavoured, the same as the one Hector dropped outside the pharmacy. Did that too fall out of Hector's pocket? If so, what was he doing in the rehearsal room? He wasn't a member of the choir. Did he poison Michael's tea? Finn slowed down as he neared the turn-off to Redmond's house. No. He was being silly, as bad as Aoife, flinging accusations around, left, right and centre at decent law-abiding citizens. Still, no harm in challenging Hector with the query when he got the chance.

Redmond lived in Derrybreen Woods. Although only about five miles from the town, his house, for want of a better word, was off-grid. Literally. It didn't have a postcode. For electricity, he had his own generator, for water a well. The property on about three acres was built among native oak and ash trees in a neglected corner of the old Chapman estate. There had been a gamekeeper's cottage on the site at one point, the ruins of which Redmond now used as a hen house. Despite the existence of the stone cottage, it was hard to believe that Redmond had received planning permission for the current dwelling. In fairness Redmond was not the type of person to ask permission for anything from anybody.

Finn parked the car on an old gravel-strewn logging road beside a battered Defender and walked up the narrow fern-lined path to his father's hut. Hanging on a rope above the door was an old copper cowbell that looked like it had been reclaimed from a bog. He rang it as an abbot must have done centuries ago, calling his monks to account.

It was an oddly shaped construction, the house, not quite rectangular, nor indeed circular, the walls made of cob, a mixture of clay and straw and sand. It reminded Finn of a cake that hadn't quite risen. The roof was a sheet of corrugated iron on a timber frame but judging from the bundles of water reed huddling in the hollow of a nearby oak tree it was but a temporary arrangement.

'Ah it's yourself.'

As well as being the most contrary man in Ireland, Redmond was also the most self-centred and most self-contained. Finn was never quite sure how to greet him. Should he shake hands, kiss him on the cheek or go in for the hug? Thanks to his indecision, it invariably ended up, as it did on this occasion, in a kind of affectionate headbutt.

'Awkward as ever. I read your book, son.'

'Oh.'
'Nice pictures.'
'Thanks, Dad.'
'I found it in the library box, you know, across from the supermarket.'

Redmond, in his trademark outfit, summer or winter, of cargo shorts and sandals, and waving a blackthorn stick, couldn't help himself. But rather than being slighted by this back-handed compliment, Finn felt strangely elated. This was a first. His father had actually read his book, a tie-in to the latest series of *Garden Nightmares*, which was more than he'd expected. The fact that Redmond preferred the pictures, which of course Finn hadn't taken, and that the book had been discarded, he was prepared to overlook.

'Tea?'

Finn knew it wouldn't be Barry's but he wasn't quite prepared for the tongue-shrivelling, face-scrunching bitterness of the mate tea his father prepared. Having spent a couple of years in the Brazilian Amazon in his twenties, Redmond came home with the nickname 'Rio', a taste for maté tea and an unwavering commitment to revolutionary causes.

'That'll put hairs on your chest, son,' his father laughed, removing an axe from the table. Although now in his seventies, his bushy grey beard still showed tinges of red.

Although Finn resented the implication that he was in some way unmanly, he had resolved never to allow himself to be rattled by Redmond's goading. Or at least not to let Redmond see that he was rattled.

'How is Isabella?'
'We've split up.'
'Marvellous. Tell her I was asking for her.'

He wasn't listening. He could have told him that Isabella was dead and his father would have nodded and said, 'that's great', so preoccupied was he with his own concerns.

As a boy Finn had camped out in these very woods with his dad. Obviously there were no tents involved or sleeping bags or energy bars or any comfort whatsoever. They built shelters out of branches covered in moss and ferns and grass. They lived on leaves – hawthorn, dandelion, wild garlic – as well as berries and mushrooms, and, if they were lucky, a rabbit. And Finn loved every minute of it. Once when he was eight years old, they spent three days and three nights knee-deep in water in Cooney's Bog up on Carrignagower, trying to spot a hen harrier. By the time they sighted the bird, Finn was delirious with pneumonia, putting an end to their adventures for that year at the insistence of his mother.

'I blame the Germans,' Redmond spat, his temper rising, when Finn dropped a loaded question about rhododendron. 'Joachim Conrad Loddiges to be precise. Bollix!'

It transpired, as Rio outlined in painstaking detail, that Loddiges introduced *rhododendron ponticum* to Ireland sometime in the nineteenth century.

'Did more damage than the Vikings and Normans and the English put together. Do you agree with me?'

'Not really. No.'

His father scoffed at his objections and ploughed on regardless. He had recruited and trained a volunteer army with members in every county to help in his quest.

'Based on the cell structure, three in each cell. They only know the other people in the cell, you see. Last year we cleared three hundred hectares.'

His father brought him outside and showed him towards

a smaller home-made shack, deeper in the woods, with his hand-carved blackthorn stick.

'We've pushed it back as far as the Cork border,' he boasted. 'There isn't a single rhodo left in the county. That's a fact. Mind you,' he darkened, 'you have to be vigilant. Look at the state of Cork and Kerry. They're on their own now, boy! Oh yes. We'll see how clever they are now.'

Redmond didn't elaborate, but Finn could tell there'd been some sort of a schism within the high command of the volunteers. And with each dastardly rhododendron flower capable of disseminating up to 7,000 seeds at a time, there could only be one winner.

'I quite like them. Rhododendrons.'

He didn't like them and secretly admired not only Redmond's philosophy but his willpower too. Yet he still retained some of that adolescent urge to challenge his father's authority.

'If they're managed properly. It's all about finding the right balance.'

Rio grunted dismissively.

'Nonsense. You have to take a stand on these things. That's why you'll never be taken seriously as a gardener.'

Ouch. His father pushed open the door of the rickety shed to reveal a makeshift laboratory and an eye-watering chemical smell.

'Herbicides! I have to say, Daddy, I'm a bit surprised.'

'Bio-herbicides,' Redmond shot back, hurt by the insinuation. 'Entirely natural.'

And lethal too, judging by the large, smoke-blackened hole in the wall of the shed. There were a couple of burlap sacks on the floor, and some jars and plastic tubs, all of them unlabelled, on a shelving unit that looked like it was about to collapse. On a crudely-made table in the middle of the floor were a number of Kilner jars, lengths of tubing, a weighing scales, a funnel and a few plastic canisters.

'I cut a little notch in the roots, you see. Pour in a soupçon of the sauce. Only needs a drop. They don't feel a thing.'

Finn's nose twitched.

'*Tamerix mannifera?*'

'Very good.'

'And if I'm not mistaken, is that— it's not *lactuca virosa*!'

'Bravo. There's hope for you yet, boy.'

'You used to give me that as a painkiller. The poor man's opium, you called it.'

'Did I? I don't remember.'

Finn could tell that he did remember. Why would he deny it, as if to care for a sick son was in some way a sign of weakness? Or was it guilt that it might have been his recklessness that was responsible for Finn's illness? Either way, Finn remembered vividly his father staying up with him all night, forcing him hourly to drink from the cup of his vile home-made medicine. Redmond was not what you might call nowadays the most 'present' dad in the world. He'd disappear sometimes for days, sometimes for months. And Finn missed him. The adventures. The danger. On those occasions, despite his mother's attempt to get Finn to knuckle down and study – like Conor, and like Harry – he preferred to be outdoors, exploring the natural world, his father's binoculars around his neck.

Redmond explained now that he had been experimenting, trying to find the perfect formula to fight off his latest nemesis. Using a soybean bran as a medium, he had been combining metabolites from fungi and bacteria, as well as extracts from various plants including methanol derived from the eucalyptus plant.

'As you correctly identified.'

Finn felt a sudden warmth in his breast. Was that a hint of pride? A pat on the back? The fuzzy feeling was quickly replaced with a chill when it suddenly occurred to him that if Rio's concoctions could wipe out a robust shrub in the wild such as a rhodo, it could do similar damage to an innocent acer minding its own business outside a community centre.

'Where were you last night, as a matter of interest?'

'And there was me thinking this was a social visit. I can't tell you where I was. Not that it's any of your business, Finn.'

His father had never been easy to track down at the best of times but since he'd renounced smartphones and credit cards, he was practically untraceable. Such were his wide-ranging interests and his boundless energy he could have been anywhere within a hundred-mile radius. He wasn't, however, put out by Finn's abrupt question. If anything, he was mildly amused. There was that familiar twinkle in his eye. It was a twinkle that suggested he didn't in fact take himself too seriously, that for a moment he could see what a ludicrous figure he cut, and furthermore that he was in a way aware of some bigger picture in which they were all just fulfilling a role. Nature's pope!

Despite the bluster and the boasting and the obstinate lunacy, Finn still credited his father with having some sort of wisdom beyond the quotidian, that he, Finn, could never possibly attain. Perhaps every son thought that about his father. Perhaps it was just a manifestation of his own low self-esteem, having so recently lost Isabella and the Chelsea

Flower Show. Either way Finn still wanted this man's approval more than anything else in the world.

'Terrible business about Michael. I had a lot of time for him, you know. But...' Redmond hesitated. 'I was going to say I loved him like a son. But that's not really true.'

He put his hand on Finn's shoulder. The perenially sore one. Finn didn't flinch, his father's hand a welcome salve.

'I did like him though.'

Finn got the impression that his father was holding something back.

'Michael. There was something a bit off about him. A bit deceptive? His accent? I'd say you knew him as well as anybody?'

Finn's fishing paid off.

'Michael ...' His father, flattered, weighed up his response. 'Michael wasn't who he said he was. For a start, he wasn't even Australian!'

Chapter 15

On her way home from school, Aoife called to see Wolfie Whelan. He lived in a terraced house on the gently sloping Pearse Street, the one freshly painted in kingfisher blue with the orangey trimmings, next door to the aquamarine one with the pink sills. It was the Tidy Towns committee who organized the painting of the houses, all of them previously a uniform grey in what was once a forlorn part of town. Some of the residents were reluctant at first to even contemplate such a makeover, afraid that people would think they were showing off, bearing in mind, Abbeyford was a town where a man was once institutionalized by his own family for wearing a cravat. Wolfie didn't mind what colour they painted his house as long as he didn't have to pay for it. He had bought the house back in the 80s for a song, literally, on the back of his one big success to date in the music business. His magnum opus. For it was he, as he often reminded people, who had composed the catchy jingle for the ad for Capital Tea.

'*No trouble with a Capital T!*'

Wolfie, although he was giving a piano lesson to a local girl, one of the D'arcy triplets – Aoife wasn't sure which one – invited her to wait in the kitchen. His dog, a schnauzer, was sitting on his hind legs in front of a bowl of dried food. He looked like he'd been sitting there a long time.

'Eat!' whispered Aoife.

The dog, not needing to be asked twice, laid into his dinner. There was a discordant crash from the living room.

'No! Aoife! No! Herbert! *No*.'

The dog stopped eating and bashfully backed away from the bowl. Wolfie, a wounded expression on his face, appeared in the doorway.

'Herbert doesn't have his dinner till six. He knows that. Don't you, Herbert? Naughty, naughty boy. You always have your din-dins with Daddy.'

A few minutes later after the D'arcy girl, Sarah, had finally played 'Ode to Joy' to his exacting standards and finished her lesson, Wolfie sat down with Aoife in the kitchen. She refused his offer of a tinned steak and kidney pie.

'That's very kind of you, Noel, but to be honest I'd prefer to eat Herbert's dried nuts.'

'Suit yourself. So now what can I do for you? If it's about Tidy Towns, you know I'd love to help but I simply can't. I have allergies.'

'The CCTV at the community centre, Noel.'

'Oh.'

'Michael is dead.'

He paled.

'You don't think I ...'

'Why did you ask Donal to switch it off? It's just ... I don't want you to get into any trouble.'

Wolfie burst into tears.

'Why would I want to hurt Michael? Aoife! Do you know how hard it is to get a countertenor these days? Like hen's teeth. Ever since the demise of the castrati,' he added, somewhat ruefully, as if this was a terrible thing altogether.

'It was their own choice to be castrated. People don't realize that. Very respectable.'

'You're not answering my question, Wolfie.'

Wolfie pouted.

'I don't want to.'

'You have to.'

'Why?'

'Otherwise people will think you did it. That you killed Michael.'

Wolfie started bawling again. Herbert jumped into his arms.

'Who'll look after you when I'm gone?'

After his comment about the castrati, Aoife couldn't help checking Herbert's undercarriage. Her fears were unfounded and in fairness she felt bad that the thought had even crossed her mind.

'Well?'

'I didn't want anybody to know,' he whispered.

'But you're the choirmaster. It's not a secret, Noel. You're the maestro, the Mozart of the South-East.'

'Thank you, Aoife. Not everyone appreciates what I do. No, I mean to say I didn't want anybody to know about ...'

His voice tailed off.

'Sorry, Wolfie. What was that?'

'AA, alright?! The AA meeting before choir practice. I didn't want anybody to know I have a problem.'

'Oh Wolfie.'

Aoife gave him and Herbert a hug.

'This is Abbeyford. I hate to break it to you but everybody knows. Everybody knows everything. And here's the thing: nobody cares.'

She followed his watery eyes as they strayed towards a

bottle of gin on the counter. With a huge effort he managed to tear his eyes away again.

'I mean we all care about you. You're a very brave man going to AA. It can't be easy, I know that.'

'You're right. It isn't easy.'

Wolfie stroked the dog with both hands.

'And do you know what the hardest thing is? The insensitivity of some people. You won't believe this. Right in the middle of the AA meeting, the night Michael died, Hector Morrissey walked in the door with a trolley.'

'Hector?'

'He was making a delivery, it must have been, twenty bottles of wine and two crates of beer.'

'No! To the AA meeting? I don't understand.'

'Yes, Aoife. Into the very room. Outrageous. The insensitivity! I'm going to have a word with the management.'

'You should.'

'It was for an Orienteering Society reception, you see, that was supposed to happen in the same room on the following day. It was cancelled of course.'

'So Hector was there?'

'Yes. He apologized. It was a mix-up. But that's beside the point. He should have had the good sense to leave it somewhere else. The booze!'

'I'm sure the Orienteering Society would have found it.'

'What?'

Aoife's humour was lost on Wolfie.

'By the way you were absolutely right. The CCTV. You did the right thing.'

'Do you think?'

'Well, look, we don't know everybody who went into that kitchenette over the last few days.'

'Sorry.'

'But sure, who needs CCTV when you have the likes of Kitty Doyle? Don't you worry, we'll catch whoever did this.'

Wolfie smiled.

'Thanks Aoife. He'll be a big loss.'

'He will. Look, if there's anything I can do, let me know.'

Whelan's ears pricked up. As did Herbert's.

'Actually . . . there is one thing.'

He stood up, doing a soft shoe shuffle.

'I've been working on a little ditty. Would you like to hear it?'

'Oh, yes, I . . . It's just I have Tidy Towns tonight. And I have to get home first.'

'It won't take a minute.'

And off he skipped to the piano. Aoife took out her notepad and crossed Noel 'Wolfgang' Whelan off the list.

Chapter 16

Back in his father's house, as Redmond pounded away manically at a clump of wild garlic with a pestle, he told Finn about the phone call he overheard Michael taking a year earlier. It was during one of the protests against the incinerator.

'He didn't know I was listening. I was up a tree at the time.'

Of course he was. Michael, it seems, had been pacing back and forth, away from the main body of protestors, and to Redmond's surprise, speaking in an English accent.

'As clear as day. I always knew there was something a bit off about his Australian accent.'

It was quite a posh English accent, 'Aynsley China' as his father put it. Michael was in very agitated state, his voice shrill, and he seemed to be under a lot of pressure by whoever it was on the other end of the phone.

At this point in the story, Redmond placed a bag of hazelnuts on the table, covered them with a tea towel and proceeded with a terrifying gusto to smash them to smithereens with a wooden mallet. He had great strength in his upper arms for a man of his age. He then continued like he'd never interrupted himself.

By the sounds of it, Michael owed a lot of money to

various 'investors', his dad intimated. And these investors, it was plain, wanted their money back. It was something to do with a festival on the Isle of Wight. Later that day Redmond confronted Michael about what he'd heard. And unsurprisingly to Finn, Michael confided in him. Redmond was a man who once he fixed you with his petroleum-blue eyes, you didn't want to let down. You didn't want him to think less of you. Besides he was good at keeping secrets. *Until now*, Finn thought. Not that it mattered to poor Michael.

'His real name was Michael St John Fitzmaurice.'
'Wow!'
'Wow is right. He was from a place called Nettlebed in Oxfordshire. Although he claimed to have some connection to Lismore Castle.'
'In Waterford?'
'That's what he told me.'

After throwing the roughly crushed nuts in with the wild garlic mush, Redmond grated some sheep's cheese from a hunk that had been hanging wrapped in a muslin cloth from a hook in a cross-beam. In a frenzy, he then mixed all the ingredients together in a bowl with some oil that he poured from an old milk bottle. Finn didn't want to imagine what plant or animal the oil came from. It definitely didn't come from Tesco.

'There you go now. Proper Irish pesto. You'll never be sick a day in your life again.'

Michael St John Fitzmaurice aka Dunlop attended the public school St Paul's. After he graduated, it seems, he got involved in event management. But Michael was ambitious. He admitted to Redmond that he had wanted to get rich quick. And so he came up with, as Redmond put it in one of his favourite expressions, 'a hare-brained scheme'. That was rich coming from Redmond.

'Crazy stuff. A Festival of Sporting Legends. In a field on the Isle of Wight.'

Michael was used to organizing book launches and garden parties to promote cosmetics. He might have had to hire the odd string quartet or somebody like Nigel Havers to cut a ribbon. Now, suddenly, he was booking Bjorn Borg and John McEnroe for an exhibition tennis match, Maradona and Johan Cruyff and the likes of Tony Currie for a five-a-side, Dennis Taylor and Steve Davis for a snooker challenge. Daley Thompson. Mike Tyson. Nigel Mansell. All the major sports were represented. There was going to be talks and giant screens reliving old memories, memorabilia stands, music, food, drinks. The works. And of course it was going to cost millions.

Michael confessed that he had borrowed substantial amounts of money from friends and other 'investors', but not only was he convinced that the festival would be a success, he assured Redmond that he had significant crypto assets himself that would underwrite any losses.

'I hope you're not in crypto, son.'

No, please, not the stump speech about gold again. He knew for a fact that, although his father was cheerfully penniless, he was, as an unbeliever in the global financial system, routinely to be found prospecting for gold in the surrounding hills.

'I think it was called "Champions", the festival, or was it "Winners"? Something like that. "Victory!" That was it. Victory.'

Needless to say, the Victory Festival was a disaster that couldn't solely be blamed on the weather. Michael knew he was in trouble when Borg asked his chauffeur to stop the car on the hard shoulder of the M25. The former tennis great refused to go any further until a hundred grand had been lodged into his account. This Michael was unable to do. He had only that morning transferred a similar amount, all that was left in the company funds, to the landowner on the Isle of Wight who was threatening to close the gates if he wasn't paid. Meanwhile, Maradona had been arrested in Argentina on a drugs charge, some of the marquees he'd been promised had been double-booked and the Hampshire police refused to sign off on the event due to concerns about the lack of a security plan in place. Michael's assistant, Julie, who had forgotten to book the Portaloos, had disappeared with the petty cash, the sponsors hadn't stumped up and yes, unseasonal winds and rain, Storm Edith to be exact, had wreaked her destructive way across the English Channel and through the festival site.

'I don't know why they have to name storms.'

Another peeve of his father's.

'Edith? Who's going to be afraid of a storm called Edith? Sounds so innocuous, doesn't it? A librarian's name. Not a storm. Do you agree with me?'

It was best to ignore him.

'They should give them proper nasty names. Like Storm Vladimir. Am I right? Or Storm Joachim.'

Michael had told Redmond that Victory had actually been a great success, for the handful of die-hard sports fans that had braved the elements. Mike Tyson by all accounts was a great sport although he did knock out cold a fifty-seven-year-old systems analyst from Basingstoke who had paid a premium to spar with him, an unfortunate mishap for which the festival was sued.

Before the weekend was out, Michael St John Fitzmaurice had changed his name to Michael Dunlop, secured a false passport – how he didn't say – and flown all the way to Sydney, Australia. Apparently, to cap it all, he had somehow lost the private key to his bitcoin fortune, meaning he was broke.

'This is what I'm saying. Crypto. It's a mug's game. You're better off in gold.'

Finn wondered if Aoife knew any of this. Did Harry for that matter? What if Harry had just found out? And enraged by the deception, had had a hand in Michael's death?

'If he was murdered, it might have been somebody from his past. One of the investors? Do you agree with me?'

It was plausible, but Finn couldn't bring himself to assent.

'Well, I mean yeah, I suppose, technically, but it's more likely it was someone from the locality, no? Someone like Barry Duggan?'

'Duggan is a lot of things, but he's not a murderer. No, I imagine he had a lot of enemies, Michael. You met him, yourself, didn't you? He could be very annoying. Besides I'm not sure he told me everything.'

Finn's curiosity got the better of him.

'It was the bit about wanting to get rich quick. I don't think he came from money like he implied. And the English accent. It was too perfect. A bit stagey.'

Rio stood up, an oily green film on his beard, signalling to Finn that the visit was over. Although still an imposing man, it gave Finn no pleasure to note that he had shrunk an inch or two of late.

'Give your mother a hug for me.'

'Why don't you give her one yourself?' Finn said, licking

his own greasy lips. On his way out the door he turned. 'That pesto was ... not bad, dad. Not bad at all.'

It was literally one of the most delicious things he'd ever tasted. But of course, he wasn't going to tell his father that.

Chapter 17

Aoife was running late now, after being detained by Wolfgang, whose new 'ditty' turned out to be a lengthy minimalist composition inspired by La Mounte Young. The piece, consisting of the same two notes played over and over again, ran to a full forty-two minutes. Eventually, as he was about to segue into another 'work-in-progress' that for all she knew might have lasted a whole day, she managed to drag herself away and called a taxi. Eddie Halfpenny turned up on Pearse Street a matter of moments later as if he'd been waiting for her call. In fairness, most of his runs, cash only, were in the morning, or late evening, to or from the airports, Dublin or Cork, and hospitals in every direction. Normally she'd be on her bike, but because Maura and Finn had given her a lift this morning, she was stranded in town.

'Howarya, me oul flower.'

She got into the passenger seat. Eddie, a small man in his early fifties, with curly red hair and freckles, like a folk singer from central casting, was originally from Dublin. The Liberties. In fact, he revelled in his true blue Dub identity, wearing a Dublin GAA jersey and singing 'The Rare Auld Times' at the drop of a hat, lest there be any doubt in the minds of 'me culchie clientele', as he put it.

'Did he do it, wha'?'

Eddie turned to Aoife, a big grin on his face.

'I told him. I said, "Wolfie, I wouldn't do tha'" but he was paranoid his ma would find out. You know, about the gargle and tha'. And her above in a nursing home in Carlow. Sure she doesn't know what day of the week it is. The poor divil.'

Everybody knows everything.

'Nothing escapes you, does it, Eddie? And you a blow-in.'

'I keep me eyes and ears open. No, luv. Amn't I in the AA myself?'

'Oh?'

'And so would you be if you seen what I seen.'

Eddie had served in the Irish army for fourteen years. He toured with the UN in Lebanon twice, not to mention Chad.

'When you're in a foxhole with your buddies ...'

He shuddered. Eddie often alluded to oblique incidents on tour. He'd start stories before correcting himself and changing the subject, leaving his listeners somewhere between bemused and deeply sceptical. Sometimes he'd stare out the window, as if he was still suffering from PTSD. One of the more cynical residents of the town reckoned that if he did have PTSD, he most likely picked it up in Dublin rather than the Golan Heights.

But just as quickly, he'd return to the here and now and revert to his good-humoured self, breaking inevitably into song.

'Raised on songs and stories, heroes of renown ...'

Despite his tall tales and his penchant for gossip, Aoife was very fond of Eddie.

'Don't mind me! Sure I'm not the full shillin', wha'? Do you get it?'

'Yes, Eddie. Good one.'

If she'd heard it once she'd heard it a million times. Eddie Halfpenny. Not the full shilling.

Eddie would also have you believe that he'd been more than just an ordinary soldier in his day. A mere peacekeeper. Aoife wasn't sure if Ireland even had special forces and if it did whether a genial soul, a chatty rogue like Eddie would make the grade. But he'd often namedrop the Ranger Wing, say, or make references to the Sudan or the Janjaweed, and regularly crowbar terminology like 'extraction' into the conversation.

'The thing about the Janjaweed – people don't realize – they know horses.'

And then he'd point at himself.

'I know horses.'

And then he'd wink and leave it at that. But he was very obliging. He would do anything for you. Stories were legion about his kindness to the elderly in particular. In the absence of a family member, Eddie would sit for hours on end next to their hospital trolleys, holding their hands and regaling them with songs and stories about heroes of renown, which no doubt included tales of his own heroics overseas. He was also punctual and worked tirelessly on behalf of the Tidy Towns. Drawing on all his military experience, he marshalled a platoon of volunteers from his own estate, Beechwood. This elite, well-drilled outfit kept what was once an unkempt and even antisocial development fastidiously clean. They planted some trees, *liquidambar* and *pyrus calleryana* 'Chanticleer', and with a donation from Barry Duggan of all people installed a community pizza oven in the common area. To Eddie's immense pride, Beechwood was singled out for special mention in the previous year's Tidy Towns judge's report.

'My money is on the husband,' pipes up Eddie.

'Harry?'

'Had them in the car last week. Picked them up out in Nicky Bow's place. Big charity thing. Some bleedin' earthquake or somethin'.'

Like most people in Abbeyford, unimpressed by titles, Eddie referred to the composer Sir Nicholas Nguyen-Bow by his previous moniker from his days in the boy band Streetwise. Aoife was listening intently.

'Next thing. Blazing row. Didn't hear what started it now. Or who started it. None of my business. You know the way people do be whispering in the car. They're the worst rows. The whispery ones. The most vicious. Anyway. Harry roars at the top of his voice. "Stop the car!" sez he. Near deafened me, so he did. You know Harry, the big jowls quivering. "Get out! Get out! Scram!" he shouts at Michael. "I never want to see your face again." Right? And Michael, he throws the keys at him, right in Harry's face, and goes, "You won't." Just like that. "You won't." Very dramatic so it was. Mentioned something about a solicitor.'

Here, Eddie put on his idea of an Australian accent.

'"My solicitor will be in touch." Anyway. Off he walks into the night. Wearing a black dinner jacket and all. Very snazzy. I started singing a bit of Molly Malone, you know, just to calm it all down. Like, it was very awkward in the car. An awkward situation. And believe me I've been in some tight spots in my time. Then Harry roars at me. "Shut up!" sez he. "Please, for the love of God, Eddie, stop singing that abominable dirge!" Imagine that. He called it a dirge. So, after I dropped him off, Harry, I came back out the road, looking for Michael. I don't take sides. But there was no sign of him. All I'm saying is, it's usually the husband. Now, here we are, luv.'

Eddie pulled up outside Aoife's cottage. He waited in the car until she was ready to go back into town.

Chapter 18

After he said goodbye to his father, Finn tried Isabella again. In fairness the signal wasn't great out by Derrybreen Woods. Mind you, it was probably a lot better than where she was now. She'd gone trekking in the Himalayas. To get as far away as possible from him, he joked to her. No, it was a trip she'd been planning for years. It just seemed to both of them like the right time to call it quits.

'Isabella. Hope you landed safely. Love you. Miss you. Shouldn't say that, I know. Sorry. But it's true. They're all asking for you here. Mammy. Daddy. Listen, I know this might sound a bit weird – and you can tell me to feck right off – but I need a favour.'

It was probably a terrible idea to leave such a message for his ex-wife, who was by now busy acclimatizing to a new altitude, literally and metaphorically, but he couldn't think of anybody better placed. He went on to ask her if she or one of her old colleagues from the newsroom could do a bit of digging for him and find out all they knew about Michael St John Fitzmaurice and the ill-fated Victory Festival on the Isle of Wight.

No doubt she'd be exasperated at such a request, and nobody did exasperation quite like Isabella. She literally stamped her foot when she was angry, like a flamenco dancer. It was one of her many endearing qualities. But she was a newshound at heart. One thing they both agreed on was that she should never have left current affairs to produce his radio show. He was pretty sure it was one of the reasons why they had reached this impasse in their relationship. Although he was slowly coming around to the idea that Michael was in fact murdered, he wasn't at all convinced by his father's suggestion that the culprit might have come from overseas. But it was an excuse to reach out to Isabella. To engage with her as a friend. To prolong their connection beyond what would have been an unnecessarily blunt cut-off point. He knew perfectly well, as she did, that the relationship was over. The rope-bridge that connected them had been washed away in a landslide. But he couldn't accept that they would simply sever all ties. He didn't want to. And he knew that she'd be intrigued as well as exasperated by his strange request, even at base camp in Nepal. She could never resist a story. If she wasn't in a position to follow it up herself, one of her intrepid friends in London surely would, and who knows what they might find.

Chapter 19

Normally the Tidy Towns committee meetings would be held in the community centre, but earlier that afternoon, the guards had belatedly declared the place a crime scene, although they assured local reporters in ambiguous Garda-speak that almost certainly no crime had been committed.

Hector Morrissey had offered them a room upstairs in his bar to conduct their business. In the absence of a lift, Happiness physically carried Maura up the stairs, Finn relegated to the role of helpless bystander, pint in hand by way of consolation.

'Hector, have you got a minute?' Finn called after the landlord as he headed downstairs out of harm's way.

'Sure.'

The bags under his eyes practically reached his chin. Was he haunted? By guilt? Finn joined him at the bottom of the stairs.

'Listen, I'm sure it's nothing. Do you always use the orange lip balm?'

'I suppose I do. You're not going to tell me it's bad for me now, are ya? I'm sick of people telling me what's bad for me and good for me.'

'It's just ... I found a ... what do you call it, a chapstick in the rehearsal room.'

Finn, all innocence, monitored Hector's face for signs of stress. Nothing. Not a flicker. That didn't tell Finn much. By all accounts Hector's reaction times were glacial. It could be days before he registered a stimulus.

'The night Michael died,' he added, 'were you there, Hector? That night or the day before maybe?'

Hector thought about it. He pulled some wisps of cotton wool out of his scraggy beard. Moisturizing that face looked to Finn like a full-time job.

'No. Haven't been near the community centre for months. Since …'

Hector looked away, embarrassed. Finn's patient, unforced manner reassured him.

'Ah look, it was a dating thing. You won't tell anyone, will ya? Not really dating as such, more a presentation, there was this company with brochures and that, more about long-term arrangements, if you know what I mean, with women from … not from here like.'

'Right. I get you. I think. And you definitely weren't at the community centre lately?'

'No.'

He shook his head firmly. It was as if the mortification of attending such an event made the venue itself a no-go zone for life.

'I have to go, Finn. Busy night.'

The Yellowbelly Suite was named counter-intuitively after the brave hurlers of the Colclough estate who, wearing distinctive yellow sashes, beat a team from Cornwall back in the eighteenth century.

'I didn't know they played hurling in Cornwall,' said Finn jovially to Aoife, outside the function room, to show her he harboured no hard feelings after their difference of opinion in Café Madremonte earlier on.

'They didn't. That's why we won so easily.'

Although she kept her idea of a straight face, like a really terrible poker player, he could see she was dying to tell him something. She looked like she had aces in the hole. Mind you, he didn't have a bad hand himself.

'So have you calmed down yet?' she asked him.

'Me? Calmed down? I was the voice of reason.'

He really believed that. It was the core part of his identity. A rock of sense in a babbling sea of inanity.

'Voice of reason, my backside. Your voice was way up there.'

She pointed towards the ceiling.

'I could barely hear you it was so high. You were like one of those ...' – she remembered the recent conversation with Wolfie – 'castrati!'

He spluttered into his pint.

'What? You're the one that lost control, Aoife, I didn't want to say it, with your outrageous allegations about Fionnuala. Big red face on you. Like ...'

He was desperately trying to think of something big and red.

'Like a ... sunset or something.'

He wasn't entirely happy with his analogy but couldn't back out now.

'I'm surprised small animals weren't falling asleep at your feet. Badgers. Squirrels.'

She started laughing.

'Your voice. It's rising again, Mr Reasonable. And I don't want to embarrass you, but you were sweating buckets in Ana's.'

'No, I wasn't.'

'I was actually worried about you. I thought you'd end up with dehydration, that you'd be on a drip in Wexford General by now. Anyway, listen, the meeting's about to start and I have news.'

She grabbed his arm and pulled him towards an alcove down the corridor. It was an S-shaped space that once housed a public payphone. Aoife told Finn that Wolfie was in the clear. Finn didn't baulk. No great surprise there. He thought for a moment she was bluffing. That she had nothing. Then she nonchalantly turned another card. She mentioned that Hector had been in the community centre the night of the fateful choir practice.

'What? Impossible. Hector told me to my face that he hadn't been in the community centre for months.'

Finn was actually quite upset that he'd been lied to.

'Why would he lie if he didn't have something to hide?'

They agreed to keep a closer eye on Hector. But Aoife wasn't finished. Like a Vegas conjuror, she started pulling cards out of thin air including the one about the big fight between Michael and Harry a few days ago. So Harry was now in the picture as a potential suspect. Finn, impressed, let out a low whistle, but reckoned he could trump Aoife. He went all in and relayed his father's revelations about Michael's past. Aoife was genuinely shocked.

'I had no idea. You think you know someone!'

There was a scraping noise outside the alcove.

'Oh! I didn't see anything.'

It was the bar manager, Eve Duggan, dragging a freestanding metal fan along the corridor. How long had she been there? What had she heard?

'It's not like that, Eve. Just picking Finn's brains about the Tidy Towns.'

'None of my business, Aoife.'

Eve smiled wanly at them. She looked like she'd been crying. Referring to the fan, she explained, 'They had some sort of a workshop in the 'Belly earlier. One of the companies in town. Pretending to be animals, they were. You'd want to have heard them. So. Bit of a whiff in there now.' Eve paused, before saying, 'He didn't deserve to die. Michael.'

She blessed herself.

'Anyway. I really hope it wasn't Harry.'

Finn and Aoife exchanged glances as Eve headed towards the meeting room.

'She heard.'

'She'll have us married by tomorrow,' worried Finn.

'Would that be so terrible?' Aoife mock-flirted.

No was the honest answer. That wouldn't be terrible at all. Not that he said that out loud. Not that he even thought it. Although he liked to think she wasn't entirely joking either.

'Listen, you're going to have to keep your voice down in future.'

'Me?'

'This is serious, Finn.'

'You're the one who was shouting.'

'In fairness to Eve, she's usually very discreet. I think.'

They agreed, if they were going to find out who killed Michael, they needed to be more discreet themselves. They also decided to visit Harry as a matter of urgency later that night. To see if he knew anything about who Michael really was. And if the temper he'd displayed in Eddie's car was a harbinger of homicidal impulses.

'Right. Wish me luck, Finn. This could get messy.'

She straightened herself up to her full magnificence and strode purposefully into the Yellowbelly Suite.

Chapter 20

There were a couple of trestle tables laid out at the front of the room behind which sat six of the eight committee members. Declan Doyle, the chair, and Aoife, the secretary, were in the middle, but the body language between them spoke volumes. You could nearly see the forcefield that separated them. Feel it. Hear it, crackling. Flanking the presiding officers were the assistant chairman and the assistant secretary. The former was the smugly handsome Gavin O'Connell with the fake tan and the collar of his polo shirt turned up as usual, like he'd just stepped off a yacht. He was the scion of Celibate O'Connell, the recently retired proprietor of O'Connell's SuperO supermarket who was still a big donor to Tidy Towns. Finn's mother, Maura, one of the original Tidy Towns committee members, was the assistant secretary. Only one of the two treasurers was present. That was Kitty Doyle, another of the founder members of the organization forty years ago. Kitty was not only Maura's friend and confidante, she was broadband personified, an indiscriminate circulator of rumours, innuendos and in fairness sometimes sound information. She was also the chairman's mother and, it should be said, belligerently indifferent to charges of nepotism. As Declan himself would say, 'Look! I have a business to run. I need all this like a hole in the head.'

The other treasurer, Dr Harry Boyle, was currently indisposed, under sedation in his loft apartment overlooking the Barrow. Only one of the executive members of the committee was able to make it on this occasion, a pious, patrician solicitor with a thin face by the name of Aloysius Sweeney, better known as Alo. As six out of eight constituted a quorum, the April meeting of the Abbeyford Tidy Towns Association, attended by a sizeable thirty or forty townspeople, got underway. Declan Doyle unzipped his gilet as if he was shedding a second skin, and opened proceedings.

'First of all, on behalf of the committee I'd like to pay my condolences to our joint-treasurer Harry Boyle on the tragic loss of his partner, Michael. *Ar dheis Dé go raibh a anam.* We're all devastated so we are.'

The attendants bowed their heads for a moment of reflection, murmuring incoherent responses in both Irish and English.

'Secondly, I'd like to welcome a very special guest to the meeting. You'll know him off the television and the radio, the celebrity gardener himself, local hero Finn O'Leary.'

There was polite applause. Some people craned their necks to have a good gawk at him. It was embarrassing. Happiness, fanning herself with an agenda, bored her eyes into him as if to say she knew better. It was something he quite liked about Happiness. She wasn't easily swayed by reputation or something as nebulous as fame.

'Aoife here, our esteemed secretary, seems to think it would be a good idea to lean in, so to speak, on Finn's what you might call expertise. Although I should point out that we haven't exactly been letting the grass grow under our feet, no, we have just recently planted a total of five thousand seedlings, so there's that . . .'

Declan declared with a rhetorical flourish hoping to elicit a clap, like a populist politician on *Question Time*, but by now the audience had the arms firmly folded in the standard impress-me pose.

'And ... and we have already repaired and indeed re-painted the various plant boxes. We're ahead of the game, so to speak, and we've ordered new hanging baskets, theft-proof hanging baskets, I might add, which, please God, should be arriving next week.'

Last year, a number of the hanging baskets had been stolen in the weeks before the judges' visit. Naturally, there was consternation in the town at such a critical moment in the campaign. Declan had placed tracking devices in some of the remaining baskets, one of which was subsequently stolen. He tracked the missing basket to a skip in the neighbouring town of Ennismore. Although the Ennismore Tidy Towns committee denied any knowledge of the crime, it has to be said, there had been a long-standing and at times bitter rivalry between themselves and Abbeyford as they vied year after year to be the tidiest town in the county, if not the country. Aoife assumed it was Ennismore who'd tried to set the picnic table on fire a couple of days ago.

'Furthermore,' Declan pointed out nasally, his jaw tight, 'we have created a really super bog garden, as you'll all agree, below in Bully's Acre. Well worth a look if you haven't already seen it. And I should say we have very, very successfully re-introduced toads in the pond there. What's it called? Not any old toad, the ... eh the cracker ... no, the natterjack toad. Loads of them. Natterjacks. So that's more or less covered. So ...'

Declan, an estate agent, was a salesman. He didn't only

sell houses, he also auctioned cattle as well, hence the affected nasal drone and the pleasure he took in the sound of his own voice.

'Now you all know my views on rewilding and biodiversity and all that lark. I'm all for bees and wildflowers. I love bees and wildflowers as much as the next man, but within reason. There has to be a balance, so to speak.'

Declan glanced at Aoife.

'If some people had their way, we'd get rid of lawnmowers altogether. Ha! The place would be completely overgrown. It'd be like the apocalypse or something. And we'd have bears and wolves roaming the town. And feckin' zombies. I'm not personally convinced that's what we want here.'

There were a few chuckles. Aoife, although remaining still like a hungry lioness, was ready to pounce.

'The good news. The application form is nearly complete.'

Declan held up a document about a foot thick.

'We're in a very, very good spot. I personally have sat up night after night for the past few months. The wife is hardly talking to me.'

He paused for a reaction which didn't arrive.

'Very annoyed with me so she is. We have a really super plan in place, capitalizing on all the hard work done over the last few years. I can honestly say, all modesty aside, it's the best plan we've ever had.'

Happiness sighed loudly.

'So while of course we would welcome input from the so-called experts, the professionals, I'm not 100 per cent sure what they could add at this stage. If you know what I mean. Unless of course they want to paint the bins.'

Finn wanted to scream. He was only at the meeting

because of his mother. And Aoife. He hoped people could see that. And didn't think he was there out of choice. Or, God forbid, that he was offering help in any capacity.

'Now before we go any further,' Declan continued, blithe to Finn's discomfort, 'I'd like to thank Gavin O'Connell and SuperO for sponsoring the hi-viz vests, which you'll find at the back of the room. Thank you, Gavin.'

There was a smattering of applause for the merch. And sure enough, there was a big pile of hi-viz vests on a table at the back of the room. Free stuff was free stuff even if it was a flimsy nylon garment emblazoned with the logo of a local supermarket. Gavin himself waved at the assembly like he was the Pope in St Peter's Square bestowing eternal blessings on the faithful. Declan, lip curled, turned to Aoife.

'Aoife, now, if you would care to go through some of the highlights of this year's campaign to date.'

The April meeting was the last chance to make changes to the proposals. The detailed submission, complete with photographs and maps, had to be lodged by the first week in May. They then had about six weeks ' – the big push – ' to implement their plans before the first visit, unannounced, from an anonymous judge. If the adjudicator was satisfied with what they saw, if the evidence of their eyes matched the plan on the page, the Tidy Towns committee had another month to make improvements before a second visit. This inspection, in July, was when the big decision would be made as to whether Abbeyford would be contending for the national prize in the Large Town category. Although they had achieved creditable Silver Medal status in two of the last three years, they had fallen short in a number of areas, not least in the Nature and Biodiversity section. To make matters worse, Ennismore had won Gold Medal status and county bragging rights every year for the last three years. Aoife, without notes, speed-skated through the key projects across all eight sections.

Firstly, she addressed Community Planning and Involvement, which was worth a total of eighty marks. The adjudicators were particularly keen on the idea of social inclusion and awarded extra marks for the participation of schools and new residents. Aoife was mindful that at this level every single point counted. This she wanted to stress to the assembly.

'It's great the Mercy is on board. Thank you to Sister Finbarr and the girls for their unstinting support. We couldn't do it without you. But it is imperative that all the schools get involved. And that includes St Joseph's.'

Giles McCabe, the headmaster of Joey's, squirmed in his seat.

'If I may, Aoife,' he interrupted. 'I'm afraid, as you well know, I can't and I won't be able to sanction that outcome. My position is clear. Cleaning the town is a job for the council. My fear is that jobs will be lost if . . .'

Everybody knew the only job Giles was concerned about was his own. Aoife nodded at the county manager, Fran Peacock, who was in attendance.

'That's just ridiculous,' said Mr Peacock. 'I have written to Mr McCabe, more than once, assuring him that nobody will lose their jobs. In fact as a council, we have taken on more people this year. And by the way, just for the record, we are fully behind the Tidy Town campaign, not just here in Abbeyford but throughout the county.'

The headmaster was undeterred.

'I have no recollection of ever having received such letters. Be that as it may, there's also the question of health and safety.'

'Dundee.'

Happiness was getting very frustrated. The heat in the room, not to mention the lingering body odour from the earlier role-playing event, was beginning to irritate her.

'Individually, the boys are welcome to assist, in a personal capacity, with the permission of their parents, of course. But as a school, no, not on my watch. I'm sorry, now. Frankly, in my view, it's not only dangerous – you know what boys are like, pushing and shoving, and play-acting – but it's a waste of time, picking up rubbish when they should be attending to their studies. It sends out the wrong message.'

'Funny, Giles, the Mercy girls manage to do both,' said Aoife sharply. 'And still somehow beat the boys hands down at exam time.'

'Amen to that,' said Happiness.

Some of the audience sat forward, unfolded their arms and rubbed their hands together. This was more like it. This was what they had come for. A bit of a ding-dong.

Aoife suspected the real reason Giles held back his forces was because of her. He seemed to see her as some sort of a threat to his authority. Not that she was after his job. She wasn't. But he resented her ease with the pupils, her popularity among staff and parents, and her progressive ways. He much preferred it when she was in prison. Aoife also suspected that he didn't want his precious charges fraternizing with the wrong sort. A sizeable number of asylum seekers had been placed in the old Rosemount Hotel outside the town, a policy that didn't sit well with everybody.

'Incidentally, we are also absolutely thrilled with the number of volunteers amongst our friends in the International Protection community,' said Aoife, staring down McCabe.

There was a mixture of enthusiastic applause and fearful mutterings from the floor at this announcement. Aoife, who unlike Finn seemed to relish confrontation, went on to share the committee's plans for the next two sections, Streetscapes and Public Places, and Green Spaces and Landscaping. Urgent work was required on the restoration of the old jail, she told them, the bridewell, in Market Square. Ultimately, over the next few years, they were going to develop it as a digital hub, but for now with the help of local artists, they were in the process of creating a temporary light installation, which could be enjoyed whether you were inside or outside the building. Declan and Gavin exchanged schoolboys smirks. Aoife ignored them. She also mentioned, as the chairman had previously, that the bins throughout the town still required repainting.

'That's my job, apparently,' said Finn, wryly, getting a bit of a laugh.

'I wouldn't hold my breath,' said Maura, getting a bigger laugh. 'He's been promising to do my house for a year now.'

'And the peace garden in the old Ball Alley,' Aoife continued, raising an obvious bone of contention. 'It needs serious consideration. A better conception for a start.'

'Personally, I think we should keep it simple as per the proposal.' Declan put his foot down.

'Either way,' Aoife went on, 'I'm sure Finn will be able to help us there too. He can be very simple and very complicated.'

'Hear, hear,' said Maura.

'Amen,' concurred Happiness.

Simple and complicated? Finn wasn't sure how to take that.

'And on a more positive note, you'll be glad to hear,

the greenway on the west side of the Barrow is nearly complete.'

There was a generous round of applause.

'Thanks to Mr Peacock and the council for providing the benches. As for Nature and Biodiversity . . .'

Aoife, standing up in readiness for her piece de resistance, took a sip of water but before she could go any further a voice from the crowd shouted, 'Otters!'

It was Nathan Kane, her nephew. Nathan, a pale 16-year-old boy, had removed his headphones. He spoke haltingly in an American accent, although he had never been to the United States. Aoife smiled encouragingly at Nathan and at his mother, her sister, Neasa, who sat next to him.

'Yes Nathan, what about them?'

Nathan, rocking back and forth, as was his wont, had read all the judges' reports pertaining to Tidy Towns that he could find online. And there were hundreds of them in fussy prose going back years about towns all over the country. Nathan had a phenomenal ability to concentrate on subjects that interested him and a prodigious memory to boot. According to him, 'Judges love otters.'

'Oh?'

Nathan blocked out the rest of the room, safe in the tunnel formed by Aoife's encouraging gaze. He then quoted verbatim the various authors' excitement at the sighting of an otter in places as far apart as Carrickmacross, Millstreet and Belturbet. He worked out actuarially that the sudden appearance of an otter, the novelty value of such a thing, was worth up to ten extra marks in the Nature and Biodiversity section.

There followed a discussion about how best to attract otters to the town. Some suggested introducing more eels to the Barrow. Others recommended building artificial holts. Eddie Halfpenny, the taxi driver, joined in.

'Look, Nathan's right. But even if we do convince the otters to move into town, there's no guarantee they'll appear on demand, is there?'

'True.'

'So why don't we like manufacture some sort of artificial otters, wha' and you know leave them lying around the place. On the riverbank.'

There was a brief silence before Aoife stepped in.

'We'll look into it, Eddie.'

'No, it's only a thought, now, don't mind me. Get your one, Fanny Whatserface, to make them. The sculptor.'

'You mean Femke. Femke Leerdam. We can certainly ask if it's feasible. Thank you, Eddie. And thank you, Nathan. If there is no objection you can be our chief otter spotter.'

The committee without hesitation unanimously adopted Aoife's resolution to co-opt Nathan as an honorary member of the board. Nathan stopped rocking and put his headphones back on. Aoife's sister mouthed a thank you.

After that digression, which briefly unified the committee, Aoife made an impassioned plea to all present, but especially to her fellow board members, to redouble their efforts when it came to biodiversity. The judges were putting a huge emphasis on it this year.

'They're on the record. And we still have time. Ennismore have pollinators coming out their asses. Who better than the Wild Man himself to help us transform Abbeyford into a biodiverse paradise? If anyone can do it, he can.'

Finn, on his second pint, reddened again when he heard his name. It was true, he was known, not necessarily in a flattering light, as the Wild Man of Gardening by a section of the British press. Mind you, he didn't share Aoife's confidence in his own abilities. Not with so little time available.

'We have one shot at this. And if we get this right, I have no doubt, it's the one thing that will sway the judges.'

'As well as otters,' said Eddie.

'As well as otters.'

The room, for the most part, roared its approval. Declan Doyle and Gavin O'Connell snorted derisively.

'It's almost as if some people don't want to win the Tidy Towns,' muttered Aoife under her breath.

'Aoife is right,' said Maura. 'What have we got to lose? I propose we let Finn cast his eye over the application before we submit. It's the one thing he's good at.'

'Thanks, Mam.'

There was a titter at this.

'And he's at a bit of a loose end at the moment now that his wife has left him.'

'Aaaah!'

Finn blushed some more. How did she even know that? He hadn't told her. Mothers must have an intuition about these things.

For forty years Maura, together with Kitty Doyle, had tried to win the overall Tidy Towns award. They had got near on occasions. At the moment, they had by any standards a decent five-year strategic plan in place. A lot of the major works had already been completed. The restoration of the old workhouse was a shining example of what could be done when the community, politicians and civil servants put their petty differences aside and came together. In terms of the remaining categories on the form, Tidiness and Litter Control, Residential Areas, Approach Roads,

Streets and Lanes, and Maps, they regularly excelled, often receiving close to full marks. But they were always missing something. A bit of magic to dazzle the judges. A theme. They needed something special to get them over the line. Was that Finn? Or would an otter, real or imagined, do the trick?

They put it to a vote. Finn wanted to be anywhere else but the Yellowbelly Suite. He felt like a pawn in somebody else's game. He felt like the demilitarized zone between North and South Korea. Maura and Aoife voted in his favour. The burgermeisters, Declan and Gavin and Alo Sweeney, voted against his involvement. All eyes were on Kitty Doyle, Declan's own mother. She thought about it, milking the tension in the room for all it was worth. All she was missing was dry ice and a swirling spotlight. Eventually she too plumped for Finn, the town's needs trumping her son's vanity. Declan looked at her uncomprehendingly. It was like the civil war all over again, mother pitted against son.

'Three apiece so. Fair enough. As chair,' said Declan, his mouth drying, 'according to the standing rules, I have the casting vote. Please don't take this ...'

'One sec, Declan, I have Harry Boyle on the line here.'

Aoife, having hastily dialled Harry and explained the predicament, put her phone on speaker. Harry's booming bass voice, a deep crevasse of sorrow, could be heard at the back of the room.

'I hereby cast my vote in favour of my good friend Finn.'

Declan, now on his phone, furiously keyed in the number of the eighth and final member of the committee, the second executive member, none other than local entrepreneur Barry Duggan. There was no reply.

'He's in Croatia,' Aoife said. 'Sorry. So I guess Finn will be officially helping us with the campaign.'

Finn grimaced. Although the denouement of the meeting was undeniably tense, it didn't feel like a victory to him.

Chapter 21

An hour after the meeting ended, and the drink-fuelled post-mortems had been held and the cliquish huddles had disbanded, the cadaverous solicitor and committee member Alo Sweeney approached Maura and Happiness. Dressed in a blue pin-striped double-breasted suit, now a size too big after a recent health scare, with a silk handkerchief trying to escape from his breast pocket, he unctuously kissed Maura's hand.

'And who is this beautiful lady?' He turned to Happiness. He raised his glasses, allowing them to rest on his forehead while he appraised Maura's companion in a somewhat disconcerting way. Again, despite Happiness' resistance, he took her hand and kissed it, his lips lingering on her skin for perhaps a fraction too long. Although slightly flattered, if wary, it was only her respect for his profession and her fear of deportation that stopped her from punching him in the face. Maura watched on with a mixture of amusement and horror as this awkward courting ritual continued. Alo was always known as 'handsy' even when his wife was still alive.

'My name is Happiness Bakare. Pleased to meet you.'

'Aloysius Sweeney,' he introduced himself in a camp voice. 'If you ever need anything, anything at all, don't hesitate to call me. May I offer you a lift?'

*

While Alo was flirting with the ladies, a still adrenalized Aoife and Finn cornered Hector outside the pub where the publican was having a contemplative smoke.

'How did the meeting go?' he asked.

'You lied to me, Hector! You were at the community centre since the bride auction or whatever it was …'

Hector looked stunned. Mind you, he always looked a bit stunned.

'That's not fair, Finn. You said you wouldn't tell anybody.'

'You were there the evening Michael was killed?'

'You delivered booze to one of the meeting rooms,' Aoife reminded him.

Hector took a long slow drag of his cigarette, as if he was a man on death row smoking his last.

'I'm sorry I lied. It was awkward. They were all giving out to me for crashing in on their meeting. I wouldn't be their favourite person at the best of times.'

Finn looked at him for elaboration.

'Owning a bar.'

'Of course.'

'Some of them blame me for their problems. I dodged in to the wee kitchen there, had meself a cup of tea. I musta dropped the chapstick. Big deal. I did nothing wrong.'

'Why did you lie?'

Hector looked hurt.

'I didn't want people blaming me. Adding two and two and getting five. Breslin, the superintendent, fell out with my father years ago. He'd only be dying for an excuse to sniff around.'

'What would he find? Traces of poison?'

Hector shook his head, the dewlaps flapping wearily.

'I run a bar. It's all cash. My books wouldn't be … how

should I put it, the most up to date,' he admitted, before adding more in hope than expectation, 'Keep that to yourselves!'

'You have my word,' promised Finn.

'Yeah right. Anyways, why would I want to kill Michael?' He turned to Aoife.

'Did Michael ever have a bad word to say about me?'

'No, Hector. In fact he thought the world of you. And your bar.'

'You see, Finn, this is nuts!'

Finn sighed. It was impossible not to feel sorry for Hector.

'You're right. This is all nuts. I'm sorry.'

He felt bad for accusing him, for accusing anybody without evidence. No wonder people get away with so much.

Twenty minutes later Aoife and Finn turned up at Harry Boyle's apartment. The place was the size of a hockey pitch taking up the whole third floor of a warehouse built circa 1830 by William Devereux, an importer of tropical fruit. It was Fionnuala who buzzed them in.

'I was just leaving,' she informed them coldly. 'Harry needs to rest. I sincerely hope he's not going to be subjected to the same sort of unsubtle interrogation as I was.'

'It's purely social, Fionnuala,' said Finn.

'Thank you. I feel *so* reassured.'

And with that, she huffily clanged the steel-framed glass door behind her, tightened her scarf and flounced out into the night. The room was dark, although light from the moon spilled fashionably through a skylight that ran the full length of the roof. Harry was reclining on a chaise covered in a chintzy fabric with a cherry motif, 'Chelan' cherries to be precise, eyes closed, clutching a bottle of Johnnie Walker

Blue to his chest as if it were a cuddly toy, opera music loudly filling the huge, soulless double-height space. Finn's self-proclaimed musical knowledge didn't stretch as far as opera. Aoife noticed his pain.

'Verdi,' she informed him.

'How can you tell?'

'Dies Irae!'

'I'd be embarrassed to know something like that.'

'Philistine.'

'I'll take that as a compliment.'

Aoife, her suspicions about Fionnuala's dispensing proclivities not in any way dispelled, approached the prone figure of Harry and felt his pulse. Harry sat up with a start, the whiskey bottle falling to the floor. Luckily it was empty.

'Unhand me, woman!' he roared in that familiar booming voice, fumbling for his spectacles.

'Oh it's you, Aoife. My profound and profuse apologies.'

He kissed her hand.

'I have these reveries in which I'm being dragged down into a stygian pit.'

Finn turned down the music. There was a spectacular view from the industrial chic windows – the tower of the old workhouse, the *Lady Jane*, and the lights of the town twinkling on the river although what they had to twinkle about right now was a mystery.

'How was the meeting? I'm so sorry I couldn't be in attendance.' Harry coughed, reaching instinctively for the stub of a cigar in an ashtray. He drew on it without success before discarding it again.

'She played a blinder, Harry.'

'She always does.'

'And you'll be glad to hear Finn is now officially on board.'

'I told you. Didn't I tell you he wouldn't let us down? Good man, Finn. Let me provide you with a modest refreshment.'

Despite their protestations, Harry conjured up a fresh bottle of whiskey and thrust tumblers into their hands. It was a stimulating tipple, each sip transporting Finn back and forward in time and triggering brief visions of other, better worlds. They did their best to jolly their distraught host until Finn's attention was suddenly drawn to two dots of light on the mezzanine level in one corner of the apartment. It was the penetrating eyes of a cat. And the cat was staring down at him from the end of the master bed. Directly at him. Menacingly. Unmistakably. And Finn was slightly afraid of cats.

'That's Esther, Michael's cat.'

Finn shivered.

'It's like Michael himself is with us,' said Harry. 'Do you believe in the transmigration of the soul?'

Harry's chest heaved. He blew his nose into a handkerchief that he produced with no little drama from his trouser pocket.

'Forgive me, you must think I'm very maudlin.'

Finn could sense that Aoife was getting restless and was wondering how to broach the sensitive subject of Michael's real identity when she, true to form, came straight to the point.

'Harry. How well did you know Michael?'

'I don't quite understand the ... the tenor of the question, Aoife.'

His voice, deeper and more gravelly than usual if that was possible, reverberated around the loft. Finn, emboldened by a combination of Aoife's directness and the exquisite whiskey, joined in.

'Did you know, for example, about the Victory Festival?'

Harry drained his glass and moistened his lips.

'Aoife, you and I are friends. And Finn, we have shared many memorable adventures in our time on this mortal coil. It would be a shame to say or do anything that might, shall we say, jeopardize our good standing. Michael is entitled to his privacy in death as in life.'

'So you did know?' Aoife pressed on.

'I'm afraid I'm going to have to ask you to leave.'

'Harry. I'm so sorry if this is a bad time,' Finn said. 'If Aoife appears insensitive . . .'

'Insensitive! That's the least of it. Rude. Boorish. There are other words I could use.'

There certainly were. Harry, his oratorical embellishments a thing of legend, never knowingly used one word where two or three would do.

'We only want to find out what happened to Michael,' said Aoife firmly.

'As your friends,' Finn added.

'And you think I might have something to do with his demise? Is that it? You have the gall, the impudence to come in here and accuse me of – let's be frank – murder? What? You think I found out about Michael's past and thus wronged and misled, in a fit of pique, disposed of him? The love of my life! Get out! Vamoose! Scram!'

Finn hadn't heard the word 'scram' in many years. Harry's mother used to tell them to 'scram' when she was tidying the house and they were under her feet but not in such an aggressive, dare one say murderous, way.

'It's the insinuation I resent. The aspersion. That I am some class of a fool. A soft touch. That what Michael and I had wasn't real? We had no secrets between us. None. Zilch.

Of course I knew about the Victory Festival. But that had nothing to do with his quietus.'

'His what?'

'His death.'

'It's Latin,' Aoife informed Finn.

Perhaps, Finn thought, doctors and teachers speak Latin to each other all the time. He got a sudden earache. The shrieking mezzo-soprano sounded like she was stuck in limbo or possibly in a Stygian pit. She seemed to be begging for some sort of divine intervention.

'It's just a little scratch,' said Harry, moving unsteadily towards the retro record player.

To Finn, the fact that the record was stuck on repeat didn't make the music any more bearable. Trying to lift the stylus from the vinyl, in his drunken grief, Harry managed to scratch the entire disc. Finn winced as if a needle had been jagged over his own nerves. Oblivious to the violence he'd just perpetrated, Harry lifted the LP carefully off the turntable and proceeded to wipe it with the arm of his chocolate-stained corduroy jacket.

'There now. Good as new.'

The two visitors watched this performance somewhat rooted to the spot. With the reverence of a Vestal Virgin, he returned Verdi to its rightful sleeve and retrieved another album from the cabinet beneath the deck. Whipping this new disc from the sleeve with a typical Boylean flourish, he inadvertently hit it against the thick stone wall of the apartment. Undeterred, Harry positioned the now chipped record on the platter and picked up the arm. Aoife and Finn, on tenterhooks now, watched aghast as the arm in Harry's hand hovered ominously for an age over the delicate vinyl. Finally they were able to relax and exhale as the needle gently hit the groove. Like a swan landing on a lake. Harry smiled in satisfaction at a job well done.

'Verdi again,' Aoife whispered.

'That's just a guess.'

'*Othello*. Act Four. Do you think he's trying to tell us something?'

'What do you mean?'

'You don't know what happens in Act Four?'

'I don't know what happens in Act One or any of the other acts. I've never read *Othello*.'

'He murders Desdemona. Othello kills his wife.'

Harry sat heavily on the chaise. The chintzy cherry chaise. No longer belligerent he looked somewhat sorrowfully, needfully at his friends with moist, slightly thyroid eyes. They took a seat opposite him in matching armchairs. They were beautiful objects, low-slung of a sleek Italian design in a burnt orange colour. Beautiful but definitely not designed for sitting in.

'Michael Dunlop was a complicated man,' he began.

'You mean Michael St John Fitzmaurice?' Finn proffered tentatively.

Harry laughed. His whole body shook. He was a substantial man, the whole room shook.

'Dunlop. St John Fitzmaurice. Hunter. Take your pick. He had many aliases. His real name of course was Michael O'Driscoll. A Corkman, his people from Baltimore. Descended from the pirates. They moved to London town when he was but a boy. Very bright boy, precocious, he won a scholarship you know, to St Paul's. Yes. We met at the tennis club shortly after he moved here. He loved tennis. I knew instantly he was the one. Everything suddenly made sense. That's immaterial. Yes, there were people after him, bad people, but he had covered his tracks. Well, until you two galoots started snooping around.'

Finn hadn't heard the word 'galoot' in a long time either, not since Harry's dad used to refer to Finn and Harry affectionately as 'a pair of galoots' when they ran around the house disturbing the peace.

'In fairness, Harry, if galoots like us could find out about Michael surely bad people with ... bad people's resources and bad people's intentions could track him down.'

'He didn't exactly keep a low profile,' Aoife added. 'I mean, he ended up in prison. His picture was in the paper.'

'He had a sweater over his head, Aoife. My own hand-knit creation, no less. The one with the cacti. No, Michael was careful. We all know who's responsible. To suggest otherwise is nonsense. A diversion.'

'Harry. I know we're being right pains in the ass.'

'Speak for yourself, Aoife,' said Finn.

'Tell me. What about that bash in Nicky Bow's place last week? Sounded like quite a bust-up, no?'

A rumbling noise, like the sound of an approaching underground train, rose from deep inside Harry's torso. He threw his head back, laughing operatically and slapping his leg.

'Naughty girl. Naughty, naughty. You have certainly done your homework. I shouldn't have doubted you.' Harry turned to Finn.

'Do you have any idea what you're getting into?'

'I can assure you I am not getting into anything.'

'Ours was a tempestuous relationship. As the great passionate liaisons tend to be.' He pointed a thumb towards the record player. 'Like our friends, pitiful Othello and dear, dear Desdemona.'

'And we all know what happened there, don't we?' asked Aoife daringly, smiling like an assassin. 'Well, apart from Finn.'

Harry chuckled sonorously again.

'Finn was always more au fait with the natural world than our mere mortal concerns. Yes, I concede, it was a good one even by our standards. A monumental tiff, as they say. He could be hurtful, Michael. You knew that. I suppose I can tell you, as my dearest friends, in strictest confidence, mind you, that he was planning to destroy Duggan.'

Having leaned forward to deliver his coup de théâtre, Harry sat back, awaiting their reaction. They remained deadpan.

'Once he got an idea into his head, Michael, it was difficult to dissuade him from his desired course of action.'

'What was on his mind?' asked Aoife.

'A cyber attack!'

'A cyber attack?' Finn blurted. 'What does that entail? Sounds a bit ambitious, no, a bit of a fantasy, a bit sci-fi. Was he serious?'

'You didn't know Michael. He didn't know Michael. He was very brilliant with technology. That was his background, you know. He had managed to hack into Duggan's computer system. The IT software. Whatever. I don't know the terminology. His accounts. Everything. He had valuable information about VAT and tax and so on, the type of people in cahoots with Duggan. Enough to put him behind bars, I'll wager. I didn't want to know the details. I begged him to desist. We almost came to blows. Almost, I admit, split up. It was the lowest point of my life. There, I've said it. You know it all now. Are you happy, Aoife? I am an empty vessel. You have sucked me dry. Like a praying mantis, you have sucked me of my sap. Begone! I wish to be alone.'

They took turns giving Harry a hug. His hugs were known to be dangerously tight. Both Aoife and Finn had tears in their eyes as they departed from Harry's huge apartment leaving him alone with his memories and what-ifs as Bocelli channelling Othello lamented the infinitely avoidable death of his beloved.

Chapter 22

Once out on the street, they decided to call it a night, to reserve judgment on the guilt or innocence of Harry. Too exhausted to even discuss the case any further, or explore their suspicions about anyone else, they parted company with a handshake. Like chess players after a game, in a spirit of mutual respect. Although, unlike chess players, Finn was convinced, she let her hand rest in his for longer than was strictly necessary.

Aoife called Eddie for a ride home. Finn decided to walk the couple of miles back to Maura's house. It was implicitly understood that they would stand down from the investigation until such time as Barry Duggan Senior, and Monika, returned from their trip to Croatia.

Over the next couple of days, Finn kept busy. He moved into the one-bed above Café Madremonte. It was even pokier then he had imagined and had a noticeably sloping floor, which was disorientating at first. There was also no hot water. Although his father would have been proud of him, Finn would have preferred to have a warm shower in the morning, the water preferably landing on his head from above in a powerful jet rather than from a hand-held hose in a feeble trickle. Furthermore, he was reluctant to force open the sash window that framed the pleasing streetscape below given how resistant it was to his exertions or even to his charming vocal exhortations. But it had to be said, the ever-present aroma of Ana's coffee disguised all the other smells in the flat. And he enjoyed his corner seat in the cafe in the mornings, observing the town stretching and yawning, delighting in the wit and banter of his townsfolk as their brains sparked into life in preparation for the dodging and weaving of the day ahead. And he was entertained too by the energetic Ana's stream of consciousness about the rights and wrongs of the world.

It was not uncommon for people to approach his table and, invited or uninvited, take a seat. Some of them had legitimate gardening questions. A middle-aged woman, close to tears, told him of her ongoing struggle with keeping a calathea alive. *Oh God*, he thought, *here we go!* Calatheas were the bane of his professional life. If he had his way, he'd ban them. Had he been a more cynical and entrepreneurial sort, he'd have opened a money-spinning nursing home for infirm calatheas. But he felt so sorry for her that he left his breakfast and went around to her house. The plant was indeed distressed, but as far as he could see she had been doing everything right. After questioning her, Finn was satisfied that it was the beneficiary of textbook care. In terms of light, air, temperature, humidity, it was in a perfect environment. In fact, the house seemed to be adapted to the needs of the plant. But the house was unusually quiet and freakishly clean. At a loss as to what to do he eventually prescribed music. Reggae music, to be precise. He felt both the plant and the lady could do with a bit of rhythm in their lives. It couldn't do any harm.

Other supplicants weren't quite as sincere. One morning while he was sampling Ana's torrijas – a particularly eggy variation on French toast – a man opened a Tupperware box containing animal excrement he said he'd found in his garden. The scats were coiled and quite dark in colour but not as foul-smelling as Finn expected. At a guess, given their sweet, violety scent, he pinpointed the pine marten as the producer of the poop.

When not studying Abbeyford's two-legged fauna, he was familiarizing himself with the foot-thick Tidy Towns application, which Aoife had delivered to the cafe. In the afternoons, he went walkabout, covering every inch of the town, visiting the specific sites that needed attention, and desperately hoping that inspiration would strike. It's not that he couldn't visualize solutions. Finn believed, arrogantly some would say, in his own ability. His own aesthetic. It was the time pressure that bothered him. He simply couldn't see how he could make a significant difference in a month or, what was it, six weeks? He was at a point in his life, a plateau he had long-aimed to reach, when he hoped not to be answerable to anybody, when he could work in his own way at his own pace. How naive! How bone-headed! He had to laugh at the situation he found himself in.

When not mulling over the plans, he spent a lot of time with his mother and Happiness, doing the crossword and drinking vermouth. He even started to paint Maura's house. Not by choice, mind you. It was when Happiness presented him with a pot of paint, a set of paintbrushes and an old T-shirt and tracksuit combination of his she'd found in the attic, that he finally took the hint. Under her strict supervision, including inspections at ten-minute intervals, he started in the hall, each stray drop of paint eliciting a howl of disbelief from Happiness.

Finn accompanied them to Dublin for Maura's three-monthly check-up at the rehab unit. After impressing both the OT and the PT with her developing motor skills, Maura was rightly chuffed. Happiness Amen-ed proudly. Finn thought he detected a smugness on her face and suspected she was inwardly taking the credit for Maura's improvement. Which was probably fair enough.

They all went to lunch afterwards in a Radisson convenient to the N11. Maura had a lifelong aversion to Dublin, preferring anonymous hostelries on the arterial routes outwards than 'stuck-up' city centre establishments. There they were joined by Happiness' daughter, Grace, and to his surprise, by Finn's sister, Eimear.

Eimear was a couple of years older than Finn, an accountant – or was it an actuary? – in an aviation leasing company, and a busy mother of two children. George and Fidelia – a bone of contention to their grandparents as well as to Finn – were attending private schools. Her body language and her constant fiddling with her phone made it abundantly clear that Eimear was doing them all a massive favour by taking time out of her impossible schedule to have lunch with them. It sickened Finn to see the condescending way she stroked Maura's arm as if their mother was a kitten. And it galled him to see the way Happiness fawned over Eimear, complimenting her on her clothes and her perfume, and asking her questions about her work. He soon copped on to her scheme. Looking from Grace to Happiness to Eimear, he understood that Happiness had somehow engineered this gathering as a way of introducing Grace to Eimear. He raised an eyebrow at Happiness, nodding in admiration as much as anything else, as if to say 'I know what you're up to.' Happiness knew she'd been rumbled. She pursed her lips and stared him down before unsubtly shifting her body weight to exclude Finn from her field of vision and, as much as possible, from the conversation.

Before she left the hotel, not quite a full half an hour after she arrived, Eimear made it abundantly clear to Finn that he was on his own now, that she, despite all the other pressures in her life and at considerable expense to her career, marriage and finances, had done all the 'heavy lifting' when it came to Maura's care and recovery and ongoing medical needs, hiring Happiness, modifying the home and basically saving their mother's life while he was off indulging in his 'hobbies'.

She also lambasted him for involving their mother in a murder investigation.

'Putting Mammy's life in danger!' she hissed while they were paying the bill out of earshot of the others.

'Who told you that?'

'Mammy. She was boasting about it. How you're all detectives now.'

'It's just a bit of fun, Eimear. She's enjoying it and besides it's good for her to get out and about.'

'Not to crime scenes, Finn. What's wrong with you? And I heard all about you and Isabella.'

'Who told you that?'

'Mammy.'

Maura, it had to be said, had always been very intuitive.

'And she told me you were already flirting with Aoife Prendergast. Typical, Finn, just typical.'

'She said that.'

'She said you'd "taken a shine" to her. I know you, Finn.'

'Oh for God's sake. Mammy's not herself. She gets these ideas.'

'You need to cop yourself on.'
Other than that, there were few tensions at the celebratory lunch in the Radisson.

Chapter 23

'They're back.'

It was Saturday morning, ten days after Michael died. Finn was in his usual spot in Café Madremonte, splashing his huevos diablos with Tabasco, when Aoife broke the news.

'Eddie collected them from the airport last night. They have no plans for the day.'

'How do you know?'

'Eddie.'

'Sorry, of course.'

'They look very watery.'

Was she referring to his eyes?

'The eggs,' she clarified.

He looked up to make sure Ana wasn't within earshot of Aoife's disparaging remark.

'Her intentions are good.'

'I know exactly what her intentions are. The point is, they're going to be at home. Monika apparently needs a vigorous workout. And Barry has to catch up on some paperwork.'

'Eddie's a sponge. Fair play to him. But we can't just march in there.'

'We don't have any more time to waste, Finn. It's been ten days.'

'What do you suggest? You of all people can't show your face at Duggan's house, surely? Under any pretext.'

'Try and stop me.'

Finn, having suddenly lost his appetite, pushed his plate to one side. Slowly, reluctantly, he extricated his wallet from his too-tight jeans. In it was Monika's business card. He showed it to Aoife.

'Monika Kovačić-Duggan, Chartered Physiotherapist.'

'She's a big fan apparently,' admitted Finn reluctantly.

'Sure who isn't?' Aoife replied.

'No. That's—'

'You could tell her you've pulled a thigh muscle. I'm sure she could fit you in.'

'No, Aoife. I don't mean.'

He paused. He quite liked it when she displayed signs of jealousy even if it was only in jest.

'I think they want to hire me, Aoife.'

'Oh?'

'To do their garden.'

'Perfect. Give her a ring. Tell her we can pop around this afternoon.'

'We?'

'I could pretend to be your girlfriend. Tell her we're inseparable. Only thing, we might have to hold hands.'

'I am not holding your hand, Aoife.'

'Well, we can pretend we're a couple who've just had a fight. Probably more convincing.'

'Wait, I promised mam I'd bring her to Lismore. To see the gardens.'

'She can come with us. She won't want to miss this.'

'And Happiness?'

'Of course. We'll need security.'

Finn was sceptical. He scratched his beard.

'Barry has huge respect for Maura,' said Aoife taking a seat at Finn's table. 'He hates me and Redmond and Michael. He *really* hated Michael. But Maura? He loves Maura. She was so good to his mother. And to his wife. First wife. He won't refuse to see Maura.'

'Oh God, Aoife. Shouldn't we just leave this one to the guards? I'll call Xavier.'

He took out his phone. She put her hand over it.

'Call Monika!'

The other brunchers, forks frozen in hand, looked around at the commotion.

'Too loud?' Aoife whispered. Finn nodded.

'You need help, Finn?'

It was Ana from behind the counter. She was holding up a knife.

'You're grand, thanks, Ana. She's just leaving.'

'This is a nice place. *Tranquillo*. We don't want no trouble.'

Ana laid down the law fiercely before breaking into a magnificent, gap-toothed smile.

'Only joking with you, Aoife.'

Ana was only mite-sized, but having heard her stories – surviving a barrio in Barranquilla, and mountain-living in the Valle del Cauca – Finn was sure nobody in their right mind would dare cause trouble in Café Madremonte. There was no doubt that she would defend her customers to the death, especially – Finn had to accept somewhat uncomfortably – her tenant in the flat above the premises. Flouting all known tenancy rights, she would regularly let herself into his private quarters, help herself to his whiskey, regale him with scary, hilarious, eye-popping stories of her life in rebel-held parts of Colombia, all the while flirting with him unambiguously and unselfconsciously. In truth, he loved the company and the overt sexual tension.

When the diminutive proprietress's back was turned, just to be on the safe side, Finn scraped his uneaten breakfast into his reusable cup and smuggled it out of the cafe. Then he rang Monika.

At 2pm the four of them, Happiness at the wheel, Maura riding shotgun and Finn and Aoife in the back of the Yaris, arrived at the Duggan residence. After an interminable inspection by a pair of fussy, restless security cameras at the entrance, the steel gate, painted white, rolled back behind an impressively thick and well-maintained box hedge. The house itself at the end of a short gravel drive was ranch style, Southfork Ranch to be precise, in the sense that it was long and low, apart from one pillar-fronted two-storey bit. There was a conventional three-tiered fountain in the centre of the lawn not currently spouting water. *That will have to go*, Finn thought, as if he was actually about to pitch for a landscaping job instead of going to question his prospective employers about their part in a potential murder. Something contemporary in granite would be preferable. Sculpted eels came to mind. Or cowbells. Maybe that was just because Aoife's earring was tingling irritatingly as they bounced over the gravel. They'll be wanting trees no doubt either side of the avenue. Beech? He always liked beech although it wasn't exactly native. It was, however, to give it its due, introduced as far back as the sixteenth century. So in that sense it was every bit as native as, well, Protestants, for example. Finn wasn't as hung up as he used to be about such vexing questions as plant nativity, which tended to bring out the zealot in people. Everything, flora and fauna, ultimately came from somewhere else. He might suggest a maze. Yew trees.

'Finn. Finn. Wake up. We're here.'

Monika was at the door, sporting a Lululemon matching crop top and shorts. Cayenne possibly in colour. Finn didn't know where to look. He'd told her on the phone that he was bringing a party to Lismore but hadn't told her who.

'Oh,' she said, before coolly offering her hand to Aoife and the others. 'Come in.'

Barry was sitting on a high stool at the island. It was a vast kitchen. In fact there were three different islands dotted around the floor, a whole archipelago. While Happiness was examining the door action of the Gaggenau oven and the various appliances, murmuring approval, Barry climbed down from the stool using the island as leverage. He had a limp.

'Doing the foxtrot in Dubrovnik.'

'Barry is such a good dancer.'

'Slipped on a feckin' napkin so I did. Otherwise, Maura, me and you, hah.'

'You wouldn't be able to keep up with me.'

Maura dropped her stick and started a little shimmy, Happiness arriving just in time to prevent her falling to the floor. Monika put her arm around her husband's back, her hand burrowing under the elastic of his tracksuit bottoms. They kissed. If Barry was at all miffed by Aoife's presence, he didn't show it.

'Monsie love, get some lemonade for the ladies, I'll show Greenfingers around.'

A trio of robot lawnmowers toiled away uncomplainingly on the expansive, undulating meadow. There was an all-weather five-a-side football pitch away to the right, complete with floodlights. With a sweep of his arm Barry indicated a hollow about fifty yards from the house.

'A lake! What do you think? In the shape of a heart. Nothing tacky now. Or the shape of Croatia. She'd love that. What's the Prendergast one doing here?'

'Aoife? Oh her, yes, she's my ... She's a friend of my mother. We were on an outing. Monika suggested we drop by.'

Finn brazened it out. But Duggan seemed to buy it.

'I'd stay well away from that one, if I was you.'

'I forgot you and her had a ... a falling out.'

'That's one way of putting it.'

Duggan sized him up. The land was featureless apart from a huge pile of metal debris not far from the patio door in front of which they were standing.

'My first lorry,' Barry said emotionally. 'Roscoe. That's what I called him. I had him took apart.'

'Bad memories?'

'Are ya joking me? I owe everything to that lorry, so I do. Four hundred and eight thousand, two hundred and thirty-nine miles. Not kilometres now. Miles!'

'Wow!'

'I was thinking. A sycamore tree.'

'Right.'

'There.'

He pointed at the heap of junk.

'Yeah? D'ya see? It would grow up through the metal.'

'Okay. Right. I see what you're saying. Yes. You want the tree and Roscoe to sort of merge?'

'Correct. I saw a tree once in Scotland with a bicycle in it.'

'A living sculpture.'

He knew the tree. It was something of a tourist attraction. And he was dubious about its origin myth.

'I couldn't put it better myself. Can you imagine? A lorry, my lorry, Roscoe, suspended above in the sky. Is it feasible?'

'Well, they do grow fast. Sycamores. But the weight might be an issue. And they're not native to Ireland ...'

'It'll be worth your while.'

'It's not that, Barry. No. If it can be done, we'll do it. I'll tell you what. Leave it with me. Might be a case of two or three trees. We'll figure something out.'

'It was supposed to be me!'

'Sorry?'

'You know that, right? I was the intended victim.'

The men returned to the house to find the three sleuths standing around one of the islands while Monika, like a dolled-up saleswoman in a department store, was holding out a handful of some herbal concoction for them all to sniff.

'You told them?' Barry asked Monika.

'I had no choice. She ...' pointing to Aoife with a toss of her immaculately coiffed hair, 'more or less accused me of murdering Michael.'

'You know me, Barry,' said Aoife smiling.

Barry with no little difficulty climbed up onto his high stool.

'He stole my cup. If yiz were any good, yiz would have seen that.'

Monika and Barry explained to Finn that Barry only ever drank from his own cup, a distinctive red-and-white chequered mug. The other ladies present, choristers all, nodded in agreement. They already knew that. Furthermore, Barry didn't drink tea or coffee as a rule. He only ever drank herbal tea made from his own recipe.

'On account of the gout. She won't let me take ordinary conventional medicine.' He pointed a thumb at Monika. 'She has a problem with the pharmaceutical industry.'

'I don't trust them. We get it from a man in Offaly,' Monika interrupted. 'A herbalist. He's very famous. He was on *The Late Late Show*.'

The others could picture him alright. Tom Lawlor. A well-known quack. They used to say he could fix anything from the wing of a butterfly to the leg of a horse. And now too, apparently, the gout of a middle-aged man.

Monika held up a handful of the stuff. Finn could see that there were bits of thistle in there. Alfalfa. Nettle.

'Yes, yes and goldenrod,' she said testily, 'And hibiscus. And *uva ursi*.'

'Ah, feckit, I should have known,' said Finn, annoyed with himself that he didn't recognize the distinctive bearberry *arctostaphylos* leaf.

'It doesn't matter what's in it. That's not the point.'

It seemed that Barry kept a jar of his special tea in the community centre. Aoife, Maura and Happiness were able to testify to that.

'And nobody else would ever dare drink it.'

'Because they're afraid of what Barry might do.' Aoife turned to Finn provocatively. Barry, with an effort, more a technique that looked like it was learned in a class or an online tutorial, controlled his temper.

'No, Miss Prendergast. For your information. Because it is so horrible,' said Monika.

'It really is disgusting,' Barry agreed.

'I wouldn't even drink it,' his wife added.

'But you're saying Michael did?' Finn asked.

'Yes. Yes, now you have it. To wind me up.'

Barry reached for a sheet of kitchen roll to dab his sweaty brow.

'Monika made my tea at the break as per usual.'

'I can never forgive myself.'

'It's okay, love. Not your fault.'

'It was on the tray.' Monika wiped away a tear. 'Michael grabbed it and ran away. How could I stop him? I had both hands on the tray.'

Aoife nodded.

'It is the sort of thing Michael would do, in all fairness,' she conceded.

'I can't believe you didn't see any of this happening. Youse that know everything. I was fit to kill him, so I was, sorry, that came out all wrong.'

'Well, why didn't you just take your cup off him, Barry? It's not like you,' said Maura.

'Oh I was going to, believe me. But Monika here, she said to drop it. Didn't want a scene, didya, love?'

'I tell him, "Barry. Barry, he's just trying to goad you. Breathe."'

'Very calming influence, she has. I don't know what I'd do without Monika.'

He kissed her on the forehead.

'Barry has a bad heart.'

'Ah for feck's sake, Monsie! What are you telling them that for? It's fine. Just a bit of a flutter now and again. Arrim . . . arrimatea.'

'Arrhythmia.'

'She won't let me take the tablets.'

She kissed his forehead.

'I just want to keep you safe, darling.'

A sullen boy, he must have been about seven years old, entered the kitchen, making straight for the fridge. He had a mullet and was dressed in a grey tracksuit not dissimilar from the one his father was wearing.

'Barry!' his mother commanded. 'Say hello to our visitors.'

Finn looked to Aoife. He mouthed the word 'Barry' and screwed up his face.

'Hello,' he said grabbing a Sprite from the cavernous fridge.

'This is Barry.'

'What a handsome boy,' said Happiness.

'Luckily, he takes after his mother,' said Barry Senior adoringly.

The boy scampered off again.

'Barry?' questioned Finn. 'I thought Barry was your other son.'

'Correct. The half-wit you doorstepped last week at the yard.'

Barry Senior stared at Finn, as if to say *Yeah, and what's the problem?*

'So both your sons are called Barry ... no? I just didn't know if that was, I mean, is that even legal? Actually, no, it makes sense.'

'That's right. They both have my name. Gives them an advantage, you know, going forward, as they say. He's Little Barry.' He pointed at the door through which the boy had just left. 'The other eejit's Barry Junior.'

'Right.'

'So there's no confusion, you see? But Barry Junior, he needs to grow up.'

'Barry!' Monika cautioned her husband to calm down, the mere mention of Barry Junior obviously raising his blood pressure. From where they were sitting, they could literally hear his heart pounding. Very arrhythmically.

'He's useless. Little Barry there could run this company better than Barry Junior.'

'Right.'

Not for a moment comparing it to his own relationship with his father but Finn felt for Barry Junior.

Maura of all people got the conversation back to the point.

'You were about to tell us why you didn't take your cup back?'

'Look. It's simple. I decided to be the bigger person. Just ignore him. I've spent my whole life fighting with people.'

He looked at Aoife.

'Objectors, the county council, rival firms. But lately, last few months ...'

Tears came to his eyes. Monika held him.

'I don't know. I look around, and see what I've got. Monika, Little Barry, this place. This town. I've mellowed, so I have.'

Aoife snorted.

'Despite what some people might think. Could you be bothered? D'ya know? I forgive you, Aoife, by the way. I forgive Redmond too. I had already forgiven Michael. In my heart.'

There was a brief silence while the party contemplated the sincerity of Barry's epiphany. Happiness, who with great concentration had been following the ebb and flow of the discussion, frowned.

'Yes. But that does not explain how Michael died? The

preparation was disgusting to taste but not harmful to the body. The tea was not malignant.'

'Don't you see? Can't you get it into your thick skulls? Somebody must have tampered with the jar.'

He banged his fist on the island.

'Somebody replaced the tea, either replaced it, or mixed in some sort of poison, in my feckin' tea. Bottom line. Somebody tried to kill me. Not Michael. *Me!*'

'And I made the tea,' Monika added, biting her lip, before bursting into tears.

Chapter 24

'Stop the car!' Aoife screeched as they rounded a corner on the outskirts of town.

Happiness stood on the brakes. Luckily she was going so slowly there was very little chance of whiplash. Aoife leapt out of the car and crouched down at the side of the road. Finn joined her thinking she was going to be sick. Granted, the case had taken a sudden, dizzying lurch. If Barry and Monika were to be believed – and their evidence was convincing – then her friend Michael had died thanks to a silly prank on his part.

'I know, Aoife. It's a big shock.'

She turned to him with a dead toad in her hand. There was a yellow stripe on its back. Its stomach was everted.

'It's a natterjack.' She was shaking, more in fury than shock.

'How did you even spot that?'

'You know what this means?'

She ran along a path through a nicely maintained public space at the side of the road. He followed her. Moments later they arrived at the bog garden in Bully's Acre. Finn was quite surprised by how well developed it was, the pond surrounded by umbrella plants and purple loosestrife.

'That your idea?'

'Yes. I got it from your book.'

A bit of ligularia *and* sagittaria latifolia *would complement what's there*, he thought, the subtle yellow bottlebrushes of the former and the arrow shapes of the latter would provide a bit more drama. And maybe they could have done a better job concealing the unsightly pond lining. Or better still getting rid of it altogether. That would be a task for next year.

'Bastards.' She pointed at the pond.

There were pellets floating on the surface of the water. Finn took off his boots.

'I didn't know you wore cowboy boots.'

The intricate stitching had been hidden by his jeans.

'They were a present.'

'Disgraceful.'

'Ah c'mon. They're not that bad. I got them in Mexico. On my honeymoon.'

'I meant the vandalism.'

He casually waded into the pond, not caring about getting his clothes wet. Would he have done it if Aoife hadn't been there watching, if he hadn't wanted to impress her? He'd like to think he would have, for the sake of the natterjacks. And the Abbeyford Tidy Towns campaign to which he was now betrothed. He scooped up some of the pellets. Aoife slipped off her shoes and waded in after him. Finn bit into a pellet.

'That's revolting,' she said.

'Mmm, alfalfa. And is it, hay, Timothy hay? And if I'm not mistaken, that's molasses. Rabbit food. They're rabbit pellets.'

Aoife picked up an empty plastic 20kg bag of Deluxe Rabbit Mix she found in a clump of foliage.

'You're good. A bit feral but I'm seeing you in a new light.'

'Who would have done such a thing? Kids?'

'Are you joking? This is sabotage. It's very calculated, specific. An act of war. It's got to be Ennismore.'

They gathered up as many of the pellets as they could. Finn said he'd come back later with a net and fish out the remainder. Apart from the one dead natterjack, there were no other casualties.

'You see what we're dealing with, Finn. Ennismore will stop at nothing.'

While he was sceptical about Aoife's claim that a nearby town might have committed such an atrocity, he had no idea Tidy Towns was such a competitive sport.

Chapter 25

'You know what this all means of course?' Finn said, helping himself to more chicken.

'What?' replied Aoife.

'You are now the main suspect.'

It was the next day. Sunday. They were sitting around Maura's dining room table. It was very shiny, a mahogany table polished to within an inch of its life by Happiness. Finn could study the faces of the other diners in the reflection without anybody noticing what he was doing. Around the table were Aoife, Maura, Happiness and, somewhat unexpectedly, Redmond.

Finn, after dropping Happiness to her service and bringing his mother to mass, took it upon himself to prepare a Sunday roast. Maura had somehow or other invited Redmond. He wasn't quite sure how the pair of them communicated with each other, given that Redmond was mostly off-grid and Maura wasn't able to use her phone unaided. Carrier pigeon, presumably. Or telepathy.

'Yes. I suppose I am,' Aoife agreed.

'That must be very exciting, Aoife. Being a suspect,' said Maura.

'You'll have to go into hiding,' Finn joked, perhaps a bit too eagerly.

They smiled at each other across the table.

'These potatoes,' Redmond complained. 'They're hard.'

'They're al dente, dad.'

'You trying to get rid of me?' Aoife asked Finn, her eyes staying on him. For some reason he felt a warm, molten sensation in his stomach.

'I'd love to be a suspect,' said Maura, wistfully.

'You were once, dear,' muttered Redmond, closely testing the texture of the cabbage with a fork. 'Remember?'

There was a loud sigh.

'They are too hard. You have to boil them first,' said Happiness with something approaching glee.

'I did boil them, Happiness.'

'Well, I think they're lovely, Finn,' said Maura. 'They could have done with another few minutes but, all things considered, they're not bad at all.'

Finn, despite the provocations from around the table, believed in his potatoes.

'What do you mean, Redmond?' asked Aoife.

'What?'

'That Maura was a suspect?'

'Nothing. No. Ignore me!'

'I was questioned about Rameses' disappearance,' Maura announced proudly.

The clatter of cutlery abruptly ceased. They all stopped eating. And criticizing the roast potatoes. The carriage clock on the sideboard chimed four times.

'Oh, it's a long time ago now. I was the last person to see him alive.'

'That would make you the killer, Maura. Not just a suspect,' said Redmond a touch patronizingly.

'Oh yes, I see what you mean. He can be very pedantic.'

'And I'm pretty sure you didn't kill him, did you?' he added very patronizingly.

'You see, I went out with him, briefly, with Rameses, before your father,' Maura confided in Finn, his eyes widening at the revelation.

It was becoming clearer by the day to Finn that he barely knew his mother.

'Before I swooped in and swept her off her feet,' Redmond clarified.

'It's a sore point with himself. That night. The night of the big snow. He came back to the house. Rameses. After Redmond had gone out.'

The story was already shaping up to be subtly different from the one his mother had started telling Finn a couple of weeks ago.

'Maura, no!'

A few years ago, Maura might have acceded to her husband's wishes and dutifully kept quiet. But that of course wasn't the case any longer, her inhibitions considerably loosened after her brain injury, and more power to her. Mind you, Finn thought he detected a note of alarm in Redmond's command, as if he was more concerned about protecting her from incriminating herself than exercising husbandly control.

'He owed money, you see. Well, that's what Rameses told me. I gave him whatever I had.'

'Whatever I had,' Redmond mumbled.

'Whatever we had. It wasn't much. Certainly not enough. Poor Ram owed a lot of money.'

'To who?' asked Finn.

'Maura! Please,' his father pleaded.

'That's why he stole the eggs. To sell them.'

'What eggs?' asked Aoife, confused.

Maura, far away, didn't hear Aoife's question.

'He had this idea that there was gold in the hills.'

'Maura!' Redmond, getting increasingly exasperated, put his fork down and stood up.

'Yes. There is gold in the hills.' He took the reins from Maura. 'It's a geological fact. There are surveys to prove it. I don't know why we have to dredge this up now. Aoife, tell me, how is Shane?'

Before Aoife could answer Redmond, Maura, in something of a trance, intoned.

'They say you can still hear him up there, Rameses, on a still night, digging away,' said Maura.

Happiness shuddered, as if a cold hand had just touched her neck.

Everyone looked at Redmond. Not normally one to bow to pressure from anyone, he seemed to Finn, who was monitoring his father's reactions in the mahogany mirror, uncharacteristically uncertain. If anything, he appeared to be slightly intimidated by his wife, this new more assertive, all-seeing Maura. Plus, the portal to the past was undeniably open now, unlocked by Michael's sudden death and Maura's vivid memories. Knitting his eyebrows, Redmond directed a disapproving look at his wife. He sighed loudly, tut-tutted and poured himself a large glass of wine. With one of his knuckles, he rubbed an eye quite vigorously. Finn was afraid his dad would dislodge the eye if he wasn't careful.

'Eamonn de Burgh, Rameses, knew those hills better than anyone, even better than me. There was always gold there of course. From earliest times. Even the Milesians knew that.'

Not the bloody Milesians, Finn thought to himself. As his father had often reminded him, the Milesians arrived in Ireland two or three thousand years before Christ. There was a serious and present danger, Finn calculated silently, although Maths wasn't his strong suit, that Redmond had approximately five thousand years of history to wade through before he got to his point about Rameses' gold prospecting misadventures. Once Redmond was on a roll it was hard to stop him. His extraordinary recall of everything he'd ever read or heard, combined with his inherent didacticism and a deep love of his own speaking voice, meant in effect that he, expertly, left little or no opportunity for interruption. After some time during which the dinner went cold, and Finn drifted in and out of consciousness, Redmond finally reached the 1980s.

'Although I warned him repeatedly not to, he spilled the beans.'

By way of synopsis, if Finn had been following the story correctly, Rameses had been prospecting for years as a pastime up around Knockanore, panning in the burns, not too far from Coomshimgaun lake. Convinced he had hit a seam of sorts, he mentioned his findings to some select people in the town, people he'd regarded as friends and who might be in a better position than he to raise the finance to conduct a proper survey. They, these merchant princes, for want of a better term, promptly bought up a lot of the land on Knockanore at knock-down prices. It was land that was long considered useless, bog and scrub, mainly used for grazing sheep if anything at all.

'Who were they?' Aoife wanted to know. Redmond, who was usually so outspoken about everything and everybody, was remarkably reticent in this instance about the names.

'Just look at the land registry if you can't contain your curiosity.'

The surveys had confirmed that there were indeed significant gold deposits in the ground. A tight circle consisting of four reasonably well-off pillars of the community closed around Rameses. Not wanting to get their own hands dirty and certainly not wanting to register their intentions with the state, they 'lent' a substantial sum of money to Rameses. They then tasked him with setting up a rudimentary but ultimately secret and illegal mining operation. He, although fully aware that he was out of his depth, but exhilarated all the same by the danger, tried his best to honour his side of the bargain. He handed over the money, some forty thousand old Irish punts, to an acquaintance of his who'd recently been made redundant by a silver mine that had closed down in Tipperary. That man, who'd promised to procure equipment and personnel, subsequently did a runner.

'Neither hide nor hair of him never seen again.'

There was a brief hiatus while the house itself seemed to exhale and the dinner party digested the information.

What the hapless consortium thought they were going to dig up with such a relatively paltry sum of money was another story. It was a ludicrous scheme by any standards, in Redmond's telling. They would extract whatever gold they could find themselves, inconspicuously, without blasting or putting cumbersome rigs in place, before fulfilling their legal obligations by reporting the discovery to the authorities. Then, they firmly believed they would be further rewarded either by being stakeholders in a proper sanctioned working mine or by selling their land at hugely inflated prices. But in the absence of any sort of a mine, the men understandably wanted their money back. Although it was hard to believe, even for a cynic like Redmond, that these particular men would resort to violence, it was not impossible to imagine that Rameses might have met with an 'accident'.

The clock chimed five times.

'Sorry, go back, what have stolen eggs got to do with all this?' It was Aoife first off the mark.

'Eagle eggs,' Finn said. 'It's a long story. We should have dessert.'

His father, who earlier on had been trying to quash Maura's telling of the story, had no qualms now, now that he had taken ownership of the story, in bringing Aoife up to speed on Rameses' penchant for collecting rare eggs.

'Whoever has the egg, the third egg, is our man. He's the one.'

'Who killed Rameses?' Finn inquired.

'If he was killed,' said Redmond, adding cryptically, 'he's the man you're looking for.'

'Ridiculous.' It was Happiness. 'The egg would have hatched.'

'Exactly. I was about to ask that very question. Wouldn't the egg have hatched after forty years?' said Finn, eliciting a why-didn't-you-then look from Happiness.

'Obviously. It would have hatched. Or deteriorated. There are methods for preserving eggs as any good oologist will tell you.'

Finn felt a seminar coming on. In fairness to his father, he kept it brief. Most likely, he surmised, the collector would have drilled a tiny hole in the egg and 'blown out' the contents.

Redmond suddenly turned very quiet. He went into himself, as they say, absent-mindedly rubbing Maura's hand.

Finn had always been intrigued by Rameses' disappearance. He studied his strangely subdued father. Remembering their endless walks together when he was a boy, it suddenly occurred to him they weren't just looking for birds and rare wildflowers. There was the time when he, at possibly eight years of age, a rope tied around his waist, was lowered into an old mineshaft by Redmond to see if he could locate some lead moss. *Ditrichum plumbicola*. But now that he thought of it, perhaps he'd actually been looking for Rameses' body. His mother had asked him about the welt around his waist. Finn had told her his underpants were too tight. His father caught his eye. It was like he could read Finn's mind. Redmond nodded, it seemed to Finn, in acknowledgment that Finn was correct about the subtext of their adventures together. That nod also seemed to act as a blessing to Finn to do something he himself had never managed to do. Find Rameses! Finn, now quite tipsy, was also intrigued by the mention of a man called Shane.

'Who's Shane?' he asked, his lips stained with red wine.

'What?'

'No. You asked Aoife earlier. How's Shane? Who is he? Shane?'

'Oh you mean Shane Delahunt. Aoife's boyfriend.'

'Oh!'

Finn was nonplussed. He had assumed Aoife was single. Not that that was any of his business, but for some reason, he was a little saddened by that news. And, irrationally, took an instant dislike to this Shane, a person he'd never met.

'Well, I wouldn't go that far.' Aoife blushed slightly.

'Oh right. I didn't ... no. That's lovely. Who's for rhubarb crumble? There's pink peppercorns in it. And pomegranates.'

'For God's sake!' Redmond, back in the room again, scoffed. 'Pink peppercorns! In a crumble? I've heard it all now.'

'Dundee!' Happiness harmonized with the doubters.

'Happiness has a new admirer!' Maura let slip.

'Maura!'

'It's true. Alo Sweeney.'

'Good God!' spluttered Redmond.

'Could do worse, Happiness,' teased Aoife. 'He's rich. And distinguished. And he keeps bees.'

'I do not need a man in my life.' Happiness' voice deepened. 'And I can buy my honey at the supermarket.'

Happiness was pretty emphatic about that. She'd never said much about her life before she moved to Ireland, not to him anyway, but Finn got an inkling that it wasn't entirely without incident. Still, judging from her reflection in the table-top, she was quite flattered by the attention she'd received from Alo Sweeney.

Both Redmond and Happiness picked the pink peppercorns out of the rhubarb crumble while they all discussed more contemporary and more urgent matters in Abbeyford. If what Barry Duggan said was true, and they were inclined to believe it was, then Michael's horrific death was entirely inadvertent. Barry was the intended victim, and one had to assume his life was still in danger.

'But what if they were bluffing?' Aoife wavered. 'What if they were trying to lull us into thinking Barry was the target. And they themselves poisoned the herbal tea?'

'Yes, but they did not know that Michael was going to take the cup.'

'You're right, Happiness.'

Even Aoife had to admit defeat. Happiness made a point of drowning her crumble in an obscene ocean of cream. The woman would happily risk a heart attack rather than show appreciation for Finn's sublime creation – a dessert, incidentally, that had earned the praise of Paul Hollywood, no less, on Finn's otherwise ill-advised and forgettable appearance on *The Great Celebrity Bake Off*.

All their intrepid work to date was, it seemed, a waste of time. It was quite hard to swallow. Their sense of failure, not the rhubarb crumble. They also felt sheepish just thinking about the various people they'd already accused. Those they'd interviewed and upset. Fionnuala. Harry. Even Wolfie. They also felt guilty about delving into Michael's past. So what if he had mysterious origins and various aliases. The fallout from the Victory Festival hardly seemed to matter now.

Soon though the guilt subsided to be replaced by a renewed curiosity and a collective, unquenchable quest for justice. In this regard, the wine helped. And when that ran out, Redmond's home-made damson wine kept the fire in the belly burning. But where to begin again? Now, with Barry Duggan the intended victim, the list of suspects was endless.

Monika quickly rose through the ranks to take pole position in Aoife's new notebook. After all, she was the one who made the tea. At a casual glance, she would have a lot to gain financially by his death. Perhaps she knew rightly what nefarious adulterants were added to the mixture? Barry Junior was clearly a candidate too. Given the way he was treated by his father, and the dismissive way his father even spoke about him, surely he carried a grievance? While it made sense to concentrate on the immediate family, there were a lot of people, local and from further afield, who'd had run-ins with Duggan over the years. Redmond and Aoife, for example both scarred by their stints in jail although they'd never show it, would most likely be classified as persons of interest in a normal murder inquiry.

'And so would Shane,' said Redmond.

Finn feigned disinterest.

'Where is he now, Aoife?' asked Maura.

'Shane? Who knows?' she replied, also feigning disinterest. 'Tanzania, I think, East Africa. You know Shane.'

Shane Delahunt, it turned out, worked for an obscure NGO, GreenHope. He was a climate-change activist currently helping to organize a protest in East Africa against an oil pipeline. It was clear too, although he hadn't been jailed, that he'd played a heroic part in downsizing Duggan's waste disposal plant. But was he in town two weeks ago when Michael died?

'A proper person,' declared Redmond pointedly. Finn rose above what he perceived to be a dig at himself. 'Not afraid to get his hands dirty. Doesn't worry about his reputation.'

That stung a little. His father in a roundabout way, it was true, had asked him to attend one of the protests against the incinerator. Without giving Finn the satisfaction of spelling it out, the implication was that Finn's presence there would have attracted more media attention. But Finn hadn't been available that day for a good reason. He'd been a guest on the panel show *Would I Lie to You?* To his father, a man who didn't have a television set and didn't understand the concept of panel games, or why someone would blatantly lie in public, that was incomprehensible. Furthermore he was appalled that a serious gardener would 'sell out', as he put it, by appearing on such a frivolous show. Finn had convinced himself that he had accepted the invitation so he could promote rewilding and biodiversity, but had to admit, as a fan of the show, he was just flattered to be asked. Since then, his father's contempt ringing in his ears, he had made a concerted effort to distance himself from the concept of 'celebrity culture'.

'Shouldn't we hand this over to the guards?' Finn said, slurring his words, in what he thought was a reasonable manner.

'*No!*'

Both Redmond and Aoife were vehemently opposed to contacting the Gardai. Happiness got to her feet. She grabbed a tea towel and waved it in the air. It was to all intents and purposes a surrogate conch which instantly bestowed upon her speaking rights. She felt strongly that they should continue their investigation.

'Independent of the police.'

But to Finn's surprise, she partially agreed with him and insisted that they share everything they'd learned 'thus far' with the Gardai. Two for and two against involving the guards. All eyes turned to Maura. Reminding Finn of the Tidy Towns meeting, it was down to her to cast the deciding vote. Maura stroked the tarantula that was Redmond's hairy hand.

'I don't think we should tell them everything . . .'

'Now Maura . . .'

'No, no . . .'

Happiness handed her employer the makeshift conch. In her soft-spoken but authoritative way, Maura quelled dissent.

'But! But we should try and find out what they know.'

'Amen!'

Finn could sense what was coming.

'Finn, you should talk to that nice lad, whatshisname...?'

'Xavier.'

'Ask him. And if that means sharing a little smidgen of what we know, so be it.'

'Mammy, it's not that simple. Xavier's a guard. He's bound by all sorts of rules. Confidentiality. GDPR. All that red tape... Besides, he might have the same idea. He might get everything out of me and give feck-all in return.'

'Now that wouldn't surprise me,' chuckled Redmond.

'I'm sure you'll figure it out, Finn. Do you know, I think I need a lie down.'

Chapter 26

Finn had given Xavier a shout ostensibly to talk about building a tree house for his children. He'd thought he might visit Xavier at his home where they might have a beer in the garden, listen to some good music, discuss dimensions and materials, and who knows, maybe the Garda investigation into the death of Michael Dunlop might come up. It didn't quite pan out like that.

Xavier, as it happens, along with Valerie, had been instructed to 'reach out' to Finn for a more formal chat about 'just what the hell they thought they were doing interfering in a Garda investigation'.

'The super, Breslin, is hopping mad. Blaming me as usual.'

Finn didn't want to be seen to be talking to the guards and so refused his old friend's invitation to go to the Garda station. Nor did he want them visiting him in the cramped confines of the café where everybody as a rule tuned in to everybody else's business. To ingratiate himself with the Gardai, he asked to be put through to Valerie. Last time they met, she had expressed an interest in reopening the De Burgh case. So, by way of an olive branch, he told her if she still wanted to know what might have happened to Rameses de Burgh that she should go to the land registry.

There, he suggested, she should take a note of who bought what in the various townlands around Knockanore in the year before Rameses disappeared.

   They'd arranged to meet on Tuesday, a full two weeks after Michael was killed, near the old handball alley. It was to be a chance encounter. The concrete floor of the alley, at Finn's request, had been jack-hammered away. In the meantime, he had purveyed a foot of what he hoped was low-nutrient topsoil, sixty by thirty feet, from a building site in Keane Street, and after mixing it with a bit of sand, had laid it down between the concrete walls. Today he was sowing wildflower seeds, all native, with neither hope nor despair. Setting aside his aversion to colour for the common good, he scattered such species as red clover, corn marigold, lady's bedstraw, corn poppy, cornflower, yellow rattle, red campion, purple loosestrife, kidney vetch, teasel and lesser knapweed. Time was of the essence. Would anything flower before the judges came to town? Would anything flower at all? In his mind, he saw what they would ideally see, a kerfuffle of colour, teeming with bees and butterflies, a novelty biodiverse garden utilizing the eyesore ruin of an existing amenity. Catnip, surely, to a box-ticking Tidy Towns' adjudicator. Even if the garden didn't bloom in time, or ever, for that matter, would that even be a problem? It was the effort that counted, wasn't it, the intent? As long as Abbeyford could demonstrate that they had a clear plan in place, they would get the extra marks.

   After sowing the seeds and rolling the soil, Finn planted a scarecrow he'd made over the weekend in the middle of the ball alley. With the help of his mother and Happiness, using straw and netting and old tights, they frankensteined a convincing creature into shape, dressing it in Redmond's old clothes. Maura joked about taking him to bed with her, which almost made Happiness laugh. In fact, she'd had to expend an enormous amount of energy working those facial muscles and that mighty diaphragm to suppress an escape of laughter. Maura, meanwhile, was laughing so much at her own ribald remark Finn thought she was going to faint. In fairness, with the hat and the old tan ranch jacket made out of hemp, and the addition of a blackthorn stick, the scarecrow did bear an uncanny resemblance to his father. Some Freudian impulse directed Finn to add a bushy reddish-grey beard to the head, and to get the proportions exactly right, the pot belly and the slightly fey stance. He resisted the temptation to stick needles in the finished article – Redmond's avatar – but did take a measure of satisfaction, a scintilla of psychic healing, from his handiwork.

He had stem cuttings of native Irish ivy, *hedera hibernica*, taking root in Maura's garden. In a week or so, he'd plant them along all three walls of the alley. By then it would be safe to remove the scarecrow. They could ceremonially bury straw Redmond after a suitable wake. In time the birds would find shelter in the ivy and join the bees and the butterflies atop the psychedelic carpet of wildflowers. It could conceivably, if he said so himself, look incredible. He actually surprised himself by his growing enthusiasm for the project. Felt elated. Then Xavier showed up. And Valerie.

Xavier looked smart, like Alain Delon, in a dark blue crew-neck pullover, trench coat flapping in the breeze. Unlike Alain Delon, he was eating a bag of crisps. Tayto cheese and onion to be precise.

'Lunch. Garda diet. Used to play tennis here against the wall, do you remember?'

'Tennis squash.'

'That's right. I had a Sampras wristband.'

He waved at the figure in the centre of the ball alley.

'Howarya, Redmond, don't see you too ... Jaysus!'

Xavier jumped backwards a couple of feet, the crisp packet leaping from his hand, at the sight of Redmond's lifeless doppelganger.

'Near put the heart crossways. So it did.'

'What's the story?'

It was Valerie, eyes scoping the scene, taking everything in, dying to find something, anything out of place. Her hair was scraped back in a severe ponytail. It looked painful. She had a Manila folder in her hand.

'You think it's all a big joke?'

'Sorry, Valerie, I—'

'Sending me on a wild goose chase in the middle of a murder case?'

Finn's ears pricked up.

'Oh. So it was murder?'

Xavier winked at him. Valerie handed him the folder.

'No iPad today?' Finn asked, trying to lighten the mood.

Xavier stooped comically with his hands over his ears, eliciting a filthy look from Valerie.

'God, Finn. Whatever you do, don't mention the iPad!'

Not waiting for him to retrieve the documents from the folder – photostats of land registry files – Valerie excoriated him.

'Shell companies! Registered in the Cayman Islands. No names apart from a solicitor above in Dublin who won't answer the phone. Do I look like a forensic accountant?'

He quickly scanned through the pages. All the land in question was owned by two companies, either Whitestairs Holdings or CosRoe Holdings. There was a click in his brain. Something about one of those company names triggered a connection.

'What?'

She was quick. She could hear clicks in someone else's brain, and had the ability to tell when connections were being triggered.

'Nothing. No. I'm just so sorry. I had it on good authority the answer was to be found there.'

He glanced instinctively towards the scarecrow. A thought, a name had sprung to mind, but Finn decided he wasn't going to tell her what it was in case he was wrong again.

'Breslin laughed in my face, didn't he, when I asked for the help of financial crime.'

Xavier nodded along, clearly enjoying the memory of their boss laughing at Valerie.

'It was the same day she dropped the iPad.'

'Xavier! I swear to God.'

'She was in a bad mood that day. Absolute fouler.'

'I'm in a bad mood every day. So you would be if you had to put up with this one.'

She pointed at her partner. He shrugged.

'She doesn't mean that. Loves me really.'

'The superintendent said he didn't have enough resources to throw at the Dunlop case never mind a cold case from forty-odd years ago.'

'In his opinion, there was no evidence of a murder,' Xavier joined in, smugly. 'I could have told her that. Or for that matter, a financial crime. He told golden girl here to stop wasting his time and do her job. It was more colourful than that, the way he put it, but you get the gist.'

'So Michael was murdered?'

'We're not at liberty to discuss an active murder investigation.'

'You just more or less told him there,' said Valerie.

'Well, you said it first. Few minutes ago. Okay, listen, Finn. Between ourselves, Michael, God rest him, was murdered. Now, look, I know Aoife was a good friend of his and I know she's got a bee in her bonnet about this and that but we have it all in hand. Trust me. The point is, it's very, very important that you guys walk away. Right now. I know you mean well. And you're sound. And we go way back. But the last thing either of us want is for Aoife or you or your mother, for the sake of argument, to be arrested and, you know, charged with … It's an offence under section 41 of the Criminal Justice Act to … ehh … she'll know the exact wording.'

He tossed his head towards Valerie.

'Article (b).'

'It was supposed to be Duggan,' Finn said, ignoring the warning.

The detectives looked at each other.

'How do you know that?'

'So it's true?'

Xavier nodded. He rubbed his jaw. Finn could tell he was dying to open up. Special wanted to impress his old school friend with how capable he was, how accomplished. He wanted acknowledgement. Respect. Like most people. What's the point of knowing stuff if you can't tell people what you know? More than most people, perhaps, in Finn's estimation, Xavier just wanted an occasional pat on the back.

'Dunlop was just unfortunate. Wrong place, wrong time.'

'You mean O'Driscoll?' interrupted Finn, watching them for a reaction.

The detectives didn't disappoint. They looked completely baffled. Xavier actually walked around in a circle.

'Let's go for a stroll,' Valerie suggested, trying to wrest back control of the conversation. They went for a walk by the river. They passed Nathan, Aoife's nephew, who was lying belly down on the grass, a pair of binoculars fixed to his face.

'Any luck?' asked Finn.

'No.'

'Shouldn't you be in school?' asked Valerie.

'No.'

Xavier looked at his watch. It was lunch break. They walked on, Finn by way of reciprocation hoping to impress his old school friend *and* Valerie with his knowledge and ingenuity. He started big, with Michael's real identity. Slowly he peeled away Michael's various guises. No slouches, they knew all about the St John Fitzmaurice incarnation and the Victory Festival. But they didn't know he was an O'Driscoll from Baltimore.

Xavier whistled.

'The pirates!'

'What?' asked Valerie, the reference escaping her.

'The O'Driscolls were a fierce pirate clan until Baltimore was sacked by even fiercer pirates from the Barbary Coast in 1641.'

Xavier seemed pleased to know something she didn't.

They sat on a bench. Two swans glided by, eyeing them suspiciously. On the opposite bank was the timber yard, the incessant saw-noise buzz-killing an otherwise tranquil scene on what was the beginning of the new greenway. Finn made a mental note to do something about the stark, steel palings around the yard, and about the sound hygiene. It would be great, he thought, to have an early warning system in place, for when the judges came to town. Something like the tsunami siren in San Francisco. As soon as a judge was spotted, the siren would go off, and the machines would instantly shut down. Mind you the siren itself might be more annoying than the saw. Maybe a circular email to all the noisy businesses around the town would do the trick. Or a WhatsApp message.

Valerie levelled with him, her ambitions to solve the case trumping her fear of Superintendent Breslin's wrath.

'Okay. We have the toxicology report. It's just preliminary now.'

'It was me,' said Xavier. 'I got my hands on it.'

'I'm all out of jelly tots,' said Valerie, getting impatient.

'No. It's just ... A friend of mine in the lab. Met her at a Pixies concert above in the Olympia a few years ago. Sorry. Go on Valerie.'

'They found traces of ...'

'Stop don't tell me.' Finn put his hand to his head like a clairvoyant. 'Barbados nut.'

The detectives swapped puzzled looks. Valerie went on.

'Traces of monkshood, oleander, hemlock, foxglove, jimsonweed, some sort of rare belladonna, they're still working on that one, lily of the valley, apricot pips in powder form, Barbados nut and ...'

'I knew it.'

'Congratulations, and castor beans. Whoever did it. They weren't leaving anything to chance.

'Do you hear that? All from memory,' said Xavier in awe. 'She's like one of those child prodigies you used to see on the Wogan show who can recite pi to a thousand decimal places. Were you raised entirely on cod liver oil, Valerie?'

Somebody had gone to a lot of trouble to make sure Barry Duggan died. Naturally, Finn recognized the plants and their infamous properties. As well as being a gardening guru, he had read detective novels since he was a child, which obviously featured all of the poisons Valerie had listed in multifarious plot contrivances. Many of them were readily available, although preparing them for such a villainous exercise would require dedication and expertise. One or two of these species might have sufficed to kill a man. All of them together would floor a herd of elephants. It was most likely the work of somebody who was not unfamiliar with flora and/or crime fiction. The murderer, Finn surmised, was also a very thorough person and/or seriously unhinged.

'We found a jar in the kitchenette off the choir room. An ordinary sweet jar.'

'Skull and crossbones drawn on it in black marker?'

'Yeah, how did you know? I think it was Duggan's idea of a joke. It was the jar he kept his herbal tea in.'

'Right.'

'The Duggans aren't co-operating by the way.'

'No surprise there.'

'No. We know somebody added this mixture to the jar between choir practice the previous Tuesday and choir practice the night Michael died. Unfortunately there's no CCTV.'

'I can help you there.'

Finn filled them in about Noel 'Wolfie' Whelan's issue. The guards seemed grateful. One less lead to follow up. And hopefully a bit of leverage for Finn.

'We have to assume it was somebody who knew he drank this particular herbal tea, somebody who attends choir practice.'

'Or somebody close to him.'

'Monika?' Finn asked.

Xavier hesitated. But Valerie's silence gave him permission to go on.

'We're thinking Barry Junior. Alo Sweeney, the solicitor, you know, tall fella, looks like a ghost, big bags under the eyes.'

'Ah yes, he was at the Tidy Towns meeting.'

'He would be alright. That would be his sort of thing. Well, Alo reported an attempted break-in at his office about a month ago. Now we looked into it; nothing was taken or anything as far as we know. They never got as far as the safe. But eyewitnesses, two different people, saw Barry Duggan Junior running away.'

'What's that got to do the attempted murder of Barry Senior?'

'I'm coming to that. Normally, we wouldn't pay too much attention to Barry Junior. You think, *that's just Barry*, Barry's always in some kind of trouble or another, nothing too serious now, you know. He's just your classic messer. But there's talk that Barry Senior had just recently made out a new will.'

'Right.'

'You see. Alo Sweeney is Barry Duggan Senior's solicitor. Look, Valerie, he's seeing the light.'

Finn nodded.

'Now of course we don't know the contents of that will but we're going on the premise that maybe Barry Junior was, let's say, concerned about what that new will might entail.'

'It might have been just a robbery.'

'It might. But there was no money in the office. Barry

Junior would have known that. He's actually very friendly with Alo. Alo Sweeney's his godfather.'

It was glaringly obvious that the police, although seemingly far from incompetent, needed help. Finn had no intention of offering any, especially after being warned, in no uncertain terms, off the case. But Finn did happen to mention that he'd been asked by Monika and Barry Senior to design a garden for them. At that, their eyes lit up. They went into a brief huddle before emerging with an offer as he knew rightly they would.

'Now look. This didn't come from us. But it would be great if you could take that job.'

'What?'

'And keep an eye on the Duggans.'

'Me?' He feigned coolness.

'We have a patrol car checking in on him every half an hour, on his house and his yard. He doesn't want it, mind you. But to have eyes inside the house would be fantastic. Wouldn't it, Valerie?'

Valerie didn't seem sure, but Xavier continued.

'It would be unbelievable.'

'I don't know.'

'We're not asking you to do anything risky, Finn, but if you happened to stumble upon the will, like. Or, you know, notice any suspicious behaviour by Barry Junior, or Monika, we would hugely appreciate it.'

'So let me get this right. Just there, a while ago, you were telling me to "walk away". You were threatening to arrest my mother if I didn't stop. And now, if I understand you correctly, you're asking me to help, no, you're actually pleading with me to go undercover, into the actual lion's den.'

Valerie, a blink betraying just a flicker of vulnerability, a tiny hint of nervousness, a momentary fear of failure, swallowed her pride.

'It would greatly help in our investigation, Mr O'Leary.'

Chapter 27

A week later, on the Wednesday, although his body still hadn't been released, there was a memorial service for Michael of the Many Names in Morrissey's Bar. Many members of the Abbeyford tennis club were in attendance, all by arrangement, wearing their red tracksuit tops bearing the club logo. Some of them also brought their tennis rackets with the vague intention of forming some sort of guard of honour although in the absence of remains the opportunity didn't arise. The choir of course was well-represented. Aoife, Happiness and Maura were safely ensconced in a banquette not far from the piano, although the company of Maura's gossipy friend Kitty Doyle, meant they themselves had to be more circumspect than usual. Kitty had inserted herself among them, knowing full well that they were actively involved in investigating Michael's death. She of course, having been actively involved in making the tea at the choir practice, was not beyond suspicion herself.

A very emotional Harry Boyle was doing the rounds, grasping hands extended in condolence with his own. Fionnuala was there in a hosting capacity, greeting family and friends and well-wishers from the community. Meanwhile, behind the bar Hector Morrissey was on his phone, live-streaming a toy-car auction taking place in Tennessee, USA.

Despite it being a poignant affair, there was a hum of excitement in the air, given that Sir Nicholas Nguyen-Bow was at the gathering. Nicky, as he insisted on being called when he was in residence at his Irish retreat, was richly tanned, his thin frame held together in an exquisitely tailored grey suit, his thinning hair structured into a bouffant quiff by some rare mousse available only to the rich and famous. His presence meant that the inevitable sing-song in honour of Michael would be of a higher calibre than previously imagined. The choir's musical director, Wolfie, was put out. He had no right to be for he had a strict, self-imposed policy of never stepping foot in a bar under any circumstances since he'd found sobriety. Mind you, being the paranoid sort, he came to the conclusion that the only reason they were holding the memorial in a bar in the first place was to exclude him.

'Himself not here tonight?'

It was the bar manager, Eve Duggan, addressing Aoife.

'Who? Shane?'

'Finn.'

'I wouldn't know, Eve. I'm not a stalker. Why don't you ask his mother?'

Aoife was unusually peevish this evening. She hadn't heard from Shane in months and she objected to the rumours going around town associating her romantically with Finn. Granted, she was quite annoyed that he hadn't turned up, not, she quickly reminded herself, because she was missing his company per se, but because he was missing Michael's memorial. And, she acknowledged after her second drink, because she was actually missing his presence too.

'Don't mind her, Eve,' said Maura. 'Finn wanted to be here but he had another engagement.'

'The life of a celebrity, hah! He must get invited to all sorts of fancy dos. Probably meeting the president or something?'

Eve, although married to Barry Duggan Junior, always seemed impervious to any hassle, slight or otherwise. Whether it was a rude remark from an irate customer, or furniture being thrown through the window at an unruly wedding, it was all the same to her. She'd worked in Morrissey's for seven or eight years. No matter how busy she was, or harassed, she remained calm and made time for everybody.

'I think he was afraid he'd have to sing in public,' said Maura, holding Eve's hand.

Eve smiled.

'Oh yeah, I heard about that. We were short-staffed that night. I couldn't get away.'

She went silent and bowed her head. A lot of people had similarly paused for reflection over the preceding weeks when they suddenly recalled the awful event that had led to this evening.

'It's back next week, the choir,' Maura announced. 'Harry insisted. We'll see you there?'

Eve, meek as she was, was a valuable member of the choir.

'I'll be sure to be there. I missed it, so I did.'

She hesitated. They all looked at her.

'Don't believe what they say about Barry, my Barry. He wouldn't hurt a fly. Same again?'

'Lovely.'

Eve cleared away the glasses just as Harry, divested now

of his corduroy jacket, his bulk restrained in a tight-fitting tank top, rested a hand on Nicky's piano. He opened his lungs and, lips quivering, launched into 'Over the Rainbow'. Nicky was best known for his commercial successes, most notably 'Checkpoint', about the fall of the Berlin Wall, and his flop 'Sabotage', which although he always denied it was actually about Brexit. But he was first and foremost in his own mind a virtuoso pianist. By the first note, thanks to the tuning and the tone and the timing, the entire audience was spellbound. By the second line, 'way up high', they were all, including Hector Morrissey who was waiting for lot number 144, a die-cast 1956 Chevrolet Bel Air, in tears.

Chapter 28

'Pass!' Barry Duggan Senior shouted at his son. He was in goal, a general leading his army from behind.

Barry Duggan Junior received the ball in space on the right wing. His first touch was heavy, the ball skidding forward, perilously close to the touchline.

'Pass the bloody ball!'

The sound of his father's hoarse voice in his ears, he chased after it with all his might, with all the grace and agility of a bag of coal. Somehow he reached the ball before Declan Doyle. After about four touches he got it under control. The fourth touch, another heavy one, fortuitously took the ball beyond a lunging Doyle.

'For feck's sake. Pass! PASS!' Barry Senior bawled.

Barry Junior, the wind in his sails now, had a clear sight at goal. He hadn't played this well for a while. It was halfway through the first half and his father's team, in pink bibs, were losing 1–0. And his father didn't like losing. This was his chance to show them all he still had it. It was all down to him. The goalie hesitated, not sure whether to come off his line or stay. He inched forward. Barry Junior, imagining a whole new future for himself – cleaning up his act, getting fit, being entrusted with his father's business – was thinking of a lob. Even his father would be impressed by that. He leaned back, preparing to use his foot as a wedge to dink the keeper, visualizing the claps on the back from his teammates, the respect of his opponents, his father's pride, when he was clattered from behind by Dominik. Big Dom, all six foot four of him, lean muscle and spite. Where the hell did he come from? Dominik, although he had the build of a centre half, was a natural athlete who covered every inch of the five-a-side pitch like a panther. Barry fell awkwardly face first on the all-weather surface sustaining for himself nasty carpet burns on his forehead and cheekbone. And, by the vacant look in his eyes, a concussion.

'I told ya to feckin' pass, ya thick gobshite!'

Barry Senior, well kitted out in goalie gloves, padded tights and knee supports, kicked a goalpost in frustration. Finn, wearing a blue bib, helped Barry up.

'You okay?'

'I'm grand,' he said, clutching a hamstring. He hobbled off the pitch towards the house, a grinning Declan Doyle giving him a sarcastic clap as he did so.

'Well played, Baz!'

Finn, now on the payroll, had been invited to play in Duggan's regular Wednesday night football match. He'd been to the house a couple of times since agreeing to 'consult' on their ambitious garden design. Like all the other players, he was searched by Dominik on the way in. Although uniformed Gardai routinely parked outside the property to deter any would-be assassins, Finn couldn't entirely relax, certainly not enough to go snooping around the house. Apart from anything else he was rarely left alone. Barry and Monika were not just keen to discuss their landscaping plans, but seemed to enjoy having him around. They liked the cachet and his celebrity-adjacent stories. This was excruciating to Finn, the anecdotes having to be forcibly extracted from him with champagne as a loosener. Despite his medium-profile career on TV and radio and occasional appearances on the likes of *Bake Off*, he didn't see himself in any way as a celebrity per se. The very term was anathema to him. Barry was particularly impressed that Finn had met the current king when he was but a prince, mind you. It was at the Chelsea Flower Show. The Prince and his consort stopped at Finn's garden. Recognizing that he was Irish, the Prince whispered to him dryly, 'Sorry about Cromwell!' Barry thought that this was absolutely hilarious and made him repeat the story to everybody they encountered in the meantime. When Barry and Monika weren't on his heels, hanging on to his every word, Dominik, one of Barry's security team and, as it turned out, Monika's brother, was usually not too far away. Just as he was on the football field – powerful, stealthy, with impeccable timing – so he was in the house. A couple of days ago, for example, he'd arrived in the kitchen to make a smoothie at the precise moment Finn had planned to access Barry's unattended laptop. If it wasn't Dominik giving him the creeps, it was his more volatile partner, the malnourished-looking skulker, Karl. Earlier in the week he'd had quite a scare.

Barry had been at work. There was no sign of either Dominik or Karl. Monika had gone for a run, bronzed in full make-up. Finn had decided to go with Barry's suggestion of a lake in the shape of Croatia as he quite liked the challenge of the croissant shape. As long as Barry didn't demand red-and-white-chequered water. He'd been working out a potential perimeter with a measuring wheel when Monika, in a high-stepping running style, had jogged past him towards the woods at the north-eastern corner of the estate where he knew there was a gate. As soon as she exited the gate, he rolled the wheel back towards the house and abandoned it at the patio door. Slung across his body was a satchel with his notebooks and pencils. A long time since he'd been so frightened, he bounded a very wide staircase up to the first floor. The entire floor, the central two-storeyed part of the mansion, consisted solely of the master bedroom suite. The bed, a super-king, was covered in an oversized gold damask bedspread that probably weighed a ton. It's a wonder Barry and Monika weren't crushed at night. The sheets were black. He didn't know what he was looking for. A safe, he supposed, preferably with the door open or, at least the number combination scrawled on a scrap of paper. Or better still, a copy of Barry's will lying on the bedside locker. A threatening letter. Some clue that would hint at the identity of the person who wanted Barry dead. In the unlikely event he did find anything incriminating or enlightening, he doubted he'd have the cop-on to recognize it.

The bedroom, together with his and hers walk-in wardrobes and the ensuite bathroom, was huge. It would take a week to search it properly. He had minutes. The double-size spa bath had two faux-leather headrests, blue-glass panels on the side and underwater lighting. That bath alone was bigger than Finn's flat. There was an exercise bike in one corner of the bedroom, parked in front of a TV screen that was flush against the wall. He went back into Barry's walk-in wardrobe and quickly searched a floor-to-ceiling bank of drawers, needing a step chair to reach the top ones. He was nervous, a hose of adrenaline spraying his insides. It reminded him of the time his father had left him at the bottom of a rock face while Redmond, in just his sandals and shorts and with a camera around his neck, climbed the cliff with the intention of photographing a peregrine falcon. Finn was convinced that his father would fall to his death and that he would be left alone, never to be found, destined to wander the mountains until he was savaged by wolves. Mind you, he thought, if he was disturbed, he could just jump into one of the oversized drawers where he could remain hidden for weeks.

There was a photograph of Barry's late wife in a silver frame resting on his bedside locker. What did Monika make of that, he wondered. He picked it up. The sleeves of her wedding dress were rolled up to her elbows, like she herself had just wiped up some punch that had spilled on the ballroom floor. She had a lovely shy smile. Finn noticed a bulge in the backboard. He took apart the photo frame, delicately prising open the soft metal tabs securing the board in place. Between the backing and the photograph was a lock of hair, Imelda's presumably, the name of Barry's wife coming to mind. While putting the photo back together, he accidentally let the glazing drop on the bedside locker. Finn held his breath. He could feel his heart thrashing deep inside his chest, thumping away like a hostage buried alive beating his coffin lid. Luckily, just a small shard of the glass had broken away. It was a clean break, meaning he was able to fit it neatly to the plate, leaving only a barely noticeable hairline crack. Satisfied with the repair job, hands on his hips, he looked around the room. There was something about the television. He sat on the exercise bike. That's it! There was no remote control. He looked under the bed, almost slipping a disc with the weight of the bedspread. On a whim, he picked up the photographs that stood on Monika's dressing table amongst the expensive creams and lotions. He wasn't that interested in who the people were in the pictures. No, thinking Monika might have the same idea as Barry, he was looking for unusual bumps in the mounting boards. Sure enough, there was one behind a photo of an old couple, Monika's parents on a boat, the father's lined face like closely spaced isobars on a weather map of a very windy day. After carefully dismantling the photo frame, he found a key, hidden between the glossy print and the foam-board backing. Curious! It was at that moment he heard the patio door opening and closing. In a panic, his hands shaking, he managed to restore the photo and the key to the frame and run to the window.

'Finn! What are you doing here?'

'Monika! I'm—'

'Are you tired? Perhaps you wanted a little sleep? In my bed?'

'Oh Monika, I'm so sorry. You were out. I . . .'

He showed Monika a notebook he'd managed to whip out of his satchel in the nick of time. Fortunately, he had already drawn some preliminary sketches of the lake, the sycamore-lorry monstrosity, the fountain, the driveway, trees, beds, hedgerows, a contemplation garden, a treehouse, a potting shed, a sandpit, various follies and even a maze. Monika smiled, her eyes glittering above her perfectly proportioned nose.

'Yes, but I don't remember asking for a tree in the bedroom.'

At this juncture, she casually removed her hoodie right in front of him.

'It's very warm today, no,' she said, enjoying his discomfort, as she entered her walk-in wardrobe.

'The lake. I just have to make sure it's in the right position.'

He was pointing a digital laser device out the window as she came back into the room. She was pulling a lurid green and ludicrously revealing mesh running vest over her head. Sweat beads were glistening on her shapely arms.

'The right angle, the distance,' he stammered, eyes on the fields, 'you know, the ... the ... the aspect. Not much use if you can't see it, is there? The lake.'

'Mmm.'

She lay on her back, splaying her legs in the air, in a jaw-dropping yoga pose.

'Perhaps you are trying to find out where I keep my supply of hemlock.'

Finn laughed nervously.

'Just doing my job, Monika. How did you know about the hemlock?'

'I guessed.'

'Not a bad guess.'

She bounced up off the floor.

'I was there. I saw Michael die. His mouth ... foaming. That is a sign of hemlock poisoning, no?'

'I wouldn't know.'

Finn could hear the front door opening.

'Monsie!'

It was Barry.

'My husband is a very jealous man. If he finds you in here with me ...'

She placed her palm on his chest.

'I don't know what he is capable of.'

Finn swallowed.

'Well, I won't tell him if you don't.'

'He might kill you,' she leaned into him, her hot breath stimulating his ear. Then she shouted.

'In the bedroom, darling.'

And with that, laughing, she skipped down the stairs. There were no wires coming from the television set. Right? No cables. And no sockets. He suspected it was a fake screen and that the safe was behind it. As for the key behind the photograph of Monika's parents, he had no idea what that was for. A cabinet of some sort. A locker. A suitcase. Maybe it wasn't important. If it was, it would be in the safe, wouldn't it? Unless she didn't want Barry to know what it was for.

By now, his legs had turned to jelly. Not normally a believer, he prayed that there was no CCTV in the master bedroom.

Not only was Finn afraid of being caught prowling around the Duggan home, he was literally afraid of being killed. If somebody did want to bump off Barry, there was a danger, as one of his current entourage, that he could get caught in the line of fire.

That night at the five-a-side, he wasn't seeing much of the ball. Mind you, his most telling contribution was a fierce tackle from behind on Declan Doyle, upending the cocky estate agent, in retaliation for the way he'd sneered at Barry Junior after Dominik had poleaxed him and, he had to admit, for the way Declan had sneered at Finn at the Tidy Towns meeting. He would have hacked down Dominik too if they weren't on the same team. Dominik, as well as tackling everything that moved, was the conductor, the chief conduit for the ball on the blue-bibbed team. He seemed to be making a point of not passing to Finn, to whom, for some reason, he'd taken a dislike. Finn was looking forward to half-time and in particular to the pints delivered to Barry by drone from Morrissey's Bar. It was a tradition that had originated during the pandemic. Barry would take receipt of four morale-boosting pints of Guinness at exactly 8.15pm every Wednesday. One for himself, and the other three he'd award to those who pleased him most on the night. You might get a drink if you scored a goal, or demonstrated some outrageous piece of skill, or committed some hilarious howler. Unless you were Barry Junior. By all accounts Barry Junior never received a pint, no matter how well or how badly he played.

Chapter 29

After a solo piece, Chopin's 'Funeral March', by Nicky Bow, Morrissey's was awash with emotion. The crowd were tantalizingly close to enlightenment. This was one of the things that Nicky loved about Ireland, or Eire as he called it. Music wasn't just a sideshow. It was central to the way people lived their lives. The other thing he loved about Eire were the generous state subsidies provided to the horse-racing industry. He closed the lid of the Steinway and went to the bar.

Harry then led a roof-raising chorus of 'What a Wonderful World', sung in swelling harmonies by everybody present, those who were able to stand, standing. Nobody wanted the song to stop. When the verses ran out, Harry started from the beginning again. Every hair on every head, every follicle – chin, nasal, or pubic – was standing on end. This was uncharted territory emotionally for the people of Abbeyford, who always prided themselves, throughout their turbulent history, on their equanimity.

Harry joined Maura's table for a drink. He was knocking back whiskeys as quickly as the well-meaning mourners were putting them down in front of him. Despite the brave face, he was drained and distracted, his grief a month after losing his partner barely underway.

'I don't know if I can go on,' he confided in Aoife, their foreheads touching across the table. Harry's phone rang.

'Forgive me! Hello, Dr Harry Boyle speaking.'

He visibly sobered up as he listened to the caller, nodding gravely at what the person was saying. After ending the call, he rose to his feet.

'Duty prevails, I'm afraid. A collapsed lung in Ballyfin. I must make haste without delay.'

Like a bishop, he blessed the table. It was an old Harry trope. To Aoife, he looked relieved. It was just the excuse he needed to leave what for him must have been an overwhelming event. A dying patient was his lifeline. Harry retrieved his jacket from a peg beside the bar and slipped out into the evening.

Kitty immediately started speculating as to who the patient might be and how the lung might have collapsed.

'It's usually an injury to the chest, a knife wound or something. Isn't it, Maura? I bet you it's your man Brendan Doran. He's out in Ballyfin. Always messing about with a chainsaw. The wife has trouble with the nerves.'

Happiness stuck her nose in the air. She didn't find Kitty as entertaining and outrageous as others did. And Kitty didn't like Happiness. She had her down as judgemental and humourless, and worst of all, she'd come between Maura and herself. The gatekeeper, she referred to Happiness disparagingly behind her back. It was incomprehensible that Maura would prefer the company of her carer to Kitty.

'I'm not sorry he's gone, to be honest with you,' Kitty continued. 'Harry, I thought he was hogging it a bit, did you, Maura? He was always an attention-seeker. Even as a boy.'

'Not really the time, Kitty,' said Aoife.

'Oh. You're a divil, Kitty,' said Maura, trying to keep the peace.

'It wouldn't surprise me if he's already moved on to Sir Nicholas there.'

'For God's sake!'

Aoife got up and walked to the bar.

'Now, Kitty, you know perfectly well, Sir Nicholas is a happily married man.'

'So was Harry. No, I don't care what anybody says, I still think he did it.'

'Why would Harry try and kill Barry?'

Everybody by now knew that Barry Duggan was the intended target that night at the choir.

'Miss Kitty,' Happiness, exasperated at the interloper's constant sniping, inquired. 'How do we know it was not you who administered the poison to Barry's tea?'

'The cheek.'

'You had the opportunity. And the motive.'

'Maura, where do you get the staff these days?'

Happiness, like everybody else, knew about Kitty's history with Duggan. Her late husband had driven a waste disposal truck for Barry. About twenty years ago, he had caught his arm in the back loader. The arm was later amputated. The Doyles sued the Duggan's for millions but lost the case. Barry, with the help of a specialist engineer, successfully proved that the lorry was in perfect working order and that the employee had received exemplary and up-to-date training. The accident, the court decided, was entirely due to Pa Doyle's negligence. Apparently he'd had a few drinks at lunchtime and shouldn't have been driving the truck at all. Kitty's husband never worked again and died a few years later.

'Anyway, maybe I did,' said Kitty, her face going pale.

'What?'

'Put something in his tea. Who could blame me? That man destroyed my family. And there's our Declan now licking his backside.'

Maura put her arm around Kitty. Tears rolled down her cheeks, not a sight you saw every day in Abbeyford. Happiness was unmoved despite Maura's eyes pleading with her to go easy.

'So did you?'

'What?'

'Put something in his tea?'

Kitty wiped her eyes with her fingers. She straightened up and smiled at Happiness.

'I did. It was a couple of years ago now. You'll remember this, Maura. Before your time, Miss Happiness. I put a laxative in Barry's jar.'

'That was you!' Maura laughed.

'It was powerful stuff. Barry couldn't hold it in.'

'This was at the choir?'

'At the choir. Around Christmas. We were practising 'The Little Drummer Boy'. He ran for the jacks, do you remember? But he didn't quite make it, did he, the bold Barry Duggan.'

Maura slapped her legs with both hands.

'You are some card, Kitty Doyle.'

'That did me. That was my revenge. And I never looked back.'

The two ladies laughed uproariously before, in unison, breaking into song.

Happiness folded her arms, satisfied with Kitty's story, a grudging respect even forming for her antagonist. Kitty finished her glass of white wine in one gulp. The tennis club assembled sombrely around the piano, rackets in hand. Nicky Bow took his seat. They proceeded to sing a passable if under-rehearsed version of the Men at Work classic 'Down Under', by way of homage to their late 'Australian' friend.

There was a brief, some would say, crass interlude to the requiem when Eve, knowing her clientele all too well, turned on the TV for the lotto results. Happiness was particularly keen, calling for shush. After her own Sunday morning service with Pastor Willy, the lotto results was the highlight of her week. Everyone quickly got over the disappointment of yet again not winning a life-changing windfall. Equally they were consoled by the fact that nobody else won anything either. Eve switched off the television. At the behest of the crowd, she was persuaded to sing one of Michael's favourite Irish ballads, 'Grace'. As most people there knew, Eve didn't take much persuading as she had a great singing voice and 'Grace' was her party piece. Unlike her, however, she faltered somewhat mid-song, crying and stumbling over the words. With the cloth she kept tucked into her jeans, Eve wiped away her tears. It was a song most people knew and they all got behind her, joining in on the chorus, the pores to the soul opening once again, the portals to wisdom and understanding widening too, for those who dared to walk through.

Chapter 30

It was Finn who noticed the drone first, coming from the direction of the town, a distance of about four kilometres. Seen as how he was being ignored by Dominik, he didn't have much else to do but look around. Gavin O'Connell had just scored an equalizer for Barry's team and done a spectacular cartwheel by way of celebration. So he was definitely getting one of the pints. Dominik after that crunching tackle on Barry Junior was surely a shoo-in for one too. As was the custom, Barry Senior would take the one with the creamiest head for himself. That left one remaining pint, Finn liked to think that his name was on it. While he hadn't excelled on the football field, he had, at Barry's request, regaled the other players with the story about the Prince and Cromwell. And he was clearly flavour of the month. Sometimes, Finn had to admit, despite his protests to the contrary, he did trade on his so-called celebrity status.

Duggan looked at his phone.

'What the feck is going on? It's too early.'

It was only five past eight. The delivery wasn't due until a quarter past. The players watched enthralled, like little children, as the drone hovered above Barry as he stood on his goal-line. Just then, his phone rang.

'Hector! What's going on?'

The others obviously couldn't hear what Hector was saying to Barry, although they found out later.

'Alright. No panic, Hector. You're grand,' said Barry. 'It's here now.'

Barry returned his phone to the backpack that contained his water bottle, snack bars and towel, which he kept inside the net. He rubbed his gloved hands together as the bag was lowered from the drone. Six feet from the ground, the bag was released and dropped at Barry's feet. He looked into the bag, his face crumpling and turning white. Seconds later, with Barry frozen to the spot, as the drone soared away back towards the woods, there was an explosion. Everybody instinctively dived onto the artificial grass. When they tentatively got to their feet, those that hadn't been hit by shrapnel in the blast saw Barry Duggan Senior lying in a bloody heap in the goals. It took a minute or two to process what had happened. Dominik and Karl, who hadn't taken part in the match, ran in the same direction as the drone. Finn, miraculously unscathed, rushed to Barry's side. It was too late though. Barry was dead.

Chapter 31

'That was beautiful, Eve, absolutely gorgeous,' said Maura.

'Ah now,' Eve replied. 'It's a great song. Sure you couldn't go wrong.'

Eve's skin was flushed and her eyes were blazing, high on the thrill of performing live. There was then a welcome respite from song in what was by any standards a highly charged room. People circulated. With a few drinks on board now, and the funereal niceties having been correctly observed, the chatter rose. Aoife rejoined the table, having apologized to Fionnuala who in fairness to her had graciously accepted her apology.

Alo Sweeney approached the table. Aoife and Maura exchanged wide-eyed glances. Happiness tried to appear nonchalant but Maura could sense her leg tapping beneath the table. The lawyer was hesitant, almost endearingly so, as he bowed and asked Happiness out to dinner. Happiness, her voice duskier than usual, said she'd think about it. Alo wrote down his number on a paper napkin and chivalrously withdrew. Within seconds Kitty was on her feet, only dying to share news of Sweeney's overture with everyone she could.

'Don't mind her,' whispered Maura to Happiness. 'She doesn't mean any harm.'

Aoife, restless, noticed a worried-looking Hector Morrissey take Eve aside. She went back to the bar to eavesdrop.

'Eve, c'mere to me, you didn't send the pints to Duggan's, did you?'

'What? No. I was up to my eyes. Did you get the car?'

'What?! No, no. Far too dear. Fifteen grand. Sure you could get a real Chevvy for that.'

'That's a terror, Hector. Sorry about that.'

'No. Listen. I can't find the drone anywhere. Have you seen it? It was in the boot.'

'I'm sure it'll turn up,' said Eve pouring a pint.

'It's a right mystery. Somebody delivered the pints.'

'I'm sure there's a simple explanation.'

At that moment, Aoife got a call from Finn. His voice sounded strange, lifeless, monotone. He told Aoife what happened to Barry Duggan. Saying it out loud, relating what he saw with his own eyes – a local businessman being murdered in a drone attack during a five-a-side football match – sounded implausible, like something you'd see in a war documentary. It was obvious by the darkening faces of most people present at Michael's memorial, that news of the appalling aerial assault had filtered through to Morrissey's Bar.

Chapter 32

Needless to say there was consternation at the Duggan estate. Monika had rushed from the house at the sound of the explosion, followed by a still dazed and hamstrung Barry Junior. Overtaking him was Little Barry in his pyjamas and his bare feet.

'Daddy, daddy,' the boy cried, as he approached the mangled remains of his father, before being gathered up in the bloody arms of Declan Doyle. Declan had edged nearer to Barry Senior as the drone approached, hoping that being in his eyeshot would help him be favoured with a pint. For all his initiative, he now had a gash on his forearm that looked worse than it was. Although not particularly close, he was a business associate of Barry's, having negotiated property deals for him in the town and elsewhere. Despite his own injury, he had the presence of mind to steer the struggling boy away from the distressing scene and back inside the house.

Barry Junior collapsed dramatically on the ground beside his father. He was sobbing loudly, and roaring at the uniformed guards who'd been outside the property when the device went off and were now desperately trying to preserve the scene from contamination. Finn was doing his best to console Monika, who was wailing in Croatian and calling for her brother, Dominik. Dominik and Karl, who like his partner was surprisingly quick, like a lurcher, were still chasing the drone towards the copse beyond the perimeter of the estate.

Within twenty minutes, Valerie and Xavier arrived alongside a grim-faced man with saucepan-grey hair that Finn understood to be Superintendent Breslin. The ambulance and fire brigade were not far behind. Finn wasn't quite sure what the fire service with their cutting equipment had to offer on this sorry occasion. Xavier, conscious of the fury in Breslin's eyes, didn't look at Finn. While they awaited the specialists – ballistics from Dublin and detectives from the National Bureau of Criminal Investigation, not to mention the state pathologist – the local brass studied the crime scene and questioned everybody who was on site at the time.

It was fairly clear that Barry had been killed instantly by the ingeniously evil device dropped from the sky. What they couldn't agree on at this stage was whether the weapon was a grenade, a crude home-made bomb or some sort of liquid explosive. The explosion had been surprisingly dull and flat and short-lived, even for Finn who was only metres away. It was like a pistol shot. There'd been a delay of about five seconds between the bomb-laden bag arriving at Barry's feet and the blast. Finn, though he had no experience of military matters, decided it must have been a grenade. Presumably its safety pin had been removed before take-off. On impact with the ground, the catch held flimsily in place with what? an elastic band? was released triggering the mechanism. Not trusting his own strong hunch, he didn't share his amateur deductions with the police.

There had been thirteen footballers present. Although it was a five-a-side game, there were three subs, one for each team, and a floater to be used as required thanks to injury or fatigue. Apart from them, the only other adults on the property were Monika and Karl. The latter had been on the sidelines acting in some sort of surveillance role for Duggan. Although, as usual, not everyone co-operated with them, the Gardai were quickly able to rule out everybody as a suspect except for Monika and Barry Junior. They were not on the pitch or pitch-side at the time of the incident. Both of them refused to speak to Valerie and Xavier. Mind you, as Xavier confided in Finn later, they were both highly agitated and not in a fit state to be interviewed even if they had been prepared to talk. Declan Doyle and other eye-witnesses placed them in the house. They could of course have been out the front or up on the roof. Either way they were the only two of the fifteen people on the premises who could feasibly have operated the drone without being seen by anyone else.

Valerie, impatient at the wait for the technical people, showed the initiative for which she was cherished. She slapped on a pair of sterile gloves, summoned a young officer to her side and embarked on a quick walkabout of the house, inside and out. She was looking for something that could control a drone, a console of some sort, before anybody could dispose of it.

She entered the kitchen. There was a laptop open on the table. And there was a man hovering over it using the finger of a yellow Marigold glove to press the keys. It was Finn.

'What are you doing?' she hissed.

'Eh ... Just getting a glass of water.'

'Check upstairs!' Valerie ordered the uniform before turning back to Finn.

'You shouldn't be here.' She closed the kitchen door. 'Did you find anything?'

'Yeah, no. She was on her email. Nothing strange. Although a lot of them are in Croatian.'

Finn scrolled down through her emails, sharing the screen with Valerie. Nothing stood out as worthy of closer inspection. Valerie nudged him aside.

'Here. Let me.'

She scanned through the recent search history. Monika had recently visited the Zadig and Voltaire website where she'd just bought a pair of ankle boots. After that she'd made a hefty contribution to Médecins Sans Frontières.

'Guilt!' declared Valerie.

'What?' asked Finn, confused, searching the screen for the evidence. 'What does that prove?'

'No. *I* do that. When I buy something nice for myself, I immediately feel bad.'

Finn was taken aback. For a start, he couldn't imagine Valerie ever buying something nice for herself. Nor did he imagine she would ever open up to anyone about her own insecurities, let alone him. He was quite moved.

'Look!'

Monika had also been on quite a few property websites in Croatia over the last few weeks. Most of the houses she viewed online were in the two to three million euro bracket.

'Wow!'

'Wow is right. Did Barry know about that, I wonder?'

There was no sign of any interest in drones. Or grenades.

'Try hemlock!' Finn suggested, remembering the conversation he'd had with Monika in her bedroom. Valerie keyed 'hemlock' into the search engine. Nothing in her history. They quickly looked through her desktop. Nothing incriminating. Apart from her interest in expensive properties, there was nothing overly suspicious on her laptop.

'Look, we can seize it anyway. Have a proper nosey.'

Suddenly, they heard a cry of pain. Leaving the kitchen, they hurried to the end of a long corridor to a room, the light spilling from the door. Turning the corner, they saw Little Barry sitting on the floor of his bedroom, console in hand, deep in concentration in front of a large TV screen playing Pigs in Goo. Finn wasn't sure if that was the actual name of the video game, but if it wasn't, it should have been. It was basically pigs slipping and sliding in pink goo, and trying to escape from the goo, and some sort of bird trying to force them back into the goo. Whatever concerns children's rights organizations might have about such activities, this particular game was a godsend for taking Little Barry's mind off his father's murder. Beside Little Barry was Declan Doyle, lying on the floor. He was writhing in pain.

'I was trying to stop a pig from slithering down a chute. Wrenched my fecking arm so I did. Aaaahhhh!'

Having been wounded by a bit of shrapnel, he was losing blood on the rug. He really shouldn't have been playing computer games.

'Listen, there's an ambulance outside, Mr Doyle. We'll look after the boy.'

'Thanks.'

Declan hoisted himself off the floor and stumbled in considerable agony down the hallway. There were a number of controllers and consoles and handsets of different shapes and sizes scattered on the floor. None of them appeared to be a key component of a drone. Little Barry, at Valerie's gentle prompting, told her that he was playing on his own, then Barry Junior was playing with him, and Barry Junior was very sad, and then there was a big, scary bang, and then the man with the sore arm was playing with him. He had Monika's greeny-purple pistachio eyes.

The Garda officer called down to Valerie.

'Detective Kilcoyne, you might want to look at this.'

Valerie, Finn and Little Barry went upstairs, Finn a little more secure in the presence of Valerie than he had been the last time he entered the Duggan's bedroom.

'I knew it.'

The television had been unhooked from the wall. There was indeed a safe concealed behind it, the door wide open. And there was nothing in it. Nothing at all, apart from a toy car, green in colour. It looked like a Merc. It was still in its original packaging. There was also a note addressed to Barry Junior. All it said was:

B.J. You'll have to do better than that, son!

There was a drawing of a clown beneath the inscription. He took a photograph of it. And one of the car.

'Luckily I didn't see that,' said Valerie dryly.

Finn, while he was there, took the opportunity to see if the key was still hidden behind the photograph of Monika's parents. It was. He didn't mention it to Valerie. It was probably nothing.

Chapter 33

Seeing as how the guards had their hands full at Duggans' place, Aoife took it upon herself to interview Hector Morrissey about the missing drone while his mind was still fresh. According to Hector, on a Wednesday night he would normally go down to his car to get the drone.

'What time would this be now, Hector?'

'About ten to eight, five to eight, something like that. Barry liked the drinks bang on time. Quarter past.'

Hector brought Aoife out the back of the pub to a yard surrounded by outbuildings.

'They would have been the stables back in the day. They say this was one of the oldest coach inns in Ireland, you know.'

Aoife had heard that many times before.

'There was a forge there.'

And that. Hector stood in the middle of the yard.

'Normally I'd do a quick test. Then I'd pull four pints. They'd be in fibreglass containers, nice little lids on them. Pop them in the bag. Send them on their way. Never had a problem. Since Covid. Duggan is what, three or four kilometres outside the town. At like forty kilometres an hour or whatever, it would usually take say four minutes. But when I went to the car, no sign of the drone.'

'Was the car locked?'

Hector chewed on that for a sec. It wouldn't be that unusual for Hector to leave his car unlocked. There were whole nights he left the bar unlocked. Before Eve came along and straightened everything out.

'I couldn't say for sure, Aoife. Yeah, probably, but I dunno. Maybe. But look, the keys were in my jacket pocket. The jacket was hanging up in the bar. Anybody could have taken them. That's if the car wasn't locked.'

They looked around the yard. It was hard to say one way or the other if the stolen drone had been launched from there.

'Highly unlikely. Sure I'm in and out all the time.'

Hector showed Aoife on his phone what the handset looked like. They searched the sheds to see if there was any sign of it. Or any sign of any materials that might have been used in making the bomb.

'I mean the drone could have been nicked any time since yesterday. That was the last time I saw it.'

'But you'd need to be fairly competent to fly it?'

'Not really.'

'No, but to land it at Barry's feet without seriously injuring anybody else?'

'I suppose.'

Hector looked up, mournful.

'I won't get the blame, will I?'

'Not unless you did it.'

His eyes widened momentarily, Aoife noted, as his mouth formed a tight O shape before quickly relaxing again. Given how passive and listless a character Hector seemed to be by nature, she wouldn't have him down as capable of murder, but that uncharacteristic flash of alarm gave her pause for thought.

'C'mon now, Aoife, I didn't care for Duggan, no more than the next man, but he was a good customer. Besides, I was in the bar all the time until I went looking for the drone. Ask anybody.'

'I will.'

'Do.'

Fully in control of his facial features now, he stared back at her.

'Is it always you?'

'What?'

'Who flies the drone to Duggan's?'

'Yeah.'

He thought about it for a moment more.

'Well, no, once or twice Eve did it.'

'Eve?'

'When I was away. She's fairly handy as a matter of fact. Show her something once, she has it down pat.'

'Could she have, you know . . . ?'

Hector laughed mirthlessly.

'Eve? Not a chance. What time did you say Duggan was killed?'

'Five past eight. Exactly. That's what Finn said anyway.'

'It couldn't have been Eve. At eight o'clock didn't she put on the Lottery? That only lasts five minutes. And sure after that, she was belting out "Grace".'

'Did you see anybody else leave the bar?'

'I didn't. But Pawel would have. We have a bouncer tonight, you know, with the big crowd and all. Pawel. He'll know.'

Aoife suddenly went weak at the knees.

'Wait. Harry Boyle left. But that was a house call.'

Hector looked dubious.

'Was it though?'

'There's no way, Hector, not Harry. It's just a coincidence. What?'

Hector picked at a bit of lint on his well-worn fleece.

'I have a lot of time for Harry. You know that. We're friends. But ... ah it's probably nothing ...'

Hector took his time. He applied some lip balm to his lips.

'Go on!'

'I did take Harry for a spin about five weeks ago now. This is before Michael died. In a wee Cessna. He was always on at me to bring him up. Now, I'm not saying anything, but he was very, very interested in Duggan's house. Made me go around and around a few times, as low as I could go.'

'What does that tell you? There's not that much to look at it around here.'

'Sure there you are. Look, if we found the controller, you'd have the co-ordinates, like, of where the journey started. And where it ended up. *Where* did it end up, by the way? If you're talking to anybody, I wouldn't mind getting it back. It's a DJI MAVIC. Cost me five thousand euros.'

'Duggan's dead, Hector. Blown to pieces. Into the back of the fecking net. I'm not sure you getting your drone back is going to be a massive priority for the Gardai.'

'Sorry, yeah. Bad business.'

Hector sighed. Life was full of disappointments.

'It could have been anybody.'

It sure could, Aoife thought, as she went back into the bar dizzy with possibilities. It could have been Hector, the most skilled drone operator in the region. It could have been Eve. She had handled that exact delivery to Duggan's on at least one occasion previously. And what about Harry? Was that phone call he received in the bar not a bit too convenient? Did his phone even ring? She couldn't remember. He certainly had the motivation, even if he had nothing to do with the first attempt on Barry's life. When she got back to the table, Finn was there, describing in hushed and urgent tones to Maura and Happiness the atrocity he'd just witnessed. He stood up when he saw her. She threw her arms around him, not caring what anybody thought.

To Aoife's list, Finn was able to add Monika and Barry Junior.

'They were always on the list.'

'I know. I'm just confirming that they're definitely still on it. Mind you, Valerie did say that Little Barry was playing a computer game with Barry Junior when the grenade went off, if you can believe the testimony of a seven-year-old boy.'

As a priority, they decided they should speak to Harry. He wasn't answering his phone. And he hadn't been seen by anyone since he'd left the pub three hours ago. They impressed upon Fionnuala their concerns. Fionnuala, although still cool towards them, had been trusted with a key to Harry's apartment and reluctantly showed them in. He wasn't there. Like the others, Fionnuala was by now alarmed for his welfare.

Chapter 34

'We found the drone.'

It was Xavier. Finn could barely hear him. Himself and Aoife were in the car now, having dropped Maura and Happiness home. They were out looking for Harry, visiting bars and hotels in the area. And looking in ditches for overturned cars. He'd drank quite a lot before going on that house call. Finn put the phone on speaker.

'I can't talk, Finn. Breslin's on the warpath. Listen, I need your help. Do you have any idea where Harry is?'

'Why?'

'Nothing. We just need to talk to him.'

'Where are you, Xavier? Where's the drone?'

'I can't tell you that, I'd be strung up.'

'I can't tell you where Harry is then.'

They could hear Xavier breathing heavily into the phone. There were panicky voices in the background.

'Jeepers, Finn. I could have you for obstruction. Alright, look, you didn't hear this from me. We're in Carney's Wood, out the Lisanisk Road, the far side of Duggan's house. I'll send you the Eircode.'

'We'll find it.'

'Whose we?'

'Aoife is with me.'

'Howarya, Aoife?'

'Grand.'

If Xavier was expecting a sudden thaw in their relationships, he was being optimistic.

'Where's Harry?' he asked.

'We're just on our way to Harry now.'

'Good man, Finn. You guys know him better than anyone. Bring him in. You'll be doing us a massive favour. And him.'

Finn hung up.

'You know where Harry is?' Aoife asked.

'Haven't a clue.'

Finn screeched to a halt, did a U-turn in the middle of the road and headed at speed towards Carney's Wood. By the time they got there, the road had been sealed off with tape about fifty yards from where the white tents had gone up. Breslin, in an unmarked Jaguar, zoomed past them, followed by a squad car. A young, gangly Garda was manning the cordon. Without hesitation, Finn pulled in outside a nearby house, the guard, engrossed, scrolling through his phone only giving them a passing glance. They casually walked through the gate, and once out of sight climbed over a fence. Crouching low, they moved through a field of cows, towards the woods, a stone wall concealing them from anybody out on the road. A floodlight above the crime scene was suddenly switched off, leaving them to walk the last few yards in darkness. Finn slipped on a cowpat. As well as his clothes, his hands and face were covered in mud. He wished, at that moment, that he was back in London, in a bath, ideally in a different decade. Activity was winding down for the evening. Just a few lamps illuminated the clearing where the drone presumably had landed.

'Excuse me. Hey. You can't be here.'

A woman in a white boiler suit stopped them from going any further.

'Oh sorry, we were just out ... collecting ... mushrooms,' improvized Aoife.

'In May?' The technician wasn't buying it.

'Morels,' Finn said with authority.

'Oh it's you.' She blushed beneath her face mask, instantly recognizing Finn's voice. 'I always wanted to meet you.'

She offered him a hand, covered in a latex glove. Finn shook it, heartily, in his somewhat friendlier 'public persona' guise, although he was pretty sure her instinctive gesture flew in the face of all known crime-scene preservation regulations. Not least as his hand had so recently been contaminated by cow dung.

There were maybe four or five people milling around including Valerie and Xavier. It was a mild evening, the copse enshrouded in a cooling mist.

'It's alright, Maeve, I'll deal with them,' Valerie intervened, striding towards them. There were cleavers stuck to the legs of her trousers.

'*Galium aparine.*'

'Speak English, Mr O'Leary, if you don't mind.'

'Sticky willies.'

'Are you being smart?'

'No, I mean your legs. They're covered in sticky willies.'

Valerie looked down at the legs of what could only be described as slacks. He looked down at his own legs.

'So are mine.'

'Where's Harry?'

Finn felt suddenly tired, stumped for words.

'It's delicate, Valerie.' Aoife took over. 'We begged Harry to come with us. But he wants to know why you're so eager to talk to him. He's afraid you're going to stitch him up.'

Hostile. Aoife's attitude didn't faze Valerie. She hadn't joined the force so as people would like her. She looked over at Xavier, who had become a guard thinking people would like him. He was currently supervizing the bagging of the drone. He shrugged.

'Come with me.'

She marched them another few yards towards the centre of the clearing.

'We think this is the spot. Where the culprit launched the drone.'

'What's that got to do with Harry?'

'We know he left the pub.'

'So?'

'Well, he might have come here.'

'He might have gone to Dublin,' said Aoife. 'Or Spain. Or the North Pole. He went on a call. To see a sick patient. A collapsed lung.'

'Where? Who? This is what we need to find out, Miss Prendergast,' said Valerie neutrally, keeping her cool. 'We just want to eliminate him from our enquiries.'

Apart from the drone itself, apparently undamaged, Finn noticed a few yellow plastic markers with numbers on them. Number two was placed beside a foil sweet wrapper. Upon closer inspection, it looked very like the wrapper of a Crunchie Bar.

'You think Harry did it? You think Harry, big, cuddly Harry Boyle, was capable of such a, such a foul, such a monstrous deed? Are you mad?'

Valerie, keeping her head remarkably still, like a Zen goddess, looked him in the eye.

'According to our information, you seemed to think he was capable of murdering Michael.'

Xavier nodded as he joined them.

'True, Finn. That's only a few weeks ago now. Hounding him, I hear.'

'Fionnuala,' Aoife muttered under her breath.

'We're all after the same thing, lads,' Xavier went on. 'No murders for the past forty-two years and now two in the space of a month. It's not good enough. In fact, it's a disaster for Abbeyford, business, et cetera. Tourism! Nobody will come near the place. Think of the Tidy Towns, Aoife. The only person enjoying any of this is herself.'

He pointed at his colleague. She didn't deny the charge.

'I eat Crunchies too,' Finn squealed, his exasperation getting the better of him. 'Love them. The whole world loves Crunchies. That proves nothing.'

Valerie and Xavier exchanged more coded looks. In agreement, they looked back at Aoife and Finn. Xavier pointed at the little yellow marker numbered 4. With Valerie's permission, they nosed forward. At first, exhibit number four just looked like a wild blackberry bush.

'What are we looking at here?'

Xavier pointed at a tiny piece of fabric snagged on a thorn. The material was corduroy. It was fawn-coloured. The very same as Harry Boyle's jacket.

Chapter 35

The fact that he was missing, incommunicado, didn't look good for Harry. It looked like he was on the run. Or worse. They tried all his friends. No joy. Aoife remembered Harry in the bar saying something about a patient in Ballyfin. Although it was late they drove out there and called at random houses. Nobody had seen him, and more pertinently, nobody knew of anyone in the townland whose lung had recently collapsed.

At one farmhouse, the farmer, a friendly sort lit a pipe and riffled through the Rolodex in his head, going through every house within a two-mile radius. He discussed in great detail everyone who lived in the parish, the Dorans and the Morans, and those who'd moved away to Australia or to England. He sized up their respective characters at length and recalled any misadventures they might have had along the way. Finally he got around to his neighbours and their ailments, right down to their most recent sneeze.

'Would you like a bath?' the man, noticing Finn's muddy clothes, asked Finn.

'You're grand, thanks,' Finn politely declined, although the offer was tempting.

'It would be no trouble, now. Might take an hour or so for the water to heat up.'

'No, no. We've taken up enough of your time.'
'A shower?'

Before they left him, the man assured them that nobody in Ballyfin had called for a doctor that evening. The old homesteader was sorry he wasn't able to help them.

'Would you like some biscuits?'

Finn sensed that he, in the absence of concrete information, desperately wanted to give them something. He got the impression that he was the sort of man who lived to help others, that he most likely waited up half the night hoping to be summoned by a neighbour or, in this case, strangers in distress, that he probably stood by the door with a rope in his hand on the off-chance that a cow needed to be pulled from a gulley, or somebody required assistance delivering a calf.

Rapidly running out of ideas, they even got Donal Kirby, the manager of the community centre, out of bed. When they were boys, Harry and Finn had often played in the then derelict belvedere of the workhouse. Once or twice, after 'running away' from home, they'd stayed overnight in the tower. Although Finn didn't want to think about it, that particular landmark was also a platform from which people were known to jump.

'Blebby's Pludhhlid.'

They were sitting in the Yaris eating chips from Gino's. The windows were all fogged up. Aoife was looking at Finn in alarm as if he was having a stroke. He eventually swallowed the hot chip that had been churning around in his mouth.

'Bressie's Saddle,' he exclaimed, placing the vinegar-soaked paper bag on his lap and shoving the car into gear.

She nodded assent, Diet Coke spilling on her skirt as the car lurched forward.

'We used to go there as kids.'

She knew the place well, having brought school parties up there on field trips on many occasions. It was not far from Duggan's waste disposal plant. You could see three counties – Wexford, Carlow and Kilkenny – and all their geographical treasures from there. In the distance, a very long distance, at a certain angle, in a specific light, under the influence of hallucinogens, you could at a push construe the limestone hilltop as saddle-shaped. The beauty spot was called after Bres, a Formorian giant and formidable horseman who reigned in pre-historic times until the Formorians were usurped by the Tuatha de Danann. That was Redmond's idea of a bedtime story. By the time he was finished telling it to Finn, it was usually time to get up for school.

They parked the car in the deserted car park and walked the few hundred yards up through a Scots pine wood until they reached the plateau.

'Hyperbolic paraboloid,' said Aoife, taking a breath after the exertion of what was a fairly steep climb.

'No, I'm not,' he retorted on the defensive, having been spooked by an owl on the way up.

'Not you. The rock. The shape of the rock. It's very unusual.'

'So are you, Aoife. That's the sort of information I'd keep to myself.'

Aoife noticed a pinprick of light, glowing in the distance. It could have been miles away, a fire around which pagans were dancing, or it could have been the tip of a cigar not twenty feet from where they stood.

'Harry!' she cried.

In the mist, they didn't realize he was sitting on the cliff edge, his legs dangling over the void. Finn was squeamish when it came to heights and held back.

'If it's not the redoubtable Nancy Drew.'

She sat down beside him.

'They're bad for you. And you, a doctor!'

He flicked the cigar towards the ether. The breeze blew it back onto his blue tweed trousers. In a panic he started beating his legs, lest he caught fire. In doing so, his weight shifted and he slid forward on the moss. Despite his fear of heights, and the attendant weakness in his legs, Finn ran towards them. Between the two of them, they managed to grab a hold of Harry and drag him backwards to relative safety. Finn noticed there was a hole in his jacket. Aoife had seen it too.

'For the record, I had no hand, act, or part in the assassination of our good friend Barry Duggan.'

'Where did you go, Harry? When you left the pub.'

'Really, Aoife? Have I not been through enough?'

He exhaled loudly, his whiskey-soused tonsils groaning in sorrow.

'I went to Ballyfin as requested. Having sworn an oath to Hippocrates in my youth, neither today or yesterday I might add, I was obliged to go. In hindsight it was strange. She said she was his sister.'

'The caller?'

'Ollie Moran doesn't have a sister.'

'Right.'

'But it was a woman on the phone?'

'That's what puzzles me. The voice was strange. Robotic. It was, how can I put it, distorted. It could have been a woman, of course, with a very deep voice. Or a man pretending to be a woman. The pub was noisy.'

'But you did go to see Ollie?'

Harry joined his hands in a prayerful pose and placed them over his pursed lips. They didn't want to rush him.

'Ollie Moran's pulmonary system, I can safely report, was in good repair, functioning like a dream. Both lungs intacto. Like bellows in a forge. As specimens, I would go as far as to say they were exemplary.'

The old farmer would be gutted to know he hadn't been informed of Harry's visit to Ollie Moran.

'You have proof of the call?' Aoife persisted.

Harry didn't answer.

'I only ask because the Gardai will want to know.'

'They think I did it?'

He looked up at her with those ingenuous eyes of his. Aoife nodded. Harry waved a desultory hand towards the cliff and the beyond.

'I threw it away. My phone. It was dinging all evening. In a most irritating fashion. It's down there. Somewhere in County Carlow.'

'Right.'

'Harry, you need to go away.'

'No, Harry. Don't listen to her. You need to go to the police.'

'Do you have friends in Europe? What about San Francisco? Conor would help.'

Finn became quite indignant. Conor might have been her brother but he was his oldest friend.

'You can't bring Conor into this, Aoife. Harry, hand yourself in. Clear your name. It's the only way.'

Harry stood up. Aoife and Finn braced themselves in case

he ran. Once he was motoring, there was no way they'd be able to stop him. He took a mini-Crunchie bar from his pocket and unwrapped it, discarding the familiar foil wrapper on the ground, and ate it in one bite. Aoife picked up the wrapper.

'Tidy Towns, Harry. Big push this year.'

'Bressie's Saddle is hardly within the stifling confines of Abbeyford town,' he sniffed drily.

He arranged himself, one hand on his lapel, the other outspread, as if he was about to break into song.

'I will present myself at the Garda station in the morning. I will face the music and dance. And ...' he punched his right fist into his left hand, 'by God, I will convince the world of my innocence.'

Harry held his head high and turned from them so that he was in profile. He reminded Finn of a stag on a postage stamp, standing heroically upon a hilltop. There was a tiny sense that Harry, guilty or innocent as he might have been, was beginning to entertain the seductive idea of martyrdom and the dramatic possibilities a grilling at the hands of the police might provide.

'What are you looking at?'

Finn was studying Harry's trouser legs.

'No sticky willies?'

'How dare you! I didn't have you down as a homophobe.'

'I mean the plant.'

That was a good sign, wasn't it, that Harry didn't seem to know what he was talking about. If there were no sticky willies on his trouser legs, that would mean he wasn't at the copse. That would mean he wasn't the operator of the drone. A glimmer of hope. Although Finn wasn't sure it would stand up in court.

'Where's your car?' Aoife asked.

'Oh,' he waved his hand vaguely again. 'I just parked it down the road among some bushes. I wasn't going to . . .'

'We know, Harry. We know. Come on!'

They led their broken friend down from the rock. And didn't rest until he was safely back in his apartment.

PART 3

Chapter 36

In the days following Barry's murder, Abbeyford was besieged by reporters. They camped outside Duggan's house waiting to catch a glimpse of Monika. She had become something of a cause célèbre. On her rare outings, she'd invariably wear a knee-length black dress, sunglasses and a black mantilla on her head. To support herself, she'd be holding onto her brother's arm. Dominik, with his striking good looks and upright carriage, had also made quite the impression on the public consciousness. A group of fangirls had made the pilgrimage from Athlone and joined the posse of newshounds outside the demesne, shrieking every time the gate rolled back.

The people of Abbeyford, circumspect as ever, generally avoided the press, refusing to answer questions about the grisly happenings in their beloved town. Finn stayed away from Café Madremonte that week as it was full of noisy, insensitive journalists, metropolitan coffee snobs, all congratulating themselves on 'discovering' Ana and her cute café and her amazing cortado.

He tried to keep busy with the Tidy Towns project, now that a visit from the judging panel was not far away. He joined Eddie and the 'Street Angels' on their litter patrols early on Tuesday morning and again on Friday morning.

It was too early for the media who'd been swapping war stories in Morrissey's every evening. If they had gotten out of bed, and hadn't been so hungover and so preoccupied with the racy sport of a double murder, they would have seen the real Abbeyford. Thirty or forty people, young and old, dyed-in-the-wool and recent immigrants, shoulder to shoulder in hi-viz vests and good humour cleaning the streets and housing estates of the town.

With Aoife's nephew, Nathan, Finn, wearing a baseball cap and sunglasses lest he be recognized by the press, repainted the bins in the commercial district. A simple gesture on the surface, he was as proud of that job as of anything he'd ever done, any award-winning garden or TV show. And it made a difference.

Throwing himself into a wholesome activity was therapeutic after all that had happened since he'd come home. He even got a call from Declan Doyle of all people, the chairman of the committee, chastened by his own brush with mortality at Duggan's five-a-side, directing him to help tidy up the old Huguenot cemetery.

Nothing too creative, was the instruction, it was mainly just weeding and cleaning headstones. A bit of dry-walling. Mind you the first thing Finn did was to plant blackthorn, the misunderstood 'crone of the woods'. It would provide protection, both physical and metaphysical, on what was a sparse, windswept burial ground for souls both dead and alive. The trees, although slow-growing, would ultimately provide shelter for birds and other creatures not to mention the moon fairies if you were to believe that sort of thing. At the very least, the living could avail themselves of the sloe berries to make their gin, and of the knobby wood to lovingly craft bespoke blackthorn sticks, which of course, as his father used to say, no self-respecting Irish man should be without.

Speaking of which, the men of Abbeyford might need a cache of such arms, Finn thought, if Aoife's suspicion about Ennismore's subversive offensive was correct. There'd been another act of hooliganism. One of the town's murals had been defaced. The one in the derelict site near Morrissey's Bar that featured Finn himself and other notables. Somebody had gone to the considerable trouble, in the middle of the night, to add a representation of the grim reaper to the group, a scythe-wielding figure hovering ominously over Finn's shoulder. In fairness it was better drawn by a talented, if somewhat malicious, artist than the caricature of Finn or the astronomer.

The weather was pleasant as May turned into June. The wildflowers were blooming in the old ball alley. On a routine inspection, on a bit of a whim, he cut from the sod the shape of a person – more a gingerbread man – with a spade. Then using his newly found dry-walling skills he made a bed in the resulting hollow from a half-ton of smooth pebbles. As he expected, lying on the bed, staring at the sky, framed by the square walls of the ball alley, was a profoundly restful experience, presenting an ever-changing picture. Combined with the scent of the flowers and the sound of the insects it was, in his humble opinion, an ecstatic encounter with the divine. Well, it was until it started raining.

Of course, he understood the obsession with winning the overall Tidy Towns Award, or at least beating Ennismore, but didn't share it. As far as he was concerned, *this* was winning. The work itself. The camaraderie. The bonhomie. The community spirit. It was a welcome contrast to the hate and violence that engendered the killings, and the cynicism of the salivating media, and the prurient interest of the wider public.

Finn didn't see much of Aoife at that time as she was busy preparing her students for the Junior Cert. Neither of them had forgotten about their burgeoning sideline in crime detection although Finn was secretly hoping they could just let the guards get on with the job.

After showing up at the station as promised, Harry Boyle had been taken into custody in Wexford town where he was held for questioning for two days. Xavier acknowledged Finn and Aoife's help in the matter by text. Although Harry was released without charge, the Gardai were reviewing the evidence and preparing a file. They had found his phone at the bottom of Bressie's Saddle and were able to confirm that Harry had indeed received a call while he was in Morrissey's at the memorial. That call, however, was made from a burner phone which couldn't be traced. A man called Ollie Moran did confirm that he had had an unexpected visit from the doctor. The guards, rather than seeing this as vindication of Harry, treated the house call as suspicious, evidence of Harry trying to engineer an alibi. The piece of fabric from his jacket was of course damming, but Harry vociferously protested that it had been planted there. He also argued, not unreasonably, that while the drone landed in the woods, it didn't necessarily leave from there. Unfortunately, since the data on the drone – the flight history and whatnot – had been deleted, nobody could say for sure from where the grenade had embarked on its deadly journey. The device, Harry was assured, would be sent to a data recovery specialist in due course.

'It might take time,' said Xavier sympathetically at the

door of the Garda station. 'If there's anything there, they'll find it. But, in my experience, I wouldn't bank on it.'

Finn was spending most evenings with his mother and Happiness, doing crosswords and odd jobs about the family home. The ivy plants were coming along well, ready to be transferred to the ball alley. One evening, he was losing heavily to Happiness at poker. She was a natural, absolutely unreadable despite never having played the game before. Gambling went against her religion, apparently. But exemptions it seemed were permissible when it came to the faithful extracting money from the faithless. Her Baptist sect was clearly an accommodating religion. He had to borrow a tenner from Maura, who despite holding her cards the wrong way around was somehow hanging in. He objected to the way Happiness hoarded her gains in big greedy piles of coins in front of her. That was just rubbing it in. It also bothered him the way she took so much time over each decision, doing some complicated actuarial calculations in her head, and staring through him, as if she could read the ruminations in his own head. Poker was supposed to be fun. It was during one such interminable wait for Happiness to raise or fold that he received a call from Isabella.

'I am so sorry. I have to take this.'

'Convenient,' huffed Happiness.

Finn got up from the table and went outside.

'Isabella!'

The signal was terrible. It sounded like she was in a blizzard.

'Where are you? On top of K2?'

'Highgate. I got home last week.'

'Oh.'

She was in their flat, a chilly but spacious three-bed

affair with high ceilings in an art deco block at the top of Highgate Hill. He could picture her padding around in the thick socks that she wore instead of slippers, the retiree in the flat below playing Chopin to the best of his ability. In fairness, the signal was always very bad there. It was what he liked least about their home. It had led to a lot of misunderstandings over the past few years.

Isabella gave him the name of a 'property developer' in London, Rufus Morgan. Her unsubtle use of the inverted commas told him all he needed to know about Rufus Morgan. He didn't have the heart to tell her that it didn't matter now, that Michael's death was a case of mistaken identity and that he'd sent his ex on a wild goose chase.

'I know that Michael Dunlop was not the intended target.'

Of course she did. Isabella was always very thorough. And by now she would have read about the drone attack on Duggan. She would have heard about that in the Himalayas. That story had made headlines around the world.

'Morgan, he's a dangerous man, Finn. According to my sources, he's in Ireland. Right now. And, by all accounts, he wants his money back.'

'By all accounts' was one of his own expressions, one that she had adopted. It pleased him that she hadn't as of yet eliminated all traces of his influence from her vocabulary.

'How are you? How was the trip?'

He knew Barley Davis had been part of her tour group. She and he were old friends from Oxford. Barley Davis worked for the FCDO, or the Foreign Office as he still insisted on calling it. A supercilious sort, he had always treated Finn as a curiosity. To him, although he never actually verbalized it, gardening was a cute, peasant occupation and television a vulgar medium for mollifying the masses. Perhaps Finn was being unfair to him, guilty of projection and inverted snobbery. Easy confidence and entitlement didn't necessarily make you a bad person. It was probably the over-familiarity with Isabella, the in-jokes and the implied primacy of their prior friendship that rankled more. Or maybe Finn, for all his easy-going demeanour, was actually a bit possessive. It would probably take some time – without the distraction of a murder case – to parse the fizzling out of their relationship. Not to mention the divvying up of their fancy flat.

While she was sharing a brief synopsis of her adventures, in her measured, understated, slightly ironic way, not feeling the need to embellish the story for comic or dramatic effect, like he would or most Irish people would for that matter, he felt an ache in his heart. Although their marriage was dead, they still had a shared history, friends and interests in common, and most importantly a shorthand. A shorthand was not to be sniffed at. One of the great advantages of a relationship was not having to spell everything out when you were tired at the end of a long day. Telepathy was surely one of the boons, nay, the cornerstones of a successful marriage? Although now that he thought of it, assuming you always knew what your partner was thinking and that she knew what you were thinking, wasn't exactly foolproof. If he ever ended up in another relationship, he resolved, he'd spell everything out.

'I need a favour, Izzy.'

'Another one? Do you think that's ... appropriate?'

He racked his brains trying to think of something that had been nagging him.

'CosRoe!'

'Sorry? The line is bad.'

'CosRoe Holdings. It's the name of a shell company, registered in the Cayman Islands.'

The phone went silent. Downstairs in number 20 the neighbour's fingers were beginning to falter on the piano, not surprisingly as he tended to play for four or five hours every evening. Finn had hooked her. Isabella, a stickler for rules, couldn't resist the merest whiff of corporate crime.

'Go on!'

'I need to know who the beneficial owner is. I've been thinking. CosRoe is Roscoe backwards.'

'What?'

'An anagram or whatever.'

'Roscoe? What are you talking about? Are you okay, Finn? Your voice. You sound like you're having a breakdown?'

'It's the signal. I should explain. Roscoe was the name of Duggan's first truck. Barry Duggan.'

'The man who was murdered, yes. You think CosRoe was his company?'

'No. That's just it. I don't. Well, I don't know. I was hoping you could ... you know, do your magic and find out.'

'And you think this will help you find the killer?'

'Yes. No. Not Barry's killer.'

'I don't follow.'

'Rameses' killer. If he was killed.'

'If you mean Rameses the third, I'm pretty sure he was killed by one of his wives in Thebes two thousand years before Christ. She cut his throat.'

That's exactly the sort of thing people who went to Oxford knew, Finn thought. He could just picture herself and Barley discussing succession rights in ancient Egypt over an expensive Ribera del Duero.

'Not that Rameses.'

'I think you need to see someone. Has there been another murder?'

'No. Not exactly. It's complicated.'

'It always is with you,' she replied, a tad irritated.

There was a lull in the conversation. Although he wasn't in the least offended by her remark, he could tell she was sorry she said it. He took the opportunity presented by her silent contrition to ask her to also delve into the ownership of the other company mentioned in DI Kilcoyne's dossier, Whitestairs Holdings.

'Vale. Vale,' she said wearily in Spanish, echoing her mother, as she wrote the names of the companies down. 'It shouldn't take too long. I have a friend in the *FT* who does this for fun. Unravelling shell companies is her Sudoku.'

'Do people still play that?' he asked.

They changed tack then, talked breezily of inconsequential things and, in a more stilted way, of consequential things, his family, her family, his new vocation as a detective, her imminent new position as deputy controller of the World Service. It was a long overdue conversation. The last thing she said to him before she hung up was, 'Be careful, Finn.'

Chapter 37

The following Monday Finn decided to brave an early breakfast in Ana's café. His attempt to remain incognito amongst the cognoscenti of the press was undone by Ana.

'Finn O'Leary!' she scolded him loudly. 'Where have you been all my life?'

She tousled his hair proprietorially.

'You think you can just walk in here whenever you feel like.'

She posed with her hands on her hips.

'What did I do to you? Did I spit in your food?'

Heads turned, even those of the more grizzled scribes. He really hoped they knew she was joking. Ana's attempts at humour, as a rule, had an unfortunate tendency to land just a few millimetres wide of the mark. He handed Ana his cup. One of the journalists, Nolan from the *Independent*, asked him for a selfie.

'For the wife,' he hastened to add, presumptuously taking a seat at Finn's table, 'She's a big fan. As am I.'

He then brazenly turned on the Voice Memos on his phone and started interviewing Finn about the murders.

'I believe you were actually present when Duggan was killed.'

Finn was wary around journalists at the best of times,

even when promoting something as seemingly innocuous as one of his TV shows. In his early days on television, he tended to be flippant in his answers, not out of cockiness but out of a sense of shyness and self-preservation. His instinct was to deflect questions particularly the more intrusive ones. Once when being profiled by a women's magazine he was asked if he ever took drugs. Annoyed by the question, a hostage to fortune, he replied with a perfectly straight face that he occasionally munched on a cocaine sandwich. And on he went in that facetious manner, even claiming that he only got into gardening as a cover to grow weed. In his mind, he was expressing disapproval for drugs generally as well as for the impertinence of the mischievous journalist. But it didn't come across that way in the article. Flat on the page, without the heavily ironic tone, Finn came across as having a very casual attitude towards drug-taking, earning him a reprimand from his employers. Mind you, it didn't do his wild man image any harm.

'Did you actually see the grenade explode?'

'The grenade?'

'That's what killed him. An M67 fragmentation grenade.'

Nolan consulted his notebook.

'Yeah. Containing one hundred and eighty grams of composition b explosive,' he reported, delighted to be breaking the news. He could see what Nolan was up to, taking him into his confidence, in anticipation of a quid pro quo. The burly hack, in a full-zip, a deep cleft in his chin, tapped his nose.

'Keep that to yourself now, son. That information hasn't been released as of yet.'

'Right,' Finn said, neutrally.

'You were a lucky man. You know a grenade like that has

a …' – he checked his notebook again – '… a wounding radius of about fifty feet. Did you feel lucky?' Nolan asked, pen at the ready, trying to put words in his mouth.

'Where would someone round here get their hands on a grenade?' Finn wondered aloud. He had a flash of inspiration as to, at least, where to start looking. But he kept that to himself.

'You tell me, Mr O'Leary,' he said, leaning forward. 'Between myself and yourself, it wasn't the shrapnel that wiped him out, Duggan, although he did end up with some pretty serious lacerations.'

Nolan smiled expectantly, waiting for Finn to ask him what exactly was the cause of death. Finn, remaining determinedly tight-lipped, didn't oblige.

'It was a heart attack. Can you believe that? None of his wounds were actually life-threatening. He died of a heart attack. Did you know Barry Duggan well?'

There'd be nothing this man Nolan and his ilk would like more than to link Finn with Duggan and Michael too, for colour and sensation if nothing else. A 'celebrity' angle, however tenuous, wouldn't do Nolan or the *Independent*'s sales figures any harm.

Ana slammed down Finn's coffee and regular breakfast on the table.

'Huevos diablos. You better eat it this time, man.'

He looked longingly at the scrambled eggs with chorizo and green peppers on her home-made cheese bread. Ana, somehow balancing another two breakfasts and two cups of coffee, pulled an envelope out of her breast pocket. During their many pleasant, sexually charged chats together, Ana had mentioned her circus skills. She was, according to herself, and not in a boastful way, an accomplished trapeze artist, a proficient trampolinist and probably the best hula-hooper in all of South America. He could well believe it. Appraizing her small stature with admiration, approaching awe, he could see that she had indeed the physique and concentrated energy of a gymnast.

'This is for you. It was on the floor when I opened the café this morning.'

There was a short pause as he studied the envelope.

'It's from your father.'

He gave her an inquisitive eye. How did she know that? She wouldn't have read it, would she?

'He wants you to meet him at the men's shed.'

She would. To give her her due, as previously noted, Ana was fiercely loyal to her customers and particularly protective of Finn. In her mind, she was probably doing him a favour, censoring his post, making sure it wasn't hate mail, or a note from a crazed stalker.

'He'll be there from two to five today. He has something that might interest you. It's urgent.'

She picked up Nolan's phone, still miraculously holding on to the other crockery, a chipolata sausage rolling perilously close to the edge of one of the plates.

'Mick! What do I tell you? Don't bring your dirty work into Café Madremonte. *Madre de Dios!* Next time I throw your phone in the toilet.'

The other journalists cheered. Ana, who was on first-name terms with everyone who frequented her café, beamed, her high-wattage smile lighting up the room. Nolan bowed mock-humbly.

'Sorry Ana.'

He withdrew towards his own table, not before dropping his card on the table.

'Call me. We should talk.'

Before Finn had a chance to tackle his breakfast, his phone rang.

'It's a disaster, Finn.'

It was Aoife.

'What's going on?'

'Gotta go. See you at Morrissey's in five.'

Finn felt the familiar panic rising in his chest. He assumed the worst, fearing there'd been another murder or, God forbid, something had happened to Harry. He was also dreading Ana's reaction if she happened to notice him slipping out of the café.

'Finn!' she shouted. 'This is the last time I make you huevos diablos. *Hijole!*'

Mick Nolan, after securing a nod of permission from Ana, tore into Finn's abandoned eggs. He looked like he'd already had a few breakfasts that morning.

'*Hijueputa. Malparido,*' she muttered to herself. Whether the curses referred to Finn or Nolan or to both men wasn't entirely clear.

Chapter 38

Aoife was outside Morrissey's issuing instructions to a number of people in hi-viz vests who were standing around her in a semi-circle. It was not yet 8.30am. As her students were that morning starting their state exams, school was finished for the year. Aoife had been enjoying a rare lie-in when Eddie Halfpenny had called, alerting her to a number of overturned bins in the town. He had left somebody at Dublin Airport in the early hours of the morning and was on his way home and back to bed when he had spotted the trail of destruction.

'That's a relief,' said Finn, as the litter squad dispersed to clean up the mess.

'A relief?' snapped Aoife.

'Well, at least nobody died.'

That was not the right thing to say at that moment. Aoife looked as if she was about to commit murder herself.

'This is the work of Ennismore.'

'C'mon. It's probably just foxes.'

That asinine opinion did nothing to placate her.

'Sometimes I wonder about you, Finn. Have you seen the sheer level of destruction?'

He looked around him. It was bad alright. After the picnic-table arson, the pollution of the pond in the bog garden, the defilement of the mural, this was an escalation. It was, as she intimated on the phone, a disaster. Even here in the centre of town, rubbish was strewn all over the street. Some of the plants had been uprooted. A nearby skip had been emptied of its contents. Traffic was backed up as far as the New Bridge.

'Do you think it was a fox that threw that old pram on the footpath?'

'I take your point.'

'Or that old fridge.'

'Look, love, we'll have it cleaned up in no time.'

He realized as soon as he said it that he'd called her 'love'. It was purely an accident, a slip of the tongue. Hopefully she didn't notice.

'What did you say?'

'No, I didn't mean ... It's just ... I was talking to my ex last night, Isabella, and ... I didn't get much sleep actually ...'

'What do you mean, "we'll have it cleaned up in no time"?'

She hadn't noticed, thankfully, so preoccupied was she with the current disaster. There was no other word for it.

'I appreciate the positivity, Finn. But it's too late.'

There were press photographers taking pictures of the debris, no doubt seeing the discarded pram as a symbol of the town's decline. Likewise, there were reporters bored by the lack of progress in the murder investigation, and bitter at the non-existent co-operation from the townsfolk, who were busy writing up the story unfolding before their eyes and no doubt linking it in their feverish minds to Abbeyford's recent murders.

'We'll be the laughing stock of the country. Ennismore

knew exactly what they were doing. At our weakest moment, Finn, they pounce. When we're on our knees. They're not going to get away with this.'

There was no doubt this attempted sabotage, if that's what it was, was a genuine threat to the Tidy Towns campaign. Images of the carnage would soon appear in the papers and on the evening news. With the context missing, it wouldn't look great.

'Will the judges even show up?'

Finn, in the short time he'd been home, apart from perhaps Michael's death, hadn't seen Aoife rattled by anything. Right now, she was clearly distraught, all her hard work having been undermined. Tears started extruding from his eyes. He couldn't do anything to intrude them again. Everything suddenly became a lot for him. It might have been the delayed shock of seeing Barry Duggan die. Or maybe it was the conversation with Isabella and the certainty that that period of his life was truly over. Or it could have been due to his own investment in the Tidy Towns campaign that was, whether he liked it or not, beginning to give his life a new definition.

'C'mon now, Finn. Snap out of it.'

Aoife gave him a quick one-armed hug, their cheeks touching for a moment, sending a slight shock wave through his synapses. She then handed him a refuse sack.

'There we are now ...' – she winked at him – '... love. We have work to do.'

Within a couple of hours, with the help of a battalion of volunteers, Aoife had made the town presentable again. Eddie, who had been up since two in the morning, was at the vanguard of that effort. When they were finished, over a sandwich in Morrissey's, Eddie complained bitterly to anybody who'd listen.

'Where's the mainstream media now, ha, wha'? Dirtbags, so they are, only interested in scandal.'

Where Eddie got his news from, nobody was entirely sure. Since he spent most of his time in his car, they presumed it was from some obscure radio station outside the normal frequency range. Although he could barely stand by now, so tired was he, he was all on for running the press out of town. And in a state of sleep-deprived delirium he was already drawing up plans for a night-time revenge raid on Ennismore.

'Now, they'll probably be expecting us,' he said, sipping from a pint glass of Coke. 'They hardly think we're going to lie down, do they? Right? So there's a good chance they'll have sentries on all the main approach roads.'

When the moment was right, when Eddie paused briefly to burp, Finn took him aside.

'Eddie, I was thinking. It was a grenade that killed Barry.'

'Yeah.'

Finn was watching Eddie carefully. The latter had adopted a gormless expression which in fairness wasn't that different from his face's usual resting state. Why didn't Eddie ask him, *How do you know it was a grenade and not an improvised explosive device or a pipe bomb?*

'Assuming it was a local person who did it, who murdered Barry, where would they have got their hands on a M67?'

Eddie shook his head, slowly, dumbly.

'Don't know, to be honest with you, now.'

He didn't bat an eyelid at the specific mention of an M67.

'You that was in the army,' he wheedled him, 'higher up in the army than you let on, I'd say, what? If anybody knows you'd know. There must be some old range or something? Some black market?'

Eddie made a show of thinking hard, making a series of popping sounds with his mouth.

'God, now that's a good one, hah. You have me there, Finn.'

He looked embarrassed, perhaps because he knew more than he was saying, or because he didn't actually know the answer at all thereby exposing himself as a charlatan, all talk. Either way, the army veteran was unperturbed possibly because he was actually daft, or highly trained in the art of misdirection.

Finn, none the wiser, left Eddie alone. Eddie resumed his monologue, during which Aoife and Finn slipped out of the pub unnoticed by him. When Eddie was in full flight, despite being a teetotaller, he was generally oblivious to who entered or exited his orbit. He'd be as happy talking to the wall.

'So I'm thinking. Parachute!'

After everybody else had drifted away, Hector, trapped behind the bar, was stuck with him, as usual.

'Hector here could fly the plane.'

'Well ...'

'Me and a couple of my old mates, we could drop down behind enemy lines, do ya get me, cause havoc, in and out in no time, if they want war ...'

'Well. now Eddie, it would depend on the VMC.'

'The wha'?'

'You were in the army. The Visual Meteorological Conditions.'

'Of course, yeah, the VMC. As long as it's a clear night. Obviously. I wouldn't be party to anything you might call reckless. Tha' reminds me. Do you know who creates the weather?'

Hector had switched off, his face, after a lifetime in the bar trade, a study in neutrality.

'The authorities! Yeah. They can make rain now. With special seeds. And fog too. If it suits them. Like, if they found out about this mission, they could sort out fog around Ennismore. Like that.'

Eddie clicked his fingers, startling Hector out of a reverie about his lost drone.

'In America, there, only a few months ago, they were actually steering the hurricanes into certain communities. I can't believe nobody is talking about this. The towns you know that vote the wrong way. That's a fact, now. Tha's not my opinion. Do you ever wonder why all the storms hit Kerry and Galway? Just the west coast?'

'The wind coming in off the Atlantic . . .'

Eddie carried on ignoring him.

'Depopulation. Tha's right. They're trying to drive the people out. So as they can sell the land to the data centres. And the bleedin' . . . whatchamacallems, the wind farms. So as they can power the data centres. Don't take my word for it?'

Hector sighed. It was going to be a long shift.

Chapter 39

Finn pulled up at the men's shed. It was an old dance hall in the Gower area of town out the Ennismore Road. The hall had been built in the early '60s to facilitate a jiving craze that had literally swept Ireland off its feet, and ultimately resulted in a population boom. People have been twitchy ever since, liable to spontaneously shake a leg in any situation no matter how inappropriate. Since then the modest premises had hosted a garage and later a furniture store from which his mother bought some old two-seater school desks with inbuilt inkwells when the Adoration convent had closed. As far as he knew they were still at home in her garden shed, never used. Now the premises was a refuge for isolated, mostly elderly men, to come together, chat, drink tea and learn new skills. Needless to say, Redmond, although more than eligible at this stage, wasn't there as one of the clientele. No. Once a week, he deigned the bemused men with his presence to tutor them in the arts of survival.

When Aoife and Finn entered the hall, there was a deathly silence. At first they thought the men were snoozing, the nap induced by some soporific lecture of Redmond's. Or, it briefly crossed Finn's mind, they were actually dead due to some gas leak or one of Redmond's denser monologues. But they were quickly taken aback to see that, today, Finn's father was teaching the men how to build boats. Redmond was instructing them in the forgotten craft of currach-making to be precise, currachs being the small wooden-framed boats covered in animal hides and more associated with the islands off the Atlantic seaboard than inland waterways. On the other days of the week the men might do crosswords, or listen to music, or chat about sport and politics. Occasionally, they would paint landscapes or maybe turn their hands to a bit of light carpentry, making birdhouses or children's toys. The library boxes outside SuperO were lovingly created in this room. But when Redmond was in town, the men had to be on their toes, age and infirmity be damned.

There were a number of cowhides laid out on the ground. One man, he must have been about eighty, was brushing them clean. Another, in his nineties at least, was on his knees removing fatty residue from the skins. Some men were deep in concentration sharpening willow rods. Redmond, with a patience he'd rarely showed Finn in his youth, was demonstrating to them how to bend and weave the rods into the desired shape of a half-walnut shell. In fairness, the men, although clearly hard-pressed by their exacting taskmaster, were fully invested. What possible good a finished currach might do them, Finn couldn't say. Surely they had more immediate needs. These were men, he imagined, who lived alone for the most part, who couldn't make an omelette, or climb a stairs without assistance, and Redmond had them engaged in the manufacture of ocean-going vessels. It wouldn't have surprised Finn to learn that his father had founded a doomsday cult and was busy prepping his followers in advance of an epic flood.

'You took your time, son,' Redmond said, when he eventually gave his charges a break.

'We had an incident,' Finn explained.

'Blatant sabotage,' Aoife added.

The men's shed was a great leveller. Looking at them now, their faces relaxed, Finn recognized the straight-laced old bank manager, Mr Meredith, in conversation with Tony 'TenPints' Ring, a former navvy and still occasional hell-raiser.

'Beautiful woman!'

'Thank you,' said Aoife, deadpan as ever.

'Bit inappropriate, Daddy, no?'

'Bella donna,' he continued ignoring his son. 'It's Italian, but then languages were never your strong suit.'

'Fair enough.'

'Remind me, Finn, what was your strong suit?'

Finn smiled tightly.

'I'm joking.'

Redmond clapped Finn on the back.

'He's very good at procrastinating, I find,' Aoife joined in.

'Don't you start!'

'No. Joking aside, I must say, among his many outstanding qualities, my son was always a very good listener.'

'Thank you,' said Finn. 'I think.'

'A friend of mine contacted me a few days ago.'

'How?' Finn asked, genuinely wondering how people got in touch with his father.

'Doesn't matter how. Alice Birdthistle.'

Aoife nodded, recognizing the name.

'Alice lives in Tullaun House with her sisters,' Redmond went on. 'I'm sure you've heard of it.'

He hadn't.

'I'm surprised. It's one of the finest gardens in Ireland.'

Aoife looked at Finn sympathetically. Sometimes it seemed that every word that came out of Redmond's mouth contained some implied criticism of his son. There followed a mercifully short history of the estate, the garden and Alice's lineage. She was descended from the Sheridans.

'The chocolate people. The shares keep her afloat.'

For all Redmond's maverick ways and close reading of Irish history, he had always displayed a high regard for the gentry. If nothing else, he liked the way they managed land. Was this what he wanted to tell him? The urgent message? Was he going to marry Alice Birdthistle, or something?

'And you and Alice ... ?'

'What?'

'Bella donna. Beautiful woman. It's okay. I have no issue, dad. You don't have to ...'

'What are you drivelling on about? Alice? Me? I wouldn't touch her with a barge pole.'

'You can't say that.'

'She's a perfectly pleasant person, but she's no oil painting.'

'Or that.'

'More like something a five-year-old would draw.'

'Daddy! No!'

'Alice wouldn't mind. I'm sure she'll be very amused when I tell her you were so offended on her behalf.'

As it turned out, although coming from very different traditions, Alice and Redmond had many interests in common, not least a loathing for rhododendron. He placed a plank of wood on top of one of the upturned boat frames that was straining at the seams. Then, to weigh it down further, he lifted a heavy chunk of masonry. Seeing him tottering under the weight, Finn went to help his father carry the broken flagstone, help his father predictably refused.

'Okay, I'll spell it out for you. I'm trying to tell you that Alice has the finest collection of belladonna in the country if not in the world. *Atropa Belladonna*. Deadly nightshade. Rare strains she has cultivated herself. One of them, *atropa donnabrutta*, I think she calls it, she's especially proud of. These Anglo-Irish dames have a touch of the macabre about them,' he declared approvingly.

In his roundabout way Redmond finally got to the point. A few weeks ago, Alice's deadliest plant, a specimen three foot tall, was stolen.

'Uprooted! Gone. During broad daylight.'

'No CCTV?' asked Aoife, knowing the answer.

Redmond laughed at the very idea.

'As you know, Aoife, these people keep to themselves. They don't trust modern gadgetry. And they're right not to.'

'I suppose they don't want any evidence of their weird rituals in circulation, ha ha, their debauched garden parties,' said Finn, attempting levity.

'Croquet is actually a very skilful game.' Redmond cut him dead. 'But then you were never really a sportsman.'

'I beg to differ.'

'The thing is, Tullaun only receives a trickle of visitors every day. Ten or twenty at this time of year, according to Alice. A coach party, maybe, or a gardening society.'

Aoife sought confirmation.

'And you think whoever stole the plant might have killed Michael. And presumably Barry?'

'Aoife.' Redmond bowed. 'The children of Ireland are in safe hands with you.'

There followed a brief debate about how one would

extract the atropine from the plant. And the dosage required to fell a man. While the shed men, now rested and sated on tea and cigarettes, were fidgeting in the background, anxious to get back to work, the trio discussed whether the roots, leaves, or indeed the berries were the best source of the lethal alkaloid. At this point, 'TenPints' started singing MacAlpine's 'Fusiliers'. There followed a slight but heated digression about the fate of the Shakespearean heroine Juliet. Aoife was adamant that the sleeping potion she took to feign death was extracted from the *atropa belladonna*. Redmond disagreed, insisting it was from the root of the mandragora plant. Finn, although out of his depth when it came to Shakespeare, sided with Aoife.

'It was definitely the nightshade that killed her.'

Redmond laughed. He turned to Aoife.

'I take back what I said about him being a good listener.'

He turned back to Finn.

'Was that before or after Juliet stabbed herself?'

Aoife spared Finn any more ridicule by changing the subject.

'So what you're saying is the poison that killed Michael could only have come from Tullaun?'

'Yes. Well, Tullaun, or the Gediz Valley in Eastern Anatolia. My money's on Tullaun.'

'Why didn't she go to the police?'

'Ha! The likes of Alice live in a parallel universe. They don't really recognize the institutions of the state. Theirs, you see, is a feudal society ...'

Finn got that unnerving twitch when he sensed his father was about to start a lengthy lecture. If Redmond was right, this was an overdue and very promising lead. With so few visitors to Tullaun, it was not beyond the realms of possibility that they might actually be able to trace some or all of the botany enthusiasts who'd ventured there on the day in question. Or at least they might be able to find a clue.

'As a matter of interest,' Finn asked his father, 'how do you know it was atropine?'

'What?'

'That killed Michael.'

'I presumed. His pupils were dilated, weren't they? Now forgive me, I have an armada to assemble. Men!'

Chapter 40

Next morning, they left early for Tullaun House. Aoife wanted to be back in St Joseph's by the early afternoon to greet her students coming out of their exams. The journey, a distance of about twenty-five miles, due east beyond Ennismore towards the Irish Sea, took longer than expected. That's because Happiness decided to drive. As Maura's chief carer it was her prerogative after all.

'Who's for an ice cream?' Aoife asked as the car, the engine whining ominously, passed through the dreaded town of Ennismore. It wasn't an ice cream Aoife wanted. Nor was it simply a break from Happiness' erratic driving. She wanted to see how they were faring in Ennismore. She wanted to compare her main rival's progress to date in their respective Tidy Towns crusades.

While Finn was buying the cones – plain vanilla for Maura, lemon sorbet for himself, strawberry for Aoife and vanilla, lemon sorbet, strawberry and chocolate for Happiness, topped with a chocolate flake and sprinkles – Aoife scanned the town in dismay. Ennismore, although it didn't have the river, had a few advantages over Abbeyford. For a start, it was a planned town, its square surrounded by imposing Georgian buildings. Off the square there was an entrance to the beautifully manicured grounds of the castle, which featured a fine collection of exotic trees. From her vantage point Aoife could see the quirky monkey puzzle avenue, dominated by the giant *araucaria* with a circumference of 400 centimetres, and some of the redwoods. The town in a sense was an offshoot of the castle, gothicized in the early nineteenth century and still in the hands of the Patterson family, renowned for their munificence to this day. Surrounded by some of the best land in the country, Ennismore attracted richer farmers than Abbeyford, and as a result was more prosperous. It didn't have the industry or the social problems or the dereliction her own town had, not that she was complaining. In fact the absence of any sort of an edge rendered Ennismore, in her jaundiced view, somewhat sterile. It gave Aoife *Stepford Wives* vibes. There was an anality about Ennismore, in her estimation, reflected in the ICU standards of cleanliness evident on the streets, and the total absence of neon or plastic on the shopfronts. Although the square was festooned with hanging baskets and bunting, as if the town was in a permanent festival mode, there were few people around. Perhaps the Tidy Towns committee, in all their zealotry, had banned people from the streets. No people, no litter. It made sense as a policy on one level but it was no way to live. Abbeyford, for all its faults – not to mention its recent double murder – was living, breathing, messy and wonderful. And more importantly it was her town.

Maura and Happiness were sitting contentedly on a freshly painted bench outside the oh-so-discreetly branded Centra. Finn handed Maura her cone, which she held with two hands like a little trophy. He then carefully presented Happiness with her quadruple ice cream and a wad of paper napkins. Unfortunately, despite its size and multiplicity of domes, hers came in a barely-fit-for-purpose double cone. Finn felt, by the suspicious way Happiness was looking at him, that she felt that he was somehow judging her and her choices. He absolutely wasn't. In fact he was insulted that she should think he was. It was a bold selection and more power to her. Granted, Finn was staring in her direction. But it was only to observe how she was actually going to manage the unwieldy treat, four scoops unevenly balanced on a flimsy wafer cone, especially now the temperature was rising. It was ambitious, to say the least. He went to join Aoife.

'She better not drop any of that,' Aoife said. 'She could be arrested.'

Aoife had to hand it to Ennismore. Yes, it was all a bit fastidious, but the town at a glance looked impeccable. Putting herself in the judge's shoes, she couldn't find any fault whatsoever. At this rate, they certainly didn't need to be vandalizing Abbeyford.

'You're not thinking of ... ?'

'No. It wouldn't be fair on the ordinary volunteers. It's the committee I have a problem with. Besides we've got you.'

Finn wasn't sure if that was a compliment or an exhortation to work even harder. Either way he felt the pressure.

'My goodness, she's done it,' he said, as he witnessed Happiness polishing off the last of the ice cream without mishap. She knew what she was doing alright. He had been studying her technique, licking a dollop from each flavour in turn, while expertly revolving the base of the cone with her fingers. Gradually, she pushed the diminishing spheres down into the hollow of the double cone with her tongue, thereby reducing the risk of a spillage. Finally, triumphantly, classically, she nibbled off the pointy tip of the cone and sucked the remaining ice cream through the resulting aperture. Not as much as a dribble. And now, as she helped Maura into the passenger seat of the car, she looked like a poster girl for satisfaction.

'Excuse me,' a voice called irately from the other side of the square. 'Oy! Oy! Do you mind?'

It was a man in his mid-forties, wearing a short-sleeved shirt with billowing arms and beige chinos.

'Foster,' muttered Aoife under her breath.

He barrelled towards them.

'What do you think you're playing at?'

'Hello, Eugene. Nice to see you too,' said Aoife. 'This is Eugene Foster, chairman of the Ennismore Tidy Towns committee. And this is—'

'I know who you are, Finn O'Leary. Aoife's secret weapon.'

He pronounced Finn's name sarcastically. And likewise the words 'secret' and 'weapon'. He was standing uncomfortably close to Finn's face, spatial awareness obviously not one of his better traits.

'Although I don't watch television myself. Too busy. And just because you're a big star, Billy Big Boots, doesn't mean you're going to get away with that.'

Foster dramatically pointed at a spot on the ground where a drop of Finn's lemon sorbet was melting.

'What?'

It was barely a dot. How did he even notice that from fifty yards away? He must have been sitting on his quad bike with a telescope.

'Wipe it up!'

'Ah, it's ... I can't see anything.'

'We run a tight ship here in Ennismore. Unlike some

places,' he said pointedly. 'I saw the pictures in the paper, Aoife. Shocking altogether. You really need to get your act together.'

'There's nothing there, Eugene. You're hallucinating. Must be the late night you had,' said Aoife, equally pointedly.

'What are you insinuating?'

'Bit insecure, are we?'

'I'm very secure.'

'You big baby. Want him to wipe your backside too while he's at it?'

Aoife leaned into him.

'I'd prefer to lose, Eugene, than to cheat. That's a stain you can never remove.'

'That's a very serious allegation, Aoife Prendergast.'

'You'll have to burn down Abbeyford to have any chance of the Tidy Towns this year.'

'It's okay, Aoife,' said Finn in an attempt to de-escalate the situation. 'Aoife, it's fine.'

Finn searched his pockets for a tissue. No joy. Foster, smugly, folded his arms. By now Happiness and Maura had got out of the car again and came over to see what the commotion was all about. Happiness handed Finn a tissue. He was strangely moved by her act of kindness.

'Dundee.'

For once she wasn't referring to him. Finn got down on his knees.

'There.'

Foster bent down to inspect the job.

'It'll have to do, I suppose. You're wasting your time with this shower, big shot like you. If you're ever looking for a proper job, give me a shout.'

He handed Finn his business card. EUGENE FOSTER, VETERINARY SURGEON, COUNTY COUNCILLOR, PEACE COMMISSIONER.

'It'll be worth your while.'

Off he went. Finn followed him to his quad bike.

'You've done a great job here, Eugene, fair play to you. The town is stunning,' he said quietly but firmly. 'But if you or any of your minions ever step foot in Abbeyford again, I will personally destroy Ennismore. I'll take it apart brick by brick. It'll be like Stalingrad when I'm finished with it.'

Foster, the swagger replaced by terror, didn't reply as he hopped on his quad and roared off. Finn felt bad, not that he'd intimidated the objectionable man, but that he'd lost his temper. In recent years, he'd learned to keep the head. And as his career progressed, he'd also become more conscious of his public image and as a result more circumspect. But with the dead natterjack toad, that for some reason had suddenly popped into mind, and the selfless, valiant efforts of Aoife and her Tidy Towns team, and the priggishness of Foster, he was furious.

'Seems like a nice man,' said Maura, as Finn rejoined them and they headed for Tullaun after their detour.

Happiness, one hand on the steering wheel, rolled down the window and before Aoife could stop her, threw out a clump of tissues and an empty drink can she'd found in the side pocket. It was a small gesture, but defiant and rebellious all the same. In her mind, it was the right thing to do, and Happiness didn't do things lightly. Finn, proud of her, took it as a sign of solidarity. He rolled down his own window and threw out Eugene's scrunched-up business card. Maura, who hadn't been quite herself all morning, joined in the fun. She rolled down her window and threw out the old vinegar-drenched fish-and-chip wrappers she'd found in her side pocket. Aoife, despite her chronic aversion to littering, didn't intervene. This wasn't quite the revenge on Ennismore she had imagined. But in the absence of suitable firepower and deep-seated malice, it was nonetheless a satisfying, symbolic act.

Chapter 41

Tullaun House, for the home of a branch of the celebrated confectionery family, was surprisingly modest. Well, compared to some of the Big Houses in the area. It was Italianate in style and classically proportioned, surrounded by about twenty acres of fabulous gardens, and some three hundred acres of farmland, most of which was under wheat. There was a ruined castle, Tullaun Castle, on the site, which dated back to 1560.

They parked on the gravel in front of the house. There was no obvious entrance to the gardens and nobody answered the front door when Happiness repeatedly pressed the bell. They peered in through the windows. Finn got a fright when he saw, in one of the drawing rooms, a woman clad only in a pale dressing gown standing before an easel. She was furiously, with sweeping brushstrokes, painting what looked like a stormy seascape. Was that a ship being tossed on the rocks? He tried to attract her attention but she ignored him.

'That's my sister. Deaf as a post.'

A woman, jeans tucked into her wellies, came striding around the corner. She was wearing a tweed jacket, prim blouse and a bolo tie. For some reason she reminded Finn of Wyatt Earp.

'We don't have a set charge as such. Just put whatever you think is appropriate in the honesty box.'

There was a metal box on a post near the hall door. It would have been beneath the descendants of the Sheridans to handle anything as grubby as cash.

'We recommend twenty euros each,' she added, firmly.

Alice, contrary to Redmond's tasteless joke, was a handsome woman, thin, with angular features, a sharp nose and chin. Finn dug deep. He only had two fifties.

'I am so sorry. We don't have any change. This way.'

Alice opened the door. There was a visitors' book in the vestibule.

'I'll sign for everybody,' Aoife volunteered.

While Alice showed the others into a rather grand hall, Aoife whipped out her phone and took the opportunity to photograph the previous pages of the visitors' book. Of course there was a good chance that whoever stole the belladonna didn't actually advertise the fact that they were there; but the other visitors that day might have seen something.

The only way to the gardens was through the house.

'It's an honour to have you here, Mr O'Leary. Ginny and Faith will be so jealous I met you.'

Alice clapped her hands in a gleeful, girlish way.

'Faith has one of her migraines. And Ginny . . . One can't disturb our Virginia when she's under the spell of the muse. This is so exciting.'

Alice gave them a perfunctory tour of the ground floor in a stiff, unenthusiastic way and quickly ushered them out to the gardens. Hospitality didn't come naturally to her. It was obviously a source of some embarrassment to be forced to open her house and gardens to the public just to keep the lights on. Perhaps their stake in Sheridan's was not what it was cracked up to be. After vaguely indicating the path to follow and mentioning some of the botanical highlights including the poisonous plants and the walled garden, Alice gratefully took her leave.

'Don't forget the bluebell meadow. As I'm sure you know they were late to bloom this year. When you're finished you can leave by the side door. Make sure you close it after you.'

The quartet made straight for the poisonous plants. There was quite an array on display in a fenced-off area. Apart from the deadly nightshade, there was at a glance hemlock, hemlock water-dropwort, lily of the valley, oleander, foxglove and lupin. It was hard to say if any of them had been tampered with many weeks after the event but one thing was certain: there was an empty space behind the label for the *atropa belladonna*.

'Why would they take the whole plant?'

'A few leaves would have done the trick.'

'Or berries.'

'And how would they get it out of here without anybody noticing?'

Happiness all of a sudden shivered and instinctively turned towards the house. There she caught a glimpse of a woman's face staring at them from an upstairs window.

'Faith, presumably,' said Aoife.

There were no obvious clues as to who had removed the plant. They rooted around in the vegetation for a good ten minutes. No footprints. No Crunchie bar wrappers. Nothing.

'I found this.'

They all jumped. It was an apparition with frizzy auburn hair, wearing a cashmere jumper.

'Faith?'

The woman nodded. Judging by the holes in her sweater,

the garment was clearly something of a playground for the moths. Faith looked like she was being choked by a string of pearls. And she was holding a rubber glove by one of its fingertips.

'It might be of interest.'

Faith Birdthistle had the same profile as Alice albeit with a slightly more pronounced chin. Her eyes were dilated, as if she'd just dropped a tincture of atropine in them. It was a thick workman's glove, blue in colour and coated in PVC or nitrile, with canvas cuffs.

'I found it out front. The day the plant was stolen.'

Like Alice, although her family had been in Ireland for at least ten generations, Faith spoke with an English accent, strangulating the vowels. Unlike Alice, she seemed slightly spaced out, with long pauses between her sentences. But her memory was clear. She told them that not only was the whole belladonna taken but that the thief did in fact take berries and leaves from the other plants.

'I was in my room, sewing. It had been raining all day. I thought at first it was Kelly, the gardener. He, or she, was wearing some sort of oilskin. I really must go.'

Faith didn't move.

'Mummy likes me to wash her feet.'

She laughed.

'Silly me. Have you seen the bluebells?'

And with that Faith drifted back towards the house.

'A very nice lady,' said Maura.

They left the gardens by the side door as instructed by Alice just in time to see a lorry roaring off. As it rounded a corner on the drive, they noticed the unmistakable pink colour scheme of the AAAAAAAAAA waste disposal company.

'Let's not jump to any conclusions,' cautioned Finn.

They went looking for Alice. No sign of her. Happiness prodded the doorbell. Finn knocked on Ginny's window. She, busily obliterating her artwork with black paint, the tempest now an internal one, either didn't hear him or chose to ignore him.

'Alice,' Happiness shouted at the top of her voice, at a decibel beyond the capacity of most human beings. Within seconds, Alice arrived, cradling a new-born lamb in her arms.

'Dreadful racket. I trust this is important.'

In answer to Aoife's query, Alice brusquely acknowledged that Duggan's company collected waste from Tullaun every Tuesday. And, no, she didn't know either Barry Duggan Senior or Barry Duggan Junior personally. It might have been just a coincidence that one of Duggan's lorries was at Tullaun the day the poison that killed Michael was procured. Then again AAAAAAAAAA did most of the commercial rubbish collections in the whole south-east. Aoife thought the glove, now in Maura's handbag, looked awfully like the ones Barry Junior was wearing the day they interviewed him at the yard. Either way they decided as a matter of urgency that it was time to speak to Barry Junior again.

Chapter 42

On the way back to Abbeyford, to be on the safe side, they decided to bypass Ennismore. This was in case Foster and his crew were waiting for them to exact retribution for their recent audacity in littering his town. And Happiness was crawling along, in low gear, even slower than usual, if that was possible, the engine of the Yaris protesting in vain. It dawned on Finn, as they rounded another hairpin bend, throwing him briefly on top of Aoife, that it was not entirely her choice. Maura, since her accident, was a nervous passenger and her body language, her imaginary braking, was a constant reminder to Happiness to slow down.

On the road, they formulated a plan. They would hand over the glove to the guards, ask them to check for DNA and see if that DNA matched Barry Junior's. In the meantime, Aoife and Finn would corner Barry. They'd give him a good grilling about the mounting circumstantial evidence against him. If only they could get their hands on a copy of Barry Senior's will. If Duggan had changed his will before he was murdered, at Barry Junior's expense, that would surely have given him a motive.

'That's a job for Happiness,' said Maura.

'I don't know about that, Mammy. Bit risky, no? She's a carer, not a ninja. No offence, Happiness.'

'She is joking, fool.'

Maura smiled salaciously. Happiness took her eyes off the road for a moment to read her employer.

'You are joking with me, Maura. Is it?'

'If anybody can find out what's in Barry's will, Happiness can.'

Aoife laughed.

'She's right, Happiness. You know what you have to do.'

Finn was in the dark.

'No, no, no, no, no, no, no. No! No way. You are barking in the wrong tree. Ah ah. *Ko şeé şe,*' she said in Yoruba.

She fixed her eyes on the road ahead.

'What?' Finn pleaded with the ladies for enlightenment.

'They are asking me to go on a date with Aloysius Sweeney.'

'For the team,' said Aoife.

'He's not the worst,' said Maura.

'That is not helping, Miss Maura.'

'And he really does fancy you.'

'And I can't blame him,' added Aoife, from behind.

Happiness was impervious to their flattery.

'He can be quite charming.' Maura tried another tack. 'In his own way. His own very strange way.'

'And generous, isn't he, Maura?' Aoife elaborated. 'He'll bring you to Lardo. Which is not terrible.'

'You are not selling it to me.'

'We'd be outside the restaurant in the car,' Finn joined in. 'You know, if he tried anything.'

Happiness turned around to give him one of her by now legendary baleful looks. An oncoming car beeped her to stay on her own side of the road. She beeped him back with interest.

'I do not want to go on a date with any man.' She beeped the horn on each syllable. 'Especially not Mister Sweeney.'

Eventually by the time they got back to Abbeyford they'd worn her down. Once she was absolutely certain that none of them thought for a moment that she might actually be interested in the solicitor, she relented. For the greater good. Her curiosity and her appetite for a challenge got the better of her. Alo was one of the few people alive, if not the only person, who knew the contents of Barry's revised will. Happiness, with her wiles and her nosiness, just might be able to find out if Barry's son had a motive.

'Or Monika,' said Finn, ever the devil's advocate.

'Listen to him,' said Aoife. 'Just dying to interview Monika again, are we? Now that she's single.'

'Alo's a very lonely man, Happiness,' said Maura. 'He'll tell you everything.'

'Yes, he will,' said Happiness, back to her haughty, self-confident self. 'Even if I have to beat it out of him.'

Chapter 43

Apart from the ice cream in Ennismore, Finn hadn't eaten all day. Any notion he might have once entertained about enjoying a quiet hiatus from life and work at home in Abbeyford had long been abandoned at this stage. The mental and physical reset would have to wait. And the more pressing concern of dinner would have to wait too now that he had the bit between his teeth after the fruitful trip to Tullaun. While Aoife escorted Maura and Happiness to Morrissey's for a bite to eat before their evening choir practice, Finn called around to Xavier's house. Most people traditionally bring a cake or a bottle of wine when dropping in on old friends. Finn brought twenty two-by-eight treated shiplap boards he'd picked up at the timber yard and some galvanized bolts.

'For the treehouse,' he explained to a bemused Xavier who had just arrived home from work and was busy making a carbonara for the children.

'I knew you wouldn't let me down. You just missed Niamh. She's on nights.'

Xavier helped Finn carry the timber out the back. The latter, no more than the former, hadn't a clue how to construct a tree house. To make things more complicated, there didn't seem to be a suitable tree in the small garden of the semi-detached house.

'So which one were you thinking of . . . ?'

Xavier pointed at the designated tree, an *amelanchier* 'Robin Hill' with mature purple berries.

'Yeah. Nice specimen alright. Bit on the small side, I fear, no?'

It was by far the biggest tree in the garden but only about seven feet tall with flimsy branches and a trunk barely a foot in girth. It would be risky hanging a birdhouse on a tree like that.

'I see what you mean, Finn. Listen, no rush. Sure, come back to me in five years.'

Off duty, DS Keane was likably laid-back. He was himself.

'Or here, better still, we could just build them a little shed? They won't mind.'

They went back inside. Xavier put on the Style Council. They ate the pasta and had a beer. Finn gave Xavier the glove and asked him to check it for DNA. Xavier, frowning, agreed to do so although he was a bit miffed that Finn wouldn't tell him where he got it, or what the angle was. Finn could see that there was something on his mind. And could see that his willpower was wilting, his Garda training no match for his urge to share, and do what he felt was right in terms of solving the case.

'Tell me, is there something going on between you and Aoife?'

'What? No. Of course not.'

'I only bring it up because she has a bloke, some tool called Delahunt. Unsavoury character, in my opinion. Bit of a temper on him.'

'I can look after myself, Xavier.'

'No, no. Just giving you the heads-up. So as you know what you're getting into.'

'I'm not getting into anything. And I'm pretty sure you have something else on your mind.'

Xavier laughed.

'I'm not inscrutable enough to be a cop, am I? What do you know about Eddie Halfpenny?'

'Eddie? The taxi driver? Well, he's not the full shilling, is he?'

Xavier smiled.

'Bit of a character alright. It's just . . .'

He looked around to make sure his children weren't listening.

'The grenade!'

'What about it?'

'You know about the grenade?'

Finn nodded.

'This town! Eddie was ex-army. A ranger apparently.'

'Was he, though? Is that not just bluff? A bit of bravado.'

'It's not much to go on, I admit, but he was overheard in Morrissey's a few weeks ago telling someone, some tourist, a rando, that he knew where he could get his hands on weapons. Ammunition, grenades, even a tank.'

Finn had to laugh, remembering the last conversation he had had with Eddie. So Eddie did know more than he'd been letting on.

'That's just Eddie. Like you say, he's a character. A fantasist. What was he on to me about the other day? Oh yeah. He doesn't believe in the moon landings, Special. In fact he doesn't even believe in the moon.'

At the reference to his old nickname, Xavier gave Finn a disappointed look. Finn held his hands up in apology. It was clearly a sore spot.

'I know, I know, I'm very fond of Eddie too . . .'

Special got up and went to the fridge to grab a couple more beers. He handed one to Finn.

'Hope you're not driving.'

'Wouldn't dream of it.'

'You didn't hear this from me. But Eddie has a brother in jail.'

'I didn't know that.'

'Not many people do. It's not one of his old stories. We checked it out. It's true. A ten-year stretch. And he blames Barry.'

Over another couple of beers, Xavier explained the background. Barry had relations in Dublin, the Dublin Duggans, who were heavily involved in crime. Post-office jobs, a high-profile Securicor robbery.

'Do you remember?'

Finn didn't.

'And there was a bank robbery in Waterford city about ten years ago. They got away with a million or something like that. Valerie would know.'

He looked like he was missing Valerie. The verbal sparring. Being corrected.

'What's that got to do with Barry?'

'There's a theory, only a theory, that Barry was the mastermind.'

'Barry?'

'Got the cousins from Dublin to do the dirty work.'

'I don't see where Eddie fits in.'

'Hold your horses, Finn. I'm coming to that.'

Finn was beginning to wish Valerie was there too. They complemented each other beautifully. And together tended to get to the point a tad quicker.

'About a year later, after a tip-off, a Thomas Halfpenny was arrested.'

'The brother.'

'Correct. Charged and convicted for the armed robbery. But the money was never recovered. Did you ever wonder why Eddie moved down here?'

'No.'

'Neither did I until a few days ago.'

'C'mon, Xavier, there's any number of reasons why someone like Eddie might have moved. Have you seen the price of houses in Dublin?'

'Yeah, yeah. Might be a blind alley, I know.'

'Could be a broken relationship, a change of scenery, anything. Who wouldn't want to live in Abbeyford?'

They both laughed.

'Or he might have come here to get close to Barry Duggan. The man, if the theory is correct, and I'm not saying it is, who got his brother banged up for ten years.'

'Ridiculous! Eddie?'

'It has to be looked at. He might have bided his time until now, 'til he got the opportunity. He had the motive.'

'I suppose.'

'And with his military contacts, he also had the means.'

'And let me guess, you want myself and Aoife to have a little chat with Eddie.'

'That would be most unethical, Finn, I mean, only if it's convenient. And very, very discreet. We could take him in, but you know yourself, he won't talk.'

Chapter 44

By the time Finn got to Morrissey's, the others had left to sing at the community centre. After a few false starts, it was the first time the choir had convened since Michael's death. It was bound to be a sombre occasion. The emporium had run out of candles. Femke Leerdam, the sculptor had been commissioned to make some sort of memorial bowl, a ceramic incense burner, that in some way would represent the deceased. Nobody was quite sure what it was, or which anatomical part inspired it, or how exactly it said 'Michael'. There was also a danger that the musical director, Wolfie, would take the opportunity to preview his new avant-garde composition, which he had dedicated to Michael. And while there was a chance the person who poisoned Michael, and by extension blew Duggan to smithereens, was going to be there, Finn decided to stay in the pub and wait for Aoife's return.

Eve Duggan was rushing out the door as Finn arrived. Although the evening was warm, she was wearing a coat.

'Oh hello.'

She blushed slightly, caught off-guard.

'Eve, how are you, off to choir?'

'I am indeed.'

'What'll Hector do without you?'

'He'll manage.'

Although she was low-key by nature, it wasn't like Eve to entirely swerve a chat.

'Do you want a lift?'

'You're grand.'

She pointed to an electric scooter resting just inside the front door. Then she seemed to force herself to make an effort to be friendlier.

'You're doing a great job on the town. I was down the Ball Alley there. Magical, so it was. Like butterfly heaven.'

'Thanks Eve. I've been meaning to ask. How is Barry?'

'Barry?'

She didn't welcome the question.

'Is he okay?'

'Not great now to be honest with you, Mr O'Leary, thanks for asking.'

'Finn.'

'Barely left the bed this past few days.'

'Sorry to hear that, Eve.'

Her voice wavering, she was in danger of becoming upset.

'He took it very bad so he did. And despite what people say, he was close to his father.'

'Right.'

'He loved him. I know old Barry could be hard on him. He could be hard on everyone. Even Monika.'

Eve looked at him for a reaction.

'Monika?'

'There was talk there. Ah it's none of my business. I better go.'

'What kind of talk, Eve?'

'Well, you know, the usual, that Monika might have been having an affair. People have nothing better to be doing than spreading gossip. I hear enough of it in the pub. Goes right over my head. Where does she go on a Friday morning? That sort of thing.'

'Every Friday?'

'It's just, if she was, having an affair, and I'm not saying she is, I don't know where she goes on a Friday, and I don't care. A house on Pearse Street, they say. It's just if Barry, Barry Senior that is, had of found out about it . . .'

Eve whistled.

'You think Barry might have found out that Monika was having an affair? She killed him before he killed her?'

'That man had some temper, is all I'm saying. I wouldn't have liked to be in her shoes.'

It occurred to Finn that Eve was trying to protect her husband, by deflecting attention on to Monika. That said, the possibility of Monika having an affair was another line of enquiry to add to what was becoming a very long list of leads.

'Do you think I could visit Barry?'

'Why?'

Eve's face darkened. Her tone changed. There was suddenly a hardness to her he'd never noticed before.

'I was there the night his dad died. I just . . . I feel so sorry for him.'

'Don't go near the house,' she insisted, before softening, 'please. It's in no fit state.'

Eve brushed away a stray hair from her forehead.

'He'll be back at work in a couple of days. I'll make sure of it. You'll find him there. But I can tell you now, he didn't kill his father.'

She hopped on her scooter and took off. Eve was surprisingly steady and fleet as she zipped away. Her coat opened in the breeze to reveal a bottle of whiskey secreted in the inside pocket. Finn wondered if Hector knew she'd taken it.

Chapter 45

The bar was quiet. The press maul had rolled back to Dublin. There were more murders in the capital. More corpses to circle over. Besides, a leading politician had just been outed for awarding his mistress a job on a state body. Hector looked up from his crossword and gave him a nod. Finn nodded back and retired to a snug to where a steady stream of pints arrived to provide him with comfort and inspiration as he tried to piece together what he'd learned so far.

There were two murders but only one intended victim: Barry Duggan Senior. That much was clear. They had suspects galore. Top of the list for the moment was Barry Duggan Junior. Finn saw with his own eyes how abominably his father had treated him. There was a possibility that Duggan had changed his will to favour Monika and his second family. Happiness was assigned to go on a date with Duggan's solicitor, Alo Sweeney, to find out if there was any merit in this contention. Being disinherited as well as disrespected would certainly provide motive. But did he have the wherewithal? The chops? Beneath that lumbering, cowed exterior, did he have the imagination and the sheer viciousness to kill his own father in such a dramatic way? Could he really have flown the drone after he'd hobbled off injured during the football match? The injury was genuine.

Of that Finn had no doubt. He was concussed. Could you even fly a drone with concussion? And this was a planned attack, timed to perfection. Of course there was the prospect of an accomplice being involved, but Finn's brain couldn't currently countenance that idea given the myriad connections between everyone in the close-knit town of Abbeyford. He was far from convinced about Barry Junior's guilt or innocence. But until Happiness reported back from her soirée with the lawyer and until himself and Aoife had talked to him they would have to reserve judgement.

Then there was Monika. She was something of a curiosity. Significantly younger than Barry Senior, rumoured to be having an affair, chaperoned by her frankly sinister brother, Dominik, she stood to inherit a fortune now that her husband was dead. She'd known about his heart trouble. She could easily have poisoned his tea. And she, not having the distraction of playing a football match, was better placed than Barry Junior to guide the grenade that exploded at her husband's feet. They would have to watch her closely over the next few days.

Harry Boyle was not out of the woods yet either. How did a piece of fabric from his jacket end up in Carney's Wood from where the drone had been supposedly launched? The GP was a passionate man. If he really thought Barry Duggan had murdered Michael, it wasn't inconceivable that Harry, in rage and grief and operatic excess, could have exacted his revenge. Hector had flown him over Duggan's property some weeks prior to the attack. Finn was pretty sure that if they didn't come up with a plausible alternative in the near future, Harry would be re-arrested and charged with the crime whether he did it or not.

He couldn't discount Hector either. Not only had he

piloted a small plane over Barry's estate, he regularly handled the drone that literally delivered murder. Although he had an alibi, and no known motive, in many ways he was the most obvious candidate.

'Ah, the very man,' said Finn reflexively as Hector put down a fresh pint in front of him.

Hector had an unnerving habit of creeping up on you. Skin and bones, he was light on his feet. He didn't say much as a rule. In fact, he barely breathed at the best of times. He could murder somebody right in front of your nose and you mightn't notice.

'That one's on the house. For all the good work you're doing.'

'Why would Barry Duggan have a toy car in his safe?'

What little blood was in Hector's face to begin with drained from it.

'I couldn't tell you.'

'Did he collect them as well?'

'I doubt it. I know most of the collectors in this country.'

'Sorry, I was just thinking out loud there. Thanks. Cheers!'

Finn raised his glass of stout as Hector walked away.

'You were talking to Barry on the phone just before the grenade exploded.'

'Well, yeah.' Hector turned around again. 'I'm still a bit you know traumatized or whatever. I should probably see somebody. A therapist.'

It would take an army of therapists a lifetime, Finn thought, *to work out exactly what was going on in Hector's head.*

'I mean you could have been operating the drone at the time. In theory.'

'I could, in theory, if the drone hadn't been stolen. And if I wasn't in the bar, serving customers.'

'So you say. Could you ... How would you trigger it?'

'What?'

He realized he'd forgotten to say the word, grenade.

'The grenade. Right? You take the pin out, I get that. How come the grenade doesn't explode over the town, in the sky? Not until it lands precisely at Barry Duggan's feet?'

'Ah. It would be easy enough. A spring of some sort. A mousetrap would do the job, a few elastic bands. Boom!'

'You seem to know a lot about it, Mister Morrissey.'

'You're drunk, Finn. I do a lot of experimenting. It's part of my business. Providing a valuable service to rural areas. You'd be surprised what you can do with a mousetrap. Anyway, I discussed all this with the guards. They believe me.'

'So do I, Hector. So do I.'

Finn didn't know what to think. There was something niggling about the timeline. It's like time itself had stopped that night. The whole town was in a stupor while somebody was manipulating that dreaded device. And now, thanks to Xavier, there was a new name firmly in the mix: Eddie Halfpenny. As if they didn't have enough to be getting on with, they were compelled to investigate Eddie, one of Aoife's closest allies in the Tidy Towns movement. He, too, had a grievance with Duggan. He wasn't at choir practice. That didn't mean he couldn't have planted the poison earlier. Half the town, it seemed, were in and out of the community centre on any given day. Nor was he in the pub the night of Michael's memorial. He could easily have stolen the drone. Being ex-army and, if as he implied special forces at that, he would have had a variety of skills at his disposal to dispense with his enemies. And if Finn's friend in the

Gardai was to be taken at his word, Eddie knew where to get his hands on a grenade.

On his own, the alcohol broadening his mind, enlarging the pool of suspects further, he saw guilt everywhere. He remembered snippets of various conversations he'd had or heard over the past few weeks. Vignettes flashed before his eyes. So many people disliked Duggan. They hated him and had reason to kill him. Kitty Doyle had cheerfully admitted to adulterating Duggan's tea with a laxative because of the callous way he'd treated her husband. Others entered the frame briefly due to something they said, or didn't say, or because of some unusual body language. Eve Duggan, for instance, had previously flown the drone from the pub to Duggan's football pitch. She presumably didn't have much time for the victim given the way he'd treated her husband.

Finn's own father, Redmond, was familiar with poison plants and where to find them. Although sometimes he thought of his dad as a bit unhinged, he couldn't imagine him actually committing murder. Thanks to Duggan, though, he did spend a stint in jail but he was sure his father wouldn't take that sort of thing personally. Knowing Redmond, he probably enjoyed the novelty, the notoriety of being a jailbird. No, if Redmond had harmed Duggan, it would have been on behalf of the environment.

Finn tried to think of any cause that would drive him to murder. He couldn't, off the top of his head. That made him momentarily quite sad. Not that he wanted to kill. But that there was no cause so dear to him. And that suggested a lack of passion, or purpose in life. There were other peripheral suspects but there was little credible evidence against them and, like Eve and his father, they had decent alibis.

While he was waiting for Aoife to return to Morrissey's

after choir practice, he wandered around the pub, admiring the memorabilia, the hodgepodge of artefacts and the hundreds of photographs depicting more innocent times. A line under one faded photo caught his eye. Big Snow. He did a double take. 12 March 1982. *Night of the Big Snow.* It was a picture of four men all in suits sitting around a table in Morrissey's Bar. That was taken, he quickly realized, the night Eamonn 'Rameses' de Burgh had disappeared, never to be seen again. Between the contemporary murders and the overload of detail through which he was currently sifting, not to mention the pressure of the Tidy Towns campaign, he had completely forgotten about poor Rameses. He took the photo off the wall. The only person he recognized straightaway was that epitome of piety, Gerry Flynn, Fionnuala Boyle's forbidding father. Before he could put names to the other faces, a crowd, including Aoife and Harry Boyle and Monika Duggan, entered the pub. Finn hastily removed the photo from the frame, stuffed it into his trouser pocket and went to join the returning choristers.

Monika was wearing black lipstick when Finn approached her at the bar to express his sorrow; she wrapped both arms around him and pulled him tightly to her.

'You must finish the garden. It's what Barry would have wanted.'

'I didn't want to intrude at this difficult time.'

'No. Please. Come any time. I insist. You have my number.'

Finn paid for his drinks and conveyed them to Harry and Aoife. Aoife raised her eyebrows to let him know she'd seen what had just transpired.

'Don't let us detain you, if you have other commitments.'

'Ignore her, Finnington, she's jealous.'

Harry was in mellow-ish form, sober, indulging in wordplay. It was a good sign, and not the sign of a guilty man.

'Look at his face, Harry,' said Aoife laconically pointing at Finn. 'Goggle-eyed. Like Mowgli in *The Jungle Book*. Bamboozled by Kaa.'

Harry's rumbling laughter filled the bar. It was a welcome sound not heard for a while in these parts. Finn didn't mind being the butt of the joke. He derived inordinate pleasure from being teased by Aoife.

'I've been thinking,' Harry intoned. 'We can safely assume that whoever framed me is the murderer.'

'Obviously.'

'The question I pose: how did they manage to cut the little piece of fabric from my jacket? I wear it all the time.'

Finn and Aoife suppressed a smile. That jacket was so well-worn it could walk on its own.

'You're not wearing it now,' she noted.

'Precisely. That's my point. The only time I don't wear my jacket is when I'm in here.'

He indicated the hook on the wall near the bar where his jacket was currently hanging.

'You're in here quite a lot, if you don't mind me saying so,' Aoife reminded him.

'True, for my sins, which gave the culprit ample opportunity to excise that sample of exquisite corduroy from the garment.'

'What are you saying, Harry?' Finn asked.

'The murderer is a customer?' Aoife took over. 'That doesn't exactly narrow it down.'

'A customer' – Harry paused for dramatic effect – 'or a member of staff!'

'Hector?' Finn spluttered.

'Eve.' Harry lowered his voice.

'Eve?'

'Eve Duggan. She's not the angel she appears to be.'

Eve, by now, was back on duty. Their eyes collectively followed her around the bar as she, in one seamless, almost balletic movement served multiple customers, cleared tables, exchanged mild banter and small talk and at one point disappeared for a few minutes, presumably to change a keg.

'You see. She's gone. Vanished. She could have left the bar for a few minutes the night Duggan was killed. Nobody would have noticed.'

'But she wasn't at choir the night Michael died, remember?' said Aoife.

'True. But she was at the AA meeting earlier that day. She could easily have slipped the poison into Duggan's tea jar.'

'Wait. Eve was an ... alcoholic?' Finn whispered.

'Eve!' Harry shook his head, knowingly. 'Eve has led a colourful life.'

Harry was Eve's doctor. Setting patient confidentiality to one side in the interest of self-preservation and justice served, he outlined to Finn the pertinent details of Eve's medical history. Of course Eve's chequered past wouldn't have been a secret to most people in Abbeyford, least of all Aoife. Harry first treated Eve when she overdosed on heroin at the age of fifteen. To say Eve came from a troubled home was an understatement. A 'tearaway', Harry called her. By the age of seventeen she'd already been arrested on numerous occasions. Shoplifting. Selling weed. Stabbing one of her mother's partners. She had served time in juvenile detention.

'On her release, she gravitated towards the metropolis.'

In Dublin, things didn't get any better for Eve, by all

accounts. Among the reports about wayward sons and daughters that filtered back to Abbeyford from time to time was one story implicating Eve in a pipe-bomb attack. Apparently she'd been caught up in an escalating feud between two small-time dealers in the Crumlin area of the city.

'And then at the age of twenty-three, Eve returned home, clean, serene and totally at peace with herself and the world. The nuns took pity on her. Gave her a job, cleaning. Milking the goats. Then Hector gave her a chance, the patient, saintly Barry Duggan Junior married her, and the rest, as they say, is history.'

Finn, ever the voice of reason, was sceptical. You could edit anybody's biography to make them seem suspicious. Granted she was capable of violence, and, quite possibly, she'd had some experience with explosives. And she was undeniably resourceful – that was plain to see – but she was a reformed character. She had turned her life around. That was surely a cause for celebration instead of wild accusation.

'She couldn't have done it,' declared Aoife, a fraction ahead of Finn.

'Oh?' said Harry.

'What time was Barry killed?' Aoife asked.

'Five past eight,' affirmed Finn. 'I could never forget it.'

His face blanched as the memory unfolded before his eye.

'Eve was right there ...' Aoife pointed to a spot on the floor near the piano, recalling her conversation with Hector the night of the murder '... singing grace at five past eight.'

'How can you be sure?'

'The lotto. She switched on the TV. For the lotto. It starts at eight. Show only lasts fifteen minutes. Then she sang.'

There was a brief silence before Harry's infectious laugh drew sympathetic glances from elsewhere in the pub.

'Oh well, there goes that theory,' he chortled. 'Back to the drawing board.'

Harry finished his shandy, clicked his heels and took his leave.

'My apologies for maligning the good name of Eve.'

Chapter 46

'By the way, she texted him.'

Aoife's eyes were shiny in excitement. Finn caught Eve's attention and gave the signal for two more pints.

'Who texted who?'

'Happiness texted Alo.'

'No?'

'During the break. He called her back straightaway. Within seconds. They're going on a date.'

'No way, when?'

'Tomorrow. In Lardo.'

'Fantastic. We need a break in the case. I have to say, I am none the wiser,' said Finn, a bit addled, in truth, thanks to hunger, excessive alcohol consumption and a clamour of voices and shadows in his head all protesting their innocence.

Aoife and he had moved to a quieter corner near the piano. Having already brought her up to speed on what Xavier told him about Eddie, they briefly discussed the plan for the next few days. Barry Junior in the morning; Eddie Halfpenny in the afternoon.

'No, leave Barry until after Happiness susses out Alo about the will.'

'Good point.'

'Eddie. We'll talk to Eddie on Thursday too. At the bridewell. He's taking the day off.'

Thursday was the day they'd earmarked for a concerted effort to fix up the old jail. This was the last of the keystone works they hoped to complete before the Tidy Towns judges descended on Abbeyford. A local semi-retired builder had shanghaied a few of his handymen buddies, including Tony 'TenPints' Ring, to do a pit of repointing and other repair works on the listed structure. While the experts would be sprucing up the exterior of the building, Eddie and his volunteers would be clearing the interior of weeds and rubble. Meanwhile, a friend of Aoife's, a lighting designer by the name of Nicolas Galatini, who lived in West Waterford but had in the past lit shows for the Wexford Opera festival, had agreed to lend his expertise. On a minuscule budget, with basic effects – gobos and gels and uplighters – and a lavish imagination, he planned to project the story of the institution and the town on to the wall of the bridewell.

'By the way, any luck with the names?'

'What names?'

'The visitors to Tullaun.'

'I didn't get a chance. I was busy looking after your mother.'

'Touché.'

Aoife took out her phone and opened the photographs. Together they looked at the list of people who'd visited the estate the day the belladonna was stolen. Thankfully, it was a very short list. There were only five visitors that day.

'Nobody knows about it.'

'Such a pity, and it's a great garden, in all fairness.'

'They don't advertise. It's like they don't want people to see it.'

'I'm sorry I missed the bluebells.'

He stared into space as his eyes moistened.

'Are you okay, Finn? Is this an age thing?'

She had a wonderful, empathetic gift. On the one hand, she noticed everything, every little shift in emotional temperature, and on the other managed to find the right words to pre-empt any lapse into self-pity.

They read the names out loud. Etienne Leclerc, Chantal Guerin, Jenny Murray, Nuala Watters, Naoise Mac Anois. None of those names were familiar to either of them. Although a tiny, distant bell went off in Finn's head. It might have been Aoife's earring, their heads being quite close together at this stage. They decided to exclude the two French names for the moment, although the killer could of course have passed themselves off as French. That left three candidates. Of those, Naoise Mac Anois sounded the most suspect. It sounded like a made-up name.

'It literally translates as Naoise Mac Now,' said the schoolteacher.

'Bit stupid of the killer to come up with such a stupid pseudonym.'

'Bit stupid of them to sign their name in the first place.'

'It would look more suspicious if they didn't. With Alice hovering.'

'Maybe,' she pointed her finger at the list. 'But my money's on Mac Anois.'

'We should look at them all.'

'Oh we will.'

'We'll get Xavier and Valerie on the case.'

For once Aoife didn't resist the suggestion of involving the police. An hour passed. The bar thinned out. They chatted playfully about this and that, while their respective brains churned profoundly in the background.

'I meant to ask, what is the significance of the bell?'

He pointed at Aoife's earring.

'Michael had a bell tattoo. My father has an ancient cowbell outside his weird house in the woods. Are you in some sort of cult?'

Aoife laughed.

'It was your father's idea. When we started the campaign against the incinerator, he decided we needed a symbol, some sort of a charm that would unite us.'

'Right.'

'St Patrick apparently used the cowbell to ward off evil spirits.'

'Does it work?'

Playfully, she shifted away from him on the banquette.

'I'm not sure.'

A few minutes later, Finn extracted from his pocket the creased photograph he'd swiped from the wall earlier on.

'Who are these people?'

'Why?' asked Aoife.

'Why do you always ask why?'

'You're drunk.'

'I haven't drank half enough,' Finn slurred. 'That's my problem. Who are these very important men?'

'That's Gerry Flynn.'

'I know that. He never liked me, old Gerry. Thought I was cheeky.'

'He was right, Finn. You are. And that fella, that's Hector's dad.'

'Right, yes, I see the resemblance. The dead eyes.'

'Exactly. Richard Morrissey. Dickie. He died years ago.'

'I remember. I couldn't make the funeral.'

Thanks to his work, and his exile generally, he hadn't managed to attend a lot of important funerals. He should have made a bigger effort given the outsized significance funerals played in the culture of his country. Nor, he flayed himself, had he made it to the weddings of many of his old friends. He didn't even show up at his father's trial. If he wasn't careful, there was a present danger of becoming maudlin. To offset the prospect, he swallowed another half a pint of Guinness.

'You were greatly missed,' Aoife cajoled him.

'You're the cheeky one.'

'Show me again.'

Aoife took the photograph from his hands.

'Why are you so interested in this?'

'Why, why, why, always with the questions.'

'The lanky one with the unfeasibly narrow head is Celibate O'Connell.'

'The supermarket king?'

She nodded.

'That's right. Gavin's father. This is the Chamber of Commerce?'

'Is it?'

'I assume.'

She noticed the title for the first time. *Night of the Big Snow.*

'Has this something to do with Rameses de Burgh?'

'I don't know. It could be. Some people put up the money for the gold thing, the shenanigans. So my father says. Who's this guy?'

Finn stabbed a finger at the fourth and final figure in the photograph. The glare from an overhead lamp had bleached out the man's facial features. Aoife wasn't able to identify him.

'Shouldn't be too hard to find out. What are you thinking?'

Finn extemporized incoherently. In the snow, Rameses left Redmond and Maura's house. He replaced two of the eggs in the golden eagle's nest. And then, Finn envisioned for Aoife's benefit, he arrived in the pub, shivering, frostbitten, frightened, where after their monthly Chamber of Commerce meeting, his wealthy benefactors were having a lock-in. Finn pointed at the photograph. The clock on the wall in the background said two thirty. Rameses offered the remaining eagle egg as compensation for the seed money he'd so carelessly lost. It was Finn's humble submission that Rameses did not leave Morrissey's Bar alive. There was an altercation. Or an accident. His body was removed at dead of night through the secret passage, if there was a secret passage, or even, given the Big Snow, through the front door. One or all of those men – Gerry Flynn, the respectable chemist and religious maniac, Celibate O'Connell, the respectable grocer and equally fervent Catholic, Richard Morrissey, the respectable publican, undertaker and regular mass-goer and the fourth man, the Man Without a Face – was responsible for the fate of Eamon 'Rameses', a close friend of his parents' and one-time lover of his mother.

'Do you want to come back to the flat?'

As soon as he said it, he knew he had made a mistake. There was an awkward silence. Out of the corner of his eye he noticed Eve hiding a smile. She certainly didn't miss much. Aoife touched the back of his hand.

'You're grand, Finn. I'm up early.'

'I mean, just for a drink. It's not ... I wasn't ... I have some whiskey.'

'Of course. No. It's just I promised one of the boys I'd help him with his French. You know, before the exam.'

'Yeah, yeah. Absolutely.'

'Justin Kirby.'

'I haven't eaten. I might get some chips.'

'That's a good idea. Some other time. Soon.'

'Do you want a lift home?'

'No!'

Too loud, she realized, but she was genuinely alarmed at the thought of Finn driving anywhere in his current state. The few remaining customers in the bar, as well as Eve, craned their necks to get a closer look. It would give them something to talk about the next day.

'Thank you, Finn. I'll call Eddie.'

Chapter 47

'And would you believe it? He faked his own death just to see who would attend his funeral.'

Alo laughed in a high-pitched squeal. Then he clicked his fingers at the waitress.

'The service here,' he confided in Happiness. 'It can be a bit patchy.'

Aloysious Sweeney, eminent solicitor and commissioner for oaths, had been waxing lyrical about a man called Alexandre Balthazar Laurent Grimond de la Reyniere, the author of a nineteenth-century cookbook.

'A gourmand, like myself.'

Happiness, sitting upright, seeing as how she was in a restaurant, remained stone-faced.

'As I was saying, it's a bird within a bird within a bird and so on. Like a Russian doll. You start with a bustard, do you have bustards in Nigeria? You stuff a turkey into the cavity of the bustard – it's a big beast of a bird, I imagine – and then a goose inside the turkey, followed by a pheasant...'

He pronounced the word pheasant as 'feezant'. Happiness, although she was looking forward to the challenge of extracting information from Alo, was finding it difficult to concentrate.

'... then you put a chicken inside the feezant. They're

all dead of course, by now, the birds, and plucked clean of feathers. You have a duck, a guinea fowl, you get the idea, teal, and so on in order of descending size, partridge inside the teal, I believe. Engastration they call it, plover ... Orla, hello. Orla, yes, we'd like to order if you don't mind, Orla, this is Happiness ... '

'Be right with you, Mr Sweeney.'

'Tsk, where was I? Yes, did I the mention the lapwing? You insert the lapwing within the confines of the plover, or is it the plover within the lapwing? It's all in the book. Of course it's illegal to shoot a lapwing these days, then there's the quail – I've always had a soft spot for quail eggs ...'

Happiness, wearing a vivid red dress and crowned with a multicoloured gele, looked around the room while Alo wittered on about birds within birds. Lardo was a conventional Italian restaurant situated above a hair salon, the tables covered in the obligatory red-and-white gingham tablecloths. Lit candles were held in squat Chianti bottles cradled in straw baskets.

'A fiasco,' Alo mansplained, when she'd sat down. 'That's the name of the bottle.'

Apt, she thought, having second thoughts about the whole charade. He had stood up as she'd entered the dining room. Dapper to an extent in a double-breasted blue pin-striped suit, pink shirt and yellow silk tie, he attempted to kiss her cheek. She was having none of it, pulling her head back at the crucial moment. That was twenty minutes ago and he hadn't stopped talking since. Happiness was not too put out by his incessant chatter, for two reasons. Firstly, she needed time to compose herself in the unfamiliar surroundings of the restaurant. And secondly, she had detected a nervousness in her suitor, which mitigated somewhat his insufferable arrogance.

'... and finally the little lark goes inside the thrush. It's a delicate operation. Now the problem is, Happiness, there are no bustards in Ireland, not anymore, as far as I know. For my birthday last year, I personally stuffed a quail inside a feezant inside a turkey. It was delicious, if I say so myself, perhaps a tad underdone ... You must come around to the house for dinner, the table I picked up at an auction, oh many years ago now, Regency style of course, there is a tiny mark on it where somebody – I won't speak ill of the dead – put down a cup of coffee. Now I always say there are two types of people, coaster people and non-coaster people, hee-hee. Have you ever imagined your own funeral, Happiness?'

Lardo was empty on this Wednesday evening apart from a younger couple canoodling in the corner, an elderly couple and their middle-aged son who all ate in complete silence, and three men, one of whom Happiness recognized as Declan Doyle, deep in conference, speaking out of the corners of their mouths.

'Are you threatening me, Mr Sweeney?'

'No, no, purely rhetorical, I assure you.'

'I am joking.'

'Yes, of course,' he laughed in that screechy way again.

His eyes, behind his glasses, were magnified, giving him a slightly manic appearance. It briefly occurred to Happiness that he might be a serial killer, and she his next victim.

'This is marvellous. You know I have dreamed of this encounter for many a day.'

He stared at her, dreamily. It would have been disconcerting if he didn't look so lonely and vulnerable.

Happiness, remembering her task, fluttered her eyelash extensions at him.

'So have I, Aloysius.'
He swallowed hard.
'Now Mr Sweeney, what can I get you?'
It was Orla, the waitress.
'I'll have the sweetbreads to start followed by the veal saltimbocca,' he replied, not taking his eyes off Happiness. 'And a helping of spinach on the side.'
'And yourself?'
Orla turned to Happiness.
'Have whatever you want!' said Alo, extravagantly. 'It's on me.'
Orla rolled her eyes.
'Insalata Caprese, please.' She took great care over her Italian pronunciation.
'Excellent choice,' said Alo.
'And bruschetta with mozzarella.'
'Mmm,' he murmured.
'And for the main course, cacio e pepe, and carciofi alla Romana.'
'Wonderful.'
'And fried potatoes.'
'I love your headdress,' said Orla.
'Thank you.'
'Yes, I love it too,' said Alo not to be outdone. 'And may I compliment you on your exquisite Italian accent. It's like Sophia Loren is at the table. Ha ha. If Sophia was an African queen.'
Little did Alo know that Happiness had studied the menu online earlier that day, and together with Maura and the help of an app on her smartphone, they had practised the pronunciation of each dish.
Alo poured the wine, a Barolo.

'The reason I ask, I have this terrible fear there will be nobody there.'

'What are you talking about?'

'My funeral.'

'Your funeral?'

'When I die.'

'Nonsense, Aloysius. You are a very important man.'

'It's very kind of you to say so. I may be important, but I'm not very ... how shall I put it? Popular.'

He sipped from his wine and wiped his lips daintily with a napkin.

'I realized after my wife died that all our friends were in fact her friends.'

Speaking frankly, in a matteroffact way, he didn't seem to be looking for sympathy. Mind you, she did feel a little sorry for him.

'I am sure the whole town will be there,' she reassured him. 'Irish people love funerals. Maura goes to every one for twenty miles. People she does not even know.'

'Perhaps.'

'Don't worry, Aloysius. They will come. For the sandwiches.'

The starters arrived. Alo raised his glasses above his eyes to make sure she was jesting.

'I am joking.'

'Yes. Ha ha. I knew that.'

'I will be there. At your funeral.'

Alo became quite emotional.

'Will you? That makes me so happy.'

'I will sing. At your funeral.'

'Oh!' he said, taken aback.

'In Yoruba culture, we sing when a great man dies; we

praise the deceased in song. You were a good man. You lived a good life.'

'Well, yes, I'm not gone just yet. But thank you. Are you married, Happiness?'

If she was wrong-footed by Alo's blunt question, she didn't show it. He fidgeted with his napkin while trying to appear suitably nonchalant. But it looked like the answer to that question might make or break him. As a rule, Happiness didn't talk much about her past, not even to Maura. But for some reason – and it wasn't the wine, and it wasn't just because she wanted to gain his confidence – she opened up a little. Maybe it was because he asked, and he was a stranger, and she hadn't talked about herself to anybody for a very long time.

'I was,' she said quietly. 'I am not anymore.'

She poured more wine for herself. And topped up Alo's glass too with the remains of the bottle. He clicked his fingers at Orla and ordered another Barolo. She surprised herself by telling him she'd left Nigeria twenty years ago for Manchester with her husband, Festus. They worked there for five years, she in care homes, he as an accountant. Then they moved to Ireland.

'With Grace. She is my daughter. She attends Trinity College.'

'My goodness, I went to Trinity. That's hilarious.'

Festus had met a Kerryman in Manchester who had convinced him to join him in a business venture.

'Spring water! From the Macgillicuddy's Reeks.'

The young family settled in Killarney. Everything went well for the first two years. Festus and his associates set up the bottling plant. They had a good brand. Killarney Spring. It was selling well. But they hit a problem. Due to contamination in the water supply, the supermarkets stopped buying the water. The company went into administration. All the jobs were lost.

'And all our savings,' she said ruefully.

Happiness, Festus and Grace were stuck in Kerry. She managed to secure a job in a nursing home. Grace started primary school and was very happy. Festus drove a taxi for most of the year but felt the cold and went back to Nigeria each winter. As time went on, the winters became longer and longer. Once the tourists went home in September, Festus was off again to his beloved village. And then one year, he didn't come back.

'I found out he had taken another wife.'

'Oh.'

'And he has two children with this woman.'

'I see.'

'It is what it is.'

Alo excused himself and went to the bathroom, stopping to exchange niceties with Declan Doyle and his clients. *Oh Festus*, she thought. He had never settled in Ireland. A proud man with big dreams, he couldn't live with the shame of the business collapse. Even though it was not his fault. It was nobody's fault. He felt he had failed Happiness. He had failed his daughter. She looked at her watch. Time to change the subject. Alo sat down again. He had swept his hair back, polished his glasses and used a breath freshener.

'I also found out he had started a new business,' she resumed.

'Who's this now?'

'Festus.'

'Oh yes.'

'Spring water. In the Ogun state. Water from a spring

that has no known source. Miracle Water is the name of the brand. Very successful all over Nigeria.'

'Marvellous.'

'He is a millionaire.'

She hoped she wasn't laying it on too thickly. Mind you, Alo seemed captivated by her story and her hypnotic voice.

'My only fear is that Festus will disinherit my daughter. Grace.'

She placed an emphasis on the word disinherit while subtly gauging his reaction.

'Grace, the girl in Trinity?' he said to demonstrate what a good listener he was.

'I'm sure you see a lot of that in your business. Disinheritance.'

Again she wriggled the word disinheritance under his nose to see if he would bite. Everything Happiness told Alo was true up to the bit about her former husband starting a new company and becoming rich. She had been wondering how to broach the subject of Barry Duggan's will all evening when inspiration struck. Like the imaginary Miracle Water, her brainwave had no known source.

'Oh I see it all the time, Happiness. I shouldn't tell you this. But I have a client. Had a client. He died in horrific circumstances. Just a few weeks ago. For reasons of confidentiality I can't disclose how he died, you understand. Suffice to say it was murder.'

He whispered the last bit. Happiness clutched her neck dramatically.

'Murder?' she exclaimed.

'Yes. Murder. He had instructed me to rewrite his will only a month earlier.'

'No!'

'Yes. He had a bad heart, you see, and wanted to get his affairs in order. Now, originally the man was going to leave his business to his son – this is his son from his first marriage, who happens to be my godson. But that is by the by, a business worth millions I should add but, and I advised him strongly against it, he decided to disinherit this poor boy for reasons I won't get into, and leave everything, the house, the business, all his assets to his second wife, a foreign lady, Croatian I believe, and her child. So if you need help with your situation, any help at all, I would be very willing to ...'

'Would you like to see the dessert menu?'

'Orla, tell Giovanni that we would like a surprise! And could we have two cognacs, if you please? Large ones.'

Normally Happiness wouldn't let anybody order anything on her behalf, but since his tongue was loosening and since it was cognac on offer, she assented. She knew it was wrong to deceive him. But she had prayed for guidance. And God, as well as Maura, has assured her that bringing a murderer to justice was more important than a man's feelings.

'Did the man, your godson, know that his father had changed the will?'

'It's possible. There was a ...'

Alo hesitated. He studied Happiness curiously. For a second, she thought she might have been too forward and that she'd been rumbled.

'I really shouldn't, dear. It's highly sensitive. Do you like antiques?' he veered off. 'There's an auction in Dublin next week, the Mid-Century Modern at Adam's. It's usually very good. Why don't you ask Maura for a day off?'

Happiness' eyes widened. This was exactly what she hoped wouldn't happen.

'You and I can take a little spin to Dublin, have dinner at the Unicorn. Grace could join us. We could all go to a show.'

He smiled hopefully, revealing a set of yellowing teeth. At this point she was on the verge of standing up and bidding him a frosty good night. Maura, Aoife and Finn were in Morrissey's waiting for her call. She would give them a good lambasting for putting her in this position.

'Perhaps we could stay the night at the Shelbourne?' Alo fantasized, throwing caution to the wind.

Happiness almost shrieked. But she had come this far and she wasn't going to retreat now. She wanted to know who killed Michael and Barry just as much as the others.

'I will think about it. The auction. And the dinner. And the show,' she said with a hard full stop.

Alo was elated. She noticed he was wearing a gold ring. It was crudely made and noticeably yellow. He took it off and let her handle it. It was soft and malleable in her fingers.

'Twenty-four carat! Made from pure gold that, panned in the hills not far from here. An old client gave it to me in lieu of a debt.'

Happiness took in the information but was not going to be sidetracked from her mission.

'Did he see the will?' she asked innocently. 'The boy, your godson.'

'No. I mean, I don't know. It's funny you should ask. I got a call from the man, now deceased, at least I assumed at the time it was the man, asking me to come to his office. When I say office, it's just a few cabins, very rough and ready, for such a wealthy man. Now he wanted to go over the will one more time. When I arrived, at the appointed time, the man wasn't there. But his son was. The son I was telling you about, my godson. He told me that his father wouldn't be long and that I should wait, it was a most uncomfortable couch, with a rug on it, like a dog's bed, he made me a cup of tea and presented me with a slice of cake, I knew there was something funny about the cake, but I ate it anyway, out of courtesy. I was also quite hungry; you see, I always felt sorry for this boy, and he had so much promise. Within minutes, I felt a rumbling in my tummy, a gurgling noise and I had to run, literally run to the facilities. When I say facilities, I mean one of those portable kiosks, a filthy plastic box, like an upright coffin, no toilet seat, no paper, normally I use baby wipes, but they were in my briefcase, and my briefcase, I left on the filthy couch in my haste to reach the loo. Tiramisu!'

Orla had put down two plates of tiramisu.

'That's hardly a surprise, Orla. I must have a word with Giovanni. Where was I? Yes, I fear in my absence, and it was quite a lengthy absence, if you''ll forgive me, Happiness, the boy, my godson, might well have removed his father's will from my briefcase and seen with his own eyes, that he was out of favour, disinherited. I believe now with the wisdom of time that I was the victim of a cruel trick. The dicky tummy was no coincidence. That boy had impersonated his own father to lure me to the office. Chin-chin.'

They clinked glasses. They sipped their cognacs. They ate their tiramisu.

'Do you think Barry killed his father?' asked Happiness, the pretence dropped.

Alo swilled his glass. He deliberated.

'No. Well. I sincerely hope not.'

Chapter 48

Barry Junior was about to start his shift when Aoife and Finn landed in Duggan's yard on Thursday morning. There was no sign of Fidelma, the birdlike secretary. Dominik Kovačić was sitting behind Duggan's desk, his long legs, clad in brushed cashmere, sticking out beneath it. There was a broccoli and stilton quiche before him, and a supersize green smoothie. His henchman, Karl, was on the roof of the top Portakabin sunning himself on a folding chair. Mind you, he did have a pair of binoculars around his neck and a shiny metal object on his lap.

'You the boss now?' Aoife, brazenly called in to Dominik.

'Why? You need rubbish collection?' He smiled, baring his teeth. 'I give you special rate.'

They found Barry Junior sitting in his truck with a takeaway coffee and a bag of doughnuts. Both of them, Aoife first and then Finn, climbed into the cab to join him. There was a smell of whiskey and cigarettes inside that made them gag. Finn remembered the bottle Eve had concealed in her coat a few evenings before, the dutiful wife catering to her husband's needs, perhaps. Mind you, he was someone to talk, he chided himself, recalling the alcohol-fuelled misunderstanding with Aoife in Morrissey's. Luckily, she seemed to have completely forgotten about his clumsy though entirely innocent invitation to his flat. There was a photo of Eve and Barry on the dashboard, both in swimsuits, Eve behind him, her arms around his neck. With their ultra-pale skin, they looked untannable. But more importantly they looked happy.

'She's an amazing woman, alright. I'd do anything for her,' said Barry following their eyes to the photo.

Even kill? Finn was on the verge of saying but had the cop on to hold his tongue.

'We heard you saved her life,' opened Aoife, gently.

'Who said that?'

Barry looked shocked.

'Lots of people.'

With his negligible levels of self-esteem, he couldn't believe people would be talking about him never mind showering him with compliments.

'Rubbish. It's just something people say. Eve sorted herself out. I just tried to show her the love she deserves.'

They reflected for a moment on this powerful proclamation. Barry offered them a doughnut. They declined. Not being trained negotiators, neither Finn nor Aoife were sure how to proceed. Finn rolled down the window to let in some air.

'We know about the will.' Aoife just came out with it.

Barry, monosyllabic at the best of times, drummed his fingers on the steering wheel. Suddenly, he started up the engine. Before they had a chance to leap out of the truck, it tore off out of the yard, the doughnuts falling to the floor.

'Where are we going, Barry?'

'I don't know yet.'

Finn noticed a knife resting on the console between the seats. It had a dark substance on it. They drove at speed past St Joseph's. It was not yet nine o'clock. The boys were milling about in the yard, about to go in and sit English paper two.

'Barry! Slow down!'

'Sorry, Aoife.'

He eased his foot off the accelerator, but not enough for them to bail out safely. Not that they wanted to jump. Not yet.

'I don't care about the money,' he said, the tyres screeching as he turned sharply onto the New Bridge. 'I'm not greedy. Like some people.'

'Careful!'

'My father always taught me to stand on my own two feet, so he did. Work hard. Be a man. Make my own decisions.'

There was a lot of emotion in his voice. He didn't sound like he didn't care about the money. Nor, as they picked up speed again as they passed the community centre, was he acting like he didn't care.

'And you know, the thing is, we were like that!' He took a hand off the wheel to wrap the middle finger around the index finger. The lorry swerved across the single white line in the middle of the road. 'We were tight, like ... like ...'

Aoife, who once had the challenge of teaching Barry at school, encouraged him as he struggled for the metaphor that best summed up his relationship with his father.

'Like a pair of ...' she prompted him.

'Like a pair of balls,' he said. 'In a pair of underpants.'

They weren't expecting that. Barry clearly hadn't expected to say it either. He was embarrassed. And they were embarrassed on his behalf.

'You know what I mean, Aoife.'

'Yes, of course. You were close. A pair of peas in a pod.'

'That's what I meant. He was my idol. I adored him. Brought me everywhere. I'd be on his knees, back when he used to drive the lorry. He ...'

Barry started sobbing.

'He really loved me too. Until ...'

They were winding up the Annamoe road, towards the incinerator. Barry's voice trailed off.

'Until Monika came along?' prompted Aoife.

'What?'

'Things changed when he "hooked up" with Monika?'

Finn gave Aoife a look of admonishment on account of her pejorative terminology. Leading the witness, he believed it was called in legal circles. And he was worried Barry would lose control of the vehicle. There were no bollards, no fencing, no protection at all on this particular stretch of road. And he was acting recklessly, like a man with nothing to lose.

'And then Little Barry arrived?' she added, also behaving, in Finn's opinion, a bit recklessly.

'What are you talking about, Aoife? Me and Monika are great friends. And I feckin' love Little Barry. He's me brother.'

'So ... ?'

'We fell out over Eve!'

'Eve?'

'He told me, he said if I married Eve, he wouldn't leave me a penny. Called her a junkie thief. Worse. A lot worse. To my face. Nicest woman ever walked the face of the earth.'

He wiped his nose with the back of his sleeve. They had learned, not least from what Alo had told Happiness, that Barry Junior had been going out with Eve since they were teenagers. He had never given up on her, waiting patiently for her during her 'lost years', as he called them. A lot of his scrapes in his youth were as a result of him protecting Eve, struggling to pay off her debts, or fighting people who had sullied her name. And no matter what she did to herself, or to him, he was always, ungrudging and non-judgemental, there for her.

'Is that why you killed your father, Barry?'

Barry slammed on the brakes. They were by now outside the incinerator.

'I didn't kill my father,' he muttered between clenched teeth.

He was breathing heavily. Finn tried the door. It was child-locked.

'How many times do I have to tell you?'

Finn looked straight ahead while his fingers surreptitiously crawled across Aoife's lap towards the knife. Aoife yelped in surprise. He sincerely hoped she hadn't misunderstood his intentions. Besides it wasn't the time for foreplay. Barry was wise to Finn's clandestine manoeuvre and grabbed the knife. He held it up in front of him.

'What?'

He licked the knife.

'It's Nutella. I don't give a damn about no money. We're moving, the two of us. To England. Next week. Eve was onto a few of the breweries there. We've three, four offers. One in Peterborough. To be honest, apart from my father being killed, life's good. We're starting afresh.'

Barry put the truck into reverse.

'Did you think I was going to blow up the incinerator or something?'

'God no.'

'Or drive over a cliff?'

That's exactly what Finn was thinking.

'I just have to deliver this load. I can give yiz a lift back to town. But I've a few pick-ups on the way. Might take a couple of hours.'

'You're grand, Barry. We'll walk,' said Aoife.

'Yes. Sorry to bother you,' said Finn.

'No problem.'

'Oh before we go, Barry, you don't happen to do Tullaun House, do you?'

'Tullaun House? Tullaun? I've heard of it, yeah. Seen it on the list, alright. But, no, never been there. Not on my route. Why?'

Was he telling the truth?

'You weren't there last Tuesday? Or a couple of weeks before that?'

He shook his head.

'Couldn't even tell you where it is to be honest. Somewhere in Wexford, yeah? That would be James or Kaspar or one of the other lads. I can show you the rota back in the office.'

'You didn't cover for any of them?'

'Look, Aoife, I want to find out who killed my father. A lot more than you do. I couldn't have done it even if I wanted to. Ask Little Barry.'

He turned away from them.

'And like, as regards the first attempt on my father's life. I wouldn't know where to get poison, you know, poison plants or anything like that.'

Was that a hint of a smirk on Barry's face? Or just anguish contorting his features? Was that a slip of the tongue? Or a bit of deliberate trolling on his part?

*

It was a nice day. Aoife and Finn walked back to town. On the way they passed the Huguenot graveyard. Finn took great pleasure in seeing Aoife's reaction to the transformation he and his helpers had achieved in such a short space of time: the walls had been repaired; the gate had been painted and rehung; the headstones were now legible. Furthermore, Nathan, Aoife's nephew, had compiled a database of everybody who'd ever been buried there. He had diligently entered their details into a ledger, which he then laminated with beeswax and placed inside a ziplock bag. This register was kept in a special cupboard made by Redmond and the men's shed that was tucked discreetly inside the gate. Aoife was moved to tears by her beloved nephew's contribution and indebted to Finn for taking such an interest in him.

While Finn's instinct was to just let the field of tombstones to continue growing wild, he couldn't resist planting some snowdrops and dwarf narcissi. None of his old colleagues on *Garden Nightmares* would believe how sentimental or partial to colour he'd become. He was definitely a changed man since he'd returned to Abbeyford.

There'd been some resistance locally to his scheme. Gerry Flynn and the Holy Joes had claimed the cemetery as their own, denying that it ever had a Huguenot heritage at all. They were still fighting Louis XIV's seventeenth-century religious wars. Their activities frowned upon by the mainstream Catholic Church, Gerry and his friends had been occasionally using this obscure graveyard as a location for their maverick services. It had been blighted by cheap, garish statues of Mary and Joseph and the miracle worker Padre Pio for whom they had a particular reverence. Gerry was not at all pleased when Finn personally delivered the unwanted plaster icons to his door.

Chapter 49

Before they headed for the bridewell to see Eddie, Aoife and Finn, hot and hungry after their unscheduled five-mile hike, nipped into Café Madremonte for some refreshment. Ana pointed to a frail old lady in the corner.

'Finn, she has been waiting for you for over an hour.'
'For me?'
'Hi Ana,' said Aoife.

Ana grunted by way of a reply and pointedly turned away from Aoife towards the grill.

'Oh my God,' Aoife whispered, a smile forming on her lips.
'What?'
'She really has the hots for you.'
'The "hots"?! Don't be childish.'
'Ana thinks you and I . . .'
'Ridiculous. I don't know what would have given her that idea. The toastie is burning is all.'

The lady was sipping tea from her own vintage Aynsley bone china cup and saucer in the orchard gold style blouse.

'Miss Wallace!' exclaimed Aoife, for Finn's benefit.

It was 'Lady' Tara Wallace, the author, wearing what looked like an orchard gold blouse. There was a notebook on the table into which she was jotting down observations.

They approached her with caution given her apparent delicacy and her disposition and her variety of nervous tics.

'Tara is writing about me,' announced Ana proudly, from behind the counter. 'I will be famous.'

Nobody had ever referred to the hermitic writer as Tara before, by all accounts, not even her own parents. The old woman smiled benignly.

'Not strictly true, of course,' Lady Tara whispered, as her guests sat down, not because she didn't want Ana to hear, but because her voice never rose louder than a whisper.

'She's a wonderful person. And may figure in a minor role.'

Finn stole a glance at her notebook. As did Aoife. The writing he could not decipher. But there was a competent drawing of a tall woman covered in leaves.

'A female Beowulf?' said Aoife.

'Sorry,' said Finn.

The two women shared a knowing and, in Finn's mind, rather patronizing look.

'I was picking Ana's brains about Madremonte,' said Tara. 'The Mother of the Mountains or the Mother of the Trees. She's a spirit in Colombian mythology, you see. Protects the forest and the animals. Bathes naked. The point is, she punishes those who harm nature.'

Ana had told Finn the story of Madremonte before and how the deity had once saved her life. He absolutely believed that Ana had lived in the forest with a rebel group. He'd believed her when she'd described how she'd been dying from Chagas disease. And although he didn't believe in deities or spirits as a rule, he believed the 'forest' had indeed cured her. Well, extracts from the leaves of the *amaryllidaceae* plant had cured her, which he supposed amounted to the same thing.

Lady Tara, it seemed, was drawing on the Madremonte myth for her latest creation, an historical novel about a noblewoman who wreaks violent revenge on people guilty of animal cruelty, set in the year before the Act of Union.

'It's an allegory of course.'

'Of course. I can't wait to read it,' said Aoife unctuously, getting a knowing knock on her knee from Finn's knee.

Lady Tara paused. She tugged the cuffs of her blouse, touched her ears, moved her pen.

'There is something I need to tell you.'

Both Aoife and Finn sat up in anticipation. It was hardly going to be a confession. Somehow they couldn't imagine Tara flying a drone. But there was a gravitas about her that demanded their attention. Tara told them that she'd heard about Michael Dunlop's toxicology report. How, she didn't say. To her horror, the melange of poisons used in the murder was identical to a concoction one of her characters had prepared in *The Lady in the Hole*.

'Great novel, Miss Wallace. One of your best,' fawned Aoife.

'I'm surprised more people didn't notice the similarity.'

'They may not have got that far,' Finn said absent-mindedly, not realizing how insulting that might have sounded to Tara.

'Yet,' he added a little too late.

She took a sip of her black tea, the brittle cup rattling in her hand.

'As I'm sure you know, I am meticulous in my research.'

'It's obvious.'

'I have a correspondent in Durham, a forensic toxicologist, with whom I work closely. The reader can be absolutely assured that my murders are convincing, indeed plausibly doable to anybody with a titter of wit and access to the relevant materials.'

Although Lady Tara clearly felt the need to unburden herself of her suspicions, Finn felt it was as much to do with pride in her diabolical plot as with such notions of duty or guilt.

'The question is, who is the guilty party?'

It occurred to Finn that Tara was more concerned with the travesty that some plagiarist had stolen her idea than with the tragic fact that they'd actually killed somebody.

'Are you going to sue them?' Finn asked.

Lady Tara, not used to cheeky confrontation, or indeed to human interaction of any sort, looked shocked by his boldness.

'Finn, how could you?' Aoife teased him.

'Sorry, Lady Tara. I was being facetious.'

'Lady? I'm not a lady. Are you mocking me, young man?' Nobody had ever called her 'Lady' to her face.

'And your mother is such a charming woman.'

'I apologize, Miss Wallace. It was a crass remark. Do you have anybody in mind?'

While her books weren't exactly bestsellers, dozens of people in town would have read them. Tara regained her composure. She permitted herself a smile, tugged her cuffs, touched her ears, moved her pen.

'I was at the doctor's a few months ago. Dr Boyle.'

Harry!

'I was having some trouble with my hip. There was a lady in the waiting room. She happened to be reading my book. *The Lady in the Hole*. Naturally, I was flattered. I enjoyed a little frisson of pleasure.'

That will be a first, Finn thought, but knew better than to say it.

'I'm sure you know what I'm talking about, Finn. I've read your book.'

He didn't really know what she was talking about. He had never seen anybody read his book in public. And he was ashamed to admit, he hadn't actually written his book. The ideas were his alright. The sentiments were his. That was undeniably him in the photographs, looking rugged and mischievous. But it was the ghostwriter who'd followed him around recording multiple interviews who deserved all the credit. It was Geoff the ghostwriter who had channelled his thoughts and wrestled them down on to the page.

'When the lady went in to see Dr Boyle – she had a flu I think – I picked up the book. It was dog-eared, a desecration in my opinion, on a certain page. No prizes for guessing which page.'

She looked up.

'Aoife is ahead of me. The passage in which Lucinda, that's my heroine, prepares the poison, do I need to tell you? Was underlined.'

'Who was the woman?'

Tara was enjoying the suspense. It was as if she was reading her novel on *Book at Bedtime*.

'She didn't notice me. It was a bad dose of the flu. But I knew her.'

'Who was it?'

'Eve Duggan.'

'Oh.'

In truth, it was a bit of an anticlimax. They had all but ruled out Eve given her alibi at the time Barry Senior was bombed to oblivion. Maybe her husband, Barry Junior, had read the book before her and highlighted the relevant paragraphs. Or Eve might have picked up the book from the shelf in Harry Boyle's waiting room. Perhaps Harry was the murderer after all. Each of them had a motive. They would have to reconsider the movements of all three. *Unless of course, it was Eddie Halfpenny*, thought Aoife.

Aoife looked at her watch.

'We better go.'

Finn looked towards the counter. Fortunately, Ana's back was turned, giving him a tiny window of opportunity to escape without once again eating his breakfast. Somehow in the seconds it took to say goodbye to Lady Tara, Ana had materialized at the door with two takeaway cartons.

'*Huevos diablos para dos personas.*' She grinned, thrusting the cardboard containers into Finn's grateful hands.

'Adios, Aoife.'

Aoife wasn't sure if that was an acknowledgement of her earlier rudeness or a veiled threat.

Chapter 50

The town was buzzing as they approached the bridewell. A decent crowd of locals and tourists alike were milling around the stalls on Market Square, sizing up the organic vegetables and the sourdough and the seaweed soap. The cheesemongers were doing a roaring trade. Even Femke Leerdam, imperiously Dutch behind her stand, managed to sell one of her risqué ceramic vases to a day-tripper from Cork. The retired chemist Gerry Flynn, Fionnuala's father, led a rosary nearby. There were four of them in cowls, holding aloft a statue of the Blessed Virgin Mary. Finn recognized her as one of the statues he'd repatriated from the cemetery. Whether they were specifically protesting Femke's obscene handiwork on this occasion or moral decay generally wasn't immediately apparent.

Nicolas, the lighting man, had already secreted his projectors in little cement bunkers and trained them on the façade of the old jail. A braided rat's tail running down his neck was the only clue to his status as a 'creative'. The rotten windows of the one-time prison had been removed and replaced with new frames and new glass panes. On the scaffold, men and women sang songs, traditional and of our time. Eddie, by the time they located him, had single-handedly filled a giant skip with debris from inside the building.

'Aoife, me oul' segotia!' he said, wiping his hands on his Dubs jersey. 'You wouldn't believe the shite that was in there.'

They sat down on the low wall surrounding the fountain. Aoife and Finn shared their eggs with Eddie, who had no compunction about digging in.

'Wha'?'

No flies on Eddie; he detected something was amiss.

'Is this about me brother?'

Finn nodded. Eddie corroborated the story Xavier had told him about his brother's involvement in an armed bank robbery some years ago. He wasn't denying that his brother was guilty. But he was very sore about his scapegoating.

'Yeah, I'd beef with Duggan. Sure, who didn't? But tha's not why I came to Abbeyford.'

'Why did you move? I realize I never asked.'

'No bother, Aoife. No. You'll think it's stupid.'

'You, stupid? Eddie, you could buy and sell us culchies.'

Aoife knew how to butter Eddie up. He didn't disagree with her.

'Don't know about that. No. I was an extra on *Saving Private Ryan*.'

'The Spielberg film?' asked a gobsmacked Finn.

'Yeah Stephen's movie. Lovely man. With the army background, you know, they needed people with experience, to show the actors how it was done. Anyway, Stephen shot the Normandy landings on the beach over there in whatdoyacallit?'

'Curracloe,' said Aoife.

'Know-all,' muttered Finn.

'The very place. Met this girl, worked in the catering department. Mairead. Lovely girl. They did a lovely cabbage.

She was from Abbeyford, you know. We hit it off. Got on like a house on fire. Eventually, after a few years, commuting, more or less, I moved down. Got a house below in Beechwood. Same house I'm in now. One tenth the price of Dublin. Mairead fecked off to Australia a year later. Darwin, of all places. Got a job spotting cattle from the back of a small plane. For real. C'est la vie. I was supposed to go out. But ... ah ... I had no idea Duggan lived here. I assumed he lived in Waterford city.'

Aoife looked at him sceptically.

'As true as God, Aoife, I didn't touch him. Sure wasn't he one of me best customers!'

Eddie was all injured innocence. Mind you, if he was the highly-trained ranger he purported to be, he wasn't likely to buckle under pressure from rank amateurs.

'Alright, listen, if you must know, I did follow him around, from time to time, tailed him and tha', kept a note,' he pointed to his head, 'up there, of where and when he'd be and who'd he meet and so on. Instinct really. I barely knew I was doing it. Out of boredom. It can be quiet on this job.'

Finn didn't know what to believe. Was he ever an army ranger? Was he even in the army? Did he actually meet Spielberg? Was there a Mairead? Eddie, much as he liked him, came across as something of an Irish Don Quixote.

'I asked you a while ago, where would you get a grenade around here?' Finn inquired, eliciting a look of disbelief from Aoife at the lack of subtlety.

'Like I said at the time, I dunno, Finn. Try one of the stalls, there.'

It wasn't like Eddie to be sarcastic. The taxi driver rocked back and forth. At one point Finn thought he was going to fall back into the fountain.

'Sorry, mate. You have me rattled. Alright, look.'

He took out his phone. He played a song, Whitney Houston's power ballad, 'I Will Always Love You', turning the volume up to the max. They looked at him in confusion.

'You never know who's listening.'

As if the statue of the curly-haired youth on top of the fountain was bugged.

'I've never told anybody this before.'

Apart from the random tourist in Morrissey's Bar, Finn thought, who then reported it to the Gardai. How many other people had he told? How many people were listening?

'I know a fella, ex-army. Lives near Ennismore, right. I'm tellin' ya the truth now. Has a small distillery there. Makes whiskey. Vinegar Hill it's called. After the battle.'

'Never heard of it,' said Finn.

'It was a very famous battle. The United Irishmen. 1798.'

'I meant the whiskey.'

'No? It's supposed to be very good. Don't drink myself.'

'Terrible name for a whiskey,' Finn mused. 'Vinegar Hill. It suggests astringency.'

'You wha'? Is that one of your fancy gardening words?'

'What's this got to do with grenades?' Aoife interrupted the men.

Eddie sighed.

'I'll show ya.'

'It sounds acidic, is all I'm saying, Eddie. Heartburn. He should rebrand.'

'Well, you can tell him that yourself. C'mon.'

They followed Eddie towards his car.

'I didn't know Finn was such a marketing wizard,' he said to Aoife.

'A man of many talents.'

'Not a very good detective tho', is he?' said a disgruntled Eddie.

Finn had to concede that Eddie probably had a point but pressed on regardless.

'As a matter of interest Eddie, where were you that evening? When Barry was murdered. I don't think you were in the pub?'

'Ha. Do ya hear him? I was on a job. Wasn't I? Bringing a fella to the airport. There's easier ways to kill a man. If I wanted to, I coulda kilt Duggan with a rabbit punch.'

'Do you have a receipt?'

'I don't do receipts.'

'Who was the passenger?'

'That is confidential information, my friend. No can do.'

'Who was it, Eddie?' Aoife asked.

'It was an actor friend of mine, Aidan O'Hara, if you must know.'

Aoife and Finn shared a sceptical smile. They recognized the name of course. O'Hara, rarely out of the papers, in his own mind at least, was the last of the hell-raisers.

'Aidan was going off to Hungary to film this new Sherlock Holmes thing. He plays both Sherlock and Moriarty. I didn't tell you that. Sure, he likes a drink now and again, and a bit of fisticuffs, but doesn't deserve the hammering he gets, unmercifully crucified by the press, so he is. We stopped a few times on the way to the aeroport. Knows I won't say a word to anybody. I'm not just his driver, you know, or his bodyguard, I'm a ... how can I put it? ... a sorta mentor, so I am, a sorta father figure. Get in.'

They got in to Eddie's car, not convinced by his tall tale, but pretty certain he wasn't a credible suspect. At any rate, it should be easy enough, Finn thought, to check out his alibi.

On the way to Ennismore, Finn's phone rang. It was Xavier. He wasn't sure if he should answer it, but Eddie and Aoife were in the front engaged in a heated discussion about vaccines.

'I can't talk.'

'You in danger?'

'No. I don't think so. What's the ... What's the weather like where you are?'

He winced, thinking he could have done a bit better than that in terms of misdirecting their chauffeur.

'The weather, what are you on about, Finn? You sure you're not in trouble? Just say, eh, fish fingers, if you are, and we'll come and get you. No, not fish fingers ... eh ...'

'Red,' Valerie shouted in the background. 'Tell him to say "red".'

'Did you get that?'

'I'm fine.'

'Right. Well, the weather is grand here. Barry Duggan Junior wasn't wearing that glove you found at Tullaun House. It was a man called ... what was his name, Val?'

'Kaspar Buczynski, and don't call me Val.'

'Kaspar drives for Duggan's alright but he's as clean as a whistle. Dropped his glove in the driveway after picking up the rubbish.'

'What about the other ... the other ... weather?'

'What?'

'He means the list of names, you plank,' said Valerie. 'The visitors to Tullaun.'

'Yes, of course. The French pair are grand. They live in Limoges. He was in a wheelchair. No issue there. Naoise Mac Anois, would you believe it, is actually a real name. And he's a real person.'

'Really?'

'Runs a hardware shop in Stillorgan. Mac Nows. Quite a famous shop. Sells everything you could want including pet food. Who knew? A pillar of the community by all accounts. Except ...'

'Go on.'

'We reckon the bold Naoise is having some sort of a fling with another name on the list ... Let me see ...'

'Nuala. Nuala Watters,' Valerie jumped in.

'Who needs AI when you have Valerie beside you, ha? They both acted very suspiciously when we interviewed them, Nuala and Naoise. We actually thought we were on to something there for a while. Until we twigged, no, they were actually on a dirty weekend, staying in that country house place near Hook Head with the spa.'

'Right. And the ...'

'Jenny Murray? Unfortunately there are about a thousand Jenny Murrays in the country. So no joy there I'm afraid.'

'Did he say "red"?' Valerie asked.

'No. I don't think so. Did you say "red", Finn?' Xavier asked him.

'No. Thanks. Thanks a million ... Mammy. Good luck.'

Eddie looked in the rear-view mirror. Aoife twisted her body around.

'Yeah, that was just Maura.' Finn said. 'Bit anxious about something.'

'And how is the weather, two miles away in Abbeyford?' Aoife winked.

'Good. Similar to here.'

'Finn,' Eddie asked, 'are you vaccinated?'

Chapter 51

'We don't normally open to the public on weekdays,' said Garrett Jackson, a genial, clean-shaven man in his early fifties, smartly dressed in a blazer and chino combination.

'But for yourself and the missus, I'll make an exception.'

'He's not my . . .' Aoife said.

'She's not my . . .' Finn said at exactly the same time.

'Not yet, sez you.' Eddie winked.

Garrett handed Finn and Aoife hi-viz jackets and hard hats.

'Eddie doesn't need one. His head is hard enough!' Garrett quipped, rapping Eddie on the forehead with his knuckles.

Eddie laughed uproariously. Garrett had been a captain in his unit after all.

'So Eddie tells me you're a whiskey connoisseur, Finn? Well, you've come to the right place.'

Finn couldn't take his eyes off Jackson's hair. It was magnificently thick. As he gave them a guided tour of the boutique distillery, he happily enlightened them on his many successes since he'd left the army. It was the currency trading that allowed him to retire early and pursue his 'hobbies'.

'I'm a serial entrepreneur, for my sins.'

As well as the whiskey, he owned a restaurant, had

invested in tech start-ups, and imported chainsaws from Germany.

'For some reason, the whiskey is not selling as well as we hoped.'

Finn looked at the imagery. The label featured a bloody head impaled on a pike, superimposed over a hill, with the brand name, Vinegar Hill, in a chilling red script. In fairness, the label was not the problem. It was the name. But Finn considered it prudent to say nothing for now. The 'tour' lasted a full five minutes and was followed by a brief tasting. It was not a great whiskey by any means, but both Finn and Aoife felt obliged not just to sample it but to buy a few bottles, each of them costing a scandalous forty-eight euros. It wasn't just the name that damaged the sales. Mind you, the purchase proved to be a judicious decision.

'Can this pair be trusted?' Jackson asked Eddie.

'With your life, Captain.'

Jackson led them out the back of the plant towards a giant warehouse. It was the size of an aircraft hangar and protected by huge hydraulic doors. They entered by a small unlocked door to the side of the building.

Aoife and Finn were genuinely shocked by the sight they saw before them.

'Count yourselves lucky, lads. He never shows this to anyone,' said Eddie, playing a blinder.

'It's nothing,' said Garrett, faux-modestly.

Garrett Jackson, as well as being a gentleman distiller, was a collector of military hardware. There were dozens of tanks, armoured cars, field guns and assorted paraphernalia displayed around the cavernous warehouse. Involuntarily, they burst out laughing. Garrett was delighted with the reaction.

'Nobody knows about this,' said Eddie. Apart from the people Eddie told. Apart from the murderer?

'Are you going to war against a neighbouring county?' Aoife asked the collector.

He laughed. The guided tour of the hangar took a good bit longer than the tour of the distillery.

'That's a T-34,' he said, pointing proudly at a tank. 'Soviet Union, World War Two.'

Most of the ordnance, he explained, consisted of Cold War items he'd picked up at fairs all across Europe, or sometimes in farmyards.

'Most of it perfectly legal.'

Eddie sniggered.

'As long as they're decommissioned and so on, you have the right paperwork – a licence and whatnot – and your background checks are in order. You'd be surprised at the number of people involved in this game. There's about seven here in Ireland alone.'

'You're not missing a grenade, are you, by any chance?' asked Finn.

Jackson chuckled.

'Is that a euphemism? Haven't heard that one before. A sandwich short of a picnic. A toolbox short of a spanner. Missing a grenade. I probably am mad. My wife thinks so anyway.'

They walked around the floor-space, Jackson giving a running commentary on the provenance of each piece of equipment, the pitfalls of importing lethal weapons into the country, the characters he'd encountered in the trade, and his long-term plan of opening a museum.

'For the moment it's a secret, until I get the necessary permissions and get a few legal bits and pieces tied up.'

They had stopped at a display case full of grenades. Aoife and Finn instantly noticed an empty space, under which a tag read, 'M-67 Fragmentation Grenade'.

'Are you sure you're not missing a grenade, Garrett?' Aoife enquired.

'No,' he replied, emphatically. 'I don't think so anyway.'

He had the air of a man familiar with the concept of manifesting, used to wishing things into being and, equally, wishing things away. Finn was conscious that they were pushing their luck in the presence of two ex-soldiers in possession of more military ordnance than the entire Irish army put together, with nothing to protect him and Aoife other than hi-viz jackets and hard hats. There was an uneasy stand-off.

'Now, will we go back into the distillery?' said Garrett. 'I have a little gift for you.'

'It was an M-67 that killed Barry Duggan.' Finn stood his ground.

Jackson looked at Eddie.

'I don't know what they're on about,' said Eddie.

Jackson inhaled deeply.

'Alright, alright. I'll tell you if you promise it won't go any further.'

Finn and Aoife nodded in agreement.

'The grenade was stolen. Yes. Somebody must have left the door open.'

'Who?'

'It was me. I left the door open.'

'Why didn't you tell the police?'

The collector explained his dilemma. That particular item hadn't been imported through the normal legal channels: it 'arrived in a consignment of chainsaws.'

He shrugged his shoulders. It was as if it had nothing to do with him. Nor, it turned out, had that particular grenade been decommissioned properly. Somebody must have accidentally dropped a live grenade into a Husqvarna box.

'I just didn't get around to it. It's a busy time of the year.'

Not in the distillery, Finn thought.

'Look, I'm mortified it was my grenade that killed that poor man. But I'm begging you, please, please, don't tell anyone.'

'Who stole it?'

Jackson didn't have a clue who the culprit might be. It had to be someone who knew about the collection. Apart from Eddie and a few trusted friends, few people had ever been inside the shed. There was CCTV, but apparently it didn't work very well at night. He showed them the relevant CCTV footage on his phone. It looked like a large potato sack was responsible for the theft.

They walked back to the distillery. Garret was disconsolate. Something had happened to his tremendous head of hair. It had sort of collapsed in on itself. He gave Aoife and Finn a goody bag each. Finn had a peek inside. It contained a Vinegar Hill branded whiskey tumbler and a Vinegar Hill miniature teddy bear on a keyring.

'I know it might be inappropriate given the circumstances, but would you mind terribly signing the visitor's book?'

Aoife's eyes lit up.

'You have a visitor's book! No problem at all, Garrett.'

While Finn and Garrett made awkward small talk, Aoife furiously leafed through the book. It occurred to her that whoever stole the grenade would have done some recon on the premises in advance. Luckily there were even less visitors to Vinegar Hill than Tullaun! One name, going back a few weeks stood out. Jenny Murray! Bingo.

'I'm thinking of changing the name,' said Garrett.

'Oh. What's wrong with Vinegar Hill?' asked Finn, innocently.

Garrett looked at him with suspicion.

'What do you have in mind?'

'Devil's Wee,' Garrett announced.

'Right.'

'What do you think?'

'Yes. Devil's Wee. It has a nice ring.'

'It has, hasn't it? Nice edge to it. We're going after the twenty-one to forty-four demographic.'

They left Garrett Jackson to his dreams and schemes. Eddie drove Finn and Aoife back to Abbeyford.

Chapter 52

Jenny Murray. That evening in his flat, Finn racked his brains. The name was not unfamiliar but he couldn't place the woman. The Vinegar Hill whiskey was no help. It was rough. The Red Army could have run their tanks on it. Finn was satisfied that they had identified the sources of both the poison and the explosive device. It can't have been a coincidence that this Jenny Murray had visited both Tullaun House and the distillery in the lead-up to the killings. But who was she? It was presumably an alias. The evidence at this stage indicated that the murderer was a woman. Signing the visitor's books was either an act of monumental folly or an act of hubris. Or was it more misdirection? According to their research to date, the woman was most likely Eve Duggan or Monika Kovačić-Duggan. But both of them had sound alibis, if not for Michael's poisoning, then certainly for the aerial attack on Barry.

His phone rang. It was Isabella. He could hear the tinkle of glasses in the background. The barking laugh of Barley Davis. It had always been an echoey flat. After dinner, they'd retire to the roof of the mansion block to admire the sweeping 360-degree views of London, from Alexandra Palace all the way down to the BT tower and the South Bank and around to the west and Hampstead Heath. He had landscaped the roof terrace pro bono with various ornamental grasses, prickly and self-sufficient like most of the residents.

'Does the name Thomas Breslin mean anything to you?' The only Breslin he knew of was the Garda superintendent.

'He's a policeman, Finn. I hope you're not getting mixed up in anything silly.'

'You know me, Izzy. It's the quiet life I'm after.'

He tried to keep it light but could feel the weight in his words, the ache in his tone. It wasn't attractive. It wasn't the impression he wanted to leave Isabella with before she rejoined her stuffy dinner party. It wasn't even how he felt. He was fine.

'Breslin was— *is* the beneficial owner of both CosRoe and WhiteStairs. I should caution you. He hasn't done anything illegal as far as my source could ascertain.'

She hung up before he could think of another favour to ask her. Who is Jenny Murray?

He retrieved the photograph taken in Morrissey's Bar in 1982 of the four burghers: Flynn, O'Connell, Morrissey and the faceless one. So Breslin, Xavier and Valerie's boss, was most likely the fourth man. It was he who had bought up the land on Knockanore hoping to make a killing in the event of a viable mine ever being established there. Whether he and his confederates were implicated in the fate of Rameses De Burgh was another story. It was not something he could bring to the attention of his friends, Keane and Kilcoyne. There was no way that they would investigate their superior officer. Whatever happened Rameses, Finn was sure the answer was to be found somewhere in Morrissey's pub.

As for the more immediate challenge of identifying the

chimera that was Jenny Murray, he formulated a rough plan. As the plan took shape in his drowsy state, he knew it was a rubbish one. But without further clues or any sort of expertise in these matters, it was the best he could come up with. Unless Aoife could think of some better use of their time, they, together with Deputy Happiness and Deputy Maura, would follow the suspects over the next few days. Propped up on three pillows to alleviate the heartburn, it wasn't the best sleep Finn ever had.

Next morning, Finn, Aoife, Maura, Happiness and Eddie met in the café below his flat to fine-tune the plan. Finn had already arranged to meet Monika at the Duggan residence at half eight to do some more preparatory work on her gardens.

'Convenient. She'll still be in her negligee,' said Aoife.

It was beneath Finn's dignity to respond. But was there a hint of jealousy again? Or was Finn just being a hopeful puppy again, tongue out for a bit of sausage? The pair of them, burying their attraction for each other beneath layers of playful banter, had relapsed, acting like coy teenagers. It was pathetic. If Eve was telling the truth, Monika would pop out for a few hours at some point, for her weekly rendezvous at a house on Pearse Street. That happened to be the same street where the musical director of the choir, Wolfie Whelan, lived. Aoife, Happiness and Maura would commandeer Wolfie's house. From his front window they could keep watch and track Monika's coming and going. Once Monika had left the love nest, they'd swoop on the house, and confront her lover.

'So what if she's having an affair?' said Maura. 'I believe it's very common nowadays.'

'It's a sin,' insisted Happiness.

'If she is having an affair,' explained Aoife, 'it gives her a motive. And, who knows, the identity of her fancy man—'

'Or fancy woman,' Maura said.

'His or her identity might lead us to the murderer,' said Aoife.

'They might talk,' said Happiness, confidently. She was still on a high after her successful date with Alo.

'Exactly.'

Meanwhile Eddie was to wait outside Eve Duggan's house. His task was to follow her wherever she went.

'What if I get a job? Can I take it?'

'Well, that would defeat the purpose, wouldn't it?' said Aoife. 'If you're away at the airport, we won't know where Eve goes.'

'Good point.'

'Nobody else but you would be able to follow her undetected.'

'True. I'd make a great stalker, so I would.'

They all looked at him, oddly.

'If I was into that type of thing,' he clarified. 'I mean, I'm not a stalker. Mairead never pressed charges. So, you know, nothing to worry about there.'

They lowered their coffees and sprang into action.

Chapter 53

Eddie dropped Finn outside Monika's house and hurried back to town to take up his station at Eve's. Dominik drove down to the gate in a golf buggy to pick him up. Impeccably dressed as ever in tailored trousers and a silk-cashmere crew neck that accentuated his pecs, he didn't say much.

'If you try to take advantage of my little sister, I will hurt you.'

No beating around the bush with Dominik.

There was an air of distraction about Monika herself. To his relief, she wasn't her usual saucy self. Understandable, he conceded, given her husband's recent murder. How do you ever get over something like that? If you had nothing to do with it. Or even if you did. She was dressed quite soberly in darker hues and less clingy fabrics for somebody who was on her way to a morning tryst. It made her even more attractive. Without conviction, she showed him where to find cups, cutlery and the toaster. For the record, it was put away in a cupboard under one of the islands. She assumed he'd want toast at some point during his deliberations. He didn't know whether to be offended or not. Although, in fairness, he did like toast as a rule on his coffee break.

Dominik, staring at Finn, cracked open twelve raw eggs

and poured them into a blender. He then swallowed the mixture whole. Finn gagged. The widow smiled wanly. There was no sign of Little Barry. Monika told him her son had been shipped off to his grandparents in Croatia.

'It's for the best.'

Finn got down to work. As well as nosing around the property, he was genuinely thinking about the project while waiting for Monika to leave the premises. Luckily, Dominik had already departed, presumably for Duggan's yard, in the G-Wagen. Over the next few minutes, he tentatively discussed the budget with his employer and raised his reservations about Barry's madcap proposal to splice the sycamore tree with the old lorry. She brushed it off, gave him a figure – a shrewd fraction of the amount Barry had been bandying about – and instructed him to do whatever he thought was best.

'Oh.'

'I never really cared about the garden. Or the house.'

She pointed at all the islands. The appliances.

'I am not a good cook.'

She was looking into a vanity mirror, applying some make up to her puffy eyes.

'I would have been happy in a little flat. But Barry, he always wanted to spoil me.'

She grabbed her car keys and put her lipstick and eyeshadow into her handbag. He noticed that she also slipped a single key into the bag.

'I loved him. People think I'm a gold-digger,' she said, pausing to see how he would react. Finn didn't wobble. 'You know I was working in the hospital when his first wife died. Imelda. I was her physio. I saw how he cared for her. The gentle way he spoke. He stayed with her every day until the end. That was the real Barry. No man ever spoke to me like that.'

She waved her finger.

'I will be gone for two hours. If you leave, you must put on the alarm and lock up.'

She smiled sensually.

'Can't be too careful. There is a killer out there.'

There was a heavy suitcase in the hall. Finn offered to help her with it. He was imagining what might be in it. Role-playing costumes? Sex toys? It even crossed his mind that it might be a body. Monika, declining his offer, effortlessly picked up the case and loaded it into the boot of her car. Then she sped off in her cute little electric-blue Peugeot EV. It was ten to eleven. He quickly called Aoife to give her the heads up. Although he couldn't be entirely sure that he was alone, out of curiosity, he ran upstairs to her bedroom. There, he quickly checked behind the photograph of her weatherbeaten parents. The key was gone.

He was pretty certain that there were no CCTV cameras in the bedroom. But remembering the wall of screens in Duggan's office, he knew for sure there were cameras placed at various points around the house and grounds. And that Dominik was probably watching him right now. So he had to be extra careful as to where he looked, while pretending to sketch drawings and measure distances.

It was while he was sifting through the old lorry parts, Roscoe's remains, looking for some token bit of metal, like an exhaust pipe, with which he would endeavour to honour Barry's wishes vis-à-vis the tree, that his eye was drawn to an incongruous item. At first he thought it was the radio from the cab. Or a walkie-talkie. But no. It was a modern gadget, the size of a man's palm, not something that belonged to an old relic like Roscoe. On close inspection Finn deduced it was the controller for a drone. On even closer examination, he determined that it was the handset for a DJI MAVIC drone. Hector's drone. The drone that was used to murder Barry Duggan.

Chapter 54

'The eagle has flown.'

It was Eddie on the phone.

'What?'

'Eve. She's on the move.'

'Good stuff,' said Finn, making toast. 'Don't lose her.'

'Some chance. Brings me back to the Leb. I tailed these fellas, Hezbollah, for three days and three nights, not a wink of sleep. You're talking alleyways, dirt roads, mountain passes, had to wee in ... Oh hold on now, she's disappeared. I'll get back to you.'

Wolfie, delighted with the company, was playing one of Aoife's old faves, the Sondheim classic 'Send in the Clowns', when Monika arrived at number 12 directly opposite his house. Herbert, his schnauzer, was barking furiously at Wolfie, begging him to stop. The tune he could abide, but not his master's voice. At the sitting room window, behind the stage curtains, Aoife, Maura and Happiness witnessed Monika remove a suitcase from the boot, take a key from her handbag and let herself in.

'Right. We're the far side of Waterford city,' reported Eddie. 'Queuing for the Passage ferry. I think she might be doing a runner.'

'Has she spotted you?'

'Are ya joking? I swapped taxis with a friend of mine.'

'Right.'

'She went into a hardware shop there at Union Quay. When she was inside, didn't I bump into Jimmy Fay, at the rank, gave me his car, no bother, Jimmy's a diamond. Why would she be in a hardware shop, Finn? Planning something big, another murder maybe, before she elopes. Oh, the ferry's moving.'

'Just keep an eye on her, Eddie. See where she goes.'

'Roger.'

Chapter 55

About an hour later, Wolfie was lost in a raucous version of 'Life is a Cabaret', playing the piano standing up, when Monika let herself out of number 12. She looked left and right before getting into her car and speeding off.

The triumfeminatus of detectives immediately ditched the disappointed Wolfie and the whining schnauzer and marched straight over to the house opposite. They rapped purposefully on the door, fully expecting to be greeted by a man with his trousers around his ankles.

'Oh, I'm so sorry. It must be the wrong house,' said Aoife.
'Is this number twelve?'
'Yes.'

It was a family of four who answered the door, a man, and a woman in a hijab with two babies in her arms. They looked frightened, but once assured that their cold-callers meant no harm, invited Aoife, Maura and Happiness into their home. Over tea, they introduced themselves. They were a family, Mohammed, Jamila and the children, Fatima and Abdul-Malek, who'd fled Afghanistan after the Taliban came to power.

The suitcase was lying open in the sparsely furnished sitting room. It was full of old clothes. Aoife recognized Barry Duggan's grey Prada tracksuit.

'Monika is so kind,' said Fatima, shy and embarrassed.

They had been living in sheltered accommodation, sharing one room with a family from Syria, when Monika befriended Fatima. She insisted they move into the vacant house in Pearse Street. As manager of Barry's extensive property portfolio, she was able to engineer this arrangement behind her late husband's back. She'd told Barry that the house was in need of redecoration. Hence the cash withdrawals, cash she handed over to Mohammed and Fatima. If Barry had known of her philanthropy, it's safe to say he'd have been furious. The plight of refugees was not high on his list of priorities. As a businessman who'd pulled himself up by his bootstraps and as a hard-headed landlord, it would have pained him greatly to give anything away for free. Hence Monika's secrecy.

Since the family had moved in, Monika had been calling around once a week to teach the parents English – heavily accented English – and to give physio to baby Abdul-Malek, whose motor skills were underdeveloped.

The ladies apologized profusely for the intrusion and regrouped in Café Madremonte.

'Definitely not an affair then,' said Maura.

'No.'

'Nor the behaviour of a killer.'

'No.'

Chapter 56

'Got sick on the boat, so I did,' Eddie said weakly. 'Very rough crossing the estuary.'
'Where are you now?'
'She's in a house. About three miles from Ballyhack. A farmhouse.'
'Send me the co-ordinates.'
'Why? Sure I'm a walking map. I never forget a place.'
'Just in case.'
'In case of what?'
'Something happens. I might need to call the guards.'
'Oh she's coming.'
Eddie lowered his head.
'She's got something in her arms.'
'What is it?'
'It's big. Covered in a blanket. Could be a bomb. She's putting it in the back seat. Right, she's off.'
'Did she see you?'
'No. I'm in a field. What will I do? Do I follow her? Or go into the house?'
'Follow her. Give me the co-ordinates. I'll get Xavier to check out the house.'
'Right. I'm on it.'
Finn could hear Eddie's tyres skidding in the mud and

the engine straining. It sounded like the car was about to blow up.

'Bit of a problem, Finn. The feckin' thing is stuck. I'm going in.'

'No, Eddie. Might be dangerous.'

'Danger! Ha! It's safety I'd be afraid of.'

Finn was in despair. What did that even mean?

'Keep your phone on.'

'I'm at the door now.'

Eddie knocked on the door of the house. He was answered by a chorus of yelping dogs.

'Eddie!'

His phone went dead.

Chapter 57

Finn put the drone controller in his satchel, locked up Monika's house, put on the alarm and walked back into town. On the way he rang Xavier.

'I have something for you.'

'And I have something for you.' the detective said.

'Oh.'

'Meet me at the station.'

'Right. And Xavier, could you do us a favour? It's Eddie. He's at a farmhouse about three miles from Ballyhack.'

'That's out of our jurisdiction.'

'He might be in some sort of trouble.'

'Did he talk?'

'I'll tell you later.'

He could hear Xavier conferring with Valerie.

'Do you have the co-ordinates?'

'No.'

'Right well, there's not much we can do. There's probably a thousand farmhouses about three miles from Ballyhack.'

Forty minutes later, Finn was at the station in an interview room with Valerie and Xavier. He handed over the handset.

'We searched the whole area around the Duggan house, didn't we, Valerie? Twice.'

She nodded.

'There's no way we would have missed that.'

'It was planted. By the killer,' stated Valerie pacing around the room. 'Somebody who had access to the estate. Barry Junior. Eve. Dominik. Karl.'

'Or Monika?' said Finn.

'We can rule Monika out.'

'Oh!' Another dead end?

'She was on a FaceTime call with her parents in Croatia at the time Barry was killed.'

'Is that what she said? C'mon. She could have messed with the timelines. She could have been on a call but walked away for the few minutes it took to direct the drone to Barry's goalmouth.'

'She thought of that.' Xavier pointed proudly at Valerie.

'We had the laptop analysed. I flew to Croatia myself, spoke to her parents.'

'I stayed at home. Not bitter,' moaned Xavier.

'Her parents actually recorded the call.'

'Weird.'

'To be honest I'd record Monika's calls,' said Xavier wistfully. Valerie looked at him in disgust.

'Sorry. Bit pervy alright.'

'They record all her calls. She didn't budge for fifteen minutes. Until the explosion. And then she ran.'

While Finn was taking in this information, glad that it wasn't Monika, the detectives quizzed him about his recent conversation with Eddie. Honouring his pledge to Eddie and Garrett, he didn't tell them about the trip to the distillery. He did, however, share Eddie's account of his journey to the airport with Aidan O'Hara the night Barry was murdered. Apparently there were a few stops along the way. Finn suggested they contact all the pubs along the route from Abbeyford to Dublin Airport to see if his story checked out.

'That's about a thousand pubs,' Xavier said despairingly.

Valerie nodded, eagerly embracing the extra workload. There was nothing she liked more than work. She looked back at the controller.

'So who do we think planted this?'

'It could have been dropped on the pile of metal by a drone,' said Xavier.

Valerie looked up to the heavens, a view she was all too familiar with by this stage.

'He has drones on the brain. We'll look into it.'

She put the gadget into an evidence bag. They looked stressed. They were clearly feeling the pressure.

'You said you had something for me?' Finn asked.

'Play him the message.'

Xavier extricated a mobile phone from another evidence bag. It was Harry Boyle's phone. They played him the message he received in Morrissey's Bar the evening Barry Duggan was murdered.

'I'm sorry. I don't recognize the voice. Couldn't even tell you if it's a man or a woman.'

'Not the voice. We think the caller used a child's toy to change their voice.'

'A voice changer,' added Xavier knowledgeably. 'What? That's what it's called. You can get them for twenty-four euros on Amazon.'

They played the message again.

'Do you hear it?'

There was a high-pitched sound in the background, a trilling noise.

'Some sort of ... of machine. A radio, a distorted signal from a radio. Something like that, no?'

Xavier and Valerie looked at each other.

'We're thinking a bird,' she said.

Finn listened to the message again.

'Maybe. Yeah. It's not a bird I'm familiar with.'

'Your father might be, though,' Valerie said. 'I believe Redmond's the resident ornithologist around here.'

The way she said it, it sounded like she was one of those people who didn't trust experts. With a flurry of fingers, she sent the audio message by WhatsApp to Finn's phone.

'It's an unusual bird. If he can identify the song, he might know where the nest is. It might help us locate the whereabouts of the killer. You've a better chance than we do of getting him to talk.'

That was an understatement.

On his way out of the interview room, Finn, remembering the last conversation he'd had with Isabella, had a sudden urge. He decided that he was going to find Superintendent Breslin's office and walk right in, whether the senior officer was there or not. It wasn't on the first floor of the bright and airy new building, so he took the stairs to the second floor, the uniformed guards, all recognizing him and greeting him cordially, not giving his presence a second thought. At the end of a corridor he found Breslin's office. Finn knocked at the door. There was no answer. Throwing caution to the wind, he took a deep breath and pushed open the door.

The corner office, windows opening towards the Barrow on one side and the cupola of the town hall on the other, was speckless, not a paper clip out of place. There were photographs of a stern-faced Breslin on the walls. His graduation photograph. Breslin with various dignitaries. Breslin with his family. Breslin on a Garda peacekeeping mission in Bosnia. Finn wasted no time in searching the office. The door had been unlocked, which suggested the super was still in the building. What he was doing, in his own mind, was probably the stupidest thing he had ever done. He was looking for an eagle egg.

He glanced through drawers and presses with no luck. There was a capacious-looking drinks cabinet on four legs with fluted glass. There were a few bottles of whiskey in it, and gin, some liquors and some mixers as well as a variety of glasses. Bingo! There were eggs in it too! On closer inspection, they were ordinary hen's eggs, still fresh. Breslin obviously liked his whiskey sours.

Finn was about to give up what in retrospect and indeed in foresight was a foolhardy exercise when he spied a safe at the bottom of one of the cupboards. It resembled an ordinary hotel safe with a keypad on its front door. He had a couple of choices. One, walk out of the room right now. Two, stay and try and figure out the code. And three, think of a very good excuse as to why he was there if he should be disturbed.

He chose option two, and keyed in with confidence the first six-digit number that jumped into his mind: 731609 followed by the hash button. It didn't work. No great surprise really. It was after all a random number and although it came to him clearly as if by divine revelation, he had to concede he was no clairvoyant. If there was a God, he muttered to himself ruefully, surely he would have revealed the correct number. He needed to relax, be more systematic, put himself in Breslin's extra shiny shoes. What would a Garda superintendent use as his secret passcode? His badge number! Finn looked desperately around the room. There was nothing to suggest what it was. Devoid of inspiration now, and beginning to panic, he resorted to birthdays. The super's diary was on his desk. He flicked through it. He'd hardly pick his own birthday, would he? Finn noted that Mary Rose, Breslin's wife, was going to be seventy-five on 8 October. That would mean diamonds for Mary Rose. His fingers hovered over the buttons on the safe. Nah, he hesitated, Breslin would be craftier than that. He'd have a foolproof code. Finn squeezed his eyes tightly, trying to force his brain to number-churn faster, or to somehow manifest the right digits if not directly from God then from the ether: 556655. It was unmistakable. The numbers danced before his eyes. He pressed 556655 tentatively with his callused fingers. Nothing. Two goes down, one left. He'd never find out what happened to Rameses now on the Night of the Big Snow. The Night of the Big Snow! When was it again? He checked his pockets for the old photograph. It wasn't there. It was definitely 1982, March, but what date? He had only one chance to get it right. He pushed the buttons, 120382 followed by the hash key. The door sprang open. In hindsight, he wasn't that surprised if he said so himself. Aoife would be so proud of him when he told her.

In the safe, there was a holstered gun. A Sig-Sauer. There were also a few envelopes containing wads of cash. A watch. And was it possible? Was that an egg? Before he could make sure, before he could photograph the evidence, he heard voices in the corridor. He momentarily went deaf and blind before the adrenaline kicked in again. Finn swiftly closed the door of the safe and jumped to his feet just as Breslin, removing his cap, and a uniformed Garda entered the room.

'What are you doing here?' Breslin snapped.

'Oh I am so sorry. I knocked. I thought I heard you say, "come in". So I ... I came in. I had to see you urgently, Superintendent.'

Breslin, without moving his head, managed to both stare threateningly at Finn and scrutinize his office at the same time.

'This is very irregular. I have a secretary. What's all this about?'

'It's about the murders. Dunlop and Duggan,' Finn hastily clarified. 'It's confidential.'

Breslin relaxed a bit. He dismissed the uniform and took a seat behind his well-appointed desk. There were occasions, Finn had to concede, when his 'celebrity' was useful, and disarming, and when he consciously exploited that fact. This was one of those occasions.

'Much as I respect you, Mr O'Leary, as a broadcaster and a gardener, I specifically requested that you stay away from my case.'

He didn't look like the sort of man who was used to being disobeyed.

Finn soon found himself babbling incontinently about their findings to date, bamboozling the officer with the detail. There was stuff he told Breslin that he hadn't even mentioned to Valerie or Xavier. He felt bad about that but felt he couldn't be blamed in the circumstance. He had no doubt that Breslin, whether or not he was involved in the disappearance of Rameses all those years ago, was genuinely desperate to solve the two recent murders. And Finn impressed on him how he was uniquely placed, given the frosty relations extant between the community and the Gardai, to help with the enquiry.

'Thank you for calling in, Mr O'Leary. And I appreciate

the information, I do, but please, I'm asking you, no, I'm telling you: desist! Stop right now!'

Finn nodded contritely.

'By the way, my agapanthus is not flowering this year.'

'Oh, sorry to hear to hear that. Is it getting enough sunlight?'

'It's a south-facing garden. This is the sunny south-east.'

Breslin was obviously a thorough man. He seemed to know what he was doing. Probably overcrowding. Common enough with agapanthus.

'Lift and divide, Super. Lift and divide. Usually does the trick.'

'Thank you. I'll give it a go.'

Chapter 58

By the time Finn arrived in the café in the late afternoon, Eddie was in situ, alive and well, and regaling the others with his morning adventures. He was stroking a six-week-old golden retriever pup, holding him protectively in his hairy, tattooed arms.

'There's dogs everywhere. About twenty of them. Trying to jump over the fence. Pawing at the back door. Howling like wolves. I honestly thought I was going to be eaten alive. So, I go into the house. Lovely lady, Joan is her name. Nice jumper, hand-knit. There's five newborns in a little area off the kitchen. I'm telling you, I near melted on the spot. They were playing and wrestling, tumbling, trying to get out of the pen, you know. Pups! Joan tells me Eve ordered a pup off her six weeks ago, when the litter was born, for her husband, Barry, because he was depressed and Eve wanted to cheer him up, so that's why she was there, to collect it. I couldn't take my eyes off them. They were gorgeous. She says to me, Eddie, she says, do you want one? Do I want one, I said? I'll take all five of them.'

He pointed to a basket under the table. There were four golden retriever pups in it.

'There ya go now. One for each of yez.'

Chapter 59

As usual Redmond was nowhere to be found when you needed him most. He wasn't at his house in the woods. Nor was he at the men's shed. He didn't have a phone. Finn considered sending up a flare of some sort. Now that he thought of it, Redmond hadn't made it to his twenty-first birthday party either. It was fine. Luckily Finn wasn't the type to harbour grudges. There was always a compelling reason – an injured eagle, a geological crisis, a good fight. The day Finn was getting married to Isabella in Seville, his father was glued to a digger near the Hill of Tara. While trying to prevent the building of the M3 motorway through an area of outstanding archaeological and cultural significance, his father had literally glued himself into the bucket of a JCB and wasn't able to unglue himself in time to catch the flight to Spain. It was fine.

'Rhododendron business,' Maura ventured, gazing into the Martini glass from which she liked to drink her vermouth.

Back at his mother's house, Finn played the recording of the mysterious phone message. Maura knew her birds too.

'Sounds like a nightjar.'

'A nightjar? What's a nightjar?'

'Exactly. It can't be. They're hardly ever seen in this part of the world, but what would I know? Mind you, your father showed me one once in the Saltees.'

The Saltees were islands off the coast of Wexford, notable for their bird population. They were also a pitstop for migrating birds from Africa, birds like the nightjar.

'I couldn't even see it to be honest. It was dark. They only come out at night, and nest on the ground. But I could hear it alright. A distinctive "churring" sound. That was the word Redmond used. "Churring". I've never forgotten it.'

Happiness placed a bowl of golden-brown cubes on the table.

'Chin chin.'

Finn raised his wine glass.

'Chin-chin.'

'No, that is what they are called. Chin chin.'

She went back into the kitchen to tend to the new puppies, Festus and Ram. When they were trying to think of suitable names for their pets, both Happiness and Maura jokingly came up with the names of foolish, head-strong men they'd known in the past. The names stuck.

'Ooh,' Maura cooed, 'she's warming to you. That's only the third time she's made chin chin since she came here. The first was when Pastor Willy came to tea, and the second time was for her daughter, Grace. If there is a nightjar in the area, your father, no doubt will have adopted it by now.'

He smiled at his mother. Despite her endless ribbing of him, she still loved her husband. That was plain to see. His passion for life and the natural world, although not always conducive to domestic harmony, still appealed to her.

'No doubt all migrating birds from Africa are obliged to call on our Redmond, to pay homage to their lord and master.'

Finn laughed. Although it occurred to him, and not for the first time, that the subtext of her joke was slightly troubling. Was this every man's destiny – to become ridiculous, to be ultimately a figure of fun? Or was it just the fate of the O'Leary men? As he walked back to his flat, a full moon in the sky, the streets of Abbeyford quiet, he pondered the question. Of course, the more one tried to offset this fate, to not be ridiculous – that is to say, the more seriously one took oneself – the more ridiculous one became. It was something he'd have to watch out for.

As he rounded Parnell Street, he got the distinct impression that he was being followed. It was a stone rolling past him on the footpath that first alerted him to the possibility. The stone didn't roll on its own. It must have been accidentally kicked by somebody behind him. He turned around sharply. Nothing. Nobody. The echo of footsteps. A shadow. Squeaky shoes. Although Finn was a big man, with a broad chest, and naturally strong thanks to years of spadework, he was not untroubled. Only a couple of hundred yards from his flat now, he quickened his pace. There was, after all, a vicious, indiscriminate murderer on the loose. It wasn't a time for bravado. Finn hurried across the deserted Market Square. The bridewell was stunningly lit in purple and red hues. Behind the barred windows, an eerie lighting effect suggested a watchman going from room to room by candlelight. He could definitely hear a shuffling sound behind him. Squeaky shoes. Heavy breathing. A clearing of the throat. A strange tinkling noise. Like a bell in the distance. He was afraid to look around. Fumbling for his keys in his plaid shacket pocket, he stumbled on a cobblestone and fell forward. The last thing he saw before he blacked out was a pink heirloom tomato, squashed into the ground. Although it was organic and fabulous, shaped like a turkey's head, it was rubbish. Litter! *Must tell Aoife*, he thought, as his consciousness dimmed, *must tell Aoife. Aoife. Aoife. Aoife.*

Chapter 60

'Aoife, Aoife, Aoife.'

'She's here, Finn,' said Ana.

He came to in his own bed in the flat above Café Madremonte.

'Who's here?'

'I'm here,' Aoife said. 'Ana rang me. You okay?'

He tried to sit up. The headache was all-consuming, even worse in the vertical position than the horizontal.

'You were calling Aoife in your sleep,' said Ana.

'Was I?'

'It was so nice! So lovely,' Ana said, bittersweetly, her voice higher than normal.

'I'm flattered,' said Aoife.

'No! No, it's not what ... It's about the rubbish on the street, the tomatoes. There was one with a ... proboscis ... is that the word ... I ... the judges will be here any day now,' he protested weakly, his shoulders hunched up around his ears doing nothing to alleviate the pain. The women looked at each other in alarm. Ana wiped his face with a damp cloth.

'Should we call Harry? Or an ambulance?'

Ana, who opened her café at 6am every morning, had found him on her way to work with a bruise on his forehead, purple and red – not unlike the light show on the old jail – and a gash on the back of his head. She had somehow managed to drag and carry him single-handedly up the stairs.

'She's superhuman,' Aoife said, as Ana was leaving with Monty, his new retriever pup in her hand. 'You're never going to see him again, you know that. She's smitten.'

He nodded, resigned.

'She likes the pup too.'

The joke was lost on Finn. He could only concentrate on one thing at a time. And currently that was pain.

'It's a nasty wound. I don't suppose you saw who did it.'

He shook his head.

'I don't have a rear-view mirror on my shoulder.'

'It could have been worse.'

It couldn't, Finn thought. Nothing could be worse than the current waves of pain crashing over his head.

'If they wanted to kill you, they would have,' Aoife reasoned.

'That's a big comfort, Aoife. Thanks.'

'Unless they were disturbed in the act. And had to run away before they could finish the job.'

'Lovely. Even better. You have a wonderful bedside manner. Did anybody ever tell you that?'

She bent down and kissed him gently on the cheek. Her bedside manner was improving. Finn was touched, the ache in his heart now matching the one in his head.

'Look on the bright side, Finn. This is a positive development. It's a warning. It means we're getting close.'

Suddenly they heard footsteps on the stairs. Just as suddenly the footsteps stopped. There was a creaking noise as the person tried to shift their balance. The whole flat seemed to sway. Maybe that was the wooziness caused by the pain. Aoife grabbed a saucepan and waited just outside the bedroom door at the top of the stairs, while Finn lay helplessly in bed. He watched as she raised the saucepan above her head.

'Aoife! That's a fine welcome.'

It was Redmond, russeted by the sun, bearing fruits of the forest. And possibly roadkill, knowing Redmond.

'What are you doing sneaking up on people? I could have—'

'I was afraid the patient might be asleep.'

Touching. Not like his father to be so considerate. Redmond entered the cramped bedroom space.

'There you are, son.'

He plonked a basket of goodies on the floor.

'I've brought some rosemary oil for the—'

'Dad! Dad!'

'No need to shout. You'll give yourself a headache.'

'I don't want rosemary oil. Or *lactuca virosa*. Or pine tree sap. Or ... I have paracetamol. Loads of it. And codeine. And it's fantastic.'

'Suit yourself. I believe you wanted to see me.'

Finn, exhausted, pointed at his phone. He didn't have the strength to pick it up.

'Aoife, play the message.'

Aoife gently lifted Finn's hand and directed his thumb towards the thumbprint recognition icon to unlock the phone. She played the recording. Redmond chuckled.

'That's Lionel.'

Finn had forgotten about his father's annoying habit of christening individual birds.

'He sings all night long?' Redmond waited for a response.

'Do you not get it? Philistines. Never mind. The unusual thing about Lionel, he lives very near town.'

Finn sat up, the headache miraculously easing.

'Oh?'

'Now, normally, nightjars live in heathland. But this little boyo, he resides in the old convent grounds off Little Richard Street.'

'Little Richard Street?'

'Up behind Morrissey's?'

Aoife and Finn were thinking the same thing.

'I heard him one night. I was on my bike about three in the morning on my way for a swim.'

Finn let that pass. His father kept odd hours. And did odd things.

'An absolutely thrilling sound, I'm sure you'll agree. The tape doesn't do it justice. I couldn't quite believe it at first. Thought I was hallucinating.'

You would be at three in the morning, Finn thought to himself.

'Luckily, I had my night vision goggles. And I was able to follow the little blighter home.'

'Right. Is he still there? At the convent?'

'As far as I know, yes. I'm delighted to see you're finally taking an interest, Finn. He was such a dreamer as a boy.'

Redmond tenderly patted Finn's arm. That unprecedented gesture was Finn's cue to scramble out of bed. With difficulty, he pulled on his jeans. Blood was seeping through the bandage Ana had wrapped around his head. Together the three of them left the flat and walked briskly the few hundred yards towards the deconsecrated convent. In anticipation of what they might find, a modicum of strength had returned to Finn's limbs. During the walk, his father explained in far too much detail how the convent grounds were, contrary to his first impression, a perfect habitat for the nightjar.

'I can see what Lionel was thinking. All his favourite comestibles are there in abundance. You have a few sheep, you see, they broke in from Rice's field next door.'

'I doubt nightjars eat sheep, Dad.'

'No, clever clogs, but they do feed on dung beetles. And dung beetles breed in the sheep doodoo. They also love a pine tree lappet moth.'

'Who doesn't?' said Aoife.

'And lackeys too. Silver Y's, the silver Y's thrive in the old convent land, why?'

Neither Finn or Aoife were listening at this stage.

'Nettles.'

They passed Morrissey's. Hector was supervising a delivery of beer barrels, a metal hatch to the basement cellar splayed open on the footpath. They waved over at him. He waved back. He looked worried. But then Hector always looked worried. His eyes followed them for a moment. He then abruptly abandoned his station and sidled into the pub.

The yard behind Morrissey's extended for fifty metres or so along Little Richard Street. After that, as the road rose in a curve, there were a few business premises, followed by a terrace of about ten red-bricked houses. And then behind a high crenelated wall and padlocked rusting gates lurked the Convent of Perpetual Adoration on a demesne of about eighty acres. Beyond the nunnery to the east was farmland and God knows what else.

In the absence of a rope ladder to scale the wall there was no way in off Little Richard Street. They carried on up past the convent and past a few detached houses. One of them Finn recognized as the former home and dispensary of Harry Boyle's parents. Redmond in the lead, they turned right on to a side street, and right again down a lane until they reached a peeling green door in the convent wall. Finn, very tired again and short of breath, leaned against the wall while his father, trying various implements – a pen, the prong of Finn's belt buckle, Aoife's hairpin – fiddled with the lock. It felt like his brain was being macerated by tramping feet. Eventually his father turned the knob and opened the door.

'Voila, mes amis!'

'Fair play, Redmond,' said Aoife. 'How did you manage that?'

'I have to confess, my dears. The door was actually unlocked. Just a bit stiff.'

Chapter 61

The convent had been vacated by the few remaining nuns only a couple of years earlier but the building itself and its immediate grounds were already in an advanced state of disrepair. If it hadn't been for the decay, and the encroaching creepers and weeds, and the unsympathetic extensions, the main building would have been quite something in its day. Even to the untrained eye, it was a treasure with gothic flourishes, turrets and intricate tracery, in warm two-tone colours of red sandstone and red-brick dressing. The cloister enclosed an atypically large quadrangle that was completely overgrown with long grasses and weeds. There was a now stagnant pond in the middle of the garden around which the nuns must have once contemplated life and the wisdom or otherwise of their decision to join the order. It looked like the set of a post-apocalyptic zombie disaster movie. In fact a low budget horror film had been shot on the grounds of the Adoration, as it was commonly known, the year before it was bought.

'*Eileen Rua*, that's what it's called,' said Aoife.

'Right.'

'It's actually not that bad. About a young girl who's kidnapped by a religious cult. They thought she was the second coming. I was in it.'

'Oh?'

'Yes. I played "woman in the queue at the post office". Harry was in it too. He had his head chopped off.'

'I'd say he loved that.'

'It was probably the most dramatic death in cinema history.'

The convent had been bought, apparently, by Barry Duggan. Nobody could say for sure though. It was just assumed that every property that came up for sale within a twenty-mile radius of the town was snapped up by the voracious late businessman. By all accounts, he had intended in the short term at least to house refugees there, subject to the usual planning laws and bureaucratic delays.

There was a fenced-off field – a paddock of sorts – behind the convent which was now also overgrown and fringed by pine trees. A biodiverse nirvana, or a tragic neglect of good pasture depending on which side of the fence you were on. This was where the nuns once kept a herd of goats, prized for their milk. People with stomach complaints and other ailments came from miles away for the cure. The field was now, according to Redmond, the domain of Lionel the nightjar, and by deduction from where the murderer had made the call to Harry Boyle the night they killed Barry Duggan.

They waded through the grass looking for evidence. The burner phone used by the killer would be the grail, their fingerprints a bonus. Finn's phone rang. It was his mother. He didn't answer it, not wanting her to be fussing unnecessarily about his head injury. Aoife's phone then went off, eliciting a filthy look from Redmond. It was also from Maura.

'It might be urgent.'

'She'll be fine. She'll be even more anxious if she knows I'm up and about.'

'Stop!' Redmond commanded.

Aoife and Finn rushed over to where he was crouching on all floors sniffing the ground.

'There!'

By his urgent tone, they were expecting to see a dead body or a live grenade or at the very least the burner phone.

'We must have disturbed him. That's where he was sleeping. Lionel.'

They couldn't see anything. No nest. No eggs.

'You can see his feathers.'

They couldn't.

'Damnit! I knew I shouldn't have brought you here. You're just too noisy. He might never come back.'

Just then, they spotted an object in the sky. It wasn't a nightjar. Or any other bird for that matter. It was a drone and it was getting closer.

'Run!'

They all ran, the attack on Barry still fresh in their minds. Redmond was surprisingly nimble for a man of his age but couldn't keep up with Aoife. She'd slipped out of her shoes and was cutting the most direct path towards the relative safety of the cloisters. Finn, his legs suddenly leaden again and his eyes blurring, lost his footing and fell headlong into a thicket of nettles. The stinging sensation was almost a relief from the hammering pain behind his eyelids. Aoife and Redmond both did U-turns and, with the drone directly above them, took an arm each and dragged Finn though the quadrangle and into one of the galleries. There, they sheltered behind the colonnade while trying to figure out a way into the boarded-up building proper. The drone was lowered to head height. Slowly, as if it was alive and had a mind of its own, it passed along each of the three arcades in turn, pausing between the columns to look for its prey.

Finn took off his belt and offered it to his father.

'You might need the prong,' he whispered.

'Very funny,' his father replied.

Aoife, meanwhile, was prising some rotting boards away from a window to the refectory. Once she'd done that, using her elbow, she broke a pane of glass in the sash window, reached in and unscrewed the Brighton fastener. She then pushed up the bottom half of the window. She and Redmond levered Finn inside and tumbled in after him, all of them landing on the obsessively varnished parquet floor of the nuns' dining hall. Although it was bereft of furniture and the walls were mouldy, the interior of the convent was in better nick than the exterior. Apart from the *Eileen Rua* film crew, it was clear that few people had gained access to the building in the recent past. There were no signs of vagrancy or illicit party debris as they toured the facility. The stained glass windows were intact. One of them featured the patron saint of bees, St Gobnait. The bees, uncannily like drones, were hovering above tortured figures who represented the damned.

'Wait!'

It was Finn. They were now on the first floor of the convent, at the end of a corridor of bedrooms. He sat down on a circular staircase that led up to one of the turrets.

'I'm sorry, Finn. We should get you to a hospital.'

'No, I'm fine. Look.'

He pointed at some withered green stalks, strewn on the floor.

'Sticky willies. Cleavers. They were here. Whoever left the evidence in Carney's Wood. The bit of Harry's jacket. The Crunchie wrappers. They pulled them off right here.'

Aoife led the way up the stairs. A cold breeze met them as they entered what looked like an oratory, a hexagonal room with a modest altar and bird droppings on the floor.

'Pigeons,' opined Redmond, sniffing the air.

One of the south-facing windows was missing. They looked out through the empty rectangular aperture and took in the magnificent view of the town. Instinctively Aoife and Redmond looked towards Barry Duggan's house. They couldn't see the pile from the eyrie in which they stood, but were able to trace the path a grenade-laden drone would have taken. This was definitely the launch pad. Apart from anything else, after a thorough search of the room, Finn spotted a piece of paper covered in Sellotape somewhat camouflaged in a mound of pigeon guano.

'Don't touch it!' Redmond warned. 'It's toxic. Affects the respiratory system.'

He reached for the scrap of paper himself.

'I'm immune at this stage,' he coughed. 'It's nothing, just a tickle.'

The note, in a careful script, read, 'If found, please return to Hector Morrissey, c/o Morrissey's Bar' followed by a phone number and an email address. It must have been taped to the underside of the machine and fallen off unbeknownst to the murderer before lift-off. But who was the murderer? Hector? They were staring out the window musing on that very conundrum, wondering if there was anything they had overlooked, when suddenly the drone appeared again, right in front of their faces. Lurching forward, it accelerated towards them. They all screamed and scrambled from the room.

They ran down the spiral staircase to the second floor, and in a panic kept going in circles towards the ground floor. The stairs continued down into the basement, which is where their momentum took them. A dreary place, echoey, the floors covered in mosaic tiles, it was home to a laundry room, a workshop where the nuns once practised lace-making, a larder and various storage areas.

Finn sat on the ground, his back resting against a giant washing machine. He was delirious now.

'Aoife.'

'Shhh.'

'How is Conor?'

'He's fine. He'll be home in August for a few weeks.'

'Great. Tell him I love him.'

'You're not dying, Finn. You can tell him yourself.'

'I guess.'

He closed his eyes. Redmond was not too far away, rattling at doors and muttering away to himself.

'Is it serious?' Finn asked.

Aoife peeked under the sodden bandage and inspected his wound.

'You're grand. It's only a scratch.'

'I mean you and Shane.'

'What?'

'Forgive me. It's just small talk.'

'We're not on holidays, Finn, with endless hours to fill.'

Aoife went quiet. He could sense her leaning over him. Her body heat. Her breath. He could smell her hair. Redmond was now outside in a concrete yard, looking into sheds, and judging by his vocal emanations, really enjoying himself.

'I'm assuming you're not well and won't even remember asking the question. I don't know, is the short answer. It was. It might be. He's fun. You'll like him.'

'I'm sure I will.'

'If it wasn't for Shane, the limbo, I'd ...'

Finn had drifted off. It might have been for seconds or hours.

'It's just ...'

He opened his eyes. His mind was now clear. Unlike his eyesight. Aoife was just a blur. A beautiful blur.

Chapter 62

'Aoife! Finn!' Redmond bellowed from outside. 'Come here, at once!'

Aoife helped Finn to his feet. They made their way into the yard, scanning the skies above to make sure they weren't being tracked. Redmond was nowhere to be seen.

'Where the devil are you?' he growled.

The voice came from a stone grotto built into the landscape beyond the yard. It looked like a hobbit dwelling but was more likely a holy well, overlooked as it was by a limestone statue of a severe St Gobnait atop a beehive. Finn and Aoife stooped to go inside the chamber where Redmond was gazing into a pool of water. There was more than enough room for all three of them to stand.

'Should we make a wish? Ask St Gobnait to tell us who killed Michael and Barry?'

Redmond ignored his facetious son. He proceeded to tell them about the importance of holy wells in pre-Christian Ireland, and how they were 'hijacked' by the Church. He told them of the significance of St Gobnait. In Celtic lore, according to the oracle in their midst, the souls of the dead often left the body as bees. The hairs on Finn's neck rose on hearing the buzzing of a bee behind him. Who was that? He wondered. Michael Dunlop? Or Barry Duggan? Nagging him for answers.

'Look behind you.'

They both turned around. An iron grille, about three foot tall, had been removed from the wall by Redmond.

'What do you think that is?'

'A gate of some sort.'

'Behind the gate?'

'I don't know, dad. Part of the well? An old mineshaft? What?'

'Aoife, any ideas?'

Redmond was acting in a particularly smug manner at that particular moment, but being respectful of their elders, they played along.

'Is it a burial chamber? A tomb?'

'Have a look. And tell me if you see any bones down there?'

Aoife approached the opening in the wall. She could see steps made of stone leading down into pure darkness.

'Aoife, no,' Finn cautioned. 'We should call Xavier.'

Aoife reversed into the hole and disappeared down the steps.

'Well?'

She switched on the torch on her phone.

'No bones, Redmond. It looks like a . . . a tunnel!'

She clambered up again.

'So it's true?' she said, a smile on her face as she alighted again in the sacred space.

'It is.'

'What's true?' asked Finn. 'Am I missing something?'

Redmond put his hand on Finn's shoulder.

'Are you missing something? I've been asking that very

question for the last forty years, my boy. If I am not greatly mistaken, this tunnel should go all the way to . . . ?'

He left the question hanging for Aoife to answer.

'Morrissey's Bar.'

'Exactly!'

'C'mon, Daddy. That's just a rumour.'

He looked at them both.

'Isn't it?'

'There's only one way to find out,' she said.

The drone, it seemed, had gone. Aoife retrieved her shoes from the field and they headed to Morrissey's for sustenance. On the way, over Finn's futile objections, they cobbled together a plan. Redmond would return to the convent later that night with a torch and some tools. He'd follow the tunnel until, if his suspicions were confirmed, it reached the pub. Meanwhile Aoife, with or without Finn, would find somewhere to hide in Morrissey's until the bar closed.

'What if there's a lock-in?' Finn asked, not confident in the charade but not wanting to miss out on the charade either.

'Don't be such a killjoy,' Aoife chastised him. 'We'll figure something out. Tell them there's a fire.'

'Good luck with that. Nobody pays any attention to fire alarms in this country, not when there's a drink in front of them.'

'Well, we'll start a fire then. Come on!'

If everything went to plan, Aoife and Finn, in the early hours of the morning, would have the public house to themselves. They would have ample time to find the other end of the tunnel, and hopefully the proof that whoever assassinated Barry Duggan used that tunnel on that black night for Abbeyford.

'*If* there is a tunnel.'

Chapter 63

Hector was at the boot of his car as they reached the pub, gathering four or five packages into his arms. Redmond went on inside to order lunch. It was the first time he'd darkened the door of the pub in years. And the first time he'd ever offered to buy lunch.

'Do you need a hand?' Aoife asked.

'No.' Hector was uncharacteristically firm.

'What is it? A bomb?'

'Sorry, no, Aoife. It's a 1967 Matchbox Mercedes-Benz 230 SL. Apple green!'

He waited for a response but when none was forthcoming, he said, 'Apple green! Can you believe it? They only went and made it in apple green. It's the only one in existence. Just came up for sale last week. I've been looking for it for years.'

'Right,' said Finn, genuinely interested.

'They reckon it's a prototype.'

'I won't ask what it cost.'

'I'd be afraid to tell you. You'd have me locked up. More than that yoke anyway.'

He nodded towards his grubby estate car. Meanwhile Finn took out his phone. He scrolled through his photographs.

'And this one's a Hot Wheels.' Hector, his hands full,

directed his eyes towards one of the other parcels. 'From America. 1971 Purple Olds. In the original box. That's it now, honest to God. The collection is complete. I'm absolutely skint so I am. I'll have to sell the pub.'

He laughed unconvincingly. Finn showed him a photo. It was picture of a 1967 Matchbox Mercedes-Benz 230 SL in apple green, sitting in Barry Duggan's safe, taken the night Barry was murdered.

'It's similar alright,' said Hector.

'I thought you said it was the only one in existence.'

Hector was furious.

'Look, this has nothing to do with anything. I don't know who you two think you are. Yes, that was Barry's car. But I bought it fair and square.'

If he could run, he would have run, but Hector wasn't a runner. He could barely walk. Trapped, he explained that Duggan was annoyed with him because he'd bought a property Duggan had wanted.

'From right under his nose.' Hector smiled somewhat maliciously at what was clearly a treasured memory.

In revenge, it seems, Duggan had bought the thing Hector wanted more than anything else in the world, the toy car to complete his collection, gazumping him at an auction. Hector had just bought it from Barry Junior.

'He needed the money. That doesn't mean I killed him. It's only a toy.'

Aoife and Finn both knew that wasn't true.

'I swear to you on my parents' grave I didn't kill Barry Duggan.'

Aoife was looking into the capacious boot of Hector's real Merc.

'Hector, is that what I think it is?'

'What?'

'Is that a drone?'

'Oh yeah. Yeah, I finally got around to getting a new one. It's only an RC M4000. But sure it will do.'

'By any chance, were you flying it just now?'

'No,' he replied, offended. 'Why?'

Aoife reached in and felt it.

'It's warm.'

'Is it? Well, it's a hot day.'

'Were you spying on us, Hector?'

Hector stalled. He was trying to hide behind his parcels.

'I was testing it, if that's what you mean? And anyway, you shouldn't have been trespassing on my property.'

'Your property? You own the convent?'

He nodded as if it was no big deal, as if buying the convent and the land around it was a perfectly reasonable everyday transaction. That was probably the property Duggan wanted.

'I bought it. So what? Thinking of turning it into a hotel.'

'Not that skint after all,' said Finn.

'What were you doing up there anyways?' Hector asked, attempting to turn the tables.

'Dad just wanted to show us the holy well. You know what he's like. He has a thing for them.'

Hector was a dark horse. The shabby car. The dowdy clothes. The hangdog cut of him. Was it all an act? With the latest additions to his toy car collection secure under his chin, he tried to close the boot.

'Does the name Jenny Murray mean anything to you?' Aoife asked.

Hector paused mid-action. His face didn't register any noticeable alarm.

'Jenny Murray. Jenny Murray. I've heard of her alright. I just can't remember exactly where or when. If it comes back to me, I'll let you know.'

Aoife and Finn studied his reaction. Nothing. Not a twitch. Mind you, his emotional range was legendarily narrow. He rarely moved, physically, at more than a snail's pace. His blood didn't flow, it trickled. He had long mastered a woebegone demeanour and Eeyorish eyes that resulted in all of them – Aoife, Finn and the whole town – underestimating his canniness. Securing the deeds to the convent on the sly, without anybody knowing he was the buyer, was an unprecedented feat in a town like Abbeyford. It begged the question, what else did he own? What else had he done?

'And here, next time you want to visit the Adoration, just ask. By the way, did you hear the news?'

'What news?'

'Oh? Sorry. I shouldn't have said anything. You should probably go up to the Ball Alley.'

Chapter 64

All Finn wanted to do was lie down. Instead, with Aoife as his crutch, he stumbled hastily towards the Ball Alley. In his current hors de combat state, the sight that greeted him there made him want to give up. The ivy, with which he'd so recently adorned the walls, had been torn down. Somebody had done figures of eight on a quad bike over his lush wildflower lawn. Literally disturbing the peace garden. He lay down on the stone bed and contemplated the sky. Aoife lay down beside him. Every cloud and all that. They lay like that for half an hour watching the clouds overhead, looking for signs and meaning. He didn't have the energy or the will to repair the damage. The way he felt, he thought he'd never have the energy or the will to do anything ever again. The universe in all its vastness kept moving above them, unaware of their earthly plight, oblivious to the rivalry between Abbeyford and Ennismore, and the narrowing distance between Aoife and Finn. She helped him to his feet. Together they vowed they would not be deterred.

After lunch, Finn returned to the flat and collapsed on the bed. Ana brought him a bowl of her sudado de pollo – a Colombian chicken stew – and Monty, the retriever pup. She tucked Monty into the bed beside him, an inspired decision which was a great comfort to him, unlike the stew. Although the chicken was ridiculously tender and the broth a taste sensation, he had no appetite. Maybe, he thought, Monty might be able save him from Ana's wrath.

At Aoife's request, Harry Boyle called around. He diagnosed a mild concussion, re-dressed the wound, and prescribed Tramadol and bed rest. The doctor told Finn to go to A&E if he started vomiting or became dizzy or if the pain didn't subside.

'Thanks, Harry. Listen, we can prove beyond doubt the drone didn't come from Carney's Wood.'

Harry, busy wolfing down Ana's chicken stew, just grunted.

'Que sera, sera.'

The pup whined at Harry, not so much because he had deprived him of the sudado de pollo, but presumably because of the cat hairs covering his clothes. Finn noticed that Harry had sewn, somewhat crudely, a patch of mismatching cloth over the culpatory hole in his corduroy jacket. Harry, in sentimental overdrive, explained that he had repaired the garment, in a typical Boylean gesture, using a piece of his beloved Michael's black velvet dinner jacket. Harry departed, as you'd expect, with a twirl. Finn made a mental note to watch the locally made horror film, *Eileen Rua*.

Despite his misgivings and the feeble state he was in, Finn had a feeling the answer to the riddle of the hole in Harry's jacket, not to mention the identity of the Abbeyford double-killer lay somewhere in Morrissey's Bar.

Chapter 65

That night, the pub was heaving. The local soccer club were raucously celebrating a rare triumph. Sir Nicholas Nguyen-Bow was in town with an entourage in advance of a race meeting later that week at the Curragh. To complicate matters further for Finn and Aoife, an emergency meeting of the Tidy Towns committee had been called. The chairman's mother, Kitty Doyle, had heard from a source in the higher echelons of the Tidy Towns movement that an adjudicator was coming down from Dublin the next day sometime in the early afternoon. For once, such was the consternation caused by this news, Aoife and the chairman, Declan Doyle, were civil to each other. Together with Maura and Happiness, Alo Sweeney, Harry Boyle, Kitty herself and Gavin O'Connell, they conferred urgently as to what, if anything, they could do by lunchtime the following day to ensure the town would be appraised in its best light.

Unfortunately, there wasn't a function room available in the pub to hold the showdown. For two reasons: firstly, a meeting of the local Chamber of Commerce had been scheduled for that very night and, naturally, it assumed precedence over every other organization in Abbeyford. And, secondly, the Yellowbelly Suite had been booked by the Go club for its monthly face-off. There were a surprisingly large number of people in the area dedicated to the Chinese board game, Go.

It was noisy and distracting in the bar, but Eve, in her inimitable, inoffensive way, wrangling a few customers away with the promise of a free drink, had found a corner for them. She even went so far as to cordon off the area with a velvet rope. If you didn't know Eve, you'd think she was taking the piss.

'There you are now. Keep up the good work!'

Happiness, who hadn't, strictly speaking, been elected to the committee, was entitled to be there as Maura's carer. She was trying to escape the attentions of Alo by reverse-parking herself between Kitty and Declan. Alo would normally have chosen the Go club over the Tidy Towns but with Happiness in attendance, there was no contest. As if it was a game of Go, he was using all his skill and strategy, to try and conquer Happiness, suavely filling the vacant space left by Kitty when she went to the loo. Gavin O'Connell, the shopkeeper, meanwhile, loyalties torn, was flitting between the Tidy Towns meeting and the Chamber of Commerce event upstairs. The latter gathering, in a nepotistic twist of fate, featured amongst others Fionnuala Flynn, daughter of Gerry, Hector Morrissey, son of Richard, as well as Gavin himself, son of Celibate, tying this fateful night to the Night of the Big Snow in March 1982.

Eddie Halfpenny, at Aoife's behest, was currently going door to door, conscripting his litter division for one last sweep of the town first thing in the morning. Aoife and Finn, if they were still standing after their nocturnal sleuthing adventures, had agreed to inspect all the major parts of the development plan one last time, the Ball Alley for all the good they could do now, Bully's Acre, the bridewell and the old Huguenot cemetery. Spotters would be in place at all the approach roads, the bus station and the car parks trying to identify the judge, man or woman. The idea was that they would track this person's movement around the town, laying palm branches, so to speak, in front of them.

'Now, look. We have to be extra friendly to every stranger,' said Declan. 'Even you, Mammy. Try and be nice.'

'Don't know what that's supposed to mean,' Kitty snapped back, grievously offended.

'In fact. Now that I think of it. You should probably stay at home tomorrow.'

'The cheek!'

Maura consoled her old friend with a tap on the leg. Happiness almost laughed. Almost. It was the closest Finn had seen her coming to losing control since he'd arrived home in Abbeyford. A promising sign.

'It's very important to keep your distance,' Declan said. 'Dress nice, be friendly, you know, open doors and that, give them free stuff, ice cream or whatever, but don't look them in the eye. Right? We don't want them to know we're onto them.'

Finn actually felt quite excited, not so much about searching the pub later, but about his work – their work – being judged. The feeling in his gut reminded him of the nervous thrill he'd experience on the eve of Chelsea or Tatton Park Flower Shows. He was proud of himself and the people of Abbeyford, who'd come together in spite of the appalling tragedies that had befallen them, and conjured up a vision of a town anybody would be happy to live in. Even the timber yard, without hesitation, had agreed to take the afternoon off. That reminded him, he was half-thinking of asking his father to have a word with the seagulls who'd ventured inland in huge numbers to keep the noise down, at least for the duration of the adjudicator's visit. At the end of the meeting, Declan took Finn aside.

'I have to say, Finn, you've done an amazing job.'

'Thank you.'

'The Huguenot cemetery is looking spectacular. It's a picture. And as for the Ball Alley, I don't know what to make of it now, but it'll certainly leave an impression.'

'Well, I'm just glad I was in a position to help.'

'Thank you.'

Declan pumped his hand.

'You're in that wee flat above the café?'

'I am.'

'I have the very place for you. New development out by the Gower. Four-bedroomed detached houses. Very tastefully decorated. Mock-Georgian. Perfect for a VIP like yourself.'

'I'm not really . . .'

'No, no. No pressure, now Finn. You don't have to make your mind up straightaway. Just wanted to give you a heads-up, do you know. They won't be around forever, like. Drop into me during the week. Good man!'

Of course there had to be a sing-song. The lads at the bar, some of them still in their pink Abbeyford FC shirts, sponsored by AAAAAAAAAA Waste Disposal, inevitably burst into song. That advertisement had prompted innumerable inane comments about how rubbish the team were across the entire south-east.

At this point Finn, fearing the worst, called DS Xavier Keane and asked himself and Valerie if they wouldn't mind raiding Morrissey's at midnight to clear it of customers.

'For feck's sake, Finn. As if we're not unpopular enough as it is.'

Although Finn wouldn't tell him why they needed the guards to intrude, Xavier accepted Finn's assurance that their help in this regard would be vital in achieving a successful outcome to the case. Finn, pushing his luck, also made one further request.

'Jeepers Finn, who do you think you are, the Garda commissioner? The attorney general? My job is on the line.'

'You're a star, Xavier.'

'You owe me. Oh by the way, your pal, Eddie, is in the clear.'

The notorious actor Aidan O'Hara and his taxi driver, Eddie Halfpenny, were in a pub in Leighlinbridge at five past eight as the drone unloaded its deadly cargo outside Abbeyford. The guards were called to the pub after O'Hara threw a cheese and ham toastie at the barman.

'He doesn't like onions apparently.'

It didn't take long before Sir Nicky was persuaded to take a pew behind his piano. For a start, he enjoyed that sort of thing. He enjoyed it inordinately. In fact, he'd secretly hoped to be invited to do exactly that. Secondly, it would do his image in the eyes of his well-heeled guests – a leading racehorse trainer, West End angels, a minor royal – no harm. He knew from experience that they would find his ease among the locals rather charming.

After an Elton John medley, sung with a rare zeal by the entire football team and, in the middle of them all, the person with the least interest in football alive, Harry Boyle, the lads called for Eve.

'Eve! Eve! Eve!' they clamoured, banging the counter-top and stamping their feet.

Eventually Eve relented, removing her glasses and putting them in the breast pocket of her blouse.

'Alright, alright, yiz all know this one. "The Belle of Belfast City". You'll have to help me out now.'

As if. Keeping the tempo high, and the good humour going, she started belting out the classic folk song. Finn marvelled at the instant and dramatic transformation singing a song brought about in Eve. She grew in confidence. And stature. You couldn't take her eyes off her. It was like she was a different person.

> *'I'll tell me ma when I get home*
> *The boys won't leave the girls alone.'*

Sir Nicky was trying to keep up with Eve on the piano. His friends' faces were glowing. This was the Ireland of their imaginations. Alo Sweeney, sitting beside Happiness on the banquette, was swooning at her. She was clapping her hands furiously hoping the song would never stop lest her cadaverous admirer grab one of them and never let go.

> *'She is handsome she is pretty*
> *She is the belle of Belfast city.'*

The place was rocking. The Chamber of Commerce had cut short its meeting to join in the fun. The date was agreed for the annual golf outing to Waterville. Any other business could wait for the next meeting. The only people unmoved by the commotion were the members of the Go club. An earthquake wouldn't disrupt the Go players.

> '*Albert Mooney says he loves her*
> *All the boys are after her.*'

Even Finn himself, despite previous humiliations associated with his singing in public, joined in. He couldn't help himself, the lyrics to the song, latent since birth, coming to him fluently.

> '*Wee Jenny Murray says she'll die*
> *If she doesn't get the fella with the roving eye.*'

Harry was by now doing a jig on the floor. Tears the size of pearls rolled down his face.

> '*They pulled my hair, they stole my comb*
> *But that's alright 'til I go home.*'

Wait! What was that? Jenny Murray! Finn turned suddenly to his right. Aoife, eyes nearly popping out of her head, was staring straight at him. Staring back at her, he nodded. They both knew. *Wee Jenny Murray says she'll die*. Jenny Murray. It couldn't be a coincidence. It was Eve using the alias Jenny Murray who visited Tullaun house and stole the belladonna. It was Eve who signed herself into the Vinegar Hill distillery as Jenny Murray and pilfered the grenade. She would have overheard Eddie bragging about his arms dealer friend at the bar. It was Eve who killed Barry Duggan in the daring, ingenious drone attack. And in an earlier attempt to murder her father-in-law, it was her who'd accidentally poisoned Michael Dunlop. And now there she was in the bar inadvertently incriminating herself in song. Eve – unassuming, under the radar Eve – must have been the monster all along, who'd coldly destroyed people's lives and blighted the town for a generation.

> *'I'll tell me ma when I get home*
> *The boys won't leave the girls alone.'*

PART 4

Chapter 66

It was one thing knowing intuitively that Eve was the culprit; it was, of course, another proving it. She had covered her tracks well. But who else could it be? If as they suspected there was a tunnel, there was a good chance she was the only one apart from Hector who knew about it. They would need to get their hands on every shred of evidence available before presenting their case accompli to Xavier and Valerie. After about an hour, the sing-song died down. The beaming composer left the pub with his friends to generous applause. The footballers, who for the record had just won a regular league game against lowly opposition and not a cup final, continued, as was the custom, to share their good news and hard-earned cash in other hostelries around town.

Soon it was just Aoife, Finn, Maura and Happiness at the table. And Alo. Alo had invited Happiness to his apartment in Majorca. Itching to share their revelation with the ladies, Aoife suggested that Alo might like to drop Maura and Happiness home. Happiness was about to raise an objection, but sensed that Aoife had a good reason, a reason that superseded her personal discomfort. To Happiness' credit, she had a very clear moral, political and philosophical code in which her own happiness tended to come way down on her list of priorities. Ironically, that made her, despite her wilful refusal to smile, one of the happier people Finn knew. Alo jumped at the opportunity to be of service, thinking he might be able to wangle his way into Maura's house for a nightcap.

'The Jag is parked in Market Square,' Alo minced. 'I'll be waiting outside in ten minutes.'

He pronounced minutes as *min-yoots*.

'You're a gentleman,' said Aoife.

Alo Sweeney grandly insisted on paying the tab for everybody before he departed. Aoife turned to Happiness.

'So! Majorca! That should be fun.'

Maura burst out laughing.

'Aoife Prendergast. I tell you solemnly. That island is not big enough for the two of us. The Mediterranean Sea is too small for me and Aloysius Sweeney.'

'You have news!' Maura asked Finn, perceptive as ever.

'Yes. Big news, Mama.'

'Don't tell me. You're engaged.'

Finn shook his head.

'No Mammy, we're ... What ... have you been drinking ... ?'

He scowled at Happiness, for allowing his mother to drink so much, before reducing his voice to a whisper.

'We know who the murderer is?'

'Oh goody,' said Maura.

The ladies leaned across the table. Finn looked over his shoulder.

'It's Eve Duggan.'

Maura and Happiness remained unimpressed. It was not quite the reaction he was hoping for.

'Ah, I could have told you that,' said Maura.

'What?'

'As soon as I heard her singing about Jenny Murray, I nudged Happiness, didn't I?'

'Your mother nearly broke my ribs.'

'But we knew anyway. Last night before bed we each wrote down who we thought the murderer might be.'

'And?'

'And we both chose Eve.'

Aoife and Finn were both slightly miffed to be trumped in this way.

'Why didn't you tell us?'

'We couldn't. Not in front of Aloysius. He's a blabbermouth.'

'He is more than a blabbermouth, Maura. He is a lot of things.'

'Well. Why didn't you call me earlier?'

'We did. We tried ringing both of you. But you didn't answer your phones.'

'What type of a son does not answer the phone to his own mother?' Happiness scolded Finn. 'If Grace did not answer the phone to me, I would instantly disown her.'

Finn wasn't quite sure how brilliant a mother that made Happiness. Or dutiful a daughter that made Grace. But he kept his concerns to himself.

'Okay, so why are you so sure it's Eve?'

Maura handed the floor to Happiness. She almost smiled. Almost.

'It was the lotto.'

'The lotto?'

'We knew she had a motive.'

'Who doesn't?'

'Stop interrupting, Finn.'

'We found out definitively that Barry Junior was to be disinherited from the will.'

'You found out,' Maura complimented her carer.

'Yes. She loved her husband and hated to see him being abused by his own father. We also know that Barry Senior could not abide Eve. He hated her. He treated her like a piece of nik on his shoe. Everybody else in the town had accepted Eve back into the community. But not Big Barry. I would be tempted to kill a man if he treated me like that, God forgive me.'

'But what's that got to do with the lotto?'

Finn was getting impatient.

'Last night, Maura and I were watching the lotto results on the television. Did you know, exactly the same six numbers came up this week and last week?'

'I didn't know that.'

'Yes.'

A car horn beeped out on the street.

'Last orders!' It was Eve. 'I never even asked you, how is the head?'

She pointed at Finn's head.

'It's fine, Eve. Just a little bump.'

'This town has gone to the dogs altogether. Did they find out who did it?'

She tilted her chin sympathetically. Finn shook his head.

'Isn't it terrible? People are literally getting away with murder these days.'

She was either brazenly pushing her luck, entirely innocent, very forgetful or an out-and-out sociopath.

'Now, are yiz sure you don't want anything before we close?'

'You're grand, Eve. Just leaving,' said Aoife. 'Lovely song, by the way.'

Aoife smiled mischievously. Eve froze for a tick before quickly regaining composure.

'Some craic alright. I'lll miss this place so I will,' she said, misty-eyed, looking around the room. 'We're off tomorrow. For good. Meself and Barry. To England.'

'Ahh, that's a shame. We'll miss you too, Eve,' said Maura. 'The whole town will. Won't we?'

The car horn beeped again. Toot. Toot. Alo clearly fancied his chances tonight. Eve continued her trawl of the pub, the pub she'd done so much to revive and enliven over the past few years, toying with the stragglers as if she was just a regular down-to-earth bar manager instead of a homicidal maniac.

'The lotto?' Finn reminded Happiness.

'Was he always like that, Maura, as a child? The lady on the television said that this has never happened before in the history of this country. The same six numbers, two weeks in a row.'

She sat back pleased with herself. Aoife and Finn scratched their heads.

'I don't see where ...'

'Wait,' Maura said. 'She's not finished.'

'Eve's skipping the country tomorrow,' Finn hissed. 'We don't have time.'

'Then I remembered,' Happiness continued at her own unhurried pace. 'Many weeks ago, the day Barry was killed, when we were all sitting in this bar, singing songs in honour of Michael, the lotto results came on the television.'

'Yes.'

'Then. The six numbers were exactly the same as the previous week.'

'Happiness takes the lotto very seriously,' Maura pointed out. 'She knows all the numbers.'

'I remember thinking at the time: that is unusual. So last night, when the lady said it had never happened before, the alarm went off in my head. I looked at all the old results online.'

The car horn blew again. Alo was getting worried.

'The night Barry died, we were not watching the lotto results live.'

She looked towards the television on the wall.

'We must have been watching a recording of the previous week's results.'

It was beginning to dawn on Finn and Aoife as to what Eve had done to misdirect the patrons of the bar. To stop time.

'Ah. The penny is finally falling in your head!' said Happiness.

'Bingo!' whispered Finn.

'Lotto!' said Happiness, exasperated. 'I am talking about the lotto.'

'No, I know, I mean "Bingo" as in, you've cracked it ... congratulations ...'

'You should say what you mean. Do not speak in riddles. It was Eve who switched on the television.'

'Why would she do that?' said Aoife, verbalizing what they all knew. 'To provide herself with an alibi, it had to be, while she launched the drone. To pull the wool over everybody's eyes.'

Aoife became very enthusiastic.

'She needed at least fifteen minutes. Five minutes to get to the convent. Five minutes to guide the drone to its destination. And five minutes to get back here. She must have started the recording of the lotto at five to eight instead of eight. Ran to the convent.'

'The convent?' asked Maura.

'Did the deed. Ran back. Which means she was singing at ten past eight and not five past eight as we thought.'

'She stopped time,' said Finn in admiration. 'I knew it.'

'She managed to shift time itself by five minutes and nobody was any the wiser,' Aoife summarised. 'So at the exact moment Barry died, she appeared to be singing in the pub. God, she's good.'

Finn admired Eve's audacity but couldn't help feeling that she had over-elaborated in deceiving the public. Nobody had seen her leave the pub. If anything she'd left a hostage to fortune by re-running the previous week's lotto results, as Happiness proved.

'This is fabulous, Happiness. I'll call Xavier.'

Aoife put her hand on his arm.

'We'll need to find the evidence first.'

She nodded towards the TV.

'You mean?'

'Yes. We'll have to take the TV ...'

'Steal it?'

'Yes. The connect box, the other ... boxes, gadgets, whatever they're called. There might be evidence of the recording.'

Finn escorted his mother and Happiness to the door, explaining to her the significance of the convent on the way. Maura was troubled, wondering how Eve could have been in the convent if she hadn't left the pub that night.

'Isn't that what Pawel said?'

Pawel? Pawel, the bouncer at Morrissey's on exceptionally busy nights, had confirmed as much to the guards. No flies on his mother. How did she even remember Pawel's name? Even if at times she appeared to be dozing, or in this case tipsy, she continuously amazed Finn with her recall. Eve was at the door to bid goodnight to her customers.

'Eve, love, I have a question for you,' Maura said. 'How did you manage to get to the convent in five minutes if you didn't even leave the pub?'

Finn was not prepared for his mother's solo run. Both of his hands involuntarily jerked towards his temples. Eve herself was clearly unsettled too.

'I don't know what you're talking about, Maura. Did this fella put you up to it?'

'Oh, don't mind me,' said Maura. 'Night, night.'

Chapter 67

Finn wasn't sure if it was a deliberate ploy on his mother's part to fluster Eve into making a mistake, or if it was just late-night confusion. Finn and Eve briefly locked eyes. He shuddered to think what was going on inside her head at that moment in time. He waved goodbye to Maura, Happiness and an over-excited Alo. It was now more urgent than ever, if that was possible, to locate the evidence that would convict Eve. It was also now more dangerous.

Just as he was going back inside, some uniformed cops arrived at the door. Eve looked on suspiciously while they began to hunt the more recalcitrant customers from the bar. Finn and Aoife took this opportunity to conceal themselves in readiness for what the night might bring. Although it was a sprawling bar, with lots of nooks and crannies, there weren't many obvious places to hide. They were going on the assumption that Eve and Hector would do a basic sweep of the premises before they locked up. They would surely check the toilets. And the snugs. They would look under the banquettes for any belongings that may have been left behind. Aoife briefly considered as an option crawling up into the chimney breast of the fireplace. It might have been a practical solution if they had had all the time in the world and there weren't two guards standing in front of it. Finn equally ridiculously investigated the possibility of secreting himself within the cabinet of the grand piano. That was, of course, already occupied by strings. He doubted those strings were as taut as his nerves. They really should have thought through their plan in greater detail.

In desperation, as soon as they were sure they weren't in view of Eve or the Gardai, they ran upstairs to the first floor. They then inserted themselves in the S-shaped alcove near the Yellowbelly Suite, which was once a phone box. It was a tight squeeze and far from foolproof. Although they couldn't be seen from the corridor, Hector lived on the floor above. He would be passing imminently to play with his new toys or do whatever else it was Hector did in the privacy of his own quarters at night. A half hour passed before the chatter and movement downstairs subsided. Furniture was moved. The door of the pub opened and closed a number of times. A glass was broken. A vacuum cleaner was employed. Finn's heart raced for all sorts of reasons – fear, fever and proximity to the intriguing, exasperating woman beside him being the main ones.

Eventually, they heard Eve say goodnight to Hector and the door of the pub shutting with a resounding finality. Hector shuffled around for a while longer. A kettle was boiled. The smell of cocoa wafted upstairs and along the corridor and into their bolthole. Finn badly wanted to take Aoife's hand, in a show of friendship and common purpose, if nothing else, but resisted the urge. Hector mounted the stairs, whistling 'Boolavogue', the ballad commemorating 1798. He opened the door of the Yellowbelly Suite and closed it again. They held their breath. There was a manic look in Aoife's eyes. It looked like she was about to get a fit of the giggles. And it was contagious. Finn's mouth started twitching. He soon discovered that he needed all of his limited strength to stop himself from laughing, forcing his neck muscles to squeeze the life out of his vocal chords and his core muscles to close off his airways. He wanted to sneeze. He needed to pee. Hopping silently from foot to foot he tried to think of grim and gruesome thoughts to take his mind from the ludicrous situation he was in now.

Hector passed the entrance to the alcove and, to their considerable relief, continued towards the door of his apartment. But he didn't go inside. Rather, he stopped. He then double-backed. What if it wasn't Eve? What if it was Hector all along? What if he was armed? At that point, Aoife quickly undid a couple of buttons on her blouse, untucked Finn's shirt, drew him towards her and kissed him full on the lips.

'Oh, sorry to disturb you,' said Hector, deadpan, rounding the corner of the alcove with a cup of cocoa in his hand.

'So sorry, Hector,' said Aoife, hurriedly doing up her blouse again. 'We just got carried away. Lost track of time.'

'Easy done, I suppose,' said the publican.

Hector eyed them up and down. For some reason – it was probably the lugubrious moustache and the slightly officious air – he reminded Finn of a minor Mittel-European railway official in the dying days of the Austro-Hungarian empire. With a weary obligation, the functionary had to decide what punishment to inflict on these insolent, ticketless travellers.

'Keep it to yourself, Hector, willya?' said Finn, still in a state of shock, not to mention arousal, as he tucked in his shirt.

A hint of a leer stretched Hector's lip.

'Not sure Shane would be too impressed,' he said.

'Moralizing now, Hector, as well as snooping?' Aoife countered.

'I do live here, Aoife.'

Fair.

'That's actually a good point,' said Finn. 'We should get going. Really sorry about this, Hector. It won't happen again.'

The shock, although it had resulted in a split lip, had been a pleasant one. Its reverberations were still playing out throughout his entire nervous system. And although fully aware of the practical reasoning behind Aoife's quick-thinking gambit, Finn indulged himself in the brief fantasy that it was somehow meaningful. Unless she was a very good actor, that kiss was real. Hector looked ashamed, as if he was immediately rueing his peevish remark.

'Sorry, Aoife. I shouldn't have said that. How is he anyway, all messing aside, Shane? I hear he's back in town.'

Aoife was clearly undone by this news.

'Shane? In Abbeyford?'

'Oh. I thought you'd be the first to know. It's just, Fionnuala, she said she's seen him in the chemist. He was probably getting some cream for his cold sore. Or whatever.'

'Yeah. Sure. No.'

She pushed past Finn and Hector to get some air in the corridor.

'It might have been somebody else. Sure everybody looks the same now with the beards, sure you could be Shane for all I know.' Hector, pointing at Finn's beard, tried to make amends.

Hector looked to Finn for forgiveness. He had something on his mind. Something that would expiate his sins.

'What is it, Hector?'
'My father, God rest him.'
He blessed himself.
'What about your father?'
'He disposed of the body. Rameses.'

Finn was flabbergasted, not just at the unexpected news but at the matter-of-fact manner in which it was being relayed.

'What?'
'Poor old Rameses de Burgh. I know he was a good friend of your parents.'
'What are you on about?'
'He had no choice, Finn. God, I've wanted to tell people this for forty years.'

Finn was reeling. Was he in a fever? Was this a delayed concussion?

'Breslin made him do it. The guard. Yeah. He was a sergeant at the time. You see, Rameses died in this pub! I was fourteen at the time, saw it with my own eyes.'

No wonder Hector always looked haunted.

Hector, colour filling his face, blood flowing through his veins as he unburdened himself, swore to Finn that he saw Breslin strike Rameses. A blow to the head. One punch.

'Rameses went down like a stone. There was nobody else around, just the three of them. And me watching from behind the bar. They didn't know I was there.'

It was Breslin, now a superintendent, the chief upholder of law and order in the region, who had killed Rameses. And it was he who ordered Hector's father to get rid of the body. This was the verification Finn needed. His impulse to search Breslin's office was vindicated.

'Where is he now? Rameses. The body?'

'No idea. If I knew I'd tell you. I ran off to bed. Never breathed so much as a word to anyone. Until now.'

'You're a good man, Hector.'

'You don't mind letting yourselves out? I'm tired.'

Hector unlocked the door to the place he'd lived in all his life. When all this was over, Finn, out of curiosity, thought he'd love to get a look inside Hector's home.

Chapter 68

Aoife opened the door of the pub. And, remaining inside, slammed it again with a ferocity that must have shook the foundations of the building.

'Do you have to?' Finn whisper-squealed. 'You'll wake the whole town.'

They quickly got to work. Finn removed the television set from the wall, and along with the various accessories, he left it by the front door. It would be something else for Xavier's friends in forensics to play with. Aoife was already behind the bar, stroppily rooting through drawers and cupboards for evidence that would implicate Eve. She found a pair of scissors that Eve could have used to surreptitiously cut a piece of fabric from Harry Boyle's jacket, but they would never be able to tie her to that. Aoife violently threw the scissors back into the drawer.

Finn was about to join her when his eye was drawn to the fireplace. Something was missing. Of course. The pike! One of the pub's most notable treasures, the pike was about twelve feet long, a wooden pole with a steel spearhead affixed to the top of it. It was formerly used, by all accounts, by a local man during the 1798 uprising. Now, in theory at least, it served purely decorative purposes.

'Down here.'

Aoife had lifted up a hatch and had already descended the wooden steps into the cellar. It was cold down there. But it had a comforting, beery smell. Resting against a wall beside some kegs were a couple of free-standing metal lockers like you'd find in a leisure centre changing room. The door was hanging off one of the lockers. The other one had a small padlock attached to it. No prizes for guessing whose locker that was. While Aoife tried to force it open using a knife as a jemmy, Finn, with the aid of a screwdriver patiently unscrewed a sheet metal panel from the back of the storage unit. It was a cheap locker after all and not a safe. Hector didn't spend his money frivolously.

There was nothing inside the locker apart from a drab fawn-coloured raincoat. Aoife searched the pockets of the coat. In them, she found a handful of puppy treats and some receipts. She scanned the receipts for evidence of malfeasance. She was clutching at straws now, looking for proof of purchase of mini-Crunchie bars, pricey Vinegar Hill whiskey, a burner phone or any other item that would suggest Eve was guilty of the two biggest crimes in Abbeyford's recent history. Nothing. Nothing obvious anyway. Aoife stuffed the receipts in her right-hand-side jeans pockets. She might, just might, against all her principles hand them over to the cops. In her left jeans pocket, she stuffed the puppy treats as a gift for the delightful dog Eddie had bestowed upon her. She'd named her Brigid, leaving her in the capable hands of her nephew, Nathan, while she turned her hand to solving murder cases.

'Hang on!' said Finn.

He looked from one locker to the other. The base of the one that had been unlocked was a couple of inches lower than the base in Eve's locker.

'Curious!'

Finn didn't need his screwdriver. The bottom of Eve's locker was on a hinge. It just needed a gentle double-tap for it to lever open. They looked into the secret compartment. Not much. Apart from a wash-bag. Aoife removed the bag and unzipped it, not exactly expecting to find toothpaste. No. Instead of hygiene products and cosmetics, they couldn't help noticing, there was money. Cash money. Rolls and rolls of fifty- and twenty-euro notes bound in elastic bands.

'Wow!'

It was evidence of something – robbery perhaps, fraud at the expense of Eve's boss – but not necessarily murder.

'I'll take that.'

It was Eve, wearing a surgical mask and wielding a pike in one hand and some sort of a canister in the other.

'Hello, Eve. Are you going to kill us too?' asked Aoife calmly. 'Like you killed Michael and Barry?'

Finn was thinking to himself that that wasn't quite the way he would have handled it.

'Eve!' he pleaded with her. 'Why don't you hand yourself in?'

'For what? I didn't do anything.'

She pointed at the wash-bag in Aoife's hands.

'Apart from that. Which, by the way, is rightfully mine. Do you have any idea what that stingy fecker upstairs pays me?'

She pointed the pike towards the ceiling.

'Feck all is what. And I literally do all the work around here.'

'We know.'

'Hand it over, Aoife.'

Aoife didn't budge.

'Now!' Eve yelled.

Her face darkened. Her eyes were crazed. She was pointing the medieval weapon directly at Aoife's chest. Given her volatile behaviour of late, Finn's confidence in a peaceful resolution to this stand-off was rapidly falling away.

'Eve!' Finn shouted. 'Please, it doesn't have to be like this. We won't say a word, will we? Aoife, give her the flipping bag.'

Aoife threw the bag at Eve's face. At the same time, Finn, bandaged head lowered, attempted to tackle the armed woman. Before he reached her, however, she managed to hit him a sharp blow on the side of the head with the less lethal end of the pole, knocking him off balance. With another swoosh of the stick, she sent him to the ground. Needless to say, Aoife wasn't standing idly by. While trying to wrest the pike from Eve's grasp, the iron spearhead caught her a glancing blow on the collarbone. Aoife leapt back, in searing pain. Fortunately it wasn't the actual pointy bit that got her and it didn't puncture her flesh but, if the pain was anything to go by, the bone was broken. Before either of them could rejoin battle, Eve sprayed them both in the face with some sort of pepper spray. Blinded, in agony and incapacitated by the gas attack, Finn and Aoife curled up together protectively on the floor. Eve patted them down, searching for their phones, which she then flung against the wall. Finn's first thought was, *oh no, my photos* – his mother's reassuring face, his holiday snaps, his gardens, the Tidy Towns project in Abbeyford. Then he placated himself, *ah but they're probably safe in the Cloud*. Then he realized, as Eve raised the pike above her head, *sure, I'm never going to get the chance to see them again anyway.*

Finn wanted to say something reassuring to Aoife. He whispered the words 'I love you' into her ear. He wasn't sure if she heard him. For at that very moment, he heard the all-too-familiar, loud, hectoring voice of his father.

'Finn, Aoife, are you there? I found it.'

'Ah, for feck's sake,' Eve cursed and wheeled around to face Redmond as he emerged from a secret door in the wall.

'Dad!' Finn shouted in warning.

His father had turned around facing the way he came to inspect the mechanics of the concealed entrance to the passageway.

'Impressive. I can't believe you didn't find it. What have you been doing at ... Oh! Eve! It's yourself.'

Eve hit Redmond roughly in the stomach with the handle of the pike and sprayed him with the tear gas for good measure. She then ran off down the tunnel.

Finn and Aoife, their eyes streaming, their whole faces stinging, the pain from their respective head and shoulder injuries unrelenting, dragged themselves over to Redmond whose fall had been broken by a keg, resulting in a nasty bang to his head. He was out cold but still breathing.

'Dad, Dad!' Finn called, slapping his father repeatedly on the face. There was probably no need for quite that many slaps. Or slaps of quite that ferocity. Aoife had found a slab of mineral-water bottles amongst the soft drinks in storage. With one arm she ripped away the plastic film covering the consignment. She opened a bottle and poured it over her eyes. It was fizzy water, not ideal, but it would have to do. She'd had experience of being gassed, once or twice, when the incinerator protest threatened to get out of hand. She handed a bottle to Finn and poured another bottle over Redmond's eyes. He came round, the effects of the gas not apparently as debilitating to him. Whether that was due to repeated exposure to the substance over the years, a badly aimed squirt by Eve, or some sort of natural resistance, Finn couldn't say.

His father grabbed him by the shoulders, saying in a faint voice: 'I don't know if I ever said this, son, but I ... I ... think you're a great lad.'

He hadn't. It was a long time coming but worth the wait.

'What did he say?' Aoife asked, issuing more bottles of water.

'I think he said he loves me.'

He looked at Aoife, his face red and raw, eyes still awash with tears.

'What a stupid thing to say at a time like this,' Aoife declared. 'People get very sentimental in extremis.'

'Yeah. You're right.'

'C'mon, we better go after her.'

'You two go,' said Redmond feebly. 'I'll be grand. I haven't had bottled stout in decades.'

He pointed towards a crate of Guinness bottles. Why hadn't Eve killed them? Perhaps she had a conscience after all. She had only come to the basement to collect her money. She wasn't expecting to find three people in her way. Maybe she didn't think she could handle all three of them. Or maybe she only assassinated arch enemies. Michael, she'd murdered by accident.

The door to the tunnel was pretty simple but ingenious. It was at the back of an old open fireplace, about two feet in depth, there since the pub had been built centuries ago. Made of brick, it would have been a working fireplace at one time. But the back wall was a sheet of copper. And it revolved with a firm push. Stooping, Aoife and Finn entered the tunnel. The ground was earthen. For the first twenty yards or so the passage was supported by brick walls and an arched ceiling. The original moles among the Morrissey clan had gone to some trouble. They must have had something to hide. After a while, although the light from the cellar no longer guided them, they sensed that the tunnel was not quite as robust as they would have liked.

'You'll need this, you fools.'

It was Redmond, following them with a torch.

'Thanks, Dad.'

'You'll find something quite interesting about halfway through the tunnel on the left-hand side.'

He passed the torch, literally and in some ways, Finn liked to think, figuratively, and scurried back to the relative comfort of the cellar and his bottled stout.

Finn and Aoife carried on. They could see that the walls now were mostly made of compacted earth. The roof was propped up intermittently by iron bars and wooden slats. They had to navigate their way around mounds of clay where parts of the roof had collapsed. Disturbingly, they could see water dripping down the walls.

'Did you mean it?'

'What?'

'What you said back there? Or were you just trying to comfort me?'

A bit more of the roof gave way. Finn was terrified. He wasn't sure if it was the fear of suffocation or the fear of opening his heart.

'Put it this way, Aoife, there is nobody I can think of right now that I'd prefer to be buried alive with.'

'Vice versa. What's this?'

Aoife shone the torch at an opening on the left side of

the tunnel. It was a narrow entrance about four feet high and two feet tall. A number of wooden boards were lying on their sides on the ground. It was clear that this section of the tunnel had been reinforced at one time. There were planks and steel struts still in place on the opposite side of the tunnel. If the boards on the left side hadn't been removed, it would never have occurred to anybody that there was a hidden chamber behind them.

Tentatively, they entered the recess. It wasn't big. According to Finn's internal theodolite, it was five feet by five feet by five feet. He felt claustrophobic. A priest hole was his first thought. Despite his father's constant tutoring in Irish history, Finn's dates were sketchy. Would the pub have even existed in penal times when Catholic priests were routinely forced into hiding? By all accounts, even if the current iteration of the pub hadn't yet been built, there had been some sort of an inn on the site. The tunnel and this offshoot could well have predated Morrissey's, as it was known and loved today. Perhaps the family had been smugglers or rebels or both. Whatever about its origins and its past, it was clearly being used for a very different purpose in the present day.

There was a sleeping bag rolled up in one corner. And a camping gas stove. There was a book on the ground, a well-thumbed copy of *The Lady in the Hole* by Tara Wallace. Sure enough, the passage in which Lucinda prepares the poison was underlined. There were mini-Crunchie wrappers strewn on the floor. And in the opposite corner was a ... a skull!

In fright, Finn stood up to his full height, banging his head off the ceiling. He had gone well beyond his pain threshold by now. Aoife, a teacher of pubescent boys, was less easily shocked. It wasn't just a skull. There was a full skeleton, bunched up, loosely attached to it. Finn didn't know which was more creepy, that somebody had been unceremoniously buried there or that Eve seemed happy to share that person's tomb. His guess was that Eve, a woman capable of grisly murder, was not going to be fazed by some old bones. Presumably familiar with the tunnel, she must have stumbled upon this hideout. It was, he imagined, a perfect place for her to plot and scheme and prepare her poison.

'Rameses!' Finn exclaimed.

'What?'

'Eamonn "Rameses" de Burgh. Here he lieth.'

Aoife gave him a sideways look.

'I mean, here he lies. That's got to be him.'

They looked carefully through the bones for proof that his hunch might be right. No sign of anything that would identify the remains. Another job for forensics.

'She'll have escaped by now,' said Aoife, somewhat defeated.

Finn didn't say anything. There was an element of satisfaction in discovering the whereabouts of his parents' old friend Ram. There was also some fulfilment to be had in convincingly unveiling Eve as a double murderer. And he had to admit, there was a tingle of anticipation at the thought of the surprise he had lined up for Aoife.

They left Eve's ghastly den and trudged onwards towards the end of the tunnel. Emerging from St Gobnait's well in the convent grounds, they were immediately dazzled by floodlights. It must have been three in the morning. When their eyes regained focus, they realized that there were guns pointing at them.

'Hands up!' demanded an armed detective.

Given the broken collarbone, Aoife wasn't able to raise her right arm.

'Ah, the dead have arisen,' said Xavier cheerfully. 'As the prophesies foretold.'

Valerie was leading Eve away in handcuffs. The pike was on the ground. A couple of technical people in white onesies were trying to figure out how to bag such an oversized item. Eve looked back at Aoife and Finn. There was no malice in her expression. If anything, she looked relieved.

'Thanks, Xavier,' Finn said, in awe at the manpower and equipment employed, while a medic tended to Aoife.

'No. You were right, Finn. Mind you, if she didn't come out of that tunnel, I'd be unemployed right now. Or in jail. I actually filled out an application form for Dunnes Stores earlier this evening. That's a fact.'

'Sorry.'

He held up a bag with a phone in it.

'No need to apologize. The burner phone! We also found cash. Oh. And she admitted everything. Ho-ho. It's not every day you solve two murders.'

Xavier was practically jiving on the spot.

'Possibly three,' Finn said.

At that point, Valerie joined them.

'What's the story?'

No gratitude. No resting on her laurels. The biggest case of her career, neatly wrapped up in a bow. No sleep. Not even a nap, or a nightcap. Onwards to the next peak.

'What's this about a third murder?'

He told her what they had found in the tunnel. He also told her who he thought was responsible. And why. And the name of a possible witness. And where she might find the key to the puzzle, an eagle's egg. Valerie whistled.

'Tricky. Leave it with me.'

To an ordinary person, the potential involvement of her boss in a forty-year-old homicide might have complicated matters. *'Hey Super, we cracked the Duggan/Dunlop case and brought great credit to you and the force but in doing so we couldn't help noticing that you're a suspect in a cold case.'* But Valerie was far from ordinary. She lived for complications.

'Right, better tidy up here,' said Xavier, on a high. 'Oh, by the way, we arrested Barry Duggan Junior. He was sitting outside the convent in a car. Knew she was robbing Morrissey's but refuses to believe Eve murdered anyone. I think he's telling the truth. Poor Barry. Best of luck tomorrow!'

'What's tomorrow?'

'Tidy Towns? I heard the adjudicator is on the way?'

The grave way he said it, it was like Judgement Day itself was coming. A chance, on the morrow, for the town to expiate its sins. Aoife and Finn didn't need reminding. The various wounds would have to wait for attention. The aches and pains would have to be borne with forbearance. The post-mortems would have to be put on hold. And the pregnant feelings between them would have to be paused.

Chapter 69

It was a beautiful morning in Abbeyford, the sun burning away the mist by the Barrow in something of a theatrical prologue to the day ahead. The water, lit by the sun, flowed lazily like so much golden syrup. A gay, holiday mood took hold as the town came to life. Many people had taken the day off work to help the Tidy Towns effort one last time. In truth, there wasn't an awful lot to do once the few stray scraps of litter had been picked up – a cheese-and-onion crisp bag had been reported on John St; there was a piece of chewing gum underneath a bench on Quay Street; and there was a nappy in the SuperO car park that had fallen off the roof of a car. Redmond, although clearly concussed not to mention gaseous after the bottled stout, insisted on fixing the wonky hinge on the library box opposite SuperO. Others scoured the streets for dog waste. Some people were extremely surprised to see Lady Tara Wallace, off her own bat, painting in an unsteady hand a mural on a traffic light control box. It was a foliage-covered woman, presumably Madremonte. Finn himself touched up a hydrant with an unnecessary lick of paint. There was a bit of pruning here, some judicious mowing there. Due to the biodiversity imperative, there was ongoing uncertainty as to how much mowing to actually do. In fact the only reason for mowing at all was to contour and highlight the carefully cultivated 'rewilded' patches of ground around the town. Although, by lunchtime, the place was pristine, it felt good to be doing something. Anything. Even the town cynics who'd gathered early to sneer as the action unfolded had to concede that it was a good show.

At 1.30pm the word went around that the judge had arrived. He was reportedly driving a hired car.

'A Skoda,' said Eddie.

'The make doesn't matter,' said Aoife, her arm in a sling. 'Has he got a camera?'

'Yes.'

'A map?'

'Yes.'

'And a clipboard?'

'Yes.'

'That's probably him alright.'

The description of the man was circulated. He was about five feet ten in height, trim, wearing a sober suit and tie that clashed with his garish AirMax runners and a pair of sunglasses. His first stop was Café Madremonte, where he was pleasantly surprised to be given a free lunch.

'It's on the house,' said Ana. 'You are my one thousandth customer.'

'Today?' he asked laconically in an English accent to the surprise of the crowd who'd discreetly followed him into the café.

Ana was momentarily wrong-footed by his sarcastic reply. She quickly recovered and started laughing, way too loudly, even going so far as to hold her sides to keep them from splitting.

'You are so funny!'

The man, after he left Ana's, took an unexpected zigzag route through town ignoring the main attractions as outlined in the Tidy Towns programme. In fact the first photograph he took was of one of the warehouses on the riverfront, the apartment building, as it happened, in which Harry Boyle lived. He had never been to such a friendly place. Everybody he met smiled and said, 'Hello. Welcome to Abbeyford.' An old man offered him a mandarin orange. Affected as he was by the hospitality, he had a job to do. He was a professional and would not be swayed. It was outside Harry's block that he was arrested by DI Valerie Kilcoyne and DS Xavier Keane.

As Xavier later explained to Finn, the man's name was Rufus Morgan. Finn immediately recognized it as the name Isabella provided him with some weeks back. Morgan was a London gangster who'd lent money to Michael Dunlop for his ill-fated Victory Festival. Coming across reports of the double murder on Sky News and seeing Michael's picture up on the screen, Morgan had come to Abbeyford looking for his money. In the absence of Michael, his first port of call was to be Michael's next of kin. Harry Boyle.

'No need to worry. His little holiday has been cut short.'

'We have an international arrest warrant from the UK,' Valerie added, ever the stickler for the rules.

'Yeah, and we've impounded the rental Skoda.'

'How is Eve?' asked Finn.

'She's not saying much.'

They talked about Eve's baroque crimes and her split personality. In advance of further interviews with the murderer, they tried to pool their knowledge to date, filling in the gaps in the sequence of events, the motivation for her various actions and how she'd managed to cover her tracks.

Her husband, Barry, was now claiming that he was in fact the culprit and that Eve was entirely innocent. It was clear to the police that he wasn't implicated at all, that he'd known nothing about Eve's more violent crimes.

'We've informed Monika. She's in Croatia with her son.'

'Breaking news, by the way,' Valerie interrupted. 'Tom Breslin's resigned.'

'The super.'

'He knows who the super is, Xavier. He's not an eejit.'

Finn was strangely chuffed that Valerie no longer considered him to be an eejit.

'On health grounds. Dementia, apparently.'

'Convenient,' said Xavier drily. 'She'll of course be looking for his job.'

'If it means getting away from you, I probably will. Breslin's not admitting anything. But if we can persuade Hector to testify, we'll nail him.'

'So tell me if Rufus Morgan is not the Tidy Towns judge, who is?' Finn asked.

'It might be that woman over there.'

Síle Dennehy-Malone, a slight fifty-seven-year-old woman in a summer dress and a straw hat, had gotten off the bus from Dublin undetected. Inconspicuously, she'd made her way around the town, diligently making notes on all the projects highlighted in the Abbeyford plan. She fancied herself as a photographer and took great care over each composition. Although she had been stung by a bee while doing a close-up of an insect motel, she regarded that as a positive sign, something to be celebrated. Now she was conversing with Tara Wallace, admiring the old lady's painting of a woman covered in leaves and wildflowers and surrounded by bees. Even the electrical boxes in Abbeyford were being rewilded! *How delightful*, Síle thought. It turned out the adjudicator was a huge fan of Tara's novels.

Turning around, she noticed a group of elderly men in boats – currachs, at a second glance – rowing gently down the river. It was an amazing sight that brought tears to her eyes. Her father had been a Connemara fisherman. The flotilla was led by a bearded man in shorts, standing precariously in his currach, a bottle of Guinness in his hand, urging his rookie sailors on.

Maura and Happiness had by now joined Finn and Aoife on the riverbank. His sister, Eimear, and Happiness' daughter, Grace, were there too, having just arrived together from Dublin. Eimear had arranged an internship for Grace for the rest of the summer in the aviation leasing company. Eimear smiled at Finn, bonding over their father's idiocy. He felt the tears bubbling up inside him. He put his arm around his mother. The whole town it seemed had congregated, as if summoned by an inaudible bell.

'An otter!' the cry went up.

Nathan, the designated otter-spotter, ran, out of breath to his aunt, his binoculars swaying from side to side on his chest.

'I saw an otter!' he said, hyperactive with excitement.

'Where?' said Aoife.

Nathan pointed south. About fifty yards away, approaching the hushed crowd, were three otters. One of them was sliding on his belly, the other two playing a tag-like game. Síle, the Tidy Towns judge, like everybody else in the audience, was entranced. Like somebody under hypnosis she was drawn closer to the river. One of the otters started juggling a pebble in its paws. It looked like he was doing it just for her.

Aoife found Finn's eyes.

'Otters,' she whispered and crossed her fingers.

A coup de théâtre. Finn looked to the heavens to acknowledge the gods' timely choreography. He was satisfied that they had done all they possibly could. He may never have won gold at Chelsea but, if he said so himself, he did help to solve a double murder and instil pride in a town.

There was only one thing left to do. He took a deep breath and turned to Aoife. There was nothing to lose. Apart from his dignity. And his self-esteem. The usual. He was just about to ask her out to Lardo when a man snuck up behind her. He whirled her around and kissed her passionately on the mouth. Unaware that she was suffering from a broken collarbone, his clumsy pass caused her considerable pain.

'Shane!'

The man stood back self-confidently, brushing a hand through his mane of thick, wavy black hair. He was undeniably handsome with a full set of straight white teeth, a mono-brow and dark, seductive eyes that were currently riveted on Aoife's face. So this was Shane Delahunt! Wearing cargo pants, a white T-shirt and a flak jacket he looked every inch the wannabe revolutionary. Oh, and he sported an earring in one ear. It was, if Finn was not mistaken, a cowbell. It matched Aoife's. The back of his head pulsed, the pain still live since the recent assault in Market Square.

'Where have you been, Shane?' Aoife was pale, shaking, while trying to maintain a strained smile.

'I wanted to surprise you, darling.' He reached into his pocket and produced a fragment of rock. 'It's from a meteorite. I got it in Somalia. There's so much to tell you.'

One for the grand gestures, Finn suspected. She should run a mile. It looked like malachite, something you could pick up at any market in the African continent.

'You must be Finn.'

They shook hands. Shane gripped Finn's hand very tightly, pulling him closer. He had sweaty palms.

'How is the head?'

'Sorry.'

'That was some bang, I'd say,' he smirked.

Finn glanced at the lump of rock now in Aoife's hand. He looked at the cowbell dangling from Shane's ear. At the runners on Shane's feet. He probably had sweaty feet too. Hence the squeaky shoes. He was satisfied beyond doubt that it wasn't Eve who'd knocked him unconscious on Market Square.

'It's grand, Shane. It'd take more than that to stop me.'

He forgave him. Given the day that was in it, he was in a forgiving mood.

'Nice to meet you, Shane. I'm sure I'll see you around.'

He moved away towards his mother and Happiness. Maura squeezed his arm. Finn squeaked. Happiness, of all people, squeezed his other arm. Finn squeaked again. To show just how much he wasn't put out by the presence of Shane and that he hadn't lost his sense of humour, he let out a little sequence of squeaks as if he was a dog toy.

Happiness started laughing. Finn did a double-take. Did that really just happen? And once she started, Happiness couldn't stop. She repeatedly squeezed Finn's arm. He squeaked repeatedly in response. She almost hyperventilated she was laughing so much. Maura was agape. Grace couldn't believe her eyes. She hadn't seen her mother like this since she was a little girl. It was infectious. Soon the whole town, Finn included, was laughing.

It was shaping up to be a good summer in Abbeyford.

EPILOGUE

Chapter 70

A few months later, in November, at a ceremony in the Royal Dublin Society, the winners of the national Tidy Towns competition for that year were announced. A delegation from Abbeyford, including Aoife Prendergast and the chairman, Declan Doyle, were in attendance. While they hadn't settled all their differences, they did travel to Dublin together, with a fair degree of optimism. In fact, they seriously hoped to win, if not the overall title, then at least the county crown.

Finn, although he was invited along, declined the offer. He preferred to watch it on TV in Morrissey's with his mother and father and many of the volunteers. It wasn't that he wasn't chuffed at their collective efforts. It wasn't modesty – faux or otherwise – on his part, although he really, really didn't want to steal Aoife's thunder. It was simply because he had another engagement later on that evening after the broadcast.

It was a long, tortuous rigmarole. Finn could tell Aoife was nervous when the camera briefly panned across her table. She hadn't eaten. When they finally got to Wexford, she could hardly breathe.

'Abbeyford,' announced the celebrity emcee, a weatherman renowned for his wink at the end of each bulletin. There followed a long pause.

'Gold medal,' he said, winking. 'Well done to Abbeyford.'

There was a whoop from Aoife, and an almighty roar from Declan. He lifted her off her feet and twirled her around, the forcefield between them having disintegrated with that historic declaration.

The town had never won gold before. Back in the pub, Maura and Declan's mother, Kitty Doyle, rejoiced tearfully. They'd been members of the first ever Tidy Towns committee in Abbeyford. The report by the adjudicator, Síle Dennehy-Malone, when it was published couldn't have been more complimentary, despite as she noted the obvious damage to the Ball Alley. Needless to say, she raved about the otters.

'Sshhh.' The call for hush went around the pub.

'Ennismore!' the weatherman said. 'Ennismore ...' he repeated for dramatic effect.

'Gold medal!'

In the pub, there followed a stunned silence eventually punctuated by Maura.

'Shite!' she said, swearing for probably the first time in her life. Redmond rubbed her back gently.

To rub salt in the wound – if Finn, studying the television closely to get a glimpse of Aoife, wasn't mistaken – Eugene Foster, the chairman of Ennismore, got up from his seat and gave the two fingers to Aoife. Finn felt like getting in the car and driving to Dublin. But he had an appointment to keep.

All hope was not lost. It was a rare phenomenon for two towns from the same county to win gold in the same year. But only one town could win the county award. There was still every chance that would be Abbeyford.

'New Ross,' the emcee rolled the R and aspirated the

esses. New Ross hadn't come close for years. The weatherman suddenly put his hand up to his earpiece.

'Sorry, ladies and gentlemen, one minute.' He nodded, repeatedly, in response to an unseen producer's voice.

The audience in the RDS fidgeted in their seats. They were all hungry at this stage. None of them had eaten for hours on what for many was the most nerve-racking night of their lives.

'Well, I don't know what to say.' The man looked shocked. He loosened his tie and undid his top button. 'There's been an unholy development, folks.'

Everybody in the pub leaned towards the television.

'This has never happened before. It gives me no pleasure to announce that the executive board of the Tidy Towns competition have been left with no choice but to strip Ennismore of their gold medal and disqualify them from the tournament.'

There was consternation in the hall as there was in Morrissey's. The weatherman, face grave as an undertaker's, didn't wink.

'It seems, and I can't believe I'm saying this, that a member of the Ennismore committee, who shall remain nameless, desecrated a peace garden in a neighbouring town on a quad bike. This act of vandalism happened to be caught by a camera attached to a drone.'

Finn looked over at Hector behind the bar. He was clean-shaven for once, his lips a picture of rosy health. A rare smile spread across his face. Finn raised his glass.

'This footage has just come to the attention of the executive.'

Fair play to Hector. A few weeks ago, he'd been doing some editing – putting together a showreel of the town's charms for a prospective bride – when he'd spotted the video of Foster on his quad bike doing his dirty work at six in the morning. With Finn's approval, and the newly-promoted DI Xavier Keane's intercession, they'd made sure the offending images got into the right hands in the nick of time.

'Now, where was I? Yes. New Ross. Gold medal.'

'Shite,' said Maura again. Redmond rubbed her back again. With Happiness on holidays, he was, restlessly, it has to be said, playing the part of a dutiful husband.

How the hell did New Ross win gold? The town was a building site. Although there was no precedent for three towns in the same county winning gold in the same year, Abbeyford could yet take home the ultimate accolade.

'And the prize for the tidiest town in County Wexford goes to ... New Ross.'

'Shite!' the whole bar erupted as one. 'Double-shite!'

Oh well, thought Finn, as he finished his pint, *there's always next year.* Not winning the county meant they couldn't win the overall award. He didn't mind but he felt for Aoife and the others. He took one last look at the television, hoping to catch sight of Aoife. He'd never seen her in a dress before.

'And we're delighted to announce the one you've all been waiting for: the overall winner. This year's Tidiest Town in Ireland ... Carrickmacross, County Monaghan.'

'Where are you off to?' Maura wondered.

'Oh you know, just out.'

'Who is she?'

No flies on Maura. It was probably the scented beard oil. The polished cowboy boots. The clean T-shirt. He checked his watch. It was already half nine. He'd better not be late for Ana.

Acknowledgements

Firstly, I'd like to thank my editor, Katherine Armstrong, who knew before I did that I wanted to write a murder mystery. As well as having powers of premonition and persuasion, she is an oracle of crime fiction, passionate about the genre, generous with her time and achingly astute with her advice.

I count myself very lucky to have been embraced by Katherine and her talented team at Simon and Schuster. To the proofreader, Djinn von Noorden, and copyeditor, Natasha Onwuemezi, I am grateful for your dedication and craft. Your observations helped to concentrate the mind and hone the story. And as for Jess Barratt and Rich Vlietstra, it has been a pleasure getting to know you as you weave your publicity and marketing magic. Thanks also to Louise Davies, Emma Capron, Georgie Leighton, Charlotte Osment, Matt Johnson, Olivia Allen, Jade Unwin, Heather Hogan, Declan Heeney at Gill Hess and everybody else involved in getting this book into the hands (and hearts and minds) of readers.

Without the steady support and diary-juggling skills of my various agents, Jane Russell at Storied, Georgie Davies and Kat Oliver at Conway van Gelder Grant, Viki Sever at Mick Perrin Worldwide and Derick Mulvey, I could not have even contemplated taking on this project.

In researching the book, I owe a heap of gratitude to Gerry Hand of the Carrickmacross Tidy Towns committee. In entertaining fashion, he walked me through the wonderful world of Tidy Towns, filling me in on the challenges and the practicalities involved in mounting a campaign. I also appreciated the crash course in drone technology given to me by my cousin, Christopher Carragher, over a pint at a graduation ceremony in Galway. And without the pep talk from my old friend, Robert Thorogood, I may not have even started the novel in the first place.

That reminds me of my admiration for all the fabulous crime writers I met at the Harrogate Crime Festival who welcomed me – a mere interloper – into the fold. For people who wade through blood for a living, they are a remarkably genial bunch. And to all the writers, crime or otherwise, that have inspired me since I was a child, I thank you for your guidance on how to read, how to write and, at the risk of overstating the case, how to live.

As ever, it is the people closest to you to whom you owe the most. With that in mind, I'd like to give my parents, Rory and Teresa, a nod as well as my brothers and sisters, wider family, friends and the Brookfield Tennis club to where I escaped at the end of a long day. In a reversal of historic roles, it is I who seek the approval of my children. Emily, Rebecca and Red are a constant source of joy and wonder to me (I really need them to like the book). And of course I can't thank my wife Melanie enough, not just for her love and understanding, the morning coffees and free pass to write, but for her specific commitment to this novel, her deep reading and re-reading of it, her belief in it and her endless encouragement.

Lastly, I'd like to apologize to professional gardeners and enthusiasts alike. While I have tried to be as horticulturally plausible as possible, I have no doubt that my green-ness in this field will be all too apparent on the page.